The poor donkey appeared petrified with fear

The Swiss Family Robinson

JOHANN R. WYSS

A HAMLYN CLASSIC

ANDREW DAKERS LIMITED

LONDON

Published by

ANDREW DAKERS LIMITED

SPRING HOUSE • SPRING PLACE • LONDON N W 5

Printed in Czechoslovakia

CONTENTS

CHAPTER I

Shipwreck, and preparations for deliverance

The tempest had lasted six days, and, far from abating, now redoubled in fury. Driven out of our course to the south-west, it was impossible to tell in what parts we were. Our vessel had lost her masts, and leaked from end to end. Every one, commending his soul to God, implored of His loving-kindness a means of escaping death.

'Children,' I said to my four boys, who clung weeping to their mother, 'God can still save us if it be His will; if He has decreed otherwise we must submit. At the worst, we shall only quit this world to be united in the better one.'

My wife dried her tears, and, following my example, assumed an enforced calmness, to inspire the children with courage and resignation.

We fell upon our knees and prayed fervently.

All at once, through the roar of the winds and waters, I heard with rapture the salvation-cry of the shipwrecked—'Land! land!' But, at the same moment, we became sensible of a heavy concussion, succeeded by a frightful cracking noise. Thereupon, from the sudden cessation of motion in the ship, and the dull plash with which the waves broke around her, I concluded that we were stranded upon sunken rocks, and that the vessel was pierced through below.

'We are lost! Lower the boats!' cried a voice, which I recognised as that of the captain.

'Lost!' repeated the children, casting upon me a look full of anguish.

'Courage, my little ones!' I said, 'despair not yet; God gives help to the brave. I will go and see what means can be taken for our safety.'

I quitted the cabin, and went up on deck. Buffeted by the winds, half-blinded by the spray, flung down once or twice by the great seas that broke over the ship, I was unable for some moments to distinguish anything. When at length I reached the side I saw the boats rocking among the waves, overcrowded with people, and obliged, for their safety, to stand out to sea.

A sailor was just cutting the last mooring rope.

We had been forgotten!

I shouted frantically, imploring them to return and save us; but my voice was lost in the roar of the storm, and I realised with horror that we were abandoned upon the wrecked vessel.

In my terrible extremity, however, I observed, with a feeling akin to consolation, that the ship had so grounded as to leave the poop, where our cabin was, thrust high up out of reach of the

5

waves. And at the same time, even through the thick, misty rain which was falling, I could perceive, at some distance to the south, a coast-line that, in spite of its barren and desolate appearance, became thenceforward the object of my highest hopes.

I returned to my family, and, affecting a tranquillity which I was far from feeling:

'Take courage,' said I, 'all hope is not lost yet. One part of the ship—so great is the mercy of heaven—is firmly fixed above the water. Tomorrow the wind and waves will subside, and we shall be able to get to land.'

The children, in all the trustfulness of youth, accepted as a certainty this bold supposition.

From the manner in which my wife received my announcement, I saw clearly that she had penetrated the truth; but I also saw that her faith in God had not diminished.

'We are about to pass a most distressing night,' she said; 'let us take some food. Nourishment for the body fortifies the soul.'

Night fell. The tempest, in all its violence, continued to beat upon the vessel furiously. I feared every moment that she would break up.

My wife having hurriedly prepared a simple repast, the children partook of it with a good appetite. Then they retired to rest and slept soundly—all excepting Fritz, the eldest, who, comprehending the nature of our situation better than his brothers, chose to sit up with us.

'Father,' he said, after a long interval of silence. 'I have been trying to think of some means of reaching land. If we had either cork or bladders, to make swimming floats for mother and the other children, there would be no difficulty. You and I could swim ashore without help.'

'A capital idea!' exclaimed I; 'and that we may at all events be prepared, if the worst should come to the worst, let us try to put it in execution as soon as posible.'

Having hunted up a number of empty kegs, and several of the tin cans in which persons at sea carry their daily allowance of fresh water, Fritz and I tied them in couples with our handkerchiefs, and fastened two under the armpits of my brave wife and each of the sleeping children. We also placed in their pockets and our own, knives, string, tinder-boxes, and other articles which we knew would be of prime necessity if the vessel should break up and we be fortunate enough to reach the shore.

These precautions taken, Fritz, reassured and very much fatigued, went to bed as his brothers had done, and speedily fell asleep.

My wife and I continued our vigil.

It was a fearful night, and we passed it in prayer. Towards the morning I fancied that the storm was less furious, and with the first glimmerings of daylight I went upon deck. The wind was fast falling, the sea growing calm, and a lovely sunrise flashed its rose-tinted rays athwart a clear sky.

Reanimated by the fair vision spread out before me, I called to my wife and my boys, who at once hastened up on deck.

The younger children were deeply concerned to see that we were alone on board.

'Where are the sailors?' they cried. 'Why have they gone away without us? Oh, what is to become of us?'

'My children,' said I, 'our travelling companions were bewildered by fright. They leapt into the boats without thinking of us; and it is not unlikely that ere this they may have perished— victims of their own precipitation. If they still live I doubt not that they have more to complain of than we. See! the heavens are clear—land is not far off; our seeming misfortune, perhaps, is a blessing in disguise. Let us trust in God, who certainly has not abandoned us yet, and see what ought to be done to provide for our common deliverance.'

Fritz, enterprising and adventurous, persisted in his idea that it would be best to throw ourselves into the sea and swim to land.

Ernest—my second son, aged about twelve—an intelligent, but withal a timid and unadventurous boy, was much alarmed at the idea of crossing the intervening waters in this fashion, and proposed that we should construct a raft.

I pointed out to him that such a contrivance, besides occupying a great deal of time in the preparing of it for sea, would, when finished and set afloat, be very difficult to manage. And seeing the force of these two considerations, he at once abandoned his idea.

'But,' I said, 'whatever we find ourselves compelled to do in the end, let us set about exploring the ship; so that while thinking upon the best means of reaching the land, we may gather upon deck everything that is likely to be of use to us when we get there.'

Each hastened to do my bidding. I myself sought out the place where the provisions were stored, to make sure of what we had to depend upon for existence. Fritz visited the armoury and magazine, whence he brought guns, pistols, powder, balls and small shot. Ernest ransacked the carpenter's shop, and returned laden with tools and nails.

Little Francis—my youngest child, aged six—not to be outdone in activity, trotted about the vessel till he found a box full of fish hooks, which he showed us with much pride. Fritz and Ernest were inclined to make fun of him, but for my part I saw no reason to despise his discovery, for it might happen that we should be driven at last to live upon what fish we could catch, and then the hooks would be useful.

As to Jack—my third son, a merry youngster of ten years—he reappeared with two huge dogs wihch he had found shut up in the captain's cabin, and which, rendered docile by hunger, allowed him to lead them each by the ear.

My wife came to tell me that she had found a cow, an ass, two she-goats, and a sow, and had given them food and water just in time to save their lives; for the poor animals had, in the confusion, been kept without nourishment of any kind for nearly two days.

Everybody appeared to me to have made some useful discovery, except Jack.

'My boy,' I said, 'you have found us a couple of terrible eaters which will consume much and provide nothing.'

'I thought, dear father,' he replied, 'that they might be useful for hunting when we get to land.'

'You are right,' I said, 'they might, but we have not yet got to land. Have you thought of any way of getting there, my pet?'

'Well,' he replied, 'why couldn't we swim ashore in tubs? I used to swim about in the pond in that way when I was staying with my godfather.'

'The very thing!' I cried. 'Let us see what can be done at once.'

Followed by the children, I at once descended towards the hold of the vessel—now filled with water—where several great casks were floating about empty. I drew four of them out upon the floor of the lower deck, at this time not much above the water-level. They were strong wooden casks, hooped with iron, and appeared to me to be well fitted for our purpose. So, aided by Fritz, I set to work to saw them in halves.

When we had thus obtained eight tubs and ranged them along side by side, I sought out a pliable plank long enough to lie under the whole of them and turn up at each end like a keel. This done, we nailed our tubs firmly to the plank and to each other, and then, to finish the matter, we got two other planks, which we nailed along the sides of the tubs and brought to a point at each end, like the prow and stern of a canoe.

Our work finished, we found ourselves in possession of a contrivance which, in a calm sea, I felt sure would enable us to get to land.

But we were now met by another difficulty. Our boat was so heavy that not with all our strength united could we move, much less launch it.

'We want a screw-jack,' I said.

Fritz immediately remembered that he had seen one somewhere and set out to find it.

In the meantime I sawed off some rollers, and when Fritz returned with the jack, I hoisted the contrivance up while he put phe rollers under; and now we could move our tub-raft to any tart of the vessel we pleased.

The children were wonder-struck to witness the power of the jack, and I promised them that the first time we had a few moments' leisure—if, under God, we were preserved at all—I would show them all about it and explain its mechanism.

A few minutes afterwards we had the pleasure of seeing our newly-made boat slide safely down the lower deck into the sea—so swiftly, however, that she would have been far away from us in an instant if I had not previously taken the precaution of securing her to one of the beams of the wreck by a cable.

The children shouted for joy to see the cumbrous machine afloat. I was not so well satisfied; I saw that it leaned too much on one side. But though discouraged for a moment, I soon remembered that we could remedy this inconvenience by the use of balast. Thereupon I laid hold of whatever heavy things first came to hand, and throwing them into the tubs, soon had the satisfaction of seeing our vessel regain its equilibrium.

Again the children shouted, and were rushing forward to see who shoud be the first to embark, when I stopped them, fearing that if they were too boisterous in their movements they might capsize the boat.

Also we lacked oars. Ernest at once set off and found four under a sailcloth.

Remembering, too, that savages employ a kind of balance-paddle to keep their canoes steady in the water, I determined to make something of the sort myself.

I found two pieces of a splintered yard which exactly served my purpose. I fastened one of them to each end of the boat—screwing them loosely, so that they might be turned in any direction. Then to the end of each of the arms that thus stretched out over the water I attached an empty keg, which, floating upon the waves, would enable the vessel to keep its balance. We then made some more oars, so that we might have at least one each.

When these various labours were ended it was too late to think of putting to sea that day, so we resigned ourselves to the necessity of passing another night upon the wreck.

This determination taken, my wife prepared for us an excellent repast, which comforted and revived us much, for we had scarcely thought during the day, of taking either a morsel of bread or a drop of wine.

Though feeling in far less danger than on the previous evening, I took the precaution of again fitting the children with their swimming floats before allowing them to retire to rest; and I advised my wife to dress herself in male clothing, which, as I pointed out, would embarrass her less than her own if the worst should happen after all.

She naturally felt a strong repugnance thus to disguise herself, but at length she yielded to my wishes. Leaving me for a few minutes, she soon reappeared in the jaunty uniform of a midshipman, which she had found in one of the sea-chests, and which became her admirably.

Sleep was not long in overtaking us, for the day had been very laborious.

The night passed without any untoward incident.

CHAPTER II

Landing, and the first day on shore

At daybreak we were all astir; for hope, like grief, is no friend to sleep.

As soon we had offered up our morning prayer together, I said to my children, 'We are now going, by the help of God, to attempt our deliverance from this peril. Give the animals on board provisions for several days; for if our endeavour should succeed, as I devoutly trust it may, we can then return and fetch them. After that, gather together everything that may seem likely to be of any use to us when we disembark; and may God speed us in our undertaking.'

I decided that our cargo should comprise, first of all, a barrel of powder, some guns and pistols, and a supply of bullets, together with bullet-moulds and lead to renew our stock when these were gone. Each of us was furnished with a game-bag, which, for the present, we filled with provisions. I provided myself with a case of portable soup made up into cakes, a can of biscuits, an iron pot, and some knives, axes, saws, pincers, nails, gimblets, and fishing-lines. I took also a quantity of sail-cloth, with which I proposed to construct a tent to shelter us from the weather.

In fact, we amassed so many things that I was obliged to leave a large quantity of them behind, though I had already exchanged for articles of necessity everything which I had at first thrown into the tubs as ballast.

Just as we were about to embark, the cocks, by their persistent and melancholy crowing, seemed to be bidding us a sad farewell; whereupon my wife suggested that it would be better to take them with us, together with the hens, the ducks, the geese, and the pigeons. I consented.

Upon that, she placed a couple of cocks and a dozen hens into one of the tubs, and I covered them over with a rude lattice-work which we made amongst us by interlacing some of the more pliable splinters strewn about the deck of the ship. As to the geese, the ducks, and the pigeons, I simply set them at liberty, feeling confident that instinct alone would take them to land, the former through the water and the latter through the air.

The children were already embarked in the order which I had assigned them, when my wife returned from the interior of the ship carrying a good-sized, well-filled bag, which she threw into the tub occupied by little Francis. I paid no attention to this bag at the time, thinking that the provident mother had only brought it to make a more comfortable seat for her child.

As soon as we were all safely stowed, I cut the cable by which we were moored to the ship, and we began to row for the shore.

In the first tub was my wife; in the second, little Francis. Fritz

10

occupied the third. The two next contained the powder, the arms, the sail-cloth, the tools, the provisions, and the poultry. Jack was in the sixth, Ernest in the seventh. I had taken the last for myself, and there, with a stern-oar in my hands, I steered our strange vessel. Each of us had one of our swimming floats strapped round us for safety in case of accident.

The dogs being very large, I judged it prudent not to embark them, and left them upon the wreck. When, however, they saw us going away they began to whine piteously. Presently they both jumped into the sea, and soon swam up to us. Fearing that the distance to be traversed was too great for their strength, I showed them how to rest themselves by placing their forepaws upon the barrels that we had hung out to balance the boat. The sagacious animals readily comprehended this manoeuvre, and were thus able to follow us without suffering from too much fatigue.

The sea was calm, its motion being of the gentlest, and its surface flecked here and there with light, fleecy foam. The sky was clear, the sun radiant. We all rowed together; the rising tide running inland favoured us. Around us floated chests, casks, and bales— strays from the wrecked vessel.

Fritz and I laid hold of as many of these as came in our way with our oars, and tying them to our tubs, towed them along with us. My wife, with her hand placed upon the head of her youngest child, and her eyes raised to heaven, prayed silently.

Our voyage proceeded prosperously; but the nearer we came to the coast, the more wild and desolate it seemed. A line of bare grey rocks was the only sight it offered to the view.

Presently, however, Fritz, who had keen powers of vision, declared that he could descry trees on shore, and among them the cocoa-tree.

Ernest, naturally dainty in his tastes, was delighted at the idea of eating freshly-gathered cocoa-nuts, which, as he had read, were so much better than those sold in Europe.

'What happiness!' cried little Francis.

The word 'happiness', trifling as seemed the occasion on which it was used, caused my wife to start and look pained.

Divining her thought, I gently took her by the hand. 'The child is right, perhaps,' I said, in a low voice; 'we should never think our sources of happiness too small to bring the fullness of joy into our hearts; all is relative in this life.'

Meanwhile a lively discussion was going on among the children concerning the reality of the trees which Fritz was endeavouring to make them see. While I was expressing my regret that I had not thought to bring away the captain's telescope with me, Jack triumphantly drew from his pocket a smaller one which he had found in the cabin of the boatswain's mate.

I was now able to take a survey of the shore. Forgetting the point in dispute, all I looked for was a favourable place for landing, and I fixed upon a creek towards which the pigeons, now far in advance of us, were directing their course as if they were our advance guard.

'And the cocoas?' asked little Francis. 'Do you see them papa?'

'Oh, yes,' I replied, smiling. 'Fritz has sharp eyes; he was not mistaken. I see in the distance trees which certainly look to me as if they were really laden with cocoas.'

'Oh, I *am* happy!' cried the little one, clapping his tiny hands together for joy.

My wife stooped to kiss him, and I think to hide a tear. But when she raised her head again it was only to show a face with a sweet smile upon it. Little Francis's happiness had communicated itself to his mother.

We plied our oars bravely, and at length reached the land at the mouth of a stream where there was not more than enough water to float our craft, and where the coast between the rocks was very low.

The children leapt lightly to land, with the exception of Francis, who was too young even to get out of his tub, and had to be helped by his mother.

The dogs, which had reached land before us, testified their joy by bounding round us with loud barkings. The ducks and geese, already installed upon the banks of the stream, welcomed us with a chorus of quacking, with which were mingled the hoarse cries of some penguins that sat immovable upon the surrounding rocks, and several flamingoes which flew away frightened at our approach.

Little Francis, during all this time, thought of nothing but the cocoa-trees.

When we landed it was necessary to proceed at once with the unloading of our boat. Everything was soon transported to the bank of the river. It was not much, but how rich did we consider ourselves in its possession!

I selected a suitable spot on which to pitch the tent that was to be our shelter. We then took one of the poles which had been used to balance the boat, and drove it firmly into the ground. To the top of it, crosswise, we tied the other, which we fixed in a fissure of the rock. This formed the framework of our tent. Over it we threw our sail-cloth, which we stretched out as far as it would reach on either side, and fastened to the earth with stakes. This done, I had the chests of provisions and other heavy articles brought in and placed round the edges to keep out the wind; while Fritz put some hooks along the edge of one side of the sail-cloth in front, to enable us to hook the two sides together and so shut ourselves in in the night-time.

Then I sent the children out to gather as much moss and dry herbage as they could find, wherewith to make our beds.

While they were thus occupied I got together some stones, and at a little distance from the tent built up a sort of hearth, upon which I placed some armfuls of dry wood that I picked up along the banks of the stream; and in this way I soon had a great fire lighted and crackling merrily.

My wife then put our pot upon my rude grate, and after she had filled it with water I threw in five or six cakes of the portable soup.

'What are you going to stick together, papa?' asked little Francis, who had mistaken the soup-cakes for glue.

His mother smilingly replied that I was going to make some soup.

'Glue-soup?' he asked, shuddering at the thought of it.

'No, no, my pretty,' replied his mother; 'nice soup made of meat.'

'Meat!' he exclaimed, staring with astonishment. 'Are you going to the butcher's then, mamma?'

His mother thereupon laughingly set herself to the task oft making him understand that the cakes which he had mistaken for glue were in reality made of the juices of meat, extracted by a peculiar process, and that each of them contained as much nourishment as a pound of beef.

'They adopt this plan,' she said, 'because fresh meat will not keep during long voyages. This supplies the place of it.'

Meanwhile Fritz, who had loaded his gun, went up the banks of the stream to look for game, and Ernest took a stroll along the beach. Jack went hunting among the broken rocks in the hope of finding mussels.

I was employing myself in getting the casks and other wreckage out of the water, when I heard Jack crying out lustily. Armed with an axe, I ran to the place whence his voice came, and there saw him up to his knees in the water.

'Papa, papa!' he cried in a tone of mingled triumph and terror, 'do make haste, I have caught such an enormous creature!'

'That is well,' I said; 'bring it along.'

'I cannot, papa; it won't let me.'

I felt inclined to laugh at the troubles of this conqueror held prisoner by his captive, but I found it was necessary to go to his help; for a huge lobster had seized him by the leg, and poor Jack tried in vain to release himself from the aninimal's pincers.

I at once jumped into the water, whereupon the lobster let go his hold and tried to escape; but I managed to seize him by the middle of the body and carry him ashore. My precipitate young friend, Jack, burning with anxiety to show his magnificent captive to his mother laid hold of the creature with both hands; scarcely had he grasped it, however, when it swung its tail swiftly round and struck him so sharp a blow in the face, that he let it fall at once and began to cry. This time I could not refrain, while offering him my consolations, from laughing heartily at his misfortune. I pointed out to him that nothing was more simple than to render his prisoner perfectly harmless; all he had to do was to take hold of the lobster by the middle of the body. This reassured him, and holding the creature as I had suggested, he set out to bear his prize in triumph to his mother.

'Mamma! Francis! Ernest! Fritz! Where is Fritz?' he shouted as he approached the tent. 'Come and see! A crab! A crab!'

Ernest, after having gravely inspected the animal, advised that it should then and there be thrown into the pot, as it would render the soup more succulent, a matter of prime importance to one of his dainty tastes. My wife did not seem disposed to rely much upon the excellence of the recipe. She decided that the lobster should be cooked separately.

Ernest then told us that he had himself made a discovery.

'I saw,' said he, 'some shell-fish in the sea, and, but that I should have wetted my feet, I would have brought some along with me.'

'Oh, yes,' replied Jack with an amusing air of disdain, 'I saw some of those things; but what are they? Nothing but mussels. I would not eat one if you were to pay me for it. Look at my lobster —that, now, is something like a shell-fish!'

'Who knows,' returned Ernest, 'but that they may be oysters, and not mussels? Judging from the manner in which they attach themselves to the rocks, and from the depth at which they are found, I should say they were oysters.'

'Very well, then, my dainty one,' said I in my turn, 'if you realy thought they were oysters, why did you not bring us some? You were afraid of wetting your feet, say you? Let me tell you that in the situation in which we now find ourselves we shall have to show a greater amount both of self-denial and of energy than we have been accustomed to hitherto.'

'I also saw,' added Ernest, 'a quantity of salt in the crevices of the rocks. I fancy the sun must have dried the sea-water there.'

'You appear to me,' replied I, 'to be a most valiant talker, Ernest. If you saw a quantity of salt, why did you not scrape some of it together and bring a bagful back with you? Go at once and· repair this negligence, in order that we may no longer be compelled to eat soup which is insipid for the want of the very ingredient you have been so fortunate as to discover.'

Ernest set out on the instant, and soon returned. The salt which he brought, however, was so mixed with sand that I was about to throw it away, when my wife prevented me.

She dissolved the white dust in water, which she passed through a cloth. This left the sand behind, and we seasoned our soup with the liquor.

The soup was at length ready, but Fritz had not yet returned. Besides, with no vessels before us but the pot, we began to ask each other, somewhat sheepishly, how we were going to eat our savoury dish. Should we be driven to sip out of the boiling cauldron in turn, and fish for the biscuits, which had been put into the soup instead of bread, with our fingers? This was impossible.

'If we only had a few cocoa-nuts,' said Ernest, 'we might use the broken shells for spoons.'

'Would not oyster-shells serve our purpose?' asked Ernest.

'The very thing', cried I. 'Run and fetch some at once.'

Ernest set out again, but was distanced by Jack, who was

already up to his knees in the sea before young Indolence had got to the beach.

Jack detached the oysters from the rocks and threw them upon the sands, while Ernest picked them up, being still very careful not to wet his feet.

At the same time that our oyster-fishers returned, Fritz put in an appearance. He advanced slowly, with one hand behind his back, and put on a hopeless kind of look, as if praying our pity.

'What, have you found nothing?' I asked.

'Nothing at all,' he replied.

But his brothers, who surrounded him, suddenly began crying out, 'Oh, a guinea-pig! Where did you find it, Fritz? Let me look at it!'

Upon this, Fritz proudly drew forth the game which he had at first so carefully concealed.

I congratulated him upon the success of his sport, but I did not fail at the same time to reprimand him for the falsehood which he had permitted himself to tell, though it was only done in fun, and intended not deceive but to surprise us.

He begged me to pardon him his error, and then he proceeded to tell us how he had crossed to the other side of the stream, and had there found that the country was entirely different to that which was on the side where we were.

'Down there,' he said, 'the vegetation is magnificent. Moreover, there are upon the shore a quantity of chests and casks, and other waifs from the wreck which the sea has cast up. Shall we permit all these things to rot there? Shall we not go as soon as possible to fetch the beasts off the vessel? The cow especially will give us excellent milk to soak our biscuit in, and down below there, there is splendid herbage for her to feed upon; to say nothing of the noble trees that will afford shelter for ourselves. Let us make our home there. Quit this barren and cheerless spot, and—'

'Patience! Patience, Fritz!' I replied. 'One thing at a time. Tomorrow will follow today, and each day has its appointed duties. But before all, tell me—did you discover any trace of our hapless fellow-travellers?'

'Nothing—neither upon land nor at sea. Nor have I seen any living thing except a troop of animals similar to that which I have brought with me. They are, I think, guinea-pigs, but of a peculiar species, for their feet are formed like those of hares. They are not at all timid, so that I was able to observe them very closely. They leap about among the herbage, and seating themselves on their hinder legs, carry their food to their mouths like squirrels.'

Ernest, putting on his most learned look, examined the animal very carefully, and finally pronounced that, according to his reading of natural history, he believed himself authorised to declare the supposed guinea-pig to be an agouti.

Jack was exerting himself to the utmost to open an oyster with a knife; but, although he put forth all his strength, and twisted his face into the oddest contortions, he could not succeed.

I relieved him of his difficulty. I took some oysters and placed them upon the hot embers. Here they very soon opened themselves.

'There, my children,' said I, 'behold the food that gourmands most prize! Taste it.'

With these words, I took out an oyster and swallowed it.

Jack and Fritz followed my example, but they at once declared that the delicacy was detestable. Ernest and Francis confirmed this judgment.

So we only made use of that part of the oyster which is ordinarily thrown away, and threw away that part of it which is ordinarily eaten. Employing the shells as spoons, we began to eat our soup. While we were feasting with an excellent appetite, the two dogs, who had no doubt good reasons of their own for desiring to follow our example, smelt out Fritz's agouti, and began to devour it in front of the tent.

Fritz jumped up furious, and, his gun being at hand, he seized hold of it and beat them so savagely with the butt end of it that he splintered the wood. Even this did not satisfy him, for when the poor creatures sought safety in flight, he flung stones at them as long as they were within range of his missiles.

This was not the first time that Fritz had shown proofs of an ungovernable temper; and, as I was desirous of repressing so vicious a trait in his character—a trait which afflicted me sorely, and which I foresaw would furnish a very bad example to his brothers—I reproved him severely, and pointed out to him that in the blindness of his rage he had not only spoilt his gun, which in our present circumstances was of the highest value to us, but that he had also run the risk of disabling the poor animals that were calculated to rendre us services of the most important nature.

He at once comprehended the justice of my reprimand, and testified the deepest repentance. I pardoned him on condition that he should make his peace with the dogs. Without hesitation he took a piece of biscuit in each hand, and in another moment the forgiving creatures were banqueting with him.

'Oh, father!' he cried, almost weeping, 'what have I done? Before taking the biscuit they have licked my hand in kindness. How could I have been so harsh to creatures so good and grateful!'

'Anger is always wrong, my dear boy,' I said; never forget that.'

As we finished our repast the sun was sinking below the horizon, and the fowls and the ducks came clamouring around us for food.

It was now that I discovered the use to which my good wife had put the sack which she had thrown into one of the tubs of our boat, as I thought, for little Francis to sit upon. She brought it out from the tent, and thrusting her hand into it, scattered abroad a quantity of grain, upon which our feathered friends pounced hungrily.

I praised her highly for her foresight, but I also remarked that it would be much better to save the grain for seed than to waste it upon animals which could be fed well enough on damaged biscuit.

Having partaken of their evening meal, the pigeons flew off to the

ledges of the rocks, and the fowls perched themselves upon the
ridge of the tent, and the ducks waddled away to take refuge in
some beds of rushes at the mouth of the stream which ran into the
bay.

We, in our turn, prepared for repose. The arms were charged and
so placed that we could lay hold upon them at the first alarm of
danger, and we offered up our evening prayer and retired into the
tent.

The suddenness with which the darkness succeeded the daylight
greatly astonished the children. For my own part, I concluded
therefrom that we were in a region near the equator, or at all
events in some part of the tropics.

I took one more look outside the tent to assure myself that all
was peaceful around us, and then closing the entrance, retired to
rest. The night was very chilly; we were obliged to lie as close
together as possible to preserve our natural warmth. This contrast
between the heat of the day and the coldness of the night confirmed
me in the opinion I had formed concerning the geographical position of the region in which we found ourselves.

My wife slept. So did the children. It was agreed between us that
I should keep watch half the night, and then awake my wife to take
my place. But sweetly and insensibly slumber fell upon me; and
God alone kept guard over us during the first night that we passed
in the land of our deliverance.

CHAPTER III

An exploring expedition

The cocks were the first to salute the rising sun, and my wife and
I were awakened by their song. We at once took counsel together
upon the occupations of the day. She agreed with me that our first
duty was to ascertain, if possible, the fate of our fellow-travellers
who had abandoned us upon the wrecked vessel. Our search for
them, too, we thought would enable us to explore the country and
fix upon the best spot for our future dwelling-place.

It was finally determined that I and Fritz should set out upon
this exploring expedition, while my wife remained in the neighbourhood of the tent with the other children. This settled, I begged
her to prepare breakfast while I called the boys. They required no
second summons. Even Ernest was promptly afoot.

I asked Jack what had become of his lobster.

He replied that he had taken the precaution of hiding it in a fissure of the rocks, lest the dogs should get at it, as shey had done
in the case of Fritz's agouti.

That is well,' I said. "It shows at all events that you know how
to be careful when your own interests are at stake, and also that the

experiences of others are not thrown away upon you. But, however that may be, are you willing to hand over to us the large claws of your prize, to furnish us with food during a journey we are about to make?'

'Oh! a journey! a journey!' cried all the children at once. 'Take me, papa! do take me!'

'It is not possible,' I said, 'that the whole family should set out upon the expedition we have now in hand; we should travel far too slowy, and in case of danger it would be the more difficult to defend ourselves. Fritz alone will accompany me. The larger dog—whom we will call Turk, if you like—will come with us. The rest of you will remain here with your mother, under the care of the other dog, to whom I propose to give the name of Fan.'

Fritz, blushing as he spoke, begged to be allowed to take another gun with him, as his own was now useless.

Breakfast was now ready: it consisted of biscuits and lobster, which my wife had cooked upon the rude hearth where we yesterday boiled our soup. The fish was, however, so tough that the greater part of it remained for Fritz and me to carry with us.

Fritz was of opinion that we ought to set out at once, before the heat of day fell upon us.

'You are right,' I said; 'we will start immediately.'

After I had counselled the children, who were to remain with their mother, to abide in unity and obedience until our return, we departed on our unknown journey. It was not without griefs and tears that we thus set out; for my wife was sorrowful with the vague fear that we might come to harm in our adventures, and for my own part, I was troubled by anxieties for the dear treasure I was leaving behind me.

We hastened our steps, and very soon the murmuring of the stream whose course we were following drowned the distant farewells of our loved ones.

In order to cross the stream, it was necessary, as Fritz had found on the previous day, to travel towards its source, to place where it leapt over the steep rocks in the form of a cascade. At the top of the fall the water was narrower and more shallow, and by stepping upon pieces of broken rock we were enabled to cross safely.

Upon the opposite bank Nature changed her aspect entirely. We found ourselves at first in the midst of an expanse of tall grass, dried by the sun, entangled in its growth, and very tough, through which we made our way slowly and with difficulty.

Scarcely had we gone a hundred steps, when we heard a strange noise behind us, and turning, we saw the rank grass agitated, as if some creature were making its way towards us.

Fritz promptly brought his gun to his shoulder, finger on trigger, prepared to receive the aggressor bravely, whatever it might be. It turned out to be only Turk our dog, whom we had forgotten, and who now came to rejoin us. I received the sagacious animal with caresses, and felicitated Fritz upon the coolness with which he had behaved himself; for not only was he not in the least frightened by the possible approach of an unseen enemy, but he had also been careful not to fire precipitately. Had he drawn the trigger, he might have killed our best friend.

Continuing our route, we came at length to the shore of the bay. Here we looked anxiously out to sea, sweeping the horizon with Jack's glass in the hope of catching some glimpse of the frail boats containing the companions of our voyage. But as far as vision extended we could see nothing but the ceaseless rocking of the restless waves. Then we carefully examined the sand, in the hope that we might find some traces of human foot-prints; but here again we failed.

We were now turning from the shore to travel inland. After we had gone about two leagues, with our eyes always on the watch, we entered a wood. We had now been walking near upon two hours, and the sun had risen to its full height. We therefore made a halt, and sat down upon the grassy bank of a little brook that rippled softly among the trees. Around us strange birds of lovely plumage fluttered and chattered, and twittered incessantly.

Fritz would have it that he saw a monkey in the branches of one of the trees. At first I thought he must be wrong. But as Turk went sniffing in the direction where Fritz was pointing, and all at once began to bark, I came to the conclusion that it was I who was mistaken, and not my boy.

Fritz at once got up to verify his discovery, and as he walked along with his eyes among the branches, his foot struck a round thing bristling with fibres, which caused him to stumble. With a touch of ill-humour at being interrupted in his purpose, he looked down, and picking up the object over which he had fallen, brought it to me, saying that he thought it must be the nest of some strange bird.

'Your nest, my dear Fritz,' I said, smiling at his mistake, 'is a cocoa-nut.'

We now resumed our journey, making our way through the wood, which seemed interminable. Very often we were obliged to cut a road with our axes through the innumerable trailing plants that interlaced themselves on every hand. At every step some magnificent shrub or strange tree offered itself to our view.

Fritz, who marvelled more and more at every new sight, suddenly cried out, 'Oh, papa! what are these trees with large swellings on their trunks?'

I recognised at once the calabash, the flexible trunk of which winds itself round larger and more stately trees, and holds drooping from its stem the gourd with its hard, dry shell. This shell, I told Fritz, was often used for dishes, basins, bottles and spoons, while some savages even employed it to boil their water in and cook their victuals.

He was much puzzled to understand how it was that a shell apparently so frail could bear the heat of a fire without being burnt.

I then explained to him the plan pursued by the savages. They did not, I told him, place the gourd on the fire. They filled it with water, and then cast in, one by one, pebbles which had previously been made red-hot. In time this caused the liquid to boil.

Oh,' he cried, 'is that all? The thing is so simple that I should have thought of it myself with a moment's reflection.'

'No doubt,' I said, 'you would have made the discovery as easily as Columbus's friends found out how to stand an egg on its small end. He showed them the way, and then they knew how to do it. Remember, my son, that the simplest discoveries are often those which remain the longest unknown.'

While chatting thus, we had each taken a calabash, which we were trying to turn into some vessel or other of use in the household. Fritz endeavoured to cut his with his knife, and not being successful, was seized with one of his impatient fits and flung it away. I pursued a different plan. I wound a piece of string round the gourd, and by dint of drawing it tighter and tigher, I succeeded in breaking the shell neatly in two, and found myself possessed of a couple of basins of equal size.

'Well,' said Fritz, 'this only shows the truth of what you were saying. An idea at once so simple and so ingenious as that would never have occurred to me. How did you think of it?'

'The merit of invention,' I replied, 'is not mine. I only remember to have read somewhere that the device is one employed by savage tribes who have no knives, and I thought that I would put it into practice.'

Fritz then desired to know how bottles were made of the gourd. 'I can easily understand,' he said, 'that after the calabash has been left to dry, a hole can be made in it and the pith withdrawn. But how is it possible to give to this round ball a more convenient form? How, for instance, can any part of it be shaped into anything like the neck of a bottle?'

I told him that to arrive at this result it was the custom to bind strips of cloth or bark around the stalk end of the fruit when it was very young. The tied part could then grow no more, while the remainder of the gourd swelled out to its proper size.

Having witnessed my own success in basin-making, Fritz took courage and set to work again-this time with string instead of a knife.

Between us we made as many vessels as we thought would be useful. These I laid out in the sun to dry, having previously filled them with sand to prevent them from being drawn out of shape in the process. Then, in order that we might be able to find them with ease on our return, we carefully noted the spot where we had placed them.

We now pursued our journey, employing ourselves as we went in cutting some spoons out of the fragments of two or three calabashes which we had broken while making our basins. We produced nothing very remarkable; but rough as they were, our gourd-spoons were marvels of convenience as compared with the oyster-shells with which we had been obliged to eat our soup on the previous evening.

Fritz jumped for joy. 'Dishes, plates, cups!' he exclaimed. 'Won't mamma be delighted! She will not know which basins to serve our soup in, she will have so many!'

And then, thinking of little Francis—'Father,' he said, 'let us find a little calabash; the spoons we have been making will stretch the little fellow's mouth from ear to ear. I will try and make him a small set of dinner-things for himself.'

And as one good thought leads to another, he next made a couple of large basins for Master Turk and Miss Fan, who, since the beating he gave them on the previous evening, had looked askance at him whenever he came near them.

When his task was completed, Fritz took some of his own biscuit, and some of the fresh water which he carried in his flask, and made Turk a sop in his new basin. As soon as the grateful beast saw the appetising morsel placed before him, his eyes glistened with tenderness, and he graciously licked the hand of his young host in token of forgiveness. All evidently was forgotten.

After having walked steadily on for about three hours, we came to a tongue of land which ran far out intho the sea, and ended in a lofty hill, up which we climbed with some difficulty and a great deal of perspiration. The view from the summit embraced a vast extent of sea and land; but, although aided by our glass, we could discover no trace of our shipwrecked companions, nor, on the other hand, any indication that the country upon which we had been cast was inhabited.

But to compensate us for our disappointment, a magnificent scene lay spread out before us. At our feet glittered the sea, sleeping calmly in an immense bay, the shores of which were clothed with a wealth of many-coloured foliage, that stretched away on either hand to a dimly-seen cape that faded softly into the blue distance. It was a scene that would have filled me with rapture, but that my thoughts were preoccupied by saddening reflections as to the fate of our companions. At the same time I could not resist a feeling of satisfaction in contemplating a country whose evident fertility gave me the liveliest hopes for our future.

'Ah, well!' I sighed, 'here we are, an isolated band of colonists, condemned to live alone or perish. God, in His inscrutable purposes, has so decided. We must submit ourselves courageously to His will.'

'As to that,' cried Fritz gaily, 'there are three times as many of us as there were when Adam and Eve began life; and who knows but that, like the patriarch of the Bible, we may turn out to be the progenitors of a great and innumerable nation?'

This nation of an Abraham of fifteen years of age made me smile.

The sun darted down his most ardent beams at the time, and

I told Fritz to follow me to the grateful shadow of a grove of palm-trees which I saw in the distance.

In order to reach the palm-grove, it was necessary to cross a large bed of reeds, so thickly grown and tangled that they impeded our journey seriously. As the place seemed to me to be a likely habitation for venomous reptiles, I advised Fritz to proceed cautiously, and in order the more readily to defend myself if attacked, cut one of the thickest of the reeds for a weapon. Scarcely had I done so, when I felt my hand wetted with a glutinous kind of liquid that exuded from the end of my reed. I touched the juice with my lips, and it became clear to me at once that we were traversing a natural plantation of sugar-canes.

I did not tell Fritz, being desirous to leave him the pleasure of making the precious discovery for himself.

He was walking before me. I told him to cut himself a reed, as that would be a far more certain weapon for use against serpents than either a pistol or a knife.

He did as he was told, and it was not long before I heard him crying out in transports of joy, 'Sugar-cane! Sugar-cane! What exquisite juice! What delicious syrup! How delighted my mother and my brothers will be! And to finish with, nothing now will be wanting to complete the happiness of Master Ernest. He will have his sugar!'

Upon this he broke his cane into several pieces, in order to get at the juice more readily, and fell to sucking them with the greatest avidity. I should have scolded him for his gluttony if I had not reflected that he must be very thirsty. Indeed, I cannot but confess that, being oppressed by thirst myself, I felt strongly induced to follow his example.

'I will take home,' he said, 'a rare bundle of these canes for my mother and the boys. They will be delighted to feast upon them; and besides that, we can use one or two to refresh ourselves upon the road.'

I advised him not to burden himself with too heavy a load, as we had yet a long distance to travel. But he cut nearly a dozen of the very largest he could find, stripped them of their leaves, and tucked them under his arm.

Hardly had we got into the palm-grove when a troop of monkeys, alarmed by our approach and the barking of Turk, sprang into the trees, from the topmost branches of which they looked down upon us in terror, uttering piercing cries and grimacing horribly.

Fritz, without a moment's reflection, flung down his burden, brought his gun to his shoulder, and had already his finger on the trigger, when I laid my hand upon the weapon.

'Why,' said I, 'are you going to kill these animals?'

'Monkeys,' he replied, 'are such malicious and mischievous beasts. See how they are menacing us and showing their teeth!'

'Let us suppose that it is so,' I returned; 'still, if these poor creatures are angry with us, have they not cause? Do we not come here disturbing and alarming them in their own native homes? And as to killing any creature whatever, without necessity, pray let us keep ourselves from that! It is already sad enough to reflect that the care of his own life should place man in a state of enforced warfare with so many of the poor animals around him. Take my advice: let these harmless monkeys live. Who knows indeed but that they may be useful to us?'

'Useful!' repeated Fritz in undisguised astonishment, 'monkeys useful! In what way, dear father, can monkeys possibly be useful?'

'You shall see,' said I.

With that I flung some stones up towards the monkeys, without any intention of striking them. At once, obeying their natural instinct for imitation, they began to pick from the tops of the palms a quantity of cocoa-nuts, which they flung down upon us in wild emulation. It was not difficult to avoid these missiles, for they were by no means well aimed.

Fritz was immensely diverted by the success of my ruse.

'Thank you, my good friends, thank you!' he cried out to the monkeys as he hid himself first behind this tree and then behind that. 'Many, many thanks for your kindness!'

As soon as the shower of nuts slackened, he gathered up as many as he could carry, and we moved off to regale ourselves at leisure out of reach of the monkeys.

First of all we opened the small apertures near the stalk of the fruit with the points of our knives, and thence drank the milk which the shell contained. To our great surprise, however, we did not find this liquor to be so good as we had thought it would be. The cream which adhered to the inside of the shell seemed to us to be better. So we broke open the nuts with our axes, scraped the cream into our calabash spoons, sweetened it with sugar out of our canes, and made a delicious meal.

Thanks to the windfall, Fritz was now able to give to Turk all that remained of the lobster and the biscuit. Even this, however, was but poor fare for a dog of his robust appetite. He ate it up to the last scrap, and then hungrily chewed the remains of the canes we had been using, and smelt about for stray remains of the kernels of the cocoa-nuts.

In the meantime I tied together all the cocoa-nuts that had stalks and slung them over my shoulder, while Fritz gathered up what remained of the canes. Then, much refreshed by our repast, we set out to rejoin the family.

CHAPTER IV

The return journey—a night adventure

Fritz, seeing that from time to time I lifted the cane he had given me to my lips, and seemed to be refreshed thereby, endeavoured to follow my example. But his efforts were in vain; he failed to extract from it the least drop of liquor. Growing impatient, he at last asked me how this came about.

'Reflect a little,' I replied, 'and I feel certain that you will find out for yourself.'

He was not long in discovering the explanation of the phenomenon. He knew that it was of no use to suck a tube which contained no passage for the air, and in order to provide such a passage in his cane he found it necessary to make a hole in the side just above the joint below the end which he placed in his mouth. The hole, once pierced, he found no further difficulty in extracting the juice, and could refresh himself from time to time as I did with the delicious beverage which was to be thus obtained.

At the same time I felt it right to remark that it would not be wise to become too expert in drawing the juice out of our canes, or we should find ourselves carrying little else than sticks to the tent.

At this Fritz seemed troubled.

'Do not be too deeply concerned at this,' I continued, being desirous of comforting him, 'for the juice itself will not keep sweet long, especially when the canes are exposed to the sun. The heat turns it sour. Indeed, it is not at all unlikely that if we had much farther to travel, we should carry home to those who are, no doubt, anxiously awaiting us, little else but a few canes full of a very acrid, instead of a very sweet, liquor.'

'Even in that case,' returned Fritz joyously, 'I can make amends. I have my tin flask full of cocoa-nut milk. I filled it when you were not looking, to give you a surprise.'

'You are a good boy,' I replied, 'and your intentions are most excellent. But at the same time it is only right that you should know, to save you disappointment, that once out of the shell, the milk of the cocoa-nut ferments and becomes acrid too.'

Fritz pulled out his flask at once, but scarcely had he touched the cork when it flew out with a pop, and the liquor same foaming out after it like champagne. We tasted this liquor, and it appeared to us to be very agreeable. Fritz, indeed, found it so much to his palate that I was compelled to counsel him to moderation. I feared that the drink might get into his head.

Whatever may have been the nature of the liquor in its new form, we felt very much refreshed by it, and trudged along more lightly than ever.

Before long we came again to the place where we had left our gourd vessels. They were perfectly dry now, and we took them up to carry back with us.

A little farther on, Turk dashed barking amongst a troop of monkeys, who were gambolling peacefully on the ground in ignorance of our near approach.

At the first barkings of the dog the nimble creatures sprang into the trees and dispersed themselves. In a moment, indeed, they had all disappeared with the exception of a she-monkey who was giving suck to her little one, and who, being less agile than her companions, was seized upon by Turk and worried.

Fritz at once rushed off to save her. He lost his hat, flung his canes and his flask behind him, and threw down his gun; but he was too late. When he reached the spot the poor beast was dead, and the dog had already begun to devour her.

Fritz indignantly tried to force Turk to discontinue his sanguinary repast; but on coming up I dissuaded him from doing so. It was evident that the dog was hungry, and it was too late to save his victim. My advice, therefore, was to let him satisfy his appetite.

The little monkey managed to escape the fangs of the dog, and, overcome by fright, sat squatting tranquilly by a tuft of herbage, grinding ist teeth, and watching the sad scene fixedly.

As soon as he saw Fritz he leapt at a bound upon his shoulder and clung there so tightly that the poor boy, in spite of all his efforts, could not relieve himself of his unwelcome companion.

It was not without some emotion that he could bring himself to beat the little creature; it was so innocent. It had evidently no intention to harm him. Separated from its mother, it seemed only to implore his protection against the terrible enemy that had just made it an orphan.

After involuntarily diverting myself for a moment with the ridiculous state of embarrassment in which my son found himself, I went up and, using all gentleness with the animal, induced it to relinquish its hold. And then, when it nestled itself in my arms like a child taking shelter in the bosom of its nurse, I felt myself overcome by a strong sentiment of pity for it.

'Hapless little being!' I said, 'what is to be thy fate I know not. For it behoves us to think twice before deciding to admit another useless mouth to our little colony.'

But Fritz interrupted me at once:

'Oh, papa,' he cried, 'do let me keep it, pray! It will die if we abandon it. Let me adopt the little thing. I have read that monkeys, guided by their natural instinct, are able to distinguish fruits that are good for mankind to eat from those which are noxious. If that is true we surely ought not to hesitate to attach this little companion to our common interests.'

'So be it, then, my boy,' I replied. 'Nothing gives me greater pleasure than to recognise in your request both the goodness of your heart, and the wisdom of your reflections. I consent to the adoption of your young favourite; but remember that it will be henceforth your duty to rear it wisely, lest at some future time we should be constrained to undo what we have now done.'

While we were discoursing thus, the abominable and imperturbable Turk tranquilly finished his odious repast.

'Friend Turk,' said Fritz, with solemnity, pointing the while at the monkey, which he had now taken on his arm, 'you have made an orphan; you have eaten the mother of this poor innocent. We are compelled to pardon you this crime because you are only an animal devoid of reason. But keep careful watch over this little one, and promise me to love and respect it henceforth. It is happily too young to be conscious of the grievous wrong you have done it. If you turn honest and repentant, I will undertake to reward you for your conversion with the best of cooked food, instead of these horrifying feasts of raw flesh.'

Turk crouched at Fritz's feet, as if he fully comprehended the gravity of this discourse. His eyes, glistening with moisture, wandered intelligently from those of his young master to those of the motherless animal which Fritz was caressing before him, in order to show that it was henceforth to be held sacred from his teeth.

This agreement concluded between Fritz and the dog, the monkey retook its place upon its master's shoulder, and sat there with as much tranquillity and confidence as if it had never known a safer haven of rest. It showed new signs of fright, it is true, when its dread enemy, Turk, began gambolling round Fritz's legs, striving to hide itself in his breast, beneath his arms—anywhere. And here Fritz was struck with a strange idea.

Desiring to assure himself that the reconciliation between the two animals was real, he again addressed the guilty Turk.

'Rascal!' he said, 'repair thy fault. Thou hast deprived this poor little one of its parent and guardian, it is only just that thou shouldst replace her.'

Then, passing a cord round Turk's neck, he gave the end of it to the monkey, which he seated upon the astonished dog's back, after the manner of a horseman. Turk accepted his new duty with a very ill grace at firts, but after a sharp reprimand he submitted; and the droll little animal, completely reassured, appeared to find the place in which Fritz had installed him convenient and comfortable.

At length we found ourselves in the midst of the family, who were awaiting us on the bank of the stream.

The dogs saluted one another afar off by loud barkings; and Turk's part in the greeting so frightened the little monkey that he again leapt upon Fritz's shoulder, and could not be persuaded to come off.

Scarcely had the children caught sight of us, when they burst into loud shouts of joy; and when, as we came closer, they saw the monkey crouching tremblingly upon Fritz's shoulder, their delight knew no bounds.

'Oh! a monkey! a monkey! Where did you find it? How did you catch it? Oh, what a pretty little creature!'

And then noticing our other burdens:

'What are those sticks? Where did you get them? What are they for? And papa, too! What art those basins for? Where did you get them? How did you make them? Oh, do tell us all about it!'

There was such a deluge of questions, indeed, that they fairly overwhelmed us and we were unable to reply to them.

The first transports of the children's joy being abated: 'In the mercy of God,' I said, 'you see us both returned safe and sound; and not only us, but we have brought you, my dear little ones, all sorts of good things. But of those who were the cause of our expedition, and whom we went out to seek—the unfortunate beings who left the ship so precipitately—we have, alas! seen nothing. Not the least trace of the companions of our voyage is to—'

'My love,' said my wife, interrupting me, 'pray do not overcloud our joy so soon! Let us thank God that at least He has preserved us all during our separation, and brought us together again in peace and safety. Come, disembarrass yourselves of your burdens, and tell us all about the incidents of your journey.'

At once we were surrounded by little hands which were busy to relieve us of our loads.

Ernest took possession of the cocoa-nuts—without, however, recognising what they were. Francis took the gourd-vessels, which were much admired, and his own dinner set made by Fritz, which he flatly declared to be far preferable to the silver one which he had been wont to use at home.

Jack took my gun, my wife my game-bag. Fritz distributed his sugar-canes among the party, and again seated the monkey on Turk's back. Then he gave his gun to Ernest, who hinted that it might possibly go off if he were required to carry it, inasmuch as he was very heavily loaded already.

My wife, understanding this indirect complaint, relieved him of the cocoa-nuts, and our little caravan set out in procession for the tent.

'Ah!' said Fritz, 'if Ernest only knew the name of those balls which he has just allowed mamma to take from him, he would by no means have parted with them so readily.'

'What are they?' awked Jack.

'Cocoa-nuts,' said Fritz.

'Cocoa-nuts!' cried Ernest, 'real cocoa-nuts! Oh, mamma! Do give them back to me! I can carry both them and the gun too quite easily; and there will be no danger of the gun's going off.'

'No, no,' replied his mother, 'you will soon grow tried of carrying them again, and I do not care to hear your continual complaints.'

'Oh, do, mamma!' cried Ernest again. 'I will promise not to say a word. Besides, I can throw away these switches that Fritz has given me and carry the gun in my hand.'

'You had better be careful what you are doing,' said Fritz dryly, 'for those same switches, as you call them, are neither more nor less than sugar-canes; and I am going to show you all how to extract the delicious juice which they contain.'

'Capital! Capital!' cried all the children together. 'Come on, Fritz, do show us how to get the juice out of the sugar-canes!'

Thereupon Fritz walked on with his brothers, and while he was explaining to them the mystery of the vent-hole, I followed on after with my wife, whose natural curiosity I satisfied with a brief account of the little adventures of the day.

None of the curiosities which we had brought home gave so much pleasure as the vessels we had cut out of the calabashes. Though very roughly fashioned and at best but make-shifts, it was at once seen that they were likely to be of the greatest utility to us.

On reaching the tent we found that our good friends who had come to meet us had made every preparation for giving us a substantial repast.

Our pot full of appetising soup stood bubbling on the top of the fire, and while fish were being grilled on one side of it, a large goose was roasting on the other—the shell of yesterday's lobster being placed beneath it to catch the fat. Hard by stood a staved-in cask filled with excellent Dutch cheese; so that we had a variety of eatables before us, all calculated to excite our appetites—which, I may remark, had been rather coquetted with than satisfied by what we had eaten during the day.

At the same time, I could not help remarking to my wife that I thought she had begun to kill our poultry very soon, and that in my opinion ,much as I should enjoy the dish when it was served up, it would have been far better to leave the creature alive in order that it might multiply its species for the future.

'Make yourself quite easy, love, on that point,' said my wife. 'Our stock of provisions will be but very slightly diminished by the meal before us. Little Francis caught the fish, I myself found the cask of cheese on the beach, and the fowl was brought down by Ernest, who gives it a very strange name.'

'I gave it the right name,' interrupted our young scholar. 'I called it a stupid penguin. As to its being stupid there can be no doubt whatever, for it allowed me to come close up to it and kill it with a stick. That it is a penguin, I know, for it has all the peculiarities of that bird mentioned in the natural histories. It has four claws, which are united by a web, and it has short legs. It sits in one position for hours together, and, as it sits, looks in shape something like a bottle. Moreover, its beak is long and strong, and curved over at the end.'

I congratulated the young savant upon the good use he had made of his reading, and then we sat ourselves in a circle on the sand to commence our repast. Each of us was furnished with a calabash basin and spoon.

The children, while waiting for the soup to cool, broke some of the cocoa-nuts and eagerly drank the milk, which, as I have said before, was none of the best. Then we attacked the soup, and after that the fish, which I cannot but confess was a little too dry. Next we fell-to upon the penguin, which had a strong flavour as of train-oil about it. This, however, did not prevent us from enjoying so sumptuous a repast; for a good appetite always makes a good dinner.

The monkey, as was natural, became an object of general attention. The children dipped the corners of their handkerchiefs into the cocoa-nut milk and gave them him to suck, thinking that by this device he would not miss his mother so much. The little creature took to his food so intelligently, and with so excellent an appetite, that we had no longer any fear of not being able to rear him. We decided that we would call him Nip.

Fritz asked me whether I did not think that with so capital a dinner before us we might venture to indulge in some of his cocoa-champagne.

'Taste it first,' replied I, 'and see if you can conscientiously offer it to us to drink.'

Scarcely had he placed the bottle to his lips when he took it away again, and with a ludicrous grimace cried out, 'Pah! why, it's vinegar!'

'I told you that was how it would be,' I said. 'But no matter. Out of evil comes good. This vinegar will do admirably to eat with our fish: it will take off the dryness which we perceived in them.'

Thereupon I poured a little of the liquid into my gourd-plate, and all the rest following my example, we soon made an end of the fish that we had previously left. Finally we took some cheese, and also used our vinegar with that.

The repast finished, and the sun fast sinking below the horizon, we offered up our evening prayer, and retired to our mossy beds in the tent.

Fritz and Jack placed Nip between them, and covered him well to keep him warm. 'He is our child,' they said laughingly.

As was the case on the previous night, I took another look outside the tent after slumber had fallen upon my family, and finding everything peaceful, closed the door, retired to my bed, and was soon sound asleep with my dear ones around me.

I could not have been asleep long, however, when I was awakened by the yelping of the dogs and the fluttering of the fowls, which were perched upon the top of the tent.

I leapt up at once, and went outside, followed by my wife and Fritz, who did not sleep so soundly as his brothers. We each of us had taken the precaution of carrying a weapon with us.

By the clear light of the moon, we saw our dogs engaged in a fierce struggle with a half-score of jackals.

Our brave guardians had already laid three of them by the heels, but seemed in danger of being compelled to give in to numbers had we not come to their succour. Fritz and I fired together. Two of our nocturnal visitors fell dead at once; the remainder, frightened by the reports of the guns, scampered away as fast as their legs could carry them.

Fritz desired to carry the animal which he had killed into the tent with him, in order to show it to his brothers in the morning, and I gave him permission to do so. We left the other four to the dogs.

We then returned to the side of our little sleepers, whom neither the barking of the dogs nor the firing of the guns had awakened.

Very soon we were all wrapped in slumber again, and nothing further occurred to disturb us during the remainder of the night.

CHAPTER V

A voyage to the wreck

At the first break of dawn I awoke my wife, in order to consult with her again as to the employments of the day.

'My beloved,' I said, 'I see so many urgent duties before us that I know not to which to give the priority. On the one hand, it is clear that if we desire to save the cattle on the wreck, and to recover the various articles there that will be of use to us, it will be necessary to make a voyage thither at once. On the other hand, I cannot fail to see that it is almost equally necessary to set about building a more comfortable dwelling-place, for at any moment a storm may overtake us in these tropical regions, and then the effect of it will be as disastrous to us on land as it will be at sea. I confess that I do not know which we ought to do first—recover all we can from the wreck, or make our habitation secure where we are.'

'Pray do not weary yourself,' she replied, 'by forecasting events. With patience, order, and perseverance, we shall overcome every obstacle. The courage of such a father, and the endurance and obedience of such children as ours, cannot but conquer in the end. Under God, I put my entire confidence in those protectors with whom in His mercy He has blessed me. Truly it will not be without anxiety that I shall see you set out on a voyage to the wreck; but, if it is indispensable, I trust I have the fortitude to see you make it. I think it is of more importance to go thither than to set about building our new habitation at once. What remains on the wreck is perishable. As to our dwelling, a day or two will make no great change in our prospects.'

'It is well,' I said. 'I shall set out for the wreck with Fritz, leaving you and the other children to do what you can on land while we are away.'

'Come, come!' I cried, 'jump up, jump up! The sun has already risen, and we have no time to lose.'

Fritz was the first to put in an appearance, and, profiting by the time spent by his brothers in rubbing their eyes and shaking off their drowsiness, he placed his dead jackal in front of the tent in order to witness the surprise which it would cause them.

He had reckoned without the dogs, who, seeing one of their

nocturnal combatants yet remaining, and believing it to be still living, flung themselves upon it, barking furiously.

Fritz had the greatest difficulty in driving them away.

The yelping of the animals, and Fritz's wild shouting at them, brought the young idlers out all the more speedily.

They made their appearance one by one, the little monkey perching upon the shoulder of Jack. No sooner did he set eyes upon the jackal, however, than he became so frightened that he flew back into the tent, and buried himself so deeply in the moss of our beds that nothing could be seen of him but his tiny nozzle.

As Fritz had expected, his brothers were greatly astonished at the sight of the jackal.

Then we took breakfast; for the youngsters were of that class whose appetites awaken with their eyes.

A case of biscuits was opened, and the barrel of cheese again laid under contribution.

All at once, Ernest, who had been prowling about among the barrels which we had fished out of the sea, cried out, 'Oh, papa, would not our biscuit be much nicer if we were to eat it with butter?'

'There you are again with your eternal "if",' I replied. 'You are always awakening our desires without giving us the means of satisfying them. Are you not content with cheese?'

'I did not say I was not,' he answered; 'but if some one would break open this barrel—'

'What barrel?' I said.

'This one,' he replied. 'I feel certain that it contains butter, for there oozes from joints of it a kind of fatty matter which has exactly the same smell.'

After having satisfied ourselves that Ernest's nose had not deceived him, we consulted gravely as to the best plan of getting enough butter for our present supply without risking the loss of the remainder.

Fritz was for removing the hoops, and taking out the head of the cask.

I thought that if this were done it would loosen the staves, and let the butter run away when it became melted by the sun. It seemed to me to be wiser to make a hole in the side with a chisel, and extract thence with a piece of stick as much butter as we wanted.

This plan being adopted, we soon had some excellent toast, the taste of which rendered us doubly desirous of saving the cow from the wreck.

The dogs, fatigued by their nocturnal combat, slept tranquilly at our feet. I remarked that they had not come out of their fight with the jackals scatheless, and particularly pointed to some ugly wounds upon their necks.

Thereupon my wife hit upon the happy device of washing the butter till she had got all the salt out of it, and anointing their wounds with what remained. The dogs patiently submitted to this dressing of their sores, and afterwards began to lick each other—a proceeding which gave me hope that they would soon be cured.

'It is important,' said Fritz, 'that they should be furnished for similar occasions with spiked collars.'

'Yes,' said Jack, 'and if mamma will help me I will undertake to make them some during the day.'

'With all my heart,' said his mother; 'I will do everything I can to help you, and we shall see how you succeed.'

'Yes, my boy,' I added in my turn, 'use all your ingenuity, and if you can hit upon a practicable plan of carrying out your design, we will do our best to carry it into execution.'

'As to you, Fritz,' I continued, 'prepare yourself to accompany me on a voyage which I propose making to the wreck. Your mother and I have decided this morning that we shall do so; and, as was the case yesterday, she will remain here with the other children while we go to endeavour to save the cattle, and whatever else is likely to be of use to us.'

Our tub-boat was soon got ready. As we were setting out, we arranged with my wife that she should set up on the shore a pole with a piece of white rag tied to it, as a sort of signal to us when we were upon the wreck. In case of distress she was to pull it down and to fire a gun three times in succession. I then induced her—so courageous had she become—to consent to our remaining on board the wreck for a night, in case we should not be able to get everything ready for an earlier departure. In that case we agreed to burn lights to show that all was well.

Knowing that there were provisions still left in the vessel, we took only our arms. I permitted Fritz to take his monkey, to whom he promised a rare feast of goat's milk.

We at lenght put off, after having embraced and commended each other to the Divine keeping.

Fritz rowed vigorously, and I did my best to assist him while steering the craft with an oar thrust out from the stern.

When we had got some distance, I noticed that a river, much larger and more rapid than that upon which we had pitched our tent, emptied itself into the bay; and I conjectured that in doing so it would form a current which, if we once got into it, would help us on our journey. We pulled in the direction of this current, which, as I had anticipated, carried us, without any further effort of our own, over more than three parts of our voyage. A few stout pulls with our oars brought us to our destination.

We boarded the vessel and moored our boat securely to its side.

Fritz's first thought was to run to the animals, which, as soon as they heard us aboard, began lowing and bleating piteously. The poor creatures displayed the liveliest satisfaction at seeing us again, and ate up the fresh provender and water that we gave them with avidity. Having fed our dumb companions, we next made an excellent repast ourselves: we had no difficulty in procuring it, for the ship had been provisioned for a long voyage.

The ingenious Fritz then tried an experiment which succeeded to admiration. He introduced his monkey to the goat, who thereupon gave him such as if he had been her own offspring. It is needless to say that Nip made a hearty and delicious meal.

'Now, Fritz,' said I, 'what will it be best to do first?'

'I think,' he said, 'that before proceeding further we ought to set up a sail in our boat.'

It did not seem to me on the first blush of the thing that this was a very urgent matter; but Fritz pointed out to me that, during our voyage across, he had noticed a strong head wind, against which we should have had to struggle stoutly had it not been for the river current; and he said he thought he knew enough about sailing to be able to utilise this wind on the return voyage. He also mentioned that he thought we should have a good deal of difficulty in getting back in any case, with all our tubs loaded and only two oarsmen, one of whom was partly engaged in steering.

This reasoning appeared to me to be so sensible that I gave in to it at once.

I sought out a piece of broken yard large enough to serve as a mast, and a slighter piece to which to fix our sail. Fritz meanwhile nailed a thick plank across one of the tubs and bored a large hole in it. Through this hole we thrust our mast, and then attached pulleys to our sail in such a manner that I could easily manoeuvre it and steer the boat at the same time.

To finish with, Fritz—who, as was natural at his age, was given to mingle amusement and work together—tied to the top of the mast a long pennon of red bunting, and watched it float out in the wind with childish delight.

While smiling at his innocent diversion, I directed towards the bay whence we set out the large telescope which I had formerly seen on the captain's table, but had forgotten to carry away with me. I saw with joy that my wife and my little ones were peacefully engaged in various occupations, without a suspicion that I was a silent observer of all they were doing.

It was now growing late, and it became clear that it would be of no use to attempt to reach land again that night. So we spent the remainder of the day in pillaging the wrecked vessel, as if we had been pirates, and in filling our tubs with whatever was likely to prove of use to us.

In anticipation of a lengthy sojourn in the uninhabited country in which we had taken our refuge, I gave the preference to tools which would aid us in our labours to sustain life, and to arms which would protect us if attacked.

The vessel, as it so happened, was an emigrant ship, whose destination was the Southern Seas—among the islands of which we and our fellow-passengers had intended to settle as colonists. She was therefore well stocked with provisions and utensils of a kind which would not have been found had she been bound upon an ordinary voyage; so we had free choice among a multitude of objects suitable for the isolated life that loomed before us in the future.

I selected a large assortment of saucepans, plates, dishes, basins, knives, forks, and other domestic utensils, while Fritz took possession of a service of plate which he found in the captain's cabin, and some bottles of wine and spirits, to which I added a few Westphalia hams. These luxuriant provisions, however, did not lead us to contemn certain sacks of wheat and maize and other grain. Also I took possession of a compass, and some spades and other garden implements, together with a further supply of guns, pistols, and ammunition. Furthermore, we supplied ourselves with hammocks, bed-clothes, cord and twine of all kinds, and sail-cloth; and even took care to place among our cargo a little keg of sulphur with which to renew our supply of matches when those we had were all used in lighting our daily fire.

I then declared our cargo complete; when Fritz arrived with a last package.

'Leave that,' I said, 'my dear boy. We have no room for anything so large and apparently so heavy as what you have there.'

'Oh! do let us take it,' he said. 'It is the captain's library, containing books of science, and natural history, together with accounts of travels, and a Bible, Ernest and my mother will be so pleased with them!'

'My dear boy,' I replied, 'you are very thoughtful. Food for the mind is as essential as food for the body, and I heartily consent to do as you desire. Your last discovery will be a treasure to all of us.'

Our boat was now so heavily laden that it sunk almost to the water's edge, and had not the sea been perfectly calm I should have lightened it. As it was, I merely took the precaution to preserve our swimming floats, in case it should founder in the night and leave us helpless.

Night fell suddenly. A large fire which we perceived upon the distant coast assured us that nothing untoward had overtaken our beloved ones on land. And by way of reply to this good news, I hung out three lighted lanterns upon the side of the wreck. Immediately the report of a gun gave us notice that our signal had been seen.

Our preparations were soon made to pass the night in our tub-boat. I did not think it safe to sleep on board the wreck, for it was so placed that the least gust of wind might overturn it, and in that case we should be in serious danger of not seeing land again.

In spite of the discomfort of his berth, Fritz was not long in falling sound asleep. As for me, I could not close my eyes for an instant. I was full of anxiety for the safety of those whom we had left on shore, and, at the same time, desirous of being ready for any emergency that might arise where we were.

No sooner did day begin to break, than I mounted the deck of the vessel and directed my telescope towards the shore. I saw my wife come out of the tent and look anxiously towards us. I immediately ran a strip of white cloth up the mast, and my wife thereupon lowered and raised her flag three times, to show that she had understood my signal.

'Heaven be praised!' I ejaculated, 'they are all safe and well. Now let us see what can be done to get the cattle to land.'

'Supposing we were to construct a raft?' said Fritz.

I pointed out to him, not only the difficulty of making such a contrivance, but the far greater difficulty—if not impossibility—of steering it when it was made.

'Very well, then,' he replied, 'let us push them into the sea. I should think they would be able to swim to land. The pig, at all events, with its fat sides, can be in no possible danger of drowning.'

'Perhaps not,' I said, 'but what about the donkey, the cow, the goat, and the sheep; will they accomplish the journey so easily? For I must tell you candidly that I would willingly sacrifice the pig, if we could thereby save the other animals.'

'I have got it, papa!' cried Fritz joyously. 'Let us furnish them with the swimming floats which we made for ourselves. It will be splendid to see animals swimming in attire of that kind!'

'Bravo, my noble Fritz!' I exclaimed. 'Your idea, however droll it may be, seems to be quite practicable. To work, boy! to work! Let us make the attempt at all events.'

Thereupon we took a sheep, and having fastened the floats to it, one on each side, pushed in into the sea.

At first the poor beast, frightened out of its wits, disappeared beneath the waves. But it soon rose struggling to the surface; and at length, feeling the support which it derived from the swimming-belt, it floated patient and immovable. We had no longer any doubt that it could swim excellently.

Thus satisfied that we had hit upon the right plan of saving our cattle, we set to work vigorously.

Every piece of cork we could find anywhere was laid under contribution for the smaller animals; and for the larger ones—the cow and the donkey—we prepared empty barrels, which we tied to their sides with cords and strips of cloth.

When all our animals were harnessed, I tied to the horns or the neck of each of them a strong cord to lead them by when we got aboard our boat.

This done, we got them all into the water without much difficulty. The ass alone, after the manner of his kind, was recalcitrant, so we pushed him in backwards. At first he struggled a good deal, but after a time he resigned himself to the necessities of the case, and began to swim with so good a grace that we could not refrain from applauding his superior skill.

As soon as we had entered our boat I unmoored her, and the

breeze filling our sail, we found ourselves drifting rapidly and easily landwards.

Fritz, supremely happy in the result of our expedition, alternately fondled his monkey, and looked proudly up to the red streamer which unfurled itself gaily to the wind. For my own part, I followed with eye and heart the movements of my well-beloved ones on land, who, I saw by the aid of my telescope, were hastening down to the beach to meet us.

All at once Fritz cried out, 'Father, Father! There is an enormous fish coming towards us!'

'To arms!' I said, 'and attention!'

Our guns were already charged and we stood ready to fire. The creature of which Fritz had just signalled the approach was neither more nor less than a shark of the very largest kind.

'Let us fire together,' said I, 'at the moment when the monster, who swims on the surface, opens his jaws to seize that sheep towards which he is making so swiftly.'

Our guns went off together, and the shark disappeared.

An instant afterwards we saw, shining upon the surface, the brilliant scales of his belly; and a long trail of blood showed us that we were rid for ever of the terrible corsair.

I ordered Fritz to re-charge his gun, and did the same myself, lest the shark, as its custom is, should not be alone. Happily my fears were ill-founded.

Without meeting with any further adventure, we at length reached the shore.

My wife and the three boys awaited us. They seized the cable that I threw them to make fast the boat. The animals, who came to land without assistance, were soon relieved of their floats. The donkey capered about the sand joyously, and translated the pleasure he felt at once more touching the solid earth into a prolonged and not over-musical 'he-haw!'

As soon as we had embraced, and congratulated each other upon meeting again in health and safety after so long and perilous a separation, we went and seated ourselves upon the grass by the side of the stream, where I gave an account of all that had befallen us during our absence. I did not refrain from giving Fritz the high praise he merited for the assistance he had rendered me in our difficult and dangerous task.

CHAPTER VI

What passed on land during our absence

Fritz's invention for transporting the cattle excited general admiration, though little Francis marvelled most at seeing the sail and the bright red pennon.

We were then required to recount, down to the smallest details, how we had conducted our expedition.

Curiosity satisfied on this point, we proceeded to unload our tubs.

Jack soon gave up this drudgery, and went off among the cattle, where, jumping upon the back of the donkey, which had not yet been disembarrassed of its barrels, he rode back towards us with a ludicrous air of mock-majesty. We had all the trouble in the world to remain serious in the face of so droll a spectacle. But what was our astonishment to see our young cavalier wearing a hairy belt, into which he had thrust a pair of pistols!

'Where did you pick up that brigand's costume?' asked I.

'It is all of our own making,' he replied, 'and so are those,' pointing to the necks of the two dogs, each of which was furnished with a leather collar bristling with the spikes of nails. 'I think they will be able to defend themselves now,' he added, with an air of supreme satisfaction.

'Bravo, my son!' I sried, 'but are these your own inventions?'

'Mamma helped me,' he replied, 'in all the sewing that had to be done.'

'But where did you get the leather, the needles, and the thread?' I asked of my wife.

'Fritz's jackal furnished us with the leather,' said Jack.

'And as to the rest,' added my wife, smiling, 'a woman of management is always well provided with needles and thread.'

I saw that Fritz was not very well satisfied that his jackal should have been thus appropriated without his permission. It is true he concealed his ill-humour as well as he was able, but on coming near Jack he held his nose, and cried out, 'Pah! what an abominable smell!'

'Yes,' replied Jack imperturbably, 'it is my belt. It will be all right when it gets dry.'

'Let Jack remain to the windward,' said I, sailor fashion, 'and then he will not annoy us.'

'Ah, ah!' said the children, laughing, 'to the windward, Jack! to the windward!'

As to the merry Jack himself, he was not in the least troubled by the odour of his belt, but strutted about, handling his pistols like a bucccaneer.

His brothers hastened to throw the offensive remains of the jackal into the sea.

Seeing that it was nearly supper-time, I told Fritz to go and fetch one of the Westphalia hams out of the tubs.

He was not long in returning.

'Oh, a ham! a ham ready to eat!' cried the youngsters, clapping their hands.

'Moderate yourselves, my children,' said my wife, 'for if you only had this ham, which is not yet cooked, for supper, you would fast a long time, I am thinking. But I have here some turtles' eggs, with which I will make an omelette in the frying-pan which papa and Fritz have been thoughtful enough to bring away from the wreck—a nice, savoury omelette, in which butter shall not be wanting.'

'The eggs of the turtle,' said Ernest, always desirous of displaying his knowledge, 'are easily distingushed by their roundness, by their membraneous shells, which are like wetted parchment, and also by the fact that the turtle alone deposits its eggs in the sands by the seashore.'

'How did you find them?' asked I.

'That,' said my wife, 'belongs to a little history which we have to tell you. But before beginning it, I think it will be best to see to the cooking, unless you would like to go to bed supperless.'

'You are right,' I said.' Make an omelette, and reserve your story for the repast. It will form an agreeable side-dish. In the meantime I and the children will stow our cargo in a safe place, and rack up the beasts for the night.'

With these words I got up, and the boys followed me to the beach. By the time my wife invited us to do honour to her supper we had finished.

Nothing was wanting to a good meal—omelette, cheese, biscuit, all were found excellent; and a table for the time first decently laid out added not a little to the agreeableness of the repast.

Francis alone, faithful to his calabash service, declined even to return to silver-plate.

'It is far nicer,' he said, 'to eat out of playthings than out of real dishes.'

The dogs, the chickens, the goats, and the sheep formed a circle of interested spectators around us. As to the ducks and geese, I did not trouble myself about feeding them, knowing that the marshy ground at the mouth of the stream would furnish them with abundance of worms and small crabs—to which latter they had already shown themselves partial.

Supper ended, I told Fritz to bring us a bottle of the excellent wine which he had found in the captain's cabin, and begged my wife to take a glass to fortify her for her narrative.

'It seems, then,' she said laughingly, 'that it has at last come to my turn to recount my noble deeds. As to the first day, I have nothing to tell—anxiety for your safety kept me upon the beach all day, and I had not the courage to undertake a single duty away from thence. I was not a little thankful, I can assure you, when I saw that you reached the wreck without impediment.

'We passed the day, then, in the neighbourhood of the tent; and I confined myself to thinking out a project whereby, on the morrow, we might seek out some spot more comfortable for a dwelling-place than this inhospitable shore. We are here exposed to the full heat of the sun by day, and the full rigour of the cold by night. I thought of the wood you and Fritz had passed through on the previous day, and determined to go thither and explore it.

'This morning, while I was again thinking over my project—without having said anything to the children, who had but just got up—Jack took Fritz's jackal, and cut out from the skin of the animal two large strips, which he deprived of the hair and cleaned as well as he was able.

'He then obtained some long nails, which he drove through one of the strips, and cut out a piece of sail-cloth with which to line it. This done, he brought his work to me, and asked me to sew the cloth to the leather in such a manner that it would at once keep in the nails and cover them. In spite of the disagreeable odour of the skin I did as he desired, and, cutting the strap in two, he put one-half round each of the dogs' necks, as you see. He then desired me to line the other strap, in order that he might wear it as a belt; but I pointed out to him that as this strap was not dry yet, it would shrink and render our labour useless.

'Ernest laughingly advised him to stretch the strap on a board, and carry it about in the sun to dry, which he proceeded very gravely to do, without perceiving the joke.

'I then communicated to the boys my plans for the day, and they fell in with them joyfully. In a twinkling they were furnished forth with arms and provisions. I took a can of water and an axe. Escorted by the dogs, we set out for the banks of the stream.

'Turk, who remembered well enough the way he had travelled with you, was evidently impressed with the responsibilities of his position. He preceded us with an air of superior knowledge, and was continually looking behing to assure himself that we were following in the right track.

'Ernest and Jack marched resolutely behind Turk, proud of carrying arms for the first times in their lives. They also were impressed with their importance, for I had hinted to them that upon their courage and address depended the security of the whole party. And I cannot but confess that, in the circumstances in which we found ourselves, I appreciated, for the first time, your wisdom in teaching them the use of arms, and the necessity for confronting every kind od danger bravely.

'We found it by no means an easy task to cross the stream, the stepping-stones were so wet and slippery. Ernest crossed first without accident. Jack held my bottle and axe, and I took Francis upon my back. The little fellow clasped his arms round my neck and clung to me with all his strength; and with some difficulty and danger we at length got safely over.

'On reaching the other side, and ascending the height whence you saw the splendid prospect that you described to us with so much enthusiasm, my heart, for the first time since our shipwreck, gave way to the influence of pleasure and hope.

'We soon descended into a dale overshadowed with foliage and carpeted with greensward.

'A small wood lay in front of us; but in order to get there, we had to pass through a large field of grass, so tall and entangled that it both concealed the children and impeded our movements. Jack, however, found a place where the grass was trodden down; and we concluded that we were then in the track which you had made and followed on the previous day. Guided by your foot-steps, we after several times losing one or two of the children in the grass, came out at the entrance to the wood.

'All at once we heard a great rustling among the leaves, and immediately saw a huge bird rise off the ground in front of us, and fly swiftly skywards.

'Each of my little men brought his gun to his shoulder, but the bird was beyond reach before they could take aim at him.

' "What a pity," said Ernest rather irritably, "that I had not got my own little gun with me! Even as it was I should have brought down my bird if he had not flown away so swiftly."

' "No doubt," I replied, "you would be an excellent sportsman if the game were to give you a quarter of an hour's notice of its intention to fly away."

' "But how was I to tell that a bird was going to rise in front of me?" he asked.

' "It is," I replied, "just such surprises as these that make shooting difficult. In order to succeed in sport, it is not only necessary to be a good marksman, but you must also possess great presence of mind."

' "What could this bird have been?" asked Jack.

' "An eagle, of course," replied Francis. "It had immensely large wings."

' "That proves nothing," said Ernest. "Al birds with large wings are not eagles."

' "I have no doubt," I interposed, "that it was sitting upon its nest when we disturbed it. Let us look about, and if we find this nest, we shall then be better able to tell what the bird was."

'Jack, the madcap, dashed instantly towards the place where the bird had risen, and another bird, exactly like the first, flew out and away, striking the little fellow in the face with its huge wing as it went.

'Jack stood wonder-stricken, and, I think, very much terrified.

'Ernest, not less astonished, made no attempt even to raise his gun towards the bird.

' "You are pretty sportsmen, truly," said I. "Is it posible that you could profit so little by what I have been saying to you? It is clear that you badly need some more lessons in shooting from your father.'

'Ernest was annoyed.

'Jack took off his hat, and, making a comic salute to the fugitive —who by this time was but a dot in the blue sky—" Farewell for the present, Mr. Bird," said he, "another time will do as well for me. I am your humble and devoted servant always."

'Ernest soon found the nest we were looking for. It was very rudely constructed, and contained nothing but a few broken egg-shells; from which latter circumstances we concluded that a nest of young ones had not long since occupied it.

' "These birds cannot be eagles," said Ernest, "for the young of eagles cannot run so soon after they are born as these birds seem to have done. The contrary is the case with ordinary farmyard hens, guinea-fowls, and other winged creatures of the same family. I am led to assume, then, that the birds whose nest we have just found are bustards; for, besides the little matter which I have just mentioned as indicating the family to which they belong, you have seen yourself that their plumage underneath is of a tawny-white colour, while above it is black, streaked here and there with red. I noticed too that the one which flew off last had long, thin feathers growing out of his beak like a moustache, which is the characteristic sign of the male."

' "Instead of making this very minute examination of the birds," said I to our young savant, who held his head perceptibly higher after this display of erudition, "you would have done better to take sure aim. You would then have run a chance of making still more satisfactory observations at your leisure. But, after all," I added, "it was perhaps better to leave the poor things alive to take care of their little ones."

'While chatting in this wise we entered the wood. The trees were filled with strange birds, who sang to us a concert of the most varied music.

'The youngsters, profiting by their last lesson, were preparing to fire; but I pointed out to them that the prodigious height of the trees upon which the gay singers were perched rendered any attempt at shooting useless.

'The form and the extraordinary girth of these gigantic trees struck us with astonishment. Their enormous trunks did not grow out of the ground like those of other trees, but were supported by powerful roots, which, lying exposed to the open air, rose into a kin of groined dome immediately under the tree, and thence ran out in all directions, dipping into the soil only here and there, and at a distance from the tree. Jack clambered up one these roots, and measured the trunk with a piece of string. Ernest calculated that the girth of the tree could not be less than forty feet, while the height of the picturesque vault formed by some sixty of the roots, between the ground and the base of the trunk, was about eighty feet.

'Nothing had ever struck me with greater admiration than the sight of this splendid vegetation. Ten or twelve trees alone formed that which we had hitherto supposed to be a wood. Their branches thrust themselves out to an incredible distance, and their foliage, which in shape reminded me of that of our own walnut-tree in Europe, threw a delicious shadow over a large extent of ground. Beneath, the earth was carpeted with a rich velvety greensward, which invited us to repose.

'We sat down. The provision-bags were opened. A stream which murmured along its pebbly course furnished us with clear spring-water, and the multitude of birds that sang over our heads gave to our repast the air of a festival. None of us lacked appetite.

'Our dogs, who had left us some time before, now returned. To our great surprise they did not show any sign of wanting food, but lay down tranquilly upon the grass and went to sleep. We concluded that they had been lucky enough to find a meal elsewhere.

'The place where we were seemed to me so excellently situated, that I did not think it worth while to seek further for a site for our future dwelling-place.

'I thereupon determined to return by the way we had come, and go down to the beach to try to collect whatever waifs from the wreck might have been cast up there by the wind and waves.

'Jack implored me, before setting out, to sew in the lining of his belt, which he had not ceased for an instant to carry in the sun as his brother had recommended, and which was now quite dry and fit for use.

'This done, he fastened the belt round his waist, stuck his pistols into it, and looking as pleased as possible, strutted off to lead the way back and be the first to exhibit himself to you, in case you should have landed before our return. So anxious was he to get there, that we were obliged to hasten our steps in order that we might not lose sight of him.

'On the beach I found but few things to carry away, for most of the objects that we could reach were too heavy for our poor powers. While we were there, however, I noticed that the dogs were bounding along the edge of the water, and every now and then drawing out with their paws small crabs, which they devoured with relish.

' "See, my boys," I cried, "what a teacher hunger is" We need trouble ourselves no more about finding food for our dogs, nor be afraid of their eating us, since the sea affords them nourishment so abundant."

' "The dogs eat *us!*" cried Jack, drawing his pistols fiercely from his belt. "They had better not make the attempt! Let them come on: I am ready for them!"

' "Droll little braggart!" I said, embracing him, "what could your pistols avail against a couple of powerful dogs like those? Before you could fire off a single charge they would gobble you up."

' "Fan and Turk are much too good to think of eating us," said little Francis, "and it is very naughty of Jack to think of shooting them. Take away those dreadful pistols, mamma, or he will do some mischief with them"

' "There, there!" said Jack, embracing his brother, "don't be troubled. I have no more wish than you have to do harm to our good dogs. I only said what I did in fun."

'On quitting the beach we saw Fan scratch up the sand, and rake out a white-looking ball, which she swallowed greedily.

' "What if that were a turtle's egg?" cried Ernest.

' "Turtle's eggs!" said Francis. "Are turtles fowls, then?"

'You may judge of the amusement which this question caused to Jack and Ernest.

'When the merriment had subsided, "Let us profit by Fan's discovery," said I, "for I have heard say that these eggs are very nice to eat."

' "They are indeed," said Ernest, who was already rejoicing in thoughts that savoured of choice dishes.

'It was not without some difficulty that we drove Fan away from a repast which she found so much to her taste. Although she had already disposed of several eggs, there still remained about a score, which we carefully put away in our provision-bags.

'Then on looking out to sea, we caught sight of the sail of your boat. Francis feared that might be a band of savages who were coming to kill us, but Ernest said he felt sure it was your vessel. And he was right; for a few minutes afterwards you came to land, and we were once more able to embrace each other.

'Such, my love, are our adventures. I sought a new dwelling-place—I have found one; and I am so delighted with it that, if you agree, we will set out tomorrow and establish our home beneath those magnificent trees. The view from it is superb, and the place itself is exquisite.'

'What!' said I jestingly, 'trees, good wife! Is that all that you have discovered towards a secure dwelling-place for us? I can quite understand, if they are as large as you say, that we could find a refuge in their branches in the night-time. But in order to get there we should require either wings or a balloon, which are not easy things to make or to manage.'

' Ah!' said she, 'you may laugh; but I am sure we could build an excellent cabin upon the branches of these trees, which could be reached easily enough by some wooden stairs. One often sees the same thing in Europe. Do you not remember, for instance, the linden in our own country, which has a cabin in its branches, and which for that reason is called "Robinson's tree"?'

'All in good time,' said I. 'We can think over this difficult matter later on.'

But night had already fallen: our conversation had caused us to forget the hour of repose. We offered up our nightly prayer, and at once retired to rest, in order that we might rise with the first beams of the morning sun.

CHAPTER VII

Projects for migration—the dead shark—the bridge

'Last night,' I said to my wife when we awoke in the morning, 'I considered your project for migration seriously. We will go and take our habitation in the wood, as you desire; but we will still keep a storehouse of provisions here, and turn the place into a kind of fortress to which we can retire in case of attack. We will also leave our powder among the rocks; for which it is of great use to us, it may prove a dangerous neighbour. This plan adopted, it will be necessary, first of all, to throw a bridge over the stream, in order to render our removal and our daily journeys between the two places the more easy of accomplishment.'

'My love!' cried my wife, 'whatever are you thinking of? The construction of a bridge will be a long labour and a painful one. Why could we not employ the ass and the cow to carry our goods over?'

I assured her that she exaggerated the importance of the work, and the obstacles which would have to be overcome in performing it.

'In that case,' she replied, 'begin, or rather let us all begin, to put your design into execution without delay, for I have the greatest desire to remove from this place as speedily as possible.'

Thus was opened the question of our change of residence. The children, whom we now awakened, and to whom we imparted our project, received the news of it with enthusiasm. They at once christened the little wood 'The Promised Land'.

They were equally desirous, all of them, that we should lose no time in constructing the bridge; but I did not pay much attention to their impatience. It is in the nature of children to wish to see everything done at once.

Morning prayer offered, each taxed his ingenuity to make the best breakfast he could.

Meanwhile I got the tub-boat ready to go to the wreck for such pieces of carpentry and timber as would be useful to us in the construction of our bridge. Feeling that I should have need of an extra assistant, I determined to take Ernest as well as Fritz.

We soon put to sea, and by making good use of our oars were not long in getting into the current of the stream, which had already aided us so materially in our previous voyage. As we were passing close by an island situated at the entrance to the bay, we saw a cloud of sea-mews, albatrosses, and other birds wheeling their flight ever-returning circles upon the shore, and uttering cries so piercing that we were tempted to close our ears.

Fritz had a great desire to fire upon the feathery flock, but I forbade him.

So numerous an assemblage of sea-birds, it appeared to me, could only be attributed to some extraordinary cause, and I desired to ascertain what it was. I hoisted the sail, which became inflated at once, and a fresh breeze carried us towards the island.

Ernest was charmed. Our pennon floating coquettishly upon the mast, the easy motion of the boat, and the smiling aspect of the island threw him into transports of joy.

Fritz did not once take his eyes off the point where the birds seemed to be gathered in the largest number.

'I see what it is now,' he cried all at once, 'They are engaged in dismembering some sea monster, and are feasting joyously without giving us the courtesy of an invitation.'

He was not mistaken. Having landed, we fastened our boat securely to the rocks, and were then able to examine everything at our leisure without being noticed by the birds, who were busily engaged in dispatching an enormous dead fish. So eager indeed were they in the work of devouring their quarry, that our still nearer approach did not put them to flight.

Fritz wondered where the dead monster could have come from, seeing that we had not noticed it there on the previous evening.

'Why,' said Ernest, 'is it not the shark which you killed yesterday?'

'No doubt about it,' I replied. 'Ernest is right. It is our pirate. Look at his terrible jaw, and at his skin—so rough that it will polish iron and file wood. It is not one of the least of the species either, for it will measure, I should judge, fifteen feet in length. Heaven be thanked once more that we were delivered from so redoubtable an enemy! We will leave these gulls to feast upon the flesh of our shark; but I think it would be as well to carry away a few strips of his skin: it may prove useful to us.'

Ernest drew the iron ramrod from his gun and advanced upon the birds, beating them to right and left. He struck some of them down; the others flew away. Fritz was then able to cut several large strips of skin from the flanks of the animal, and we returned to our boat.

As we were about to put out to sea again to go to the wreck, I saw, some distance along the shore of the island, a large number of beams and planks that had been cast up by the tide. There was, therefore, no need to continue our voyage, for we found close at hand all the materials that were necessary to our projected construction.

I chose from among the mass whatever would suit our purpose best, and fastening the pieces together after the fashion of a raft, tied them with a long rope to the stern of the boat, and put about to return to the point whence we had set out. The wind being favourable, there was no need for rowing. All I had to do was to steer.

Fritz nailed the pieces of shark's skin to the mast in order to dry them.

Ernest made a searching examination of the sea-mews which he had killed.

He failed not to address to me many question upon the nature of these birds, and I answered him as well as I was able. Then he desired to know to what use I intended to put the strips of shark's skin. I told him that I proposed to make rasps of them; and I added that in Europe it was generally dressed in such a manner as to make 'shagreen'.

The voyage was finished. On landing, we were surprised to find none of the family awaiting us; but no sooner had we shouted for them than they came running towards us.

Francis had a fishing-net slung over his shoulder, and Jack

carried a carefully tied handkerchief dangling from his hand. When he had come up to us he opened a corner of it and showed us a large number of fine crabs.

'It was I, father—it was I who found them,' cried Francis proudly.

Yes,' replied Jack, 'but it was I who caught them. I went into the water up to my knees and took them while they were dining. as they supposed, in security off the remains of Fritz's jackal. I should have taken a great many more if I had not been called away so soon.'

'We have already more than we shall need,' said I; 'and I am thinking that it would be as well to throw the least of them into the water again, in order that they may grow larger.'

'No need to do that,' replied the careless boy; they are to be found by the millions: the stream is full of them.'

'It does not matter how many there are,' I said. 'It is necessary to use the gifts God has given us with economy. If we destroy the young we cannot expect in the future to be provided with the old or the young either.'

Upon that Jack hastened towards the banks of the stream, begging me to go with him. He was desirous of showing me, he said, that he had been gravely considering the question of building the bridge.

I asked him to explain himself a little more clearly.

Thereupon he told me he had been seeking up and down the stream for the most convenient point at which to throw the bridge across, and that he believed he had found it.

'That is well!' I cried delightedly, 'and I congratulate you upon the fact that you have been able at last to steal a few moments from your habitual thoughtlessness to devote to the general good our little colony. I shall not be slow to assure myself whether in this, your first attempt, you have shown any proof of sagacity. If it should so happen that the point you have fixed upon should seem to me to be well chosen, we will occupy ourselves in floating the beams and planks thither while your good mother prepares our dinner.'

Jack at once conducted us to the spot where he thought the brigde might most readily be built, and, after a careful examination, I was of opinion that it was the one of all others which offered the least difficulty.

After a few journeys to and fro, the transport of materials was duly effected, and everything was ready to commence the construction of our bridge.

At the point which Jack had chosen, the stream was narrower than at any other, and the banks on either side were of about the same height. Besides this, there were trees on both sides to which we could fix the cross-beams.

'Now,' said I, when everything was ready to commence operations, 'the first thing to be done is to measure the width of the stream, in order to see whether we have any pieces of wood long enough to reach across.'

'It seems to me,' replied Ernest, 'that nothing is more easy. It will only be necessary to tie a stone to the end of a piece of twine, and fling it across the stream. We can then draw it towards us till it reaches the edge of the water on the other side, and the length of the twine will give us the measure we seek.'

Having put in practice this plan—which, as it occurred to me, was as simple as it was ingenious—Ernest calculated that the stream at that point was about eighteen feet in width.

I concluded it to be necessary that the principal beams should have a resting-place of at least three feet on each bank of the stream; and therefore selected from our store three of from twenty-four to twenty-five feet in length.

The greatest difficulty yet remained to be overcome. It was how to lay these enormous pieces of wood across the stream. I proposed to my boys that we should resolve this difficulty over our meal, which had been awaiting us some time.

We thereupon returned to my wife, who had been somewhat impatiently expecting our coming, for the crabs were ready for eating a quarter of an hour since, and she was afraid that our dinner would be spoilt.

But before sitting down we could not forbear admiring the patience and ingenuity the careful housewife had displayed in preparing panniers of sail-cloth for the ass and the cow to remove our goods in. We applauded her skill still more when we learned that, for want of needles of a large size, she had pierced the holes for the twine with nails, and had thus painfully sewn her material strongly together.

The repast was short, for each of us was anxious to get back again to work. Although we discussed at length the best means of getting our beams across, none of the children hit upon a feasible plan. Happily I was better inspired.

As soon as we got back to our miniature dockyard, I put into execution the plan I had conceived.

I affixed a rope to that end of the first of my huge beams which was nearest to the bank of the stream upon which we were standing, and tied the rope to one of the trees that overshadowed us. To the other end of the beam I fastened a longer rope, and walking boldly through the stream, carried it over to the other side, where I ran it over the wheel of a pulley which I hung upon the branch of a large tree upon that side. Then I came back again, and attached the end of this second rope to the ass and the cow. I bade them pull together, which they did, and I had the satisfaction of seeing my beam first rise out of the water, and, next, swing slowly across to the other side of the stream.

The children, astonished to see a difficult piece of work accomplished so easily, jumped for joy, clapping their hands, and shouting triumphantly at the top of their voices.

The most difficult part of our labour was now at an end. The two other beams were laid, in a similar manner, parallel with the first, and nothing remained but to nail a series of planks across them to finish the bridge.

We had the happiness of bringing our work to an end before nightfall. But we were all very much fatigued; and never since our landing had we slept so soundly as during the hours of darkness which followed the greatest of the labours that we had yet achieved.

CHAPTER VIII

Removing—the porcupine—the 'Promised Land'

At the first dawning of day I woke up the children, to whom I thought it right to give a few instructions concerning their duties during our removal.

'We are going,' I said, 'to traverse a strange and, for aught I know, dangerous tract of country. Let none of you venture alone. The same risk menaces those who go too far ahead and those who fall off in the rear. Let us all travel as closely together as we can, and if an enemy presents itself, leave me to direct the attack or the defence.'

Morning prayer offered, and breakfast at an end, we prepared to set out. The animals were driven in, and the ass and the cow were loaded with the panniers which my wife made on the previous evening, and which we had filled with all such articles as were likely to be of the greatest use to us. We took care, too, not to forget a little of the captain's wine and some butter.

As I was about to complete the loading of the animals with our bed-clothes, our hammocks, and a quantity of cordage, my wife interposed and claimed a seat for little Francis, as well as for the sack which she called her enchanted bag. She also pointed out that it was obviously necessary to take our fowls and pigeons with us, inasmuch as they would most certainly disperse and be lost as soon as we ceased to feed them. I gave way to her wishes. A comfortable place was found for Francis on the back of the donkey, where he was safely seated between the panniers, with the enchanted bag at his back to lean against.

It now remained to catch the fowls and pigeons. The children ran after them and did their best to capture them, but without taking a single bird.

Wiser than they, my wife stood still, and told them that in that position she would undertake to catch all the birds, scared as they were, without any trouble whatever. 'Ah, well!' said the youngsters, 'we shall see! We shall see!'

'I intend you to do so,' replied their mother.

Upon that she scattered a few handfuls of grain around the

entrance to the tent, and in a twinkling all our winged friends were around us. After they had eaten their first meal, she scattered a few more handfuls of grain, this time not outside, but inside the tent. Pigeons and fowls at once rushed in after it, and soon found themselves in a trap.

'More is to be done by address than by violence, you see, young gentlemen,' said my wife, as she closed the entrance to the tent.

Jack was allowed to creep in to hold our feathered prisoners while we tied their legs together; and this done, we placed them on the back of the cow, shielding them from the sun with a cloth which we spread out upon a couple of sticks bent into the form of an arch. Thus hid away in the shade, they did not worry us with their cackling.

Everything we proposed to leave behind us that could be injured either by the rain or by the sun we shut up in the tent, the entrance to which we carefully closed up with stakes, and barricaded with casks and chests, some full and some empty.

Then I gave the signal to set out.

We were all well armed, and each of us carried a game-bag filled with provisions and ammunition. We were in the best of humours with ourselves and with each other.

Fritz, gun under arm, placed himself at the head of the procession. Behind him came my wife, leading in the cow and the ass, who walked side by side. On the latter was seated little Francis, who amused us greatly from time to time by his droll sayings. Behind the cow and the ass came Jack and the goat, and behind these Ernest and the sheep. I myself formed the rearguard. The dogs ran here, there, and everywhere, sniffing and barking, and constantly on the alert.

As we approached the bridge, the sow, which had at first appeared but little inclined to follow us, rejoined the party—not, however, without manifesting by her impatient gruntings the displeasure which so long a journey occasioned her. It may be as well to add that we did not trouble ourselves very seriously concerning her ill-humours.

We had not gone far when we saw our dogs bounding round a thicket, and barking excitedly, as if they were attacking some ferocious animal that had taken refuge there.

Fritz, with gun to shoulder and finger upon trigger, advanced resolutely to the charge.

Ernest uneasily took refuge nearer his mother; not, however, without making ready to fire should occasion require it.

Jack dashed intrepidly after his elder brother, with his gun slung carelessly over his shoulder.

I was hastening after to protect him if he should fall into danger when he cried out at the top of his voice, 'Oh, papa! Come along! Make haste! A porcupine! An enormous porcupine!'

I hurried to the spot, and was not long in descrying what indeed was a porcupine, as Jack had said; but it was not nearly so large as he had given me to understand.

The dogs were still barking, and gnashing their teeth with rage to find themselves confronted by an animal which they could not attack without running the risk of paying dearly for their temerity.

The porcupine was carrying on the battle after the fashion of his tribe. He had turned tail upon his adversaries, and, with his head hidden between his paws, was thrusting himself backwards against them, with all his quills bristling and shaking in a manner which produced a strange rattling sound, that daunted the dogs as much as his odd method of fighting. Every time Turk or Fan pounced upon him they returned from the charge with a number of small but irritating wounds. At length their mouths and muzzles bled profusely.

Fritz and I stood watching for an opportunity fo fire at the creature without danger of hurting the dogs.

Jack, however, more impatient, and not comprehending our hesitation, drew one of his pistols and, without more ado, shot the porcupine dead on the spot.

Jack, with his habitual lack of caution, had already laid hold upon the animal with his hands, and, in consequence, was bleeding from several wounds in them.

'Go and get a piece of string,' said I, 'you can then tie its feet together, and throw it over a stick, which you can carry between you, one holding each end.'

But, impatient to show his game to his mother and younger brothers, Jack drew out his pocket-handkerchief, tied it round the neck of the porcupine, and dragged the animal along the ground to the place where the caravan awaited us.

Ernest, who now came up, examined the porcupine very attentively and with his usual deliberateness. He then remarked that it had in each jaw two long incisor teeth of the same kind as those of the hare and squirrel, while its ears were short and rounded, and had some distant resemblance to those of the human species.

My wife and I, meanwhile, had seated ourselves on the ground, and were engaged in drawing out the points of the creature's quills which still remained in the muzzles of our dogs.

Determined to carry the porcupine along with us, I placed round him a thick covering of herbs, and tied him up in some of our bed-clothes. I then fastened the bundle to the crupper of the donkey behind little Francis, and we proceeded upon our way.

At length, and without further adventure, we reached the 'Promised Land'.

'Magnificent!' cried Ernest, when he saw the huge trees which we were approaching. 'What gigantic vegetation! The great spire of Strasburg is not nearly so high. How glorious are the works of nature, compared with those of man! What a delightful idea that was of mamma's, to quit the desolate place where we first put up our tent in order to live here!'

Then he asked me if I knew the names of these trees.

'So far as I am aware,' I replied, 'they are not described any-where; and I have little doubt that we are the first Europeans who have been privileged to see them. I defy the most agile of bears to get at us when we have established our dwelling-place at the top of these huge bare trunks'.

'So you like our trees now you come to see them for yourself?' said my wife.

'I can now understand why you admired them so,' I replied. 'I think your choice perfect.'

'And yet you were so unhappy at the idea of leaving our old dwelling for this!' she said, pointing her finger at me playfully, and laughing. 'Fie, incredulous man! You must see before you will condescend to believe, must you?'

I smilingly accepted the amicable reproach.

We halted. Our first care was to unload the beasts of burden, and turn them out to feed along with the sheep and the goat, first taking care to tie their forefeet loosely together so that they might not stray away. The sow alone was left entirely mistress of her movements.

We then let out the fowls and pigeons. The fowls at once began picking insects out of the grass around us. The pigeons flew away into the branches of the trees, whence, however, they failed to descend at the first distribution of grain.

We then sat down upon the elastic greensward with which the whole soil thereabouts was carpeted, and took counsel together concerning the construction of our house in one of the giant trees.

CHAPTER IX

The tiger-cat—the wounded flamingo

As it did not seem at all probable that we should be able to install ourselves in a new dwelling before the morrow, I became anxious concerning our means of passing the night in safety; for at present we were exposed to the weather, and had no defence against wild beasts.

I called Fritz, who I thought was among us, to tell him that I intended to attempt the ascent of one of the trees at once.

He made no reply; but two shots fired in succession, a short distance away, told us that he was not wasting his time. 'Hit! Hit! There he is!' we heard him crying excitedly.

In a few moments he made his appearance, carrying by the hind legs a magnificent tiger-cat, which he proudly held up for us to look at.

'Bravo, my young hunter!' cried I, 'you have rendered us a signal service in delivering our fowls and pigeons from this redoubtable neighbour; for they would not be safe from his clutches even if they were perched upon the topmost branches of these high trees.'

'I found it close by,' said Fritz. 'I noticed something moving among the leaves of one of the trees, and going stealthily up to the foot of it, saw this creature among the branches. I fired at it, and it fell at my feet. As I was going to take it up, it got upon its feet, and was about to make off, when I brought it down dead with a pistol-shot.'

'You may consider yourself fortunate,' I replied, 'that it did not, when you had only wounded it, fly at you instead of trying to run away. For these animals, although so small in build, are terrible when they are defending their lives. I can say this with the more certainty inasmuch as I think I now recognise in the animal which you have just killed, not the tiger-cat properly so-called, but the margay, or cayenne-cat, which is very common in South America, and is famous for its rapacity and audacity.'

'However that may be,' said Fritz, 'look at its magnificent coat— at those splendidly glossy black and brown spots upon the ground-work of gold! I trust Jack will be considerate enough to refrain from hacking the skin of my margay to pieces as he did that of my jackal.'

'Never fear,' said I. 'If you only tell Jack that you want to keep a thing, he will not think of injuring it. But what do you propose to do with this skin?'

'I was just going to ask you what I should do with it,' replied the young hunter. 'I shall follow your advice in the matter. Let it be understood, also, that I have no wish to use it exclusively for my own benefit.'

'Well said, my son,' replied I. 'In that case, as we have no need at present to draw upon furs for our clothing, I should advise that you turn the skin of the body and legs into cases for our silver dinner-sets which we found in the captain's cabin on the wreck, and that with the skin of the tail you make yourself a handsome hunting-belt to carry your knife and pistols in.'

'And I, father?' asked Jack in his turn, 'what shall I do with the skin of my porcupine?'

'Why, my boy,' replied I, 'after we have pulled out the quills to make needles or to tip arrows with, I fancy we shall be able to turn the skin into a kind of armour for the protection of our dogs in any future fights they may have with ferocious animals.'

'Capital! capital!' cried Jack. 'It will be great fun to see Turk and Fan dressed up in that fashion!'

And the impetuous fellow would give me no rest till I had shown him how to skin his porcupine.

To this end, I hung the animal up to a tree by the hind legs, and proceeded to flay him—an operation in which I succeeded to perfection.

Fritz, who watched me attentively, did the same by his margay.

We then nailed the two skins to the trunk of a tree to dry. A portion of the flesh of the porcupine was cut off for the repast which my wife was beginning to prepare; the rest was put by to be salted.

Ernest, meanwhile, had been collecting some large stones, and building a fireplace with them.

'Don't you think,' he asked me, after proceeding with his work in thoughtful silence for some time, 'that these strange-looking trees belong to the mangrove family?'

I answered that his supposition seemed to me to be a very reasonable one but that I could not speak positively upon the point until I had consulted the captain's library.

'Ah! those dear books!' he exclaimed enthusiastically. 'I do so long for the time when we shall have leisure to read them through and through.'

'Patience, my dear child, patience!' said I. 'We must first of all devote our energies to the indispensable. It will not be long before we shall find ourselves with leisure to do as we please.'

Francis, who had been sent by his mother to gather dry wood to make the fire with, returned dragging a number of small branches behind him, and munching some fruit which he seemed to enjoy greatly.

He threw down the branches at once, and began pulling out of his pocket a number of small figs, which he was about to throw away. I took one or two from him, and examined them.

'So,' said Ernest, 'these are fig-trees after all.'

'So it appears,' I replied, 'but not the dwarf species such as we used to see in Europe. These belong, as you supposed at first, to the family of the mangroves, and, as I believe, to the species called the "yellow mangrove", which so far as I remember, is said to thrust out its enormous roots in arches such as we see here.'

While gossiping thus, and while my wife, aided by little Francis, was getting the dinner ready, I employed myself in making needles out of the porcupine's quills. The point had been already made by nature; it only remained to pierce a hole through the other extremity, which I did with a long nail that I made red-hot in the fire. In a short time I turned out a large assortment of excellent needles, which my wife was very glad to accept.

The children, who never ceased to wonder at the prodigious height of the trees amongst which we had determined to fix our dwelling made many ineffectual attempts to climb up them. I was at first as much puzzled as they to hit upon a plan of reaching the branches where we were to build our hut; but as I was thinking over the matter an idea struck me, of which, however, I deferred the execution.

The repast being at length ready, we seated ourselves around it on the grass, and fell-to. The flesh of the porcupine and the soup in which it had been boiled were found excellent, and we finished our meal with butter and Dutch cheese.

Thus refreshed, we determined to make the best use of the few hours of day that remained to us.

I told my wife to make us some straps as quickly as she could, in order that with these and a few lengths of rope we might go down to the beach and bring up what timber was necessary for our projected building operations. She set to work at once.

Meanwhile I took the precaution to prepare our hammocks for the night, lest we should find ourselves without a bed to lie on. I hung them to the arched roots of one of the mangroves, and stretched a piece of sail-cloth over the top to preserve us both from the dew and the mosquitoes, of which latter there were swarms.

This done, I went down to the coast with Fritz and Ernest to see if we could find some pieces of wood that would serve for the steps of a ladder, which I intended to construct of stout cord.

Ernest discovered, at the edge of a morass, a quantity of bamboos which were half-buried in the ooze.

We pulled some of them up, and having cut them into lengths of three or four feet with our axes, made them up into three bundles—one for each of us.

At some distance from the place where we found the bamboos, and a little nearer the centre of the marsh, I espied a thick bed of reeds, towards which I directed my steps in order to cut some for the purpose of making arrows of them. Fan, who was walking beside me, suddenly dashed forward, barking loudly; and immediately a flock of magnificent flamingoes flew off with extreme swiftness.

Fritz, who was never taken at unawares in emergencies of the kind, had just time to lift his gun to his shoulder and fire before the birds were out of range.

Two of the flamingoes fell—one of them stone dead, the other only wounded in the wing. This latter would in all probability have made good its escape, had not Fan at once bounded off in pursuit of it. She soon overtook it, and sagaciously held it by the wing until I came up and took it from her.

Desirous that the incident should not prevent me from taking possession of my coveted reeds, I set to work cutting a number of the longest of them, remarking to the boys that I intended to use them for measuring the height of the tree in which we proposed to build our habitation.

The two boys were silent.

Then, laden with our bamboos, our reeds, and the dead and the living flamingo—which latter I had tied by the legs—we returned to the family.

Jack and Francis welcomed the live flamingo with shouts of joy; but their mother looked troubled as she reflected that we were adding another useless mouth to the already large number of our domestic animals.

Less prone than she to be anxious on such a subject, I set myself to examine the creature's wounds. I saw that the ends of both its wings were fractured—in the one case by Fritz's gun-shot, in the other by the teeth of Fan. I dressed each of the wounds with a sort of ointment which I compounded of butter and salt and wine. This done, the flamingo was tied by a cord to a stake driven into the ground near the stream. Left to itself, it tucked its bill under its wing, supported itself upon one of its long legs, drawing the other close up to its body, and went off to sleep.

While I was engaged with my surgery, the youngsters had tied several reeds together, end to end, and were raising them against one of the mangroves to measure its height. Their measuring-rod, however, scarcely reached to the place where the aerial roots sprang from the trunk; and I heard them expressing anew their doubts as to the success of the plan which I had hinted at, but had not yet explained to them.

Leaving them to their useless and incredulous gossip, and smiling at their perplexity, I took several of the reeds, which I pointed at one end, and garnished at the other with feathers plucked from the dead flamingo. I weighted the arrows thus formed by filling the hollow of the reed with sand. Then I constructed a bow by taking a bamboo-cane, shaving it off thin at each end, and drawing it into an arc with a piece of cord.

Jack and Fritz were not long in finding out what I was doing, then ran towards me, shouting, 'Oh! a bow! a bow and arrows! Papa, let me shoot with it! Do let me try! You shall see that I know how to do it.'

'One moment, children,' I said. 'Surely, if I have had the trouble of making the bow, I ought to have the honour of taking the first shot. Besides, do not suppose that I intend to use it merely as a toy. I have a useful end in view; and, if you will be patient an instant, I will show you what that end is.'

I then asked my wife if she could find me a ball of coarse cotton. 'It is just possible that I may,' she replied with a smile. 'I will consult my enchanted bag.'

She put her hand into the bag and drew it out again, saying, 'There, that is the article I think you require.'

Having unwound the greater part of the ball of cotton, I fastened the end of it to one of the arrows. Then, adjusting the arrow upon the bow, I drew in the direction of that part of the highest man-grove where we proposed to build our new dwelling. The shaft fell on the other side of one of the branches, upon which, therefore, the cotton hung suspended.

It was easy enough now, by drawing, the arrow back to the branch, to get a length of cotton equal to the height of our intended domicile, and thus to judge of the length of ladder it would be necessary to construct.

We found that we should want one about fifty feet long. I measu-red off something like a hundred feet of strong cord, which I divided into two parts, and laid out in parallel lines upon the ground.

I then told Fritz to saw the bamboos into lengths of two feet each, and, assisted by Jack and Ernest, I placed these ladder-wise between the ropes, and fastened them at each end—first with a knot to fix their position, and then with a nail to prevent them from slipping.

In less than an hour and a half the ladder was finished. In order to hoist it into its place, I employed the same means which had served me so well in measuring the height. Another arrow was shot off. The cotton lodged as before. But to the first thread I had attached a triple one, to that a piece of twine, to that a strong cord, and to that the ladder. All I had to do, therefore, was to pull the arrow-end of the cotton until I had drawn the ladder into its place. I then had the strong cord to fasten it by to one of the arched roots of the mangroves, and our stairs were complete.

Jack and Fritz fell into a dispute as to who should first ascend. I gave the preference to Jack, who was lighter than his brother, and as agile as a mouse. Before allowing him to start, however, I advised him not to venture a single step until he had ascertained that the rung of the ladder upon which he was next to tread was solidly fixed and strong enough to bear his weight. I also counselled him to come down as swiftly as he could on perceiving the least danger.

He instantly commenced the ascent, paying very little attention to my recommendations, and in a few moments reached—Heaven be thanked, without accident!—the first branch, across which he seated himself astride as upon a horse, shouting:

'Victory! victory!'

Fritz was the next to mount. With a few pieces of rope he made the ladder still more secure, and I then hazarded the ascent myself.

Landed safely among the branches, I took a careful survey of the whole trunk at that part, with a view of fixing upon the best spot for our future habitation.

Night fell suddenly while I was thus employed, but by the light of the moon I managed to fix to one of the branches a large pulley which I had brought with me; and this served in the morning to enable us to draw up our building materials.

Our careful housewife, who had milked the cow and the goats, gave us some excellent porridge, and afterwards brought out the remainder of the porcupine left from dinner. We made a hearty meal.

We tied up the beasts near our hammocks beneath the arched roots of the great tree.

Ernest and Francis had employed the time we had spent aloft by gathering together, in accordance with my instructions, a great quantity of dead wood, which enabled me to keep in a large bonfire all night for the purpose of frightening away the wild beasts.

Our evening prayer being offered, my wife and the children were not long in getting to rest in the hammocks which swung from the overhanging roots.

For myself, I rested not. I had resolved to keep watch, so that our fire might not go out while we slept.

CHAPTER X

The building in the tree

Immediately after breakfast my wife ordered Jack and Ernest to harness the ass and the cow with the straps which, under my instructions, she had made on the previous evening. Then, with the three younger boys, she made preparations for a journey to the beach to bring up what timber might be necessary for the construction of our aerial habitation. When she had set out I ascended the tree with Fritz, and chose a spot in the centre of the lower branches, where, aided by saw and axe, we prepared a place for the erection of our hut. The branches themselves, spreading out horizontally, served us to a thought as joists for our flooring. We left a few some six or eight feet above these on which to hang our hammocks. A few others a little higher were so trimmed as to form rafters for the support of our sail-cloth, which was to be used for roofing.

These preliminary preparations were not achieved without difficulty; but in the end we had the happiness of finding that we had cleared a large open space in the thick branches of the mangrove, which would serve admirably as a site for a dwelling-house.

The beams and planks, which had in the meantime been brought in large quantities from the beach, were now drawn up into the tree by the pulley—a contrivance which multiplied our strength even more than we had anticipated.

The floor was laid, and a hand-rail placed all round it.

We worked with so much ardour, that the middle of the day overtook us before we had one thought of eating.

We contented ourselves with a light lunch, and after the repast returned with renewed vigour to our task.

Our first business was to stretch our sail-cloth across the higher branches—a labour requiring not a little address and exertion. We finally decided to draw it over one branch and fasten it to the hand-rail on either side, thus forming a kind of gable. This done, our hut, of which the huge trunk of the tree formed one of the walls, was hermetically closed on three of its sides. The fourth, which faced the sea, was left open for the present, but I had hit upon a plan of closing it in case of need. I determined to cover it with another sail-cloth fixed upon a roller like a blind, so that we could draw it up or pull it down at will.

When we had slung our hammocks to the branches which we

had left for that purpose our habitation was ready for occupation at night.

The sun was already sinking to rest.

Fritz and I descended from the tree; and, although I was very tired, I at once set to work upon the remaining planks and posts, and constructed a table and some seats upon the site of our late dwelling-place. It seemed to me a fitting spot for our future dining-room.

The last labour accomplished to the intense satisfaction of the whole family, I threw myself, worn out with fatigue, upon one of the benches I had just constructed. Wiping my forehead, which was bathed in perspiration, I said to my wife, 'I have worked today like a negro, and I will rest the whole of tomorrow.'

'I agree,' said my wife. She then called the boys, who, though scattered in all directions, were not long in hastening in and seating themselves around the table upon which dinner was already laid.

After dinner we ascended the tree. Fritz, Jack, and Ernest went first, and accomplished the ascent with the agility of cats. Their mother followed, slowly and with the utmost precaution.

Left to the last, I had a little more difficulty than the others, for I had thought it wise to unfasten the ladder from its stake at the lower end, in order that I might draw it up after me; moreover I carried tied to my back our little Francis, whom I did not like to trust alone.

I reached my destination without mishap, and when I had drawn up the ladder, the boys compared our new dwelling-place to one of those enchanted castles of ancient chivalry which were impregnable to all assaults.

However that might be, I did not neglect to load the arms in readiness to fire upon any ill-intentioned visitor. Our dogs keeping guard at the foot of the tree would signal the enemy's approach: we could do the rest ourselves.

Our precautions thus taken, each retired to his hammock. Sleep fell upon all of us, and the night flowed by in sweet tranquillity.

CHAPTER XI

Sunday

Morning.

Jack begged me to lend him my bow, which I did. Shortly afterwards I found him endeavouring to tip his arrows with porcupine quills.

I advised him to melt one of the soup-cakes in a small quantity of water, and see if that would serve the purpose.

He adopted my suggestion, and soon had the satisfaction of finding himself armed with a number of arrows which would be deadly in the hands of a skilful archer.

Fritz, who had decided to use up the skin of his margay in the manufacture of cases for our dinner-sets, as I had recommended, came to consult me upon the best means of currying his leather.

I advised him to rub it with ashes and sand, and to soften it afterwards with butter and the yolks of eggs.

While Fritz was engaged in his amateur currying operations, Francis, already the possessor of a small bow and arrows, which he was learning to shoot with skill, came to me to beg that I would make him a quiver, which he could sling over his shoulder and use for carrying the arrows I had made for him from the reeds. I made him one with four pieces of bark cut off to a point and nailed neatly together. Thus equipped, the infant Nimrod set out joyously in search of adventure.

Ernest had taken the Bible, and, seated at the foot of the tree, seemed absorbed in what he was reading there.

It was not long before my wife called us to our dinner.

While we were dining I told my boys that I desired to lay before them a very important proposition.

Their eyes were all fixed upon me at once with the utmost curiosity.

'It is,' I said, 'to give names to the various points of the island which we have visited and become acquainted with. By the aid of these names we shall be the better able to understand each other in conversation, and shall not have to use so many words to describe where we have been or intend to go. We will abstain, however,' I added, 'from giving names to places on the coast, for it is not unlikely that European navigators have already discovered and christened them, and in that case we must be careful to respect the work of our predecessors.'

'A capital idea! an excellent thought!' cried all the children at once. 'Let us invent some names on the spot.'

'To commence with the bay where we debarked from the wrecked vessel, I propose that we call it Deliverance Bay,' said Ernest.

'Agreed! agreed! Deliverance Bay!' they all cried in unison.

All the points in our domain received names in succession. The place of our first habitation was called Undertent; the small island in the bay Shark Island, in memory of the courage and address of Fritz. Then came Flamingo Marsh and Jackal River. Our new dwelling-place received the name of Falcon-nest, 'for,' said I to my boys, 'you are as hardy and adventurous as young falcons, and as much disposed to deeds of pillage in the immediate neighbourhood of your home.' The promontory from the top of which Fritz and I had vainly sought far and wide for traces of our unfortunate fellow-voyagers was named Cape Disappointment.

These useful designations fixed upon, we rose from table and each of the boys was again set free to amuse himself as he listed.

Fritz still busied himself in the manufacture of cases for the dinner-sets. He fashioned four out of the feet of the skin, thrusting in a wooden mould which he had made to give them the proper form.

Jack begged me to assist him in getting ready for Turk the coat of mail which I had previously suggested should be made out of the thorny skin of the porcupine.

I surrendered myself to his wishes.

After having cleaned the skin in the same manner as I had recommended to Fritz for his margay, we fastened it with straps to the back and breast and shoulders of the dog, who, thus decked out, wore an aspect altogether warlike. He was very docile while we harnessed him, and appeared to have no thought of disembarrassing himself of his strange armour.

Fan, however, was far from finding her companion's costume to her taste. Every time she approached him, as her habit was, to caress and sport with him, she returned from the charge with a cruelly punctured hide. She was puzzled. Thereupon it was sagely decided that war trappings were not a thing to be abused, and that Master Turk should only be fitted out with his coat of mail when we were about to engage in expeditions of the first importance.

Of the remains of the skin Jack made himself a bristly cap, which he poised jauntily upon the side of his head, soldier-wise, observing that a helmet of that kind would, he hoped, effectually put to flight any band of savages which it might be our lot to encounter in the future.

The sun was now past the meridian: the heat had descreased. I proposed to walk. We deliberated upon the direction we should take, and for several reasons fixed upon Undertent. Certain of our provisions were running short, and it was thought well to look to our magazines. Fritz and Jack wanted powder and shot. My wife wanted butter. Ernest hit upon the idea of bringing home a couple of the ducks, which he explained would find good water in the stream that ran beneath Falcon-nest.

'Let us set out at once, then,' said I, 'and prepare ourselves for a little fatigue. We are going to take a longer route than that by which we came.'

We were soon on our way. Fritz and Jack, armed, as I and Ernest were, with their guns, took the lead—the one decorated with his jackal-skin belt, the other brave in his famous porcupine helmet. Even little Francis carried his bow and quiver. My wife alone was unarmed.

The monkey, who insisted on being of the party, leapt precipitately to his accustomed seat upon the back of Turk; but finding himself sorely pinched by the spikes of the dog's new coat of mail, put on for the occasion, took refuge upon the crupper of Fan, who benevolently consented to give the impudent little cavalier a mount.

Our flamingo, who also desired to be of the party, put himself gravely at the tail of the caravan. He was a droll addition to our company, marching wide upon his stilts, and curving his long neck as he went. I think it right to say that he looked incontestibly the most reflective and self-satisfied of the whole troupe.

Coasting the stream—Falcon-nest Stream—we fell into a most agreeable route. My wife and I walked slowly side by side. The boys ran on before, wandering now to the right and now to the left.

Before long Ernest came running towards us, holding in his hand a stalk from which depended three or four small balls of a light green colour, and crying out, 'Potatoes, papa! I have found some potatoes!'

I had no difficulty in pronouncing his judgment to be accurate, and I could not refrain from commending his spirit of inquiry and observation, which in this instance had resulted in the most important discovery we had made since our sojourn on the island.

Ernest, in a glow of gratified excitement, pressed us to make all haste to a spot whence he would show us a larger potato-field than we had ever yet seen, 'for,' said he, 'at the place where I gathered this stalk the whole plain is covered with potatoes.'

We were not slow in making our way to this precious natural plantation. Jack at once threw himself upon his knees, and commenced grubbing up the earth to get at the potatoes. The monkey, leaping off Fan's back, failed not to imitate its young master. In less than five minutes they brought to light between them a large quantity of excellent fruit, which Francis piled in heaps as fast as Nip and Jack threw them upon the ground.

The whole of the potatoes thus obtained were stowed away in our bag, and we resumed our journey, after carefully observing the situation of the field; for we had resolved to return next day and complete the harvest.

We crossed the stream at the foot of a little chain of boulders, over which the water poured in the form of a cascade. Not only was the fall itself charming, but the view all round was as varied and beautiful as it was extensive. We might have fancied ourselves in a European hot-house, except that the flower-pots and the stages on which they stand were replaced by pile on pile of broken rocks, from whose fissures sprang plants of the most magnificent descriptions, both in beauty and dimensions. What are commonly called 'grasses' were in especial abundance. There were also the Indian fig-tree, the aloe, the cactus, with its prickly stalk and flame-red bloom; the plantain, with its long, sinuous arms endlessly interlaced; and, though last not least, the ananas, bearer of the most delicious of fruits. The boys, assisted by Ernest, quickly recognised the latter, and applied themselves to its appetising treasures with an avidity which I was obliged to repress. I feared they might make themselves ill.

Among other plants, I lighted upon the karata, a kind of aloe, of which I gathered several sprigs. Showing them to the children, I said, 'See here! I have found a treasure far superior to the ananas, which you have been devouring so greedily.'

'What!' cried Jack, with his mouth full, 'those scrubby-looking bunches of leaves? Impossible! There can be nothing there like the ananas. The ananas is the fruit for me.'

'Gluttonous boy!' I said, interrupting his panegyric, of which I saw by their looks the other boys highly approved; it is necessary that you should learn not to judge by appearances. See here, Ernest—you are the most sensible of the four—take this steel and the flint of my gun, and give me a light: I want one particularly.'

'But, father,' replied the young savant, looking perplexed, 'I have neither a sulphur match nor touchwood; how am I to get a light?'

'How should we proceed,' exclaimed I, 'if it was necessary to get a light at all hazards?'

'Well,' replied Jack, 'I have heard that when savages are in a similar difficulty they procure a light by rubbing two pieces of wood together till they burn. I suppose we should have to do the same.'

'A tiresome and barren method for people not accustomed to so painful an exercise!' I exclaimed. 'I think I may safely venture to tell you that you would have to rub for days without getting a single spark.'

'In that case,' said Ernest, 'I suppose we shall be compelled to search for touchwood.'

'Such a search,' said I, 'is superfluous.' And I took a dry twig of the karata, from which I peeled off the bark and extracted the pith. Then I laid the pith upon the gun-flint, and struck it a smart blow with the steel. The first stroke set the substance on fire.

'Hurrah! hurrah!' cried the children in astonishment, 'a touch-wood-tree! a touchwood-tree!'

'You are surprised thus far,' I said, 'but you have not yet seen half the usefulness that lies concealed beneath the bark of this wonderful plant.'

As I spoke I stripped off one of the leaves, from which I drew out several lengths of a very strong though very fine thread.

'Really,' said Jack, 'the karata is a far more valuable plant than I had supposed. But these thorny things that lie scattered all around us can be of no possible use.'

'You are altogether in the wrong,' I replied, 'in concluding so hastily that these are useless. The aloe, for instance, produces a juice which is very much used in medicine. Then there is the Indian fig, with its battledore-shaped leaves. This plant grows in the most arid soils, where, but for the timely succour of its fruit, many a weary traveller would be in danger of perishing by hunger.'

At these words Jack dashed among the foliage to gather some of the fruit; which he was impatient to taste; but the long prickles with which they were covered pierced his hands in all directions, and he returned crestfallen and crying, regarding the fig-tree with a look of unmitigated disgust.

His mother hastened to remove the thorns from his fingers, and while she was thus employed I showed the other children how to pluck and eat the fruit without running so much risk.

Having taken a short stick and pointed it, I stuck the sharp end into one of the figs, which I could then harmlessly skin with my knife.

Ernest, who, so soon as this was done, examined the fruit attentively, ascertained that it was covered with myriads of small insects, which appeared to be spending their time in sucking its juice.

'Do look here, papa,' he said, 'and tell me what these little creatures are. I think I know something about them, but I may be in error.'

I at once recognised the cochineal, and exclaimed, 'Fortunate in the extreme! We have certainly lighted upon a day of discoveries. I am not sure, indeed, that this last is not the most precious that we have yet made, though to make proof of that we ought to be able to traffic with the people of Europe, who buy cochineal at a very costly rate, to make a scarlet dye.'

'However that may be,' said Ernest, 'we have at least found a second plant which is superior to the ananas, of which we at first boasted so much.'

'You are right,' I replied, 'and to prove it I will tell you of yet another use to which the Indian fig may be put. Its dense prickly leaves make excellent hedges to protect dwellings against the attacks of savages, and plantations against those of beasts of prey.'

'What!' cried Jack, 'these tender leaves serve the purpose of a barrier against animals! Why, with the cut of a knife, or the stroke of a stick, I could demolish them at once.'

With that he began to slash away vigorously at a large fig-tree.

But one of its battledore-leaves struck his leg, and pierced him with its spikes till he roared again.

'Ah! ah!' laughed I. 'Do you understand now how it is that an enclosure of these trees may prove impregnable to half-clad savages, and to animals that try to break through them with no other weapons but those furnished them by Nature?'

'We must plant a hedge of them round Falcon-nest,' said Ernest.

'And I think,' added Fritz, 'that we should collect as many cochineal insects as possible. Their red dye may be of use to us some day.'

'So far as I am concerned,' I said, 'I think it would be far wiser to confine ourselves to works of utility. The agreeable must be reserved for a future occasion, Master Fritz.'

Arrived at Jackal River, we crossed it without difficulty, and after a few minutes' walk found ourselves at Undertent, where all remained in the order in which we had left it.

Fritz furnished himself abundantly with powder and lead. I helped my wife to fill her tin flask with butter. The younger children endeavouring to catch the ducks, which had become wilder than heretofore, and would not allow themselves to be approached.

Ernest, determined to capture them, adopted a stratagem which succeeded to perfection. To the end of a piece of string, he attached a morsel of cheese, and let it float upon the water. The greedy birds soon darted after the bait and swallowed it, and then Ernest had no difficulty in drawing them gently to the edge of the river. By dint of repeating this manoeuvre several times he made himself master of the rebels. Once taken, they were each tied up securely in a handkerchief, and thus enveloped, were placed in our game-bags.

We next took in a supply of salt from the cave, though we did not get so much as we wanted, for we were too heavily loaded already.

We were even obliged to relieve Turk of his coat of mail, and make him for the time being a beast of burden.

The redoubtable but scarcely useful cuirass was left in the tent.

'It is the same with armour as with soldiers,' said Ernest; 'when there is no fighting to be done it is good for nothing.'

We set out for Falcon-nest again. The laughter and fun provoked by the contortions of our feathery prisoners, and the comic aspect of our caravan, helped us to forgetfulness of the weight of our burdens. It was not until the journey was ended that we felt fatigued.

Our good housewife at once filled our pot with potatoes, and while we made up the fire she milked the cow and the goat, in order to prepare for us our evening repast.

Our table was soon spread.

The expectation of a good supper, and of partaking of the potatoes, which formed the dish of honour, kept us awake; but as soon as the meal was finished, the children were glad to retire to their hammocks.

In a few minutes profound slumber fell upon our household.

CHAPTER XII

The sledge—the salmon—the kangaroo

I had remarked during our journey to Undertent that the beach was covered with a quantity of pieces of wood, which I thought were suitable for the construction of a kind of sledge, with the assistance of which we might be able to transport such articles as were too heavy for the backs of our beasts.

So I set out at daybreak to bring some fo them home, accompanied by Ernest and by the donkey, both of whom I was obliged to awaken, so soundly did they sleep.

The sledge took less than an hour to construct.

At the point of starting, Fritz presented us with a margay-skin sheath, which would either hold a knife and fork or a small axe. I praised his ingenuity and industry; and having embraced the rest of the family, Ernest and I set out.

The ass and the cow were harnessed to the sledge. Ernest and I, armed with a bamboo cane each to supply the place of whips, and carrying our guns slung to our backs, walked one on each side of our new conveyance. Fan followed us.

We took the road leading by the stream, and after a journey entirely unmarked by adventure, we came to Undertent.

The beasts were detached and set free, while we loaded our sledge with the firkin of butter, a barrel of powder, bullets, cheese, and other provisions.

I felt that a bath would refresh us both after the fatigue of the day. Thereupon, I went down to Deliverance Bay and soon succeeded in finding a place where the rocks rose in clusters from a bottom of fine sand, forming, so far as privacy was concerned, a long row of natural bathing-rooms.

I swam in the water something like half an hour, and then, as Ernest did not put in an appearance, I dressed myself and went to seek him. I had scarcely gone a hundred steps when I heard him crying out:

'Father! Father! Pray come and help me! Make haste, or he will drag me in!'

I ran, and soon came in sight of our young philosopher lying prone on the sand, not far from the mouth of the river, and holding with both hands a line, at the end of which an enormous fish was struggling with all its might.

I came up just in time to spare the ambitious fisherman the anguish of seeing his magnificent capture escape him; for he was breathless, and his strength was well-nigh exhausted.

I took the string and drew the fish into a shallow, where it was easy enough to take him—especially after Ernest had waded into the water and stunned him with a blow of his axe.

It was a salmon, weighing at least fifteen pounds.

I opened the fish, and sprinkled it with salt, to keep it fresh. I then packed it in the sledge with some other fish of various sizes which Ernest had also caught and had tied up in his handkerchief.

This done, I replaced the planks in the bridge; and when my son returned, we harnessed the beasts and retraced our steps to Falconnest.

We had been walking about a quarter of an hour, and were making our way along the prairie, when all at once Fan dashed barking towards a slump of tall grasses. Immediately there rushed out of the clump an animal nearly as large as a sheep, which made its way off, not by running, but by a series of extraordinary bounds. I fired—too hastily, however—and I missed.

Ernest, warned by my shot, and being at the time nearer the fugitive than I was, fired also, and killed it on the spot.

We hastened to examine the strange game which we had thus bagged.

The creature's coat and muzzle were like those of the mouse, its ears like a rabbit's, its tail like a tiger's, its fore-legs very short, and its hind-legs excessively long. I examined it for a long time and could not tell what it was.

As to Ernest, the pleasures of victory left him no time to make his accustomed investigations. He was wholly occupied with the important achievement of having killed the creature.

'Oh!' he cried in an ecstasy, 'what will my mother and my brothers say when they see game of this size, and learn that it was I alone who killed it?'

'Truly,' I said, 'you have a good eye and a sure hand; but I should very much like to know the name of the animal. Let us make a minute examination of it, and perhaps we shall arrive at some—'

Ernest interrupted me.

'It has,' he said, 'four incisor teeth, and therefore it must belong to the rodent order of animals.'

'Well reasoned,' replied I, 'but it also has a pouch below the breast, and that is a distinctive sign of the Marsupialia. And if I am not very much deceived, I think we shall find ourselves the possessors of a female kangaroo, an animal unknown to naturalists until the discovery of New Holland by the celebrated Captain Cook, who was the first to examine and describe it. You may, therefore, flatter yourself that you have brought down an extra-ordinary head of game.'

The kangaroo was placed upon the sledge, and as we proceeded on our way I told Ernest all I knew about the animal, of its fore-legs which were too short, of its hind-legs which were too long, and of its tail, which, as a kind of compensation for its inequalities of limb, served its purpose almost as well as a fifth leg.

As soon as the children left at Falcon-nest saw us coming they shouted for joy, and ran to meet us. As they came in sight we could not help laughing heartily: they were so comically attired. One was enveloped in a long white shirt; the body of another was concealed up to the armpits in a pair of huge blue trousers; the third was habited in a waistcoat which came down to his knees, and gave him the appearance of a walking portmanteau.

Seeing them thus attired, walking towards us with the gravity and solemnity of theatrical heroes, I desired them to tell me the cause of this masquerade.

They replied that during our absence their mother had thought it proper to wash their clothes, and that until these were dry they had been obliged to dress themselves in what they could find among the contents of the chest which I had turned into a sledge.

After we had minutely inspected and laughed long and loudly at their strange accoutrements, they passed round the sledge to examine its contents.

Our housewife failed not to thank us warmly for the butter, the salt, and the fish we had brought; but the attention of the children was concentrated wholly upon the salmon and the kangaroo, which Ernest exhibited with no little pride.

The sledge being unloaded, I made a distribution of salt among the animals, who had gone without for some time, and enjoyed their feast immensely.

The kangaroo was hung up to a neighbouring branch, and we sat down to a supper consisting of the small fish caught by Ernest and a dish of potatoes.

Night fell, and we retired to our aerial dwelling-place.

CHAPTER XIII

A second voyage to the vessel—the turtle—tapioca

The next morning, very early, I called Fritz, and told him that I desired him to accompany me again on a voyage to the wrecked vessel.

I then descended from the tree and employed myself in denuding the kangaroo of his beautiful grey skin. The flesh I divided into two portions—the one to be eaten fresh, the other to be salted for future use.

We breakfasted, and after the repast I told Fritz to furnish our game-bags with food and our gourd-bottles with drink, and to make ready such arms as we should require to take with us.

Soon afterwards our tub-boat was drifting swiftly with the current towards the vessel, which we reached without accident.

My first care was to seek for materials with which to construct a raft, upon which, in accordance with a plan laid down by Ernest on the preceding evening, we could bear to land a much heavier load than our boat was capable of carrying.

I had the good fortune to find between decks a large quantity of empty water-casks. We picked out a dozen of them, which we fastened together with pieces of wood strongly nailed to the tub-staves. I then made a flooring of planks, and surrounded the whole with a hand-rail about two feet high.

This work occupied us during the greater part of the day. At all events, when we had finished it, it was too late to hope to return to land with our new construction properly loaded.

This being so, we determined to make a tour of inspection all over the vessel, and take an inventory of what we judged it best to carry ashore. We then retired to the captain's cabin, and after a frugal repast, the sweet restorer—sleep—overtook us as we lay at full length upon a couple of exellent mattresses.

The next morning at daybreak we were afoot refreshed by our night's rest and in good health and spirits.

We at once set about building our boats. The apartment in which we had slept was the first to be stripped. Our second visit was made to the cabin we had ourselves occupied during our unfortunate voyage. I brought from thence everything that was useful

or had an interest for us as a souvenir of bygone days. The other
cabins we took in turn.

Locks, bolts, window-fastenings, the windows themselves, even
the doors were taken off and made ready for transport. Two trunks
abundantly furnished with necessaries were among the booty;
but what gave me the greatest pleasure of all was to find two
larger chests, one filled with carpenter's tools and the other with
those of a gunsmith. A casket containing gold and silver watches,
snuff-boxes, rings, and other valuables dazzled us for an instant;
but our attention was soon drawn more seriously towards a large
store of oats, peas, and maize, and a number of European fruit-
trees, which were carefully preserved for planting on the distant
continent to which the doomed vessel was directing her course
when she was wrecked.

But what was our joy to find, besides these, a stock of iron bars,
wheels, pickaxes, and spades, and above all a hand-mill! Nothing
which could be of use in a young colony had been forgotten in
fitting out this vessel which was to have borne us to the New
World. We could not bear everything away. A coffer full of coin
scarcely attracted our attention. Of what value was money to us
when compared with the rude implements which would supply our
first necessities? From the jewellery casket we took the two
watches which we had promised to the younger children, and from
the coin-chest a handful of coins; it was all we removed of that
which is conventionally called valuable.

Fritz begged me to let him take a fishing-net, a pair of harpoons,
and a reel of line which he found by chance.

I gave him permission.

Our loading occupied us half the day. At length the time for
setting out for the shore arrived. It was not without considerable
difficulty that we got our overcharged boats in motion. Happily
a favourable wind came to our aid, filling the sail that I had spread,

I was at the helm. The sail, bellied well to the breeze, prevented
me from seeing what Fritz was doing in the fore part of the vessel.
All at once I heard the whistling of the reel of line as it ran swiftly
out of the boat.

Great heaven, Fritz' I cried, 'what are you doing?'

'Struck! Struck!' cried he in a transport of joy. 'She can never
escape that!'

His exclamations referred to an enormous turtle which he had
perceived sleeping upon the surface of the water and had bravely
and adroitly harpooned.

The animal, pierced in the neck, darted off, drawing our boat
after it at a terrific speed.

I struck sail hastily, and rushed to the prow of the vessel to cut
the line of the harpoon; but Fritz entreated me not to permit so
splendid a prey to escape, assuring me that he would cut the line
himself if he found ourselves in the least danger.

Thus conducted by the animal, we cut through the water with

incredible swiftness, and I had the greatest difficulty in handling the rudder in such a manner as to neutralise the effects of the strange motion which our singular tug gave to the vessel. Perceiving at length that the turtle was directing his course towards the open sea, I hoisted sail again. The wind was blowing inshore, and the animal, finding the resistance too great, changed his course and swam landwards.

We touched the bottom within gun-shot of the shore opposite Falcon-nest. I leapt into the sea with the intention of finishing the turtle with my axe, but the creature had run head first into the sand, and was stranded. At the first stroke of the axe I severed its head from its body.

Fritz, delighted beyond measure at his achievement, fired a gun to advise the family of our return, and in a few moments they were all running down to the beach to meet us.

Then Fritz told the story of the turtle.

His mother trembled as she heard the record of the danger to which we had been exposed; and all expressed their admiration at the skill Fritz had displayed in taking such excellent aim at the precise part of the animal which, as Ernest explained, was always protected by the carapace, or vaulted back-shell of the animal, except when its wearer was asleep.

The two younger children were sent up to Falcon-nest to fetch the beasts of burden, with which they soon returned, having in the meantime harnessed them to the sledge. Upon this primitive means of transport we placed our mattresses and the turtle, which together weighed somewhere about three quintals: it required our united strength to lift them. The remainder of the cargo was carried up the beach beyond the reach of the tide, and our tub-boat and raft were anchored by means of large lumps of lead buried in the sand.

During the walk to Falcon-nest the children overwhelmed us with questions. The jewellery casket, of which Fritz had spoken, specially excited their curiosity. Jack claimed his watch: little Francis made himself happy with a purse full of coin.

His simplicity caused us to laugh heartily.

Arrived at Falcon-nest, I at once set to work to remove the turtle from its shell. Then I cut off some steaks from its flesh, which I desired my wife to broil for supper.

'Well, my dear Fritz,' said I, 'how do you propose to make use of your carapace?'

'I think,' he said 'that I should make a tank of it, so that my mother could always have a supply of fresh water without going down to the stream for it.'

'An excellent idea,' I cried, 'and one which must be put into execution as soon as we can find some clay to set our tank in.'

'When the tank is put in its place,' said Ernest, assuming his scholarly air, 'I shall take leave to set some roots in it which I have found today. They appear to me to be a species either of the common radish or of horse-radish.'

After examining them carefully: 'If I am not mistaken,' I said, 'you have made a most valuable discovery, which, added to the potato field, will always preserve us from famine. I believe I recognise in these roots those of the tapioca plant, with which the Indians in the West make a species of bread called cassava. But in order to be put to this use, it is necessary that the root should undergo a process which shall remove from it a certain poisonous substance that it contains.'

This conversation did not prevent us from setting vigorously to work to unload the sledge.

As soon as this was done, I made another journey to the beach to bring up a second load before nightfall. My wife remained behind, in company with little Francis, who never disdained to play the part of scullion, being well assured by previous experience that he would become the possessor of some choice tit-bit during the preparation of the meal. I told his mother and him in setting out that we expected to reap the reward of our labours in a right royal feast.

Arrived at the raft, the sledge was loaded with a mass of articles, of which the hand-mill, by reason of the discovery of the tapioca-root, appeared to me to be by far most useful.

This labour achieved, my wife called us to supper.

Fritz's turtle, excellently cooked, was enjoyed by all of us.

'It's an ugly brute, is that turtle,' said little Francis as he went to his new bed, 'but it was very nice to eat—eh, Jack?'

Jack was fast asleep.

Our mattresses had done their work.

CHAPTER XIV

Third voyage to the vessel—a discovery—the penguins

Not feeling at all satisfied about the safety of the raft and tub-boat, which were simply made fast to the beach with leaden weights, I got up before daybreak, determined to pay them a visit.

All my family were buried in a profound sleep.

I descended softly from the tree. The dogs were already awake, and began gambolling round me, and giving every sign of pleasure, as if they understood as well as I that I had determined upon an excursion. The chickens, beating their wings joyously, quitted their perch. The goats were already browsing the fresh morning herbage.

The donkey, whom I had determined to take with me, still lay extended at his ease. Much to his displeasure, I made him get up, and harnessed him to the sledge. I did not wish to fatigue the cow before she had been milked.

Accompanied by the two dogs, I then set out for the beach.

I found our craft perfectly safe, left high and dry upon the sand by the tide which had now gone down. I did not load the donkey heavily, being desirous both to keep him fresh for further work during the day, and to return myself as soon as possible to Falcon-nest.

We made a hasty breakfast, and hurried off to the beach to finish hauling up the things that remained there.

Two journeys were made in a very short time; and as I saw that the rising tide was then beginning to cover the beach, I determined to take advantage of it to float our craft round into Deliverance Bay, where they would be safer than on the coast of Falcon-nest.

I sent my wife and the three younger boys home, and waited with Fritz in the tub-boat till the rising tide set us afloat.

Seeing Jack, who remained behind upon the beach, looking at our operations with longing eyes, I put the top-stone to his enjoyment by taking him with us.

We were soon rocking pleasantly upon the waves, and seduced by the fairness of the weather, in place of steering towards Deliverance Bay, I sailed once more towards the wreck.

But when we got there it was too late to think of carrying away anything like a large or an important cargo.

Nevertheless, we explored the vessel in every direction, as much for the purpose of getting things ready to bring away another time, as to avoid going back quite empty-handed.

Jack soon made his appearance wheeling a barrow, and smiling complacently at the thought that for the future he would not have to carry burdens so heavy as had been the case heretofore.

Fritz ran to tell me that he had found, in a part of the ship partitioned off from the rest by boards, a pinnace, carefully taken to pieces and stored away, with all its rigging complete, and a couple of cannon to mount in case of necessity.

This news caused me inexpressible joy, and I left everything else to verify Fritz's communication. He had not been deceived, but I saw that it would involve an immense deal of labour to put our new-found craft to sea.

We put off this task till another day, being content for the present to take away with us a few articles for household use, such as coppers, kettles, saucepans, iron trays, plates, glasses, and so on. I added to these a few nutmeg-graters, a grindstone, a fresh barrel of powder, and a new supply of gun-flints. Not only did we not forget Jack's barrow, but we took several others, the discovery of which was almost as agreeable to Fritz and me as was the first one to Jack.

It was necessary to embark in haste, in order that we might not be met by a shore wind, which rose every night, and which might carry us out to sea.

While we were rowing towards the land, we saw standing upon the edge of the sea a troop of little creatures looking like diminutive human beings dressed in white.

'It seems to me,' said Fritz, 'that we have before us simply a regiment of birds, for I can see their beaks; and what we have taken for their arms are, without doubt, their wings.'

'You are right, my boy,' I said; 'these fantastic beings are penguins. They can swim very well, and that is all. Nature has given them wings so short in comparison to the size of their bodies, that they cannot fly very well. Their feet are so strangely formed that they cannot walk far. It is therefore very easy to come up with them on land; and such is their natural indolence that they will scarcely make an effort to get away.'

When we were within a few pulls of the shore 'Jack, armed with an oar, unexpectedly jumped into the water, and before the penguins were well aware of his arrival, had knocked several of them over. The others, not finding this salute much to their liking, plunged into the water all together, as if at the word of command, and disappeared.

Those who had been stunned by Jack's attack were tied together by us and deposited upon the beach.

It was too late now to proceed with the unloading of our cargoes. We simply placed upon our barrows the penguins, some tobacco, and a few cooking utensils, and drove off with them to Falcon-nest, where, as usual, we were received with the liveliest demonstrations of joy.

Our dogs welcomed us with enthusiastic barkings. My wife was delighted to see the barrows, the contents of which were the subject of considerable curiosity. The nutmeg-graters excited a little pleasant irony, which I affected not to notice. The penguins especially were very carefully examined. Several of them had by this time recovered from the effect of the blows dealt them by Jack, and these I tied to the ducks and the geese, in order to accustom them to domestication among the other poultry.

Our vigilant housewife, in her turn, showed me a plentiful supply of potatoes and tapioca-root, which had been dug during my absence.

Little Francis now approached me, saying with an air of mystery, 'You will be surprised one of these days, papa. We shall have a harvest of maize and oats, and plenty of pumpkins and melons. Mamma has sown such a quantity!'

'Naughty little chatterer!' cried my wife. 'Why have you betrayed me? I was counting upon giving your father a pleasant surprise.'

'Again I have to thank you for your forethought, my love,' I said, embracing her. 'But where did you get all these different seeds from?'

'Once more the enchanted bag,' she replied, smiling and looking fondly at the children, who this time did not contest the forethought of their wise mother. 'Seeing you were always occupied with your voyages to the wreck, I thought you would not find time to lay out a kitchen garden for us; so I determined to do it myself. I chose our newly-found potato-field for a site, and I have had no harder work to do than to fill the place of every root we have pulled up with the seed of some other plant.'

I felicitated her upon this excellent idea, and Fritz attempted to add to her pleasure by announcing the discovery of the pinnace. But our sea voyages caused my dear wife too much real alarm to leave her free to rejoice in the discovery of a means by which we should be able to extend them.

Nevertheless, she gave in a little when I showed her that, since these voyages must be made, it would be much better to make them in a sea-worthy vessel, than in the wretched tub-boat and raft which we had ourselves constructed.

Night fell. In giving the word for bed, I told my sons to hold themselves ready to be taught a new trade on the morrow.

CHAPTER XV

Baking

As soon as they were awake, the children, full of curiosity to know the meaning of my last words on the previous evening, hastened to ask me what was the new trade which I was about to teach them.

'The trade of the baker,' I replied.

'But,' cried Jack, 'we have neither an oven nor flour!'

'We shall get our flour,' I replied, 'from the tapioca-roots; and as to the oven, we shall supply its place with some of the iron utensils which we brought from the wreck yesterday.'

As I saw from their astonished looks that they required fuller details, I explained to them the properties of the tapioca-root, and the use made of it by people who were not yet civilised.

I then told my wife to make me a bag of sail-cloth, while each of the boys, furnished with one of the nutmeg-graters, awaited my instructions to enter upon his unknown task. The roots had been carefully washed, and I distributed them among my young millers to be grated.

They set to work with ardour—not without laughing a good deal at their new occupation—and we soon had a large quantity of flour that looked like damp sawdust.

My wife herself did not seem to be very confident in my talent as a baker, for I noticed that after finishing the bag I had asked her for, she put a supply of potatoes upon the fire, to provide against my possible non-success. Knowing what I was about, I did not allow myself to be disconcerted by her evident doubts.

I soon announced to my young labourers that our supply was plentiful enough.

The wet flour was then put into the bag which my wife had made, and we tied the mouth of it up tightly. In order to press it, I placed some planks close by one of the arched roots of the tree, laid the bag between them, and thrust a strong beam under the root in such wise that it lay over the uppermost plank. On the end of the beam farthest from the root I placed stones, iron, and other heavy articles, and thus produced the effect of a powerful lever. Very soon we saw the juice oozing from the bag abundantly.

I spread the flour in the sun to dry. Afterwards I took a small quantity of it, which I moistened with water and carefully kneaded. Then I made a cake in the shape of a roll, which I laid upon one of our iron dishes, and placed upon a brisk fire. In a very short time we had a bun, of which the colour and the agreeable odour held out the promise of a rich treat.

When the cake had cooled sufficiently, I crumbled it before the monkey and the fowls, and I was glad to see that they ate it up with avidity. Nevertheless, I delayed for the present trying the same experiment on ourselves.

A good dinner of potatoes appeased the fierce appetite which the savoury smell of the cake had awakened in the boys.

After dinner we went to visit the poultry. To our great relief we found them as lively as ever; while the grotesque gambols of Master Nip at our approach showed us that his health and spirits had undergone no alteration for the worse.

Thereupon I again ordered the boys to the task of bread-making. 'To work! To work!' I cried. 'Let us see how we shall succeed in our second attempt.'

I distributed to each the utensils of which he had need. They all danced for joy. In an instant the fires were lighted, the temporary kneading-troughs established in their places. Cakes were soon turned out in every conceivable shape, for youth makes sport of everything. Ranged upon iron trays, they were placed on the fire, and removed as soon as they were baked, to make way for a fresh supply.

As our fowls still remained in excellent health, I no longer had any hesitation in allowing the children to taste our new food. It was found excellent, especially when crumbled in milk.

Never since we had been cast ashore on this desert island had we made so delicious a repast. Our animals were delighted sharers in the feast, being supplied with such of the cakes as had been burnt or badly made.

The remainder of the day was spent in transporting, upon our barrows, the things that had been left upon our craft on the beach.

CHAPTER XVI

The pinnace

I had not once ceased to think of the pinnace which Fritz had found upon the wreck, nor had I given up my intention to take possession of and utilise it. Although my wife was seriously alarmed at the bare mention of a new voyage, I contrived to overcome her scruples, and at length succeeded in obtaining her concurrence in a plan I had formed for making one more journey in the tub-boat, and taking with me the three eldest children; for I knew that as many arms as we could bring to the spot would be necessary for our contemplated enterprise.

After promising her to return the same evening, and furnishing ourselves with a plentiful supply of tapioca-bread and baked potatoes, and also our cork swimming-belts, in case of accidents, we set sail once more upon the waters of Deliverance Bay.

As soon as we reached the wreck, our first care was to make a collection of whatever seemed to us to be the most useful, in order that we might not return empty at night. The pinnace was then examined. I found with the utmost satisfaction that all its parts were numbered, and that, little as we were skilled in the craft of ship-building, we should be able, with patience, to put them together.

The greatest difficulty I had to face was that of getting the vessel into the sea when we had put it together. I saw no prospect of launching it from the place where it was stowed away, and I equally saw no means at hand for getting its heavier woodwork transported to a more commodious part of the vessel. Some of the beams were so large that, as I foresaw, our united strength would be insufficient to stir them. I thought over the matter a long time, pausing over plan after plan, only to abandon each as soon as its difficulties grew upon me.

At length, overwhelmed with incertitude, I determined to leave the result with Providence, and called my boys to aid me with their hatchets in removing the partitions of the room in which the pinnace was enclosed.

The evening came upon us before we had advanced far with our task; but the desire to possess a convenient vessel sustained our ardour, and we made up our minds to return on the morrow and finish our work.

Counting upon our promise, my wife, accompanied by little Francis, awaited us upon the beach.

She announced to me that she had determined to quit Falcon-nest, and take up her residence at Undertent during the continuance of our voyages to the wreck. I was pleased to witness the attachment she displayed for our first residence on the island, in thus choosing to reinhabit it during our absence. We presented her with the new store of provisions we had brought with us, among which were two firkins of salt butter, three of flour, some sacks of rice and wheat, and several household utensils, all of which she accepted with tearful pleasure.

Our voyages to the wreck were continued daily for at least a week.

We set out each morning at daybreak, and did not return till sundown. A joyous repast, followed by a long conversation, caused us to forget the fatigues of the day.

At length we brought the construction of the pinnace to an end. She was light in build and elegant in shape, with a little quarter-deck in the prow, and rigging complete. We had tarred her outside, and even fixed the cannon in their places.

But though our little craft was charming to the eye, she remained immovable upon her keel, and we knew not what means to employ to launch her into the sea.

It was out of the question to think of making an opening in the sides of the wrecked vessel: they were so stoutly built. But at the same time we were very unwilling to lose the fruits of our labour. At last I hit upon an extreme measure to relieve us from our difficulty, and I determined to put it into execution without saying a word about it to the boys.

I procured an iron mortar, such as chemists use with a pestle, and also a stout board, and with these I proceeded to fashion a formidable engine of destruction. To the board I fastened some hooks, and then grooved it down the centre, and laid into it a slow match, made to burn two hours. Then I filled the mortar with powder, and fastened the board on the top of it by the hooks, which I fixed firmly to its rim. I next caulked all the joints with tar, and thus found myself in the possession of an enormous petard, sufficiently powerful to open for the pinnace a way to the sea.

When everything was ready for action, I left the wrecked vessel in haste with my boys, to whom I had communicated nothing concerning my plans, which I still feared might miscarry.

On our return, after the explosion, I noticed with satisfaction that neither flame nor smoke was visible on the wreck, round which we made a cautious tour before venturing to go aboard.

Arriving opposite an immense opening in the side of the vessel, I saw that the pinnace, though careened by the force of the explosion, remained whole, and was in an excellent position for being launched. All around the sea was covered with splinters, and my children were so concerned at the havoc that had been made that they could in no wise comprehend the joy which I manifested.

I then explained to them the stratagem I had adopted. Their satisfaction was every whit as great as mine, and they were in ecstasies at the happy result of my plans.

With the aid of a screw-jack, we hoisted the pinnace into an upright position upon the rollers which we had placed under its keel, and then with our united strength we succeeded in launching it into the sea, where at length we had the satisfaction of seeing it riding gracefully upon the heaving waves.

The sight of the trim little vessel, with its two cannon, its pro-visions of powder, and its armoury well filled with guns and pistols, awakened warlike ideas in the breasts of my boys. They saw themselves already defying and exterminating any band of savages which might have the hardihood to attack us. I bade them, however, pray that we might not be placed under the necessity of making a bloody trial of our new-found heroism.

It now remained to rig our vessel with its masts and sails; but as the day was too far advanced for this, we were obliged to return to Undertent. We agreed on the way thither to say nothing of our doings to my wife, whom we wished to surprise one of these days by a triumphant entry into Deliverance Bay.

It took us two more days to finish the fitting out of the pinnace.

When all was completed I gave the signal for setting sail. I took the rudder. Ernest and Jack placed themselves, one at each cannon, with the intention of announcing our arrival by a double salute. Fritz manoeuvred the sails.

A favourable wind wafted us towards the shore. Our pinnace cut through the water with great rapidity, although she had to tow the tub-boat, which we had tied astern.

When we were within a short distancee of the beach, Fritz, who had assumed the command of the vessel, cried out to the young gunners: 'Number one—fire! Number two—fire!'

In an instant the rocks resounded with the echoes of the double detonation.

Fritz at the same moment discharged his two pistols, and all four of us sent up a chorus of hurrahs!

We very soon reached the shore, where my wife and our youngest child awaited us. Our cannonade had frightened them, and the sight of our new vessel had caused them the greatest surprise. Finding that it was ourselves, they ran swiftly down to the beach to meet us.

'Oh, mother,' cried Fritz, 'do come on board the pinnace, just for a minute. We have given it your name, *The Elizabeth*. See, it is painted upon the door of the captain's cabin!'

My wife thanked us warmly for this mark of attention, and we all made a promenade over the pinnace, to the great joy of the children, who were enchanted to see their mother relieved of her fears.

When we had disembarked from our little vessel, 'Do not think,' said my wife, 'that Francis and I have remained inactive during your absence. Our labours, depend upon it, have not been of less value than yours, though we are not able to announce them by the sound of cannon. Follow me, and judge for yourselves.'

This said, she led the way to that part of Jackal River where the cascade fell over the rocks. There we saw a kitchen garden excellently laid out.

'Behold the results of our labour!' she said. 'Here I have planted potatoes, there tapioca-roots. On that side lettuces, and farther on is a bed reserved for sugar-canes. I have also sown melon and cabbage seeds, peas, and broad beans; and around each bed I have sown maize, in order that its tall stalks may defend the young plants from the heat of the sun.'

I felicitated my wife upon her ingenuity and her activity, and forgot not to praise little Francis for the assistance he had rendered to his mother.

The pinnace was unloaded, and fastened securely to the beach with an anchor; and then, as nothing necessitated our further stay at Undertent, we set out for Falcon-nest, which my wife had only visited two or three times during the ten days for the purpose of giving food to the animals.

CHAPTER XVII

A walk—the bustard

The next day was Sunday. It was devoted, as our custom was, to prayer, singing, reading of the Scriptures, pious instruction, and bodily exercise—to which my boys abandoned themselves with delight.

I gave them a lesson in gymnastics, and in particular taught them the way to climb a loose rope. I did so to prepare them for the work of manoeuvring the pinnace.

While they were occupied in outdoing each other at their now feats of strength and agility, I employed myself in affixing two balls of lead to the extremities of a long cord. ·

Ernest, who was the first to notice what I was doing, asked me what my purpose was.

'Well,' I replied, 'I am trying to make an arm analogous to that which is so redoubtable in the hands of some of the people who inhabit South America. I speak of the lasso, of which the Mexicans and the Patagonians make such excellent use. These intrepid men set out, mounted upon a swift horse. When they see the animal they desire to catch, they spur on, and pass it at a gallop, flinging with all their strength the lasso, which they have previously whirled with great rapidity above their heads. The thongs, meeting with an obstacle, twist themselves round it, in virtue of the momentum of the balls. In this way buffaloes, wild horses, and other powerful animals are brought to a dead stand at their highest speed, and fall, with firmly-bound limbs, victims to this singular arm, and the no less wonderful skill of the hunters.'

The idea of hunting in this fashion proved a very seductive one to my eldest sons, and they begged very hard to be allowed to make a trial of the new weapon against an adjacent tree.

I told them I would try first and show them the way.

As it so happened, my first attempt was a masterly one. The cord wound itself so tightly round the tree, that the boys not only believed in the skill of the American hunters, but in their own power to acquire it.

The next day, all our little colony were afoot betimes, for I had promised them a family visit to Calabash Wood for the purpose of laying in a new stock of gourd-vessels.

The donkey was harnessed to the sledge, upon which we placed our provisions and our hunting stores.

As was the custom, Turk, fitted out with his coat of mail, led the van. In the second rank came the children, formidably armed. My wife and I formed the rear-guard, followed, however, by Fan, who found herself seriously embarrassed by her cavalier, Nip.

We made a tour round Flamingo Marsh, and came out beyond upon a plain, whose beauty we could not sufficiently admire.

Here Fritz—always indefatigable when sport was in question—strayed away from us, taking Turk with him. The thick undergrowth hid both of them from our view.

In a few minutes we heard the dog barking, and in the midst of the noise the report of a gun. Immediately a huge bird, which had taken wing to fly away, fell to the ground. But being only wounded, it got up and made off as fast as its legs could carry it.

Turk dashed away in pursuit, Fritz exciting him to the chase both by voice and gesture. Fan found it impossible to remain indifferent. With a few vigorous jerks she disencumbered herself of Nip—who came to grief ludicrously—bounded into the brake, cut off the retreat of the fugitive, caught it by the wing, and held it fast till Fritz came up.

Fritz then called upon me, and I hastened to his aid as quickly as the weight of my baggage and the impediments offered by the thick scrub would let me.

Watching a favourable opportunity, I threw my handkerchief over the head of the huge bird, which, finding itself blinded, almost immediately ceased struggling. I tied the legs and wings of the prisoner with a piece of string which I had in my pocket. Then we returned with our capture to our companions, who awaited us on the confines of the marsh.

'It is a bustard,' said our young naturalist after examining the bird.

After binding the bird upon the sledge, we resumed our journey towards Monkey Wood.

Arrived there, Fritz related with great glee to his brothers how, on our first visit, we had made the monkeys our purveyors of coco-nuts.

CHAPTER XVIII

The wax—the parrots' nest—the india-rubber tree

The next morning I set out with Fritz for the purpose of making an excursion to the other side of the chain of rocks, in order to get some idea of the extent of the island upon which we had been cast.

Our dog and the donkey alone accompanied us.

The journey was somewhat difficult, in consequence of the tall plants and numberless exposed roots that encumbered our pathway. From time to time we came upon some crystal rivulets, where we slaked our thirst. Potatoes and tapioca grew in abundance.

Some distance on, I remarked in a thicket a number of shrubs, the berries of which were covered with a kind of wax, which adhered to our fingers when we touched it. I knew that a kind of shrub was to be found in America, which the botanists called the *Myrica cerifera*, or wax-bearer, and, to my great joy, I had no doubt that we had come upon a grove of it.

Fritz, who had observed my delight, asked me of what use these berries could be to us.

I replied that they yielded a wax which burned as well as that manufactured by bees, and that when burning it gave forth a most agreeable odour.

He thereupon collected an ample supply, which he placed in a bag upon the donkey's back.

A little farther on, a singular spectacle excited our curiosity. This was a colony of birds, in shape like our European finches, but covered with a brown plumage, mottled with white. They seemed to be living altogether in one huge nest, fixed in an isolated tree, and constructed with wonderful skill. It appeared to us to have been built for a large number of families, and it was surmounted by a kind of roof made of rushes, bound together with fibrous roots. Around the sides were many openings, which seemed to form the doors and windows of each separate apartment of the common dwelling-house. The whole resembled an enormous sponge. A flock of birds poured in and out incessantly, without being in the least disturbed by our presence.

While we were examining this strange colony, we saw a number of small parrots, which flew swiftly here and there, and did battle with the little colonists, as if these were disputing with them their entrance to the nest.

Fritz, desirous of taking some of these birds, laid aside his gun and climbed the tree. On reaching the nest, he thrust his hand into one of the holes, and laid hold upon a brood of young ones which he found there; but all of a sudden he felt himself so severely pecked that he uttered a cry of anguish, and withdrew his hand, shaking it convulsively. However, he would not relinquish his attempt. As soon as the pain was gone off a little, he again put his hand into the hole, this time more cautiously, and drew out a bird, which he thrust into his waistcoat. Then he slid down the trunk of the tree, and reached the ground again safe and sound.

He at once examined his little prisoner. It was a small Brazilian parrot, of a beautiful green plumage.

Fritz begged to be permitted to take it home, in order that he might domesticate it and teach it to talk.

I consented with all my heart. What could we do better to cheer our solitude than to people it with new friends?

In all probability the nest we had robbed belonged to the parrots, while the brown birds which we had seen at first were doubtless intruders, who desired to possess themselves of so desirable a residence. Hence the fierce little combats of which we had been witnesses.

While we were thus talking together, we came upon the borders of a wood filled with a kind of tree that was strange to us. It was not unlike in form to the wild fig, and it grew to a prodigious height. Fritz remarked that there oozed out of the wrinkled bark a kind of resin, which grew hard in the air. He broke off a small piece, which he rubbed between his fingers; and when he found that it grew soft and expanded with the heat, so that he could stretch it without breaking, he came to me crying, 'Father! father! I believe I have found an india-rubber tree!'

'What!' I exclaimed, no less pleased than my boy, 'an india-rubber tree! Then indeed you have found what will prove an inestimable treasure to us!'

Having examined the gum for myself, I saw that Fritz had not been deceived; and as he asked me of what use it would be to us, I told him that, among other things, it would make us excellent shoes.

The curiosity of the youth was awakened, and I was obliged to explain to him, as we walked along, the means by which we could arrive at the result I had indicated.

'India-rubber, as you have just seen,' I said, 'oozes drop by drop from the caoutchouc-tree. As it does so it is caught in vessels. While it is still in a liquid state, a thin coating of it is laid upon a bottle or vase made of common clay, and then dried by exposure to the smoke of a fire, which gives it the black colour with which we are familiar. This done, the bottle which has served for a mould is broken in pieces, and shaken out of the neck of the flexible and unbreakable india-rubber vessel formed upon its surface. I should follow something like the same process to make shoes. I should fill a pair of stockings with sand, paint them over with caoutchouc, let the caoutchouc dry, empty out the sand, and then I think we should find ourselves in the possession of a good, serviceable pair of perfectly waterproof boots.'

Well satisfied with our discovery, and shod already, in imagination, in our india-rubber boots, we now resumed our journey.

Presently we came to a new cocoa-tree wood.

'Here,' said I to Fritz, 'let us make a halt for a time.'

In attentively observing the trees growing around us, I lighted upon some which I believed to be sago-palms. Not only did I perceive in the trunk of one of them, which had been broken down by the wind, a quantity of the succulent powder which is sold in Europe under the name of sago, but—to confirm me in my surmise —I also discovered the large white grubs or worms which the Indians of the West seek in the sago-tree as a toothsome article of diet. Determining to test the taste of the Indians in this matter,

I spitted a number of these grubs upon a ramrod, which I then suspended by two forked sticks over a fire that had been lighted by Fritz while I was preparing the raw material for our dinner.

At the first sight of the singular dish which he saw me preparing, Fritz vowed that he would not touch a single morsel of it. But before long my grill gave forth an odour so agreeable that fancy succumbed to appetite, and my young epicurean was the first to fall-to upon the dish he had so loftily disdained.

After this repast, our donkey was harnessed to the sledge, which we had left on the previous day, and in the evening we once more found ourselves at Falcon-nest, where the family were beginning to grow anxious by reason of our prolonged absence.

The story of our journey formed the subject of conversation for the rest of the evening. But what excited the greatest delight among the children was not so much our story as our trophies, especially the parrot. Each of them clamoured to become its tutor, until it was necessary, in order to put an end to all disputes, for Fritz to declare that he would bring the bird up himself, and suffer no one else to interfere with him.

As to our good housewife, she was especially delighted at the discovery both of the caoutchouc and of the wax-berries. With the help of the latter, she hoped to see herself furnished with candles. I promised that in the morning I would try and make her some.

CHAPTER XIX

Candle-making—butter-making—the last voyage to the wreck—the buffalo—the young jackal

From the rising of the sun my children gave me no rest until I had kept my promise of the previous evening. I strove to recall to mind all that I knew about the candle-maker's craft, and then set to work. In the first place I boiled the berries in a cauldron of water. The wax soon rose to the surface, and I gathered it into vessels, which I placed near the fire to prevent it from congealing.

When my wife had finished the wicks, which under my direction she prepared from threads drawn out of the sail-cloth, I dipped them into the wax, and hung them in the air to harden. By repeating this dipping several times we found ourselves in the possession of a supply of waxed candles which, though neither so shapely nor so finished as those which are made in moulds, nevertheless, bad as their light was, freed us from the irksome necessity of going to bed at sundown.

This first success encouraged me to put in execution another project which I had formed, and which, if successful in the result, would, I knew, make glad the heart of our good housewife.

It troubled her a good deal to see the cream which accumulated on our dishes of milk put to no good use, when by the aid of a churn—a utensil we did not possess—she might have made good butter of it.

In order to supply the place of this useful machine I took one of our largest calabash bottles, and filled it with something like three quarts of cream. I then corked it hermetically, and laid it upon a square piece of sail-cloth, whose four corners I attached to stakes. This done, I set each of my boys between the stakes, and bade them shake the cloth backwards and forwards with a regular motion, which occupation proved so amusing to them that they looked upon it as a recreation.

At the end of an hour I opened the gourd, to find that we had a pound or two of excellent butter.

My wife knew not how to express her satisfaction, while the boys, who were always delighted at the discovery of a new dainty, were not less pleased.

The success of these different attempts inspired me with the necessary hardihood to undertake an operation far more lengthy and difficult than any which I had yet accomplished. It was to construct a carriage to replace our sledge, which the animals could not draw without a great waste of strength.

I fancied that I had sufficiently examined every species of carriage in Europe to be able to construct a little car, but when it came to the making of the wheels and the fixing of the axle-tree, I found myself in great difficulty. So true is it that the most humble trade requires an apprenticeship.

At length, after many attempts, and a great deal of bungling, I completed a two-wheeled car—heavy, ugly, and altogether clumsy, I agree; but likely, as it seemed to me, to save us a world of useless labour in the work of haulage.

At length the deplorable condition of our clothes necessitated another voyage to the wreck, where there still remained several chests of linen and other garments. I overcame my wife's scruples in the matter, and on the first calm day sailed away in the pinnace to the vessel.

We found that it had been very seriously damaged by a recent storm, and that the chests of clothes and the powder had suffered with the rest of the cargo. We loaded our little craft with every kind of object that we thought would be useful to us, such as cooking utensils, arms of all kinds, and even several pieces of cannon; and then, after taking away, during several successive voyages, whatever we had thought it necessary to put on board, we determined to blow up the wreck, in order that its timbers might be floated ashore by the winds and the waves.

To this end I rolled beneath the keel of the exposed end of the vessel a barrel of gunpowder, into which I had fixed a slow match, lighted at one end. Then we rowed the pinnace away as swiftly as we could.

As soon as we had disembarked and arrived at Undertent,

I proposed to my wife to take our supper to a point of the rocks in full view of the wreck.

She consented.

We had not been seated here above an hour when the darkness, which in these regions follows the day without the intervention of twilight, suddenly closed around us.

All at once a terrible explosion resounded through the air, and a huge column of fire shooting up from the sea to the clouds apprised us that the destruction of the wreck was complete.

We were on foot early next day, in order to go down to the beach to collect the timbers which we rightly opined would be thrown up during the night. Among them I saw with satisfaction several casks, to which I had attached some large copper boilers that we had not been able to take on board the pinnace, but that I had thought it well to secure for the establishment of a small sugar refinery.

For several days we were occupied in collecting these waifs and strays. My wife, while we were thus engaged upon the beach, discovered that two of our ducks and one of the geese had hatched numerous broods of young, whose engaging little ways reminded her of and caused her to regret her feathered family at Falcon-nest.

All of us desired to return there, and I announced that we would do so on the next day.

On the road thither Ernest remarked that the young trees planted for the avenue were not vigorous enough to hold themselves erect by their own strength, and he proposed that we should make an expedition to Cape Disappointment, in order to bring thence a supply of bamboos to prop them.

This excursion became indispensable, for our stock of candles was growing short, and we required a new supply of wax-berries. Also, we wanted some more sugar-canes. In short, each of us found some pretext for the journey; and I determined to make it as much as possible a pleasure-trip.

On the morrow the weather was fine in the extreme, the air pure and fresh. The whole of the colony put themselves *en route*.

We journeyed all day, and in the evening, while we were resting, our donkey, who was quietly browsing at the foot of a tree, all at once burst into a loud 'he-haw', began kicking as if tormented, and then rushed at full gallop clean out of sight. We ran after him, but without being able to discover the way he had taken. We returned in a state bordering on despair. His sudden disappearance troubled me. In the first place, we had lost a very useful animal; in the second, I feared that he had been frightened by the pro-pinquity of some wild beast, which might bode us as much harm as it had done him.

This latter consideration led us to light large fires in the neigh-bourhood of a hut we had constructed to shelter us from the cool night air.

The night was serene. My family lay extended upon soft beds of moss. As for myself, I could not sleep, I kept guard over all who were dear to me until daybreak, when I snatched a few moments of repose.

In the morning, after returning our thanks to Almighty God for His watchful care of us, and partaking of a good breakfast which was prepared by my wife, I set out to seek the ass.

I took Jack with me, leaving the two elder boys to take care of their mother and little Francis.

After a half-hour's search I found traces of the wanderer's shoes, which a little farther on became mixed up with the hoof-prints of a number of larger animals.

In following the trail we found ourselves upon a vast plain, extending before us until it was lost to view on the horizon. In the far distance we fancied we descried troops of animals, which seemed to be about the size and shape of horses. Thinking it not unlikely that our friend the donkey might be among them, we set out for the spot where they were. We found ourselves within something like a hundred paces of the animals which we had seen from a distance, and which I now recognised as buffaloes.

All at once our dogs, which were in our rear, darted forward barking furiously. Our efforts to restrain them were in vain. At the sight of the buffaloes they precipitated themselves into the middle of the troop.

The fight became terrible. The buffaloes rushed hither and thither, uttering the most appalling bellowings, tearing up the earth with their feet and horns, and throwing themselves furiously upon the dogs, who, nothing daunted, laid hold upon the ears of their adversaries, biting them severely. This gave us time to charge our arms, and to retire some paces. In a few moments we saw our brave dogs approaching us, holding firmly by the ears a young buffalo which bellowed frightfully as they dragged him along.

We had yet to conquer the young buffalo, which still did valiant battle with the dogs. We did not like to use our guns, for I had made up my mind to take the animal alive if possible, to replace our donkey, which we were too tired to seek further.

Jack hit upon the lucky notion of making use of the lasso, and he threw it with so much address that, bound tightly by the hinder legs, the buffalo fell an easy prey upon the sand.

I ran to the spot at once, drove away the dogs, and replaced the lasso with shackles. But it was necessary to make the beast follow us, and this was not a task easy of accomplishment. Driven to adopt the expedient instead of the just, I had recourse to a plan which, it is true, was cruel, but which nevertheless was sure. While the buffalo lay with its legs securely tied, and a dog at each ear, I pierced with the point of my knife the partition of its nostrils, and passed through the hole a cord sufficiently strong to lead it. By this cord I tied it to a tree.

After partaking of some refreshment, we set out again for the family, leading by the nose the young buffalo, who behaved himself much better than we could have expected.

As we were walking up a little hill, our dogs turned up a female jackal, which they pursued and caught just as she was entering the cleft of a rock, where her young were awaiting her. After disabling the mother, they fell upon the little ones.

Jack, prompt as he was to rush to the spot, could only save one alive, which he begged that he might keep.

I consented the more willingly, perhaps, as I reflected that the little animal, if properly trained, might assist us in our hunting excursions.

Jack was overcome with joy, and could not sufficiently admire the beautiful appearance of his future pupil, with its golden coat and its glistening, half-closed eyes.

I had myself made a discovery of some importance. I had recognised among the vegetation surrounding us the dwarf palm, which, with its prickly leaves, would make us a capital hedge of defence against every kind of enemy. I determined to transplant some roots of it to the grounds around Falcon-nest.

It was not until nightfall that we returned to the family, who were awaiting us with anxiety. We were deluged with questions, to which Jack replied with his habitual vivacity.

His story of our adventures so captivated his audience, that supper was ready before I had time to ask my wife what she and our other children had been doing during our absence.

CHAPTER XX

The sago—the bees—the stairs

In answer to my question, my wife said she had little to relate beyond praising the three boys I had left with her for their skill and industry. During my absence they had cut down, unaided, the enormous palm from which Ernest had on the previous day taken the top. Their only tools were their hatchets and a saw, with which they cut through the trunk; then, with a long rope, fastened to the higher branches, they had pulled the tree to the ground without accident.

While they were thus occupied, a band of monkeys had invaded the hut, and done so much damage before they could be driven away, that it took considerably over an hour to repair it.

Fritz had captured a large bird, which I recognised as the Malabar eagle. I recollected to have read somewhere that this bird was easily trained, and I advised Fritz to rear it in such wise that we might use it in our hunting excursions, as a hawk is used in falconry.

The young buffalo, to whom my wife gave a meal of potatoes moistened with milk, became so tame that we handed him over as a companion to the cow.

We had a cheerful supper. Afterwards we took the same precautions for safety during the night that we had taken on the previous evening, and then went to bed upon our couches of moss, which soon drew us off into a profound sleep.

The next morning, after breakfast, I gave the signal for setting out again to Falcon-nest; but the young people had another project.

'We do not like to leave here, my love,' said my wife, 'without taking with us at least a part of the palm-tree which the boys have cut down. Ernest tells us that the interior of it is full of the pith of which they make sago; and if he is right, I should be delighted to avail myself of an article of food which is at once so delicious and so strengthening.'

I examined the tree, and found that the young scholar had not been deceived. But, on the other hand, it was no light labour to open the trunk of a tree which measured at least fifty feet in length. Nevertheless, I made known to the assembled family that we had given up our design of returning to Falcon-nest, and were about to devote ourselves to the preparation of sago.

It required unheard-of efforts to split the tree; but what with repeated blows of the axe, and the insertion of wedges in each slit made, we at length succeeded. While employed in the operation, I conceived the idea of preserving the two halves of the enormous trunk to make gutters, wherewith to bring water from Jackal River for the watering of our kitchen garden.

One of the ends of the tree was scooped out to make a trough. In this we placed the sago pith as we got it out, and wetted it up with water; two of the boys, with their sleeves turned back, kneading it as one does dough.

When the paste appeared to me to be of the proper thickness, I attached the pierced side of one of our nutmeg-graters to one end of the trough, and then, pushing the mixture against it, we had the pleasure of seeing small grains of sago oozing through at every hole. These grains were caught in a cloth, and placed in the sun to dry.

It then struck me that I might as well make some vermicelli. In order to do this I had only to mix the paste a little thicker, and to bear with a continuous and equal pressure upon the nutmeg-grater. The sago then poured through the holes in long threads, which curled themselves upon the cloth as they fell.

The next day at dawn we were on our way to Falcon-nest. The cow and the buffalo were harnessed to the car, and we could not but congratulate ourselves upon the docility of our new-found beast of burden. The road we took led us to the spot where we had concealed our bag of wax-berries, and also by Caoutchouc Grove, where we found our gourd-vessels filled with liquid india-rubber.

As we were going through the little plantation of guavas, our dogs dashed, barking furiously, into a thicket, whence they speedily returned. Fancying that they had been disturbed by some wild animal, we marched round the wood, arms in hand.

All at once Jack, who had laid down and was peering anxiously into the thicket, cried out, 'Oh, papa, it is the sow again, and she has a litter of pigs!'

A well-known grunt followed the exclamation of the excited youngster, and as it had nothing very imposing in it, the fierce hunters of an imaginary wild beast burst into loud laughter.

The poor beast was suckling six little pigs which appeared to be four or five days old.

After deliberating as to what we should do with the young animals, we resolved to take two only home with us, and to leave the others to multiply in the woods.

Our arrival at Falcon-nest partook of the nature of a triumphal entry. We were overcome with unutterable joy in rejoining our domestic animals, who, in their turn, received us with every noisy demonstration of affection of which they were capable.

The buffalo and the jackal were tied up, till custom should teach them to obey our voices and not stray away. The eagle was also tied up, but Fritz had the imprudence to remove from its eyes the bandage with which I had instructed him to blindfold it. Instantly the bird began dealing blows right and left with its claws and its beak so furiously, that no one could for the time being come near it. It tore the parrot limb from limb in a twinkling.

Fritz, on seeing the bleeding remains of his little favourite, went into a towering rage, and was about to punish the feathered murderer with death.

'No, no,' said Ernest, 'do not kill it; give it me to bring up for you. I will tame it in no time.'

'Not I,' replied Fritz. 'It is mine. I caught it, and I shall keep it. Tell me how you will tame it.'

'If you keep the eagle,' returned Ernest, 'I shall keep my secret.'

I was obliged to intervene in the discussion.

'It is hardly fair,' said I to Fritz, 'to ask your brother to reveal his secret without offering him any kind of compensation.' They agreed to strike a bargain: Fritz was to give Ernest his monkey, and Ernest in return was to tell him how to tame his eagle.

The plan was very simple. All Fritz had to do, so Ernest said, was to blow some tobacco-smoke into the bird's nostrils, whereupon, as if seized with vertigo, it would lose all its ferocity and become calm in an instant.

Fritz refused to believe in the efficacy of the plan, and talked about having his monkey back.

I advised him not to condemn the receipt till he had tried it. Ernest took a pipe and some tobacco which we had brought from the wreck, and began smoking under the place where the eagle was perched. At the first few whiffs the bird became quite docile, and then, losing its strength little by little, first tottered on its legs and then fell from its perch immovable.

Fritz, who thought the bird was dead, regretted at first that he had given his brother permission to try his experiment; but in a few moments the creature recovered its sensibility, and at once became quiet and tractable.

There was no need to repeat the experiment often, which was fortunate, for it was almost as disagreeable to Ernest as to the eagle. The bird was very soon domesticated with our other animals.

The next day the bamboo props which we had brought from Cape Disappointment were fixed to the shrubs along Jackal Avenue.

We set out early with a good load of them, and an iron dibble to make holes to set them in, leaving my wife and little Francis at home, with instructions to prepare us a good dinner of palm-cabbage and sago.

As the cow was strong enough to draw the car, we left the buffalo in the stable. I did not like to use him until the wound in his nostrils was healed.

The props proved to be of the first utility, for our trees were bent almost to the ground by the fierce winds which for some days past had blown inshore.

Towards noon we finished our labours and returned to Falconnest, where an excellent dinner awaited us.

The execution of a project which we had had in mind for some days past occupied the afternoon.

Our desire was to erect a solid flight of stairs, to take the place of the ropeladder by which we had hitherto been in the habit of ascending to our aerial habitation. Hitherto I had only been able to think of building our stairs round the outside of the tree, which would have been a labour very difficult, if not altogether impossible. I now hit upon the idea of building them inside the trunk, which I believed to be hollow, because a swarm of bees had found a home in it. Before all, it was necessary to expel these from their hiding-place—a work of some peril, as the result will show.

In order to ascertain whether I was right in my supposition that the tree was hollow, the boys and I took an axe each, with the backs of which we began sounding the trunk in every direction. The noise disturbed the bees. They swarmed out in hundreds, and furiously attacked my giddy-witted boy Jack, who, in spite of every warning to the contrary, had placed himself directly in front of the hole which served as an entrance to the hive. In an instant his face and hands were covered with stings, which gave him the most exquisite pain. I relieved his anguish by rubbing his wounds with wet earth.

This accident showed me that in order to dispossess our terrible little neighbours, we must have recourse to means less violent.

While I was beating about for a solution of this problem, I noticed an unaccustomed disturbance at the mouth of the hive. The bees were flying in and out and going and coming with an amount of agitation which seemed extraordinary, and I came to the conclusion that a new swarm was about to leave the parent hive.

I was right. In a few moments an innumerable army poured out of the trunk, circled for some moments in the air, and then settled in a heap upon the branch of a small tree, where they hung like a huge bunch of grapes. I had several times been a witness of the hiving of a swarm of young bees in Europe, and I determined to adopt the same method with these.

As a measure of precaution, I covered my head with a piece of cloth, which I pierced with holes to enable me to see and breathe, and my hands with a handkerchief. I then approached the little tree, and turned the hive which I had prepared bottom upwards upon the grass. My plans thus completed, I gave the tree a sharp shake with my foot. The greater part of the swarm fell off into the hive, which I at once turned over and placed upon a plank laid handy for the purpose. This most difficult part of the operation was at an end. I had left an opening by which the bees could come and go, and I watched anxiously to see if my little prisoners had any disposition to escape. A noisy stream soon established itself between the tree and the hive, and in the course of an hour the whole swarm had taken possession of their new dwelling-place.

In the evening, when the bees were asleep, we carried the hive into our kitchen garden, and turned the opening towards the south. On the following day the little republic began work on its own account and ours.

Being thus the possessors of a swarm which promised, by multiplying itself, to assure us a supply of honey and wax for the future, we had the less regret in resolving to sacrifice the bees which still remained in the trunk of our fig-tree. We corked up the opening, having previously thrown in a few lighted sulphur matches, and killed the whole swarm remorselessly.

The next morning we were able not only to possess ourselves of a supply of honey and wax, the result of the accumulations of years, but to set to work, without further obstruction, upon the formation of the stairs.

I probed the tree with a pole, and found to my satisfaction that the trunk of it was hollow from the roots up to the branches where we had fixed the floor of our hut. It was clear, therefore, that we could build a winding staircase inside with ease. So, without losing time, I set to work, aided by my three eldest sons.

We made at first an opening in the foot of the tree, to which we fixed the door of the captain's cabin. Thus our dwelling was capable of being firmly closed while we slept.

A long and stout beam from the wreck was fixed upright in the centre of the trunk, and the stairs were laid thence to grooves scooped out in the sides of the tree. Holes were cut here and there in which we fixed the windows brought from the vessel, until at length the work was finished, and we found ourselves in the possession of a sort of tower, at the top of which was our house, half hidden amongst the leaves.

This labour, which occupied us several days, no doubt left much to be desired in point of architectural elegance; but it was solid and convenient, which was all we needed; so we thought it superb.

While we were building our stairs, Fan presented us with a couple of puppies, one of each sex, of the pure Danish breed, and I permitted Jack to allow his jackal to feed with them. The good-natured Fan made no objection to her adopted child, and it throve under his new régime amazingly.

The two goats nearly at the same time presented us with a couple of kids each, and the sheep with five or six lambs.

We saw our flocks increase with pleasure; but in case they should take pattern by the ass and stray away, Jack hit upon the happy idea of fastening to their necks some small bells which we had found on the wreck, and which, if they wandered, would put us upon their track at once.

The incision which I had made in the nose of our buffalo was by this time healed, and I passed through the hole, after the manner of the Hottentots, a small stick, which protruded at each side and enabled us to lead him about as easily as if he had been bridled.

Thanks to this expedient, he became easy to manage; but it was not without considerable trouble that we could bring him to the understanding that it was his duty to be ridden and to carry burdens.

CHAPTER XXI

The onager—flax — the rainy season

One morning, as we were about beginning work, we were startled by a series of the most extraordinary noises, which seemed to be borne upon the wind from a distance. They consisted mainly of a sort of howling, which was mingled with hissing and whistling, and ended in a succession of lamentable wails.

Fearing a hostile attack, we hastened to drive our animals beneath the arched roots of our tree, and then took to our castle among the branches. Our dogs, pricking up their ears, put themselves on the alert.

Perfect silence lasted for some minutes, and then the strange noises were heard again—this time much nearer and louder.

We were all looking anxiously in the direction whence the unknown sounds proceeded, when all at once Fritz, who had sharper eyes than the rest of us, threw aside his gun and, bursting into a loud laugh, cried, 'It is our donkey, and he is giving a flourish of trumpets to signalise his return! What delightful music, to be sure! Liberty seems to have improved his voice!'

The other boys looked piqued at being alarmed by so trivial a cause.

I felt less assurance than any of them.

'It is not at all unlikely,' I said, 'that our ass may have something to do with this extraordinary music; but he could hardly make so much noise alone.'

'You are right, father,' said Fritz, who was still looking out among the trees, 'for I see now that he is bringing company with him.'

I looked in the direction indicated by Fritz, and saw a magnificent onager, or wild ass, trotting along by our own Longears and braying hideously.

Without delay I cast about for some means of capturing the beast. I descended softly from the tree, followed by Fritz, cautioning the boys meanwhile to remain where they were, and make as little noise as possible.

I then took a long rope, one end of which I tied to one of the roots of the tree, while in the other I tied a slip-knot, inserting a small stick to keep it open.

With a piece of bamboo I made a sort of cleft-stick, of which Fritz, who was very curious on the subject, tried in vain to guess the use. In his impatience to catch the onager he wanted to use the lasso; but I stopped him, observing that my plan, which was the Patagonian one, would prove the better on this occasion.

Fritz fell in with my views, and I instructed him how to proceed.

As the two animals approached the tree the onager caught sight of us, and as ours were probably the first human faces he had ever seen, he started back affrighted.

Fritz held out to our donkey a handful of oats. Master Longears was not too well fed to resist temptation. He ran up so fast that the onager, judging there was something worth having in the wind, followed him without mistrust.

I profited by the opportunity to slip my noose over his back, by means of a pole at the end of which I held it.

Immediately the onager made a sharp bound backwards, and was turning to fly, when the knot closed round his neck, and the rope brought him up so suddenly that he fell to the ground as if suffocated.

I hastened to loosen the cord, lest it should kill him, and replaced it by the halter of our own donkey. Then, before he could recover himself, I closed his nostrils with my bamboo cleft-stick, the open ends of which I tied tightly together with a piece of string, thus employing to tame the animal the method adopted by farriers when they have to shoe a vicious horse.

This done, I fastened the halter with two long ropes to the roots of our tree, and waited for the captive to come to his senses again, in order to see what more was necessary to be done to bring him into complete subjection.

In the meantime the whole family had descended from the tree;

and as we stood round the prostrate animal we could not but admire the grace of form which almost raises this species of ass to the same level of beauty as the horse.

At the end of a few minutes the animal leapt up and made a brave struggle to regain his liberty. The bamboo cleft-stick, however, troubled him exceedingly, and considerably damped his ardour, so that before long he became quiet enough to be led to the place that served us for a stable.

This accomplished, it became necessary to take measures to prevent another desertion on the part of our own donkey, our confidence in whose fidelity was very naturally shaken. Having fettered his fore-legs, I tied him up beside the onager, thinking that his enforced society might be a means of teaching the new animal the kind of life he would be expected to lead in future.

We found it no easy task to train our onager. We condemned him to privations and even to blows, but we could do nothing with him until we adopted the American plan of clipping his ears. This finished his education.

At the end of a few weeks, Lightfoot—this was the name we gave him—was so well broken in that we were able to mount him without fear. In order to manoeuvre him, I attached to his halter a sort of cavesson, or nose-band, into which I fixed a couple of switches, that touched either the right or left ear according as we pulled the right or left rein. The ear being the most sensitive part of these animals, the cavesson proved to be as effectual as a bridle and bit.

During the time spent in training our onager, a triple hatching among our fowls made us the possessors of more than forty little chicks, which ran about in every direction piping joyously.

This increase in our poultry, joined with the acquisition of the buffalo and the onager, recalled to my mind a project I had formed some time since for building a substantial stable and fowl-house before the rainy season—which I knew could not be far off—came on in its intensity.

Upon the arched roots of our tree we laid a roof made of bamboos and reeds interlaced with each other, covering it with moss and clay, and finishing it off with a coating of tar. We thus had a solid roof upon which we could walk without fear of falling through. We surrounded it with a neat balustrade, which gave it the appearance of a terrace, and in this way rendered the useful ornamental.

The interior of the hut was divided into several compartments, some serving the purpose of stables and barns, and others being set apart for dairy work and provision stores. We knew it would be necessary to gather in a large stock of the latter, because the rainy season, which is the winter of these tropical seasons, would keep us indoors entirely.

Very few days passed in which we did not enrich our magazine with some new acquisition.

One evening, as we were returning from digging potatoes, I proposed to my wife that she and the younger children should drive the cart home to Falcon-nest, while Fritz and Ernest accompanied me to the oak wood, to add to the spoils of the day a supply of acorns. Fritz rode proudly upon the onager. Ernest carried his monkey on his shoulder.

We carried empty sacks with us, intending to fill them and place them on the back of the onager, which had rendered us similar services before, though he flatly refused to assist our donkey in drawing a cart.

When we had reached the middle of the wood, I tied Lightfoot to a tree, and we set to work filling our sacks. Our labour was soon at an end, for the acorns were plentiful and easy to pick up.

Just as we were coming away, the monkey suddenly dashed into a thicket, before which he had been sitting with his ears pricked up; and in another instant we heard the screaming of a bird, accompanied by a furious beating of wings. We judged that a battle was in progress between Master Nip and some denizen of the brushwood.

Ernest, who was first upon the scene of conflict, advanced with caution, and we soon heard him crying out, 'Fritz! Fritz! come here! Here is a nest full of eggs! Come and get them while I hold Nip, who is struggling to get at them! The bird is trying to escape!'

Fritz ran to the bust at the top of his speed, and a few minutes afterwards returned with a fine Canadian heath-fowl, similar to one he had fired at and missed some days before. I helped him to tie the legs of the creature, which, as it appeared to me, would be a very valuable addition to our poultry-yard.

Ernest, who had at last got rid of Nip, brought his hat full of eggs, covered over with leaves similar to those of the iris. In showing them to me he said, 'I brought these leaves of which the nest was made because they are so long and thin, and altogether so curious that they will serve to amuse Francis.'

Our full sacks were then laid upon the onager in such a manner as to leave room for Fritz, who always rode the animal. Ernest carried his eggs, I the fowl, and in this order we set out for Falcon-nest.

My wife was delighted with our new capture. She carefully laid the eggs in a new nest, induced one of our hens to sit on them, and at the end of twenty days presented us with fifteen young heath-fowls.

A day of two afterwards, when the long sword-like leaves which Ernest had brought home for Francis had become dry, and were blowing about on the grass, Fritz said to his brother, no doubt with the intention of amusing him: 'Come on, Francis, let us make some whips of these toys to drive our cattle with!'

Thereupon he proceeded to split each leaf into three or four thongs, which he plaited together into a long cord.

By accident I saw him at work, and noticing the flexibility of the leaves, I examined them more attentively. If gave me intense joy to find that they were leaves of the *Phormium tenax*, a plant which serves the Indians as an admirable substitute for the flax of Europe.

My wife was no less delighted than I was. She cried our enthusiastically, 'Bravo! bravo! This is the best discovery we have made yet. Get as many of these leaves as you can, and I will soon make you new clothes of every kind!'

She forgot, the dear creature, how far the raw material in this case was removed from the manufactured article.

While I was endeavouring to explain this to her, with the intention of softening down the disappointment which often follows misplaced enthusiasm, Fritz mounted the onager, Jack the buffalo, and the pair of them disappeared at a gallop in the direction of the oak wood.

In a quarter of an hour they returned, like true foraging hussars, their beasts laden with large bundles of the new flax-plant, which they threw down at our feet.

I commended them for their promptitude, and promised my wife that, whatever might come of our attempt, we would do our best to prepare her some flax.

'First of all,' I said, 'we must submit our grass to the process of steeping.'

'What is steeping?' asked Fritz. 'Must we make a fire, and heat some water?'

'No,' I replied, 'there is no need of a fire. Steeping consists in exposing the flax alternately to moisture and the open air, in order to allow the plant to decay to a certain extent. The soft parts are then easily separated from the long and tenacious threads. The vegetable glue which binds them together is dissolved, and they are obtained by pounding or stripping the stalk.'

'But do not the threads perish with the rest?' asked Fritz.

'That may happen,' I replied, 'if the steeping process lasts too long. At the same time the wonderful toughness of the fibre renders such an accident very rare. Besides, we have nothing to fear if, in place of exposing the grass to the heat of the sun, we carefully put it to decay in stagnant water.'

My wife was of opinion that it would be better, owing to the tropical heat of the country in which we found ourselves, to adopt the latter method of steeping, and suggested that Flamingo Marsh would be a good place to carry out the process.

The idea was an excellent one, and next morning we harnessed the ass to the car, upon which we piled our bundles of flax, leaving room for little Francis and Nip in the centre. Thus prepared, we set out, I and the boys following the convoy with our pickaxes and shovels.

Arrived at the marsh, we separated our flax into little bundles, and, tying a stone to each, sunk them in the water till they were entirely submerged.

At the end of fifteen days our good housewife, thinking that the flax was sufficiently steeped, asked us to go and fetch it. We did so, and laid it out on the grass in the sun. In a single day it was quite dry. We then brought it back to Falcon-nest, putting off till another day the pounding and other processes.

As I foresaw the speedy approach of the rainy season, I thought it wise to devote our attention to our stock of edibles.

For some days past the weather, which had hitherto been warm and serene, became at times gloomy and threatening. The heavens were often obscured by thick clouds, the wind moaned up heavy with moisture, and once or twice slight showers had fallen.

All the potatoes and tapioca we could get were brought into the storehouse and piled in heaps; for these roots were to form the staple of our provisions for the winter. We also brought in large supplies of coco-nuts and acorns.

In the place of potatoes and tapioca I sowed wheat, for, notwithstanding the many and delicious natural products of the island, we all missed our bread. It is an article of food of which one must be deprived before he can learn the full value of it. Little Francis, who had never cared for bread at home, was more clamorous for it now than any of us.

We took care also to transplant to Undertent a quantity of young coco-trees and sugar-canes.

In spite of all our activity and foresight, the rains came upon us before we expected them. They fell in such torrents that little Francis, seriously alarmed for his safety, asked me if there was not going to be another flood, and if we had not better set about building an ark like the patriarch Noah.

We soon found that we could no longer live in our aerial dwelling: the winds and the rain distressed us to the last degree of endurance. So we took up our habitation under the roof which we had thrown over the arched roots of our tree. The chambers, however, were so full of provisions, and animals, and tools, that we had hardly room to move. Nor was this the worst. We could not light a fire without being almost suffocated by smoke.

In order to make room, a large number of articles were piled up the winding staircase, and all our animals were housed in one stall. We were thus enabled to work, and could almost lay ourselves out at full length to sleep. As to cooking, we did as little of it as possible. Our desire for warm food gave way before the terrible ordeal of enduring the smoke which resulted from preparing it.

Besides, we had gathered in but a very limited supply of firewood. So we had every cause for thankfulness when we found that the only effect of the rains upon the atmosphere was to render it humid. Had the winter been cold as well as wet, we should have suffered dreadfully.

Our stock of forage for the animals was not large, and we could not add to it from our own stores of potatoes without being in danger of perishing by hunger ourselves. We therefore decided to give freedom to those of our dumb companions which were indigenous to the country, in order that they might find food for themselves. At the same time, as it was important not to leave them to resume their wild life, Fritz and I, several times during the day and each evening, went to seek them and bring them back to the foot of the tree.

My wife, seeing that we returned each time wet to the skin, hit upon the idea of making each of us a waterproof garment.

To that end she took two sailors' canvas shirts, to which she sewed a kind of hood which we could pull over our heads, and then covered the whole with a coating of caoutchouc. Encased in these garments, we could go out in the heaviest rain without danger to our clothes or to our health.

It was during the first part of this winter that I began, as a pastime, to write a detailed account of our life in this desert island. Many times I was obliged to have recourse to the memory of my wife and my boys for a recital of events which had occurred since our shipwreck.

The captain's chest of books had been opened, and we found them a great relief to us. The box contained some very useful volumes, consisting of dictionaries, scientific works illustrated with cuts, and a great many handbooks for arts and handicrafts. These volumes were not by any means perfect. We often found the authors at fault, especially when they treated of the tropical plants, trees, and animals which had fallen under our own observation.

Of all my labours, that which pleased my wife the most was the making of a card for the purpose of combing our flax.

In order to do so, I rounded and sharpened with a file a number of long nails, which I laid at equal distances one from the other on a square piece of tin. Then I folded the tin over and poured melted lead between the pieces to fix the nails solidly in their places. The next process was to nail the contrivance to a piece of wood, and the flax-comb was complete.

My invention appeared so strong, and so well fitted to its purpose, that my wife prayed for the end of the winter, in order that we might get to flax-carding at once.

CHAPTER XXII

Return of the fine season—the salt cavern—a shoal of herrings—salmon—sturgeons—the maize-field

In towns the winter has its compensations. Comfortable houses, family reunions around the domestic hearth, pleasant evenings, and warm beds to lie in, often cause those whom fortune has thus favoured to forget that the cold season is a time of acute suffering for the poor. No one, however, is insensible to the advent of the spring and summer.

As to us, it would be impossible to describe our joy when, after long weeks of privation and forced seclusion, we at length saw the skies clear up and the sun shining radiantly upon the glorious face of nature. It was with transports of delight that we abandoned our unhealthy dwelling-place to breathe the fresh air again, and to contemplate the beautiful scenery by which we were surrounded.

Everything seemed to be putting on a new youth. We ourselves felt inspired by such excellent spirits that we cast far behind us all remembrance of our past weariness and suffering, and gave our minds wholly to the labours which lay before us, and which seemed in our new condition of mind to be little more than pleasant pastimes.

One of our first cares was to make a tour of inspection over the enclosed lands which we called our domain.

Our shrubbery was in excellent condition. The seeds which we had sown were springing up. The new leaves of the trees were budding forth. The fertile soil was covered with flowers, whose soft odours were borne upon every passing breeze. The music of birds of the most brilliant plumage resounded everywhere. We had never hailed the return of a spring-time so gay and so smiling.

My wife wished to proceed without delay to the carding of our flax. While, therefore, the younger children were employed in getting in fresh forage for the animals, Fritz and I spread the bundles of flax in the sun. When they were sufficiently dry we all proceeded to the work of pounding, stripping, and carding.

The boys, armed each with a large staff, beat the stalks. My wife, aided by Francis and Ernest, did the stripping. I devoted myself to the carding, and succeeded so well that my impatient wife begged me without delay to make her a spindle, in order that she might turn my rude heaps of flax into thread fit for weaving.

By dint of skill and application—what cannot a willing man accomplish?—I contrived to make, not only a spindle, but a spinning-wheel and a winder.

My wife, transported with zeal, at once set to work without even taking a day's airing, although she had been shut up so many weeks. She consented voluntarily to stay at home with little Francis, while Fritz, Ernest, Jack, and I made an excursion to her favourite Undertent—her sole desire at this time being to provide us with a new supply of clothes to take the place of our old ones, which were fast wearing out.

We found the tent in a deplorable condition. Half of it had been carried away by the wind, and the greater part of our provisions were spoiled by the rain.

We at once took measures to dry everything that we thought could be saved by this means.

Happily our pinnace had suffered no harm. Our tub-boat, on the contrary, was a complete wreck.

The loss which troubled me most was that of two barrels of gunpowder, which, being open, I had left in the tent for current use instead of carrying them to the magazine in the rocks, where, fortunately, I had stored the remaining four barrels.

This accident led me to conceive the project of building substantial winter quarters, where we could find shelter, not only for ourselves, but for our provisions during the heavy tropical rains.

I dared not hope to carry out a bold project of Fritz's, to excavate for ourselves a dwelling in the rocks; for, with such tools and strength as we had at our disposal, I saw that this would be the work of several summers. But I determined, in any case, to try to make a cave large enough to serve as a provision-store.

With this view I set out in the morning, accompanied by Fritz and Jack, who were armed, as I was, with crowbars, pickaxes, and hammers. We chose a place where the face of the rock was even and almost perpendicular to the soil. On this I marked with charcoal the shape of the opening we intended to make; and then we began work vigorously.

At the end of the day our labours showed so little result that we were on the point of abandoning them. However, we took courage on observing that the rock became softer the further we dug into it, and that in some places we could even remove it with a spade.

We had penetrated to a depth of about seven feet, when Jack, who was working inside the cavity, and was trying with his crowbar to loosen a large piece of rock, suddenly cried out, 'I am through! I am through!'

'Through what?' I asked, 'the rock ,or the world?'

'Through the rock!' he cried excitedly. 'Hurrah! hurrah!'

'He is right!' cried Fritz, who had rushed in to see what was going on. 'His crowbar has pierced a hole, and fallen through on the other side.'

I went in, and was soon convinced of the truth of what Fritz had said. I struck the rock a sharp blow with my pickaxe, and a mass of it fell away, revealing a large opening, into which the boys were about to rush without further thought.

I stopped them instantly, for the air which came out of the hole was foul in the extreme—almost overpowering me when I approached to look in.

I took advantage of the opportunity to teach the boys what were the conditions under which air would sustain life by respiration.

'It is necessary,' I said, 'that the gases of which air in its normal condition is composed should be in their exact proportions, and not mixed with any other gas emanating from nature. And there are many ways both of discovering whether these proportions have been duly kept, and of avoiding their injurious effects if they have not. The surest test is fire. It not only will not burn except in air which is fit to breathe, but it may be used in one way to drive away the noxious gases from impure air.'

We made a first experiment by throwing into the opening some bundles of dry grass which we had set alight. They went out instantly.

I then had recourse to a means which I believed would be more efficacious.

We had saved from the wreck a case of rockets and grenades, such as are used on board ship for giving signals at night. I took some of these, placed them on the edge of the opening, pointing inwards, and then lighted their fuses. The matches hissed for a time, the grenades and rockets exploded, and by the light which they spread abroad we could see the whole interior of the cave. It appeared very deep, and its sides glittered as if they had been cut with as many facets as a diamond.

In an instant all was in darkness again, and nothing was to be seen but the huge waves of thick smoke that floated out of the mouth of the grotto.

When we had fired into the cave two or three times more, I made a second trial with the lighted grass. This time it burnt up brilliantly.

I concluded, therefore, that there was no longer the least danger of asphyxia. Nevertheless, as the cave was in total darkness, and there might be precipices and pools of water in it, I judged it prudent not to enter without a light.

I dispatched Jack to Falcon-nest to announce our happy discovery to the other members of the family, to get them to come along with him and assist in the work of exploration, and also to bring enough candles to examine the cave throughout its extent.

While Jack was away, Fritz and I enlarged the entrance to our grotto, and cleared away the rubbish that lay before it.

We had just finished when we saw our good housewife and the three younger boys approaching, mounted upon our chariot, of which Jack had constituted himself the noisy driver, Ernest and Francis waved their hats as a sign of triumph.

We entered altogether into the cavern, each of us carrying a lighted candle. Fritz and I took a tinder-box, lest any of the candles should go out.

Our expedition had an air of gravity, if not of solemnity, about it. I led the way myself, cautiously sounding the earth, and looking round on every hand as I went. My boys, spurred on by curiosity, followed me courageously.

The floor of the cavern, which a providential hand seemed thus to have prepared for our reception, was solid and level, and covered with a very fine, dry sand.

Having examined the disposition of the crystals in a piece of stone which I chipped off the side of the cavern, and placed the fragment to my lips, I found that the grotto was formed in a vein of rock-salt.

This discovery gave me the liveliest satisfaction, for it assured us of a plentiful supply of salt both for ourselves and our animals, without the labour of gathering it as we had hitherto done upon the sea-shore.

Penetrating farther into the cavern, our admiration knew no bounds. The reflection of the lights which we carried played over the crystallised walls in colours the most brilliant and forms the most captivating.

Some steps farther on, I came upon some pieces of crystal which seemed to have fallen from the roof.

This discovery led us to fear that these droppings might be continual, in which case it would be dangerous to inhabit the cave; but seeing no more about, I came to the conclusion that our explosions had loosened these fragments, and that in ordinary circumstances the roof was perfectly safe.

Nevertheless, to make quite sure, I sent everybody out of the cavern, and fired off a gun two or three times into the mouth of it. A few more pieces fell; but on sounding the roof with a pole, we found that these pieces were only exceptions, and that, as a whole, the top of the grotto was as solid as its sides.

When we had finally decided to take up our winter quarters in the cavern, no one knows the projects that were conceived for fitting it up.

Falcon-nest was to remain as a summer residence, but we thought no more of the improvements we had resolved to make there to fit it for the rainy season. Our attention was wholly concentrated upon our subterranean house. In the first place we carved out a handsome doorway, and in the next, we made apertures in the face of the rock. To these openings we fitted the doors and windows of the tree at Falcon-nest; for since the latter was henceforth to be only a summer residence, there was no need of closing it up so carefully.

The cavern being very large, we divided it into separate apartments by partitions. To the right of the entrance were placed our sitting and sleeping rooms; to the left, the kitchen and the workshop. Farther back were placed our cellar and store-room. We had four apartments in that side of the cave which we had set apart for habitation. The first was intended as a sleeping-apartment for my wife and myself; the second was the dining-room; then came a bedroom for the boys; and behind this was a large sittingroom, where we placed the books, the arms, and certain curiosities that we had collected from the wreck and during our sojourn on the island.

In the room intended for the kitchen we constructed a large fireplace, with a chimney passing out at the top of the rock in which the cave was situated.

All our provisions and tools had places of their own; but, notwithstanding the enormous extent of the cavern, the greatest ingenuity was requisite to find room for our poultry and animals. Never since we had been on the island had we displayed so much skill and activity. At the same time, we were continually stimulated to fresh labours by the satisfactory results we achieved.

While we were employed in fitting up our grotto residence, we were obliged to take up our habitation at Undertent, and our food consisted chiefly of turtles' eggs and the flesh of a turtle or two which we caught as they came up on the beach to lay. It occurred to me that it would not be at all a bad thing to keep turtles, so that we could provide ourselves according to our needs, without the trouble of waiting to capture them. I also hit upon a plan for carrying out my idea. Whenever we saw a turtle on the beach, Fritz ran out and cut off its retreat to the sea while we caught in and turned it over upon its back. Then with a drill we bored a hole on the edge of its shell, through which we passed a long cord that we fastened to a stake. The turtle was thus at liberty to plunge into the sea again or to walk about on land as much as he pleased; but he was not the less our prisoner, and we could make use of him when we wanted him.

One morning, as we were making our way from Falcon-nest to Deliverance Bay, we were arrested by a strange sight out at sea. About a thousand paces from the shore, a vast extent of water seemed to be boiling, and sparkled vividly in the morning sun. Just over this briliant wave-mass sailed a great cloud of sea-mews and other birds, which were screaming loudly.

A few moments of quiet observation put me in possession of the truth. It became evident that we were witnessing the arrival of a shoal of herrings.

I determined to organise a fishing excursion, in order to profit by this new resource that Providence had sent us.

Fritz went into the sea with a basket, which it was only necessary to submerge in order to fill it with fish; I threw the herrings upon the sand. Francis picked them up and carried them to Ernest and Jack, who, with the help of their knives, desembowelled them in accordance with a method which I described. This done, I fetched the remaining casks of our old tub-boat, and placed the herrings in them in layers, between each of which my wife scattered a good sprinkling of salt. When I had in this way filled all the casks, I closed them with some pieces of board, which I nailed down securely; and then, with the help of our donkey and cart, we transported our spoils to the new store-house in the grotto.

About a month after we were visited by the shoal of herrings, Jackal River was invaded by a quantity of salmon and sturgeon, which came up the stream, as their custom is, to spawn in fresh water.

Jack, who was the first to notice these new visitors, took them for young whales.

I had no difficulty in pointing out to him his error; and I cast about for some means of capturing a few of these fish, of which the flesh is very delicate eating.

Jack, who remarked, or rather, perhaps, divined the nature of my reflections, darted off at full speed, crying, 'Wait a moment, papa! Wait a moment! I think I know of a plan for catching sturgeon and salmon.'

It was not long before he returned carrying a bow, some arrows with barbed points, a ball of stout string, and two or three bladders which we had taken out of dog-fish.

Curious to see what he was going to do with these implements, his mother, his brothers, and I went with him to the bank of the river.

Arrived there, he tied a piece of string round one of the bladders, and then fastened it to an arrow. The other end of the string he made fast to a huge stone at the water's edge. Then, drawing his bow, he sighted a huge salmon. The arrow sped swiftly on its mission, and buried itself in the side of the fish.

'A hit! A hit!' cried the young archer, dancing with delight.

The salmon darted off like a flash of lightning, but soon found itself pulled up by the weight of the stone and the air in the bladder. The injury caused by so sudden a stoppage, joined with the rankling of the iron in his flesh, soon wore him out, and we were able to draw him to the bank without much difficulty.

Jack's ingenuity and success drove us all to emulation. Fritz went to seek the harpoon and windlass. I armed myself, like the god Neptune, with a trident. Ernest furnished himself with fish-hooks, which he baited with pieces of the first salmon caught. Salmon-fishing in every fashion began in earnest.

Jack held to the method whid had already stood him in such good stead. He discharged two or three arrows without hitting his mark, and when he did strike home, it was not without great difficulty that he landed his new victim.

Ernest got a bite from a sturgeon, which, with the aid of little Francis and his mother, he managed to pull out.

I struck two fish in succession, but could not capture either of them. My implement was the rudest of all.

As to Fritz, he economised his labour. He refrained from throwing his harpoon till he saw passing within range a sturgeon which measured at least ten feet in length. Struck full in the back, the enormous creature struggled fiercely, leaping and making the water fly in every direction. We were obliged to let out all the rope in the windlass to prevent our important catch from escaping. Then, little by little, we drew him into the shallows. Even then, however, we were obliged to go into the water and slip a noose over his gills before we could drag him to land.

The morning's sport at an end, we cleaned our fish, and put aside the roe of the sturgeon and the bladders for a particular use to which I designed to put them. The greater part of the flesh, after being cut in slices, was salted after the same manner as the herrings.

I determined to cure the rest in the same fashion as they cure the tunny-fish on the coasts of the Mediterranean. For this purpose I had some water boiled and strongly salted, which I poured into a tub containing the slices of fish, together with a small quantity of oil.

My wife, thinking not that the roes and bladders were of any use, was about to throw them into the water, when I stopped her, observing that I intended to prepare from the roes a very choice dish which the Russians called 'caviare', and from the bladders a valuable gelatinous substance called 'fish-glue'.

Without further delay, I carefully washed the roes, which in the mass weighed about thirty pounds. We then laid them to soak in salt water for several hours. It now only remained to press them into our calabash sieves, where the water was all drained off, to obtain a dozen hard and compact cakes of caviare, which were afterwards smoked in our curing-hut. Our stock of provisions for the winter was thus augmented by a delicacy for which kings have sometimes sighed in vain.

I recollected to have read or heard tell the process whereby fish-glue was prepared, and I resolved to put it in practice. I cut the bladders into strips, which I first laid in water to soften them, and then in the sun to dry them. We thus obtained a kind of shavings which, thrown into boiling water, would dissolve and yield a very pure gelatine. This gelatine, poured upon a flat surface, formed in cooling a highly transparent film, which I hoped would serve to glaze our windows.

The garden at Undertent was remarkably fertile, and yielded, almost without culture, excellent vegetables of every kind. We had only to water it to bring forth its products in rich abundance; and even this operation gave us very little trouble, for by this time we had laid down the two halves of the sago-palm, and a plentiful supply of water was thus brought upon the ground from Jackal River.

The greater part of the plants were perfectly acclimatised already. The trailing stalks of the melons and cucumbers were loaded with fruit; the ananas gave rich promise od future treasures; the maize showed ripening ears everywhere. Judging by the condition of the garden close to our home, it augured well of those farther removed from us. In the morning we set out in a body to visit them.

On the road to Falcon-nest we made a halt in the old potato-field, which my wife had sown with all kinds of seeds after gathering in her harvest of tubers. There also we were met by marvels in vegetation. Barley, peas, lentils, millet, oats, and several other cereals were growing in abundance.

I wondered where my wife had managed to find enough seed to sow so large a piece of land; and I was especially struck with a part of the field which was covered with a tall and thick growth of maize, come to full maturity. The richness of the vegetation had, no doubt, brought a great many destructive parasites to the spot: we could see their traces everywhere. As we approached the maize-field to cut some of it for present use, we disturbed a half-dozen bustards, which flew off with a great beating of wings; while a large number of smaller birds, amongst which I recognised the quail, ran away as fast as their legs could carry them. Two or three kangaroos also went hopping away, and our dogs followed them, but without being able to make a capture.

Fritz, who had his eagle with him, put it up, and it pounced skilfully upon one of the bustards, which it brought down, merely wounding and not killing it, however, so that we were able to add it to our other poultry.

Jack's jackal, which began by this time to be a keen hunter, brought in something like a dozen quails, which were very fat, and furnished us with an excellent repast.

We now resumed our journey, and by the middle of the afternoon found ourselves once more at Falcon-nest. As the heat of the day and our long walk had made us very thirsty, my wife proposed to prepare us a new beverage. Bruising some grains of the maize, which were still very soft, she squeezed them in a cloth, and obtained a thick liquid, which she diluted with water and sweetened with the juice of some sugar-canes. This done, she presented each of us with a cup of milky liquid, as pleasant to the taste as it was refreshing.

The remainder of the day was employed in removing our maize from the husk, and in making preparations for the execution of a project which I had conceived some time before. My idea was to establish in the open country a sort of colony of animals, which, if they acclimatised themselves and propagated their species, would relieve us of the troublesome task of tending and feeding them. I felt that there was no great danger in making the attempt, for by this time our barn-yard was so full of poultry and other livestock that we could risk the sacrifice of at least one of each species without feeling the loss of them.

CHAPTER XXIII

The cotton plant—Forest Grange—the pirogue—Francis's charge

The next morning then, at daybreak we set out, having previously loaded our car—in addition to a supply of provisions—with ten fowls, two cocks, three young pigs, and two pairs of goats. The cow, the buffalo, and the ass were yoked to it. Fritz, mounted on the onager, went on some distance in front of the caravan to reconnoitre.

Our course was directed towards a point of our domains which we had not yet explored—that is to say, towards the region which extended from Falcon-nest to the large bay beyond Cape Disappointment.

At the outset of the journey we had frequently to open a road with our hatchets, for we traversed fields obstructed with high grass and thickets; but soon the caravan reached a small wood, on leaving which we saw before us a plateau covered with shrubs, which appeared to be loaded with white flakes.

'Snow! snow!' cried Francis joyously, and he jumped up from the bottom of the carriage, where he was sitting. 'Here is a country where they have winters of the right sort. It not is like Falcon-nest, where it does nothing but rain half the year.'

And repeating 'Snow! snow!' he ran forward quickly with the intention of making a snowball.

We all laughed at the simplicity of his remarks.

It was not long before I got an insight into the nature of the supposed snow. 'Well,' said I to our young scholar, who was still greatly amused at his brother's mistake, 'do you know the name of these shrubs?'

'As far as I can judge,' he replied, with a certain air of importance, 'they are the cotton plant; and if it should prove so, it will be easy to make an ample provision of cotton without much trouble.'

He was right. The field presented a very curious spectacle. The pods of the plants, arrived at maturity, had burst, allowing the escape of the down with which they were filled. Part of it still fluttered on the branches of the shrubs. A large quantity had been stripped off by the wind, and lay scattered about, whitening all the ground.

This discovery was a source of much rejoicing to us all. My wife was particularly delighted. She immediately asked me if it would not be possible for us to construct a weaving-loom, for she already foresaw a means of renewing our stock of linen, which was much worn.

I promised her that I would think of some method of meeting her wishes.

Meanwhile we made a point of filling those of our sacks which were empty with the cotton. My wife collected also a quantity of the seeds of the plant, which she proposed to sow in the vicinity of Undertent, with the view of obtaining a supply of cotton nearer home.

Our harvest finished, we continued our journey. Soon we reached a small hill, from the top of which we obtained a magnificent view. The sides of it were covered with the most gorgeous vegetation. At the foot of it was the plain that we proposed to traverse, fertilised by a large river.

A tent was soon erected. A fire was made, and our good housewife, assisted by Francis and Jack, occupied herself in preparing a repast.

I remarked a group of trees placed so conveniently each with regard to the other, that I resolved on making them serve as the pillars of the farmery which we proposed to construct.

Our plans completed for the next day's work, we returned to the tent, where an excellent supper awaited us.

My wife distributed the cotton we had collected into bundles, so that we all had comfortable pillows for our heads, and we enjoyed our slumbers that night more than we had done for a long time past.

The trees which I had chosen for the construction of the hut were six in number, and formed an oblong, one side of which faced the sea.

In the trunks of the first three—I thus designated those which were nearest the shore—I cut, at about a dozen feet from the ground, some notches, into which I fixed a strong pole. I then repeated the process with the trunks of the other three trees—here, however, fixing my pole at a height of only eight feet. I then laid a row of smaller poles from the higher to the lower level, to form a roof, which I covered with strips of bark, to supply the place of tiles.

With wild vines and flexible reeds, woven strongly together, I then built up four outer walls to the height of five feet. In the open space between the top of these and the roof I placed some trellis-work, which allowed the air and light to penetrate to the interior.

The door was made facing the sea, in what we intended to be the front of the building.

The inside was so fitted as best to meet the end we had in view, with the least expenditure of wood.

A partition, raised to half the height of the building, separated in into two unequal divisions, the largest of which was intended for the sheepfold. I set apart here a place for the fowls, shutting it off from the rest of the compartment by a palisade, the bars of which, while allowing free ingress and egress for the feathered tribe, were too close together to permit of the passage of larger animals.

A door led from the sheepfold into the other part of the cabin, which we fitted up as a temporary lodging-place for ourselves.

All this had been done very quickly, and by consequence somewhat roughly; but I promised myself to endeavour to improve matters when we had a little spare time. For the present it sufficed that our livestock had a place of shelter.

In order to accustom them to return in the evening to their stable, the troughs were filled with grain mixed with salt, and it was agreed that this enticement should be renewed until our winged and four-footed colonists were habituated to their new dwelling.

The next day, after having supplied with an abundant provision of food the livestock which we left behind, we quitted the farmery, to which we had given the name of Forest Grange.

In the first wood which we passed through on our route we encountered a troop of monkeys, that welcomed us with the most horrible screams, accompanied by a shower of fir-cones. I fired into the air several times, in order that we might be relieved of their embarrassing attentions. On examining some of the cones which they had thrown at us, I found they had a very agreeable taste, and were of a kind that would yield an excellent oil. I recommended the youngsters to make an abundant provision of them. We then resumed our journey, and were not long in arriving at Cape Disappointment, on which I had resolved to put up a hut, which should serve us as a fishing-place when we made excursions along the coast.

We set vigorously to work. Our experience at Forest Grange had given us the skill which comes with practice; and in less than a week we finished the building, which was honoured by our young scholar with the name of 'Prospect Hill'.

For some time I had been on the look-out for a tree, the bark of which I had read would make a canoe, combining strength and lightness; and although my search had been so far fruitless, I had not lost all hope of succeeding in my object.

As soon as the hut was finished, my boys and I explored the surrounding neighbourhood, which abounded in rare trees. We found several that we should have deemed oaks by their height and foliage, had not their fruit, although much resembling acorns, shown us otherwise by their extreme smallness.

After having chosen one that seemed to me most suitable for the object we had in view, Fritz and I attached to the lower branches of it the rope-ladder which we had brought with us from Falcon-nest. Mounted upon this, Fritz proceeded to saw through the bark at the top of the trunk until he came to the wood, while I performed a similar operation at the base. I then stripped off a narrow riband of bark, extending from the one incision to the other, and by means of wooden wedges, cautiously forced into the opening, separated the rest of the covering in one solid piece. As the tree was full of sap, and the bark consequently very flexible, that portion of our task was perfectly successful; but the most difficult part still remained to be performed, and that was to convert the spoil into a pirogue or savage's canoe.

While the bark was yet moist and supple, I gave it the shape required. I cut with my hatchet a slit in the two ends, lapped the parts thus separated over each other, and nailed them together again in such a manner that they formed a point at each extremity. We had thus advanced one stage in the work of shaping our contrivance for easy navigation. Still, the pirogue was entirely flat in the middle; so I had recourse to ropes, and by a judicious tying down here and bracing up there, managed to get the sides of the boat into something like their proper shape.

But as I could not finish my task without the assistance of my tools, I sent Fritz and Jack to the tent to bring the truck, to which I had fixed the wheels of a cannon found aboard the wreck, proposing to place the pirogue on it and transport it to a more convenient spot, in order to finish it.

While waiting for their return, Ernest and I made an excurison into our immediate neighbourhood, where we found a certain tree called Fire-wood by the Indians, and which they employ when requiring a light for their nocturnal expeditions. I cut, on our journey, some pieces of wood of a shape that would serve for the ribs of the pirogue. We also discovered at the same time a new resin which, when dry, was firm and impervious to water; and remembering that it would be far preferable both to the gums we had and also to turpentine for coating our pirogue, we collected a quantity of it.

Fritz and Jack did not rejoin us until darkness had begun to set in; and as it was then too late to commence operations, we put off work till the morrow.

The first thing in the morning we placed our canoe on the car, together with the pieces of wood and other things which we thought might prove useful to us, and set out for Undertent. We stopped at Falcon-nest about two hours, which gave us sufficient time to dine and feed our animals.

We reached the tent some time before sunset, but were too tired to do anything that evening. The whole of the next day was employed in finishing the boat. In order to strengthen it, I nailed a piece of curved wood to each end, and furnished it with a solid keel running its whole length. Along the top we placed a ledge of flexible laths and poles, furnished with rings, through which to pass the cordage belonging to the mast.

I threw into the bottom as ballast some stones and clay, and covered it over with a floor, upon which we could stand and walk about comfortably. Movable seats were placed across. Our mast, furnished with a triangular sail, was placed in the middle. A rudder was fixed astern.

A happy idea occurred to me, whereby our little craft could be rendered more buoyant. I got my wife to make some air-tight bags from the skin of the dog-fish. These I filled with air, and after having given them a coat of varnish, I fastened them to the outside of the bulwarks. These air-bladders not only aided us in launching our vessel, but also prevented it from being capsized and submerged.

I have omitted to mention in its proper place the fact of our cow having presented us with a male calf, a little while after the rainy season. This animal was already grown to a size which I thought could be turned to account; and so one evening, when we were all assembled, I called Francis to my side.

'Come, little man,' I said, 'what do you say to undertaking the education of the calf?'

'The very thing, father!' cried he, clapping his hands. .'The calf is a gentle creature; I will be kind to him, and give him everything that he likes; and although I am young I shall succeed in the end. First and foremost, I will call my pupil "Grumbler"; for before his education is finished, I have no doubt he will give vent to many growls and murmurs.'

The name was considered appropriate by the boys, who straightway set to work to find names for the buffalo and the two puppies. Jack proposed to call the buffalo 'Storm'; for it would be a fine thing, in his view, to hear his brothers cry out when he approached, 'Here comes Jack, riding on the "Storm"!' The dogs were called, the one 'Brown' and the other 'Fawn', in accordance with their respective colours.

During two whole months we were employed in putting up partitions to separate the cavern into compartments, in order to render our habitation as agreeable as possible; the embellishment and finishing off our work we reserved for the winter.

The great quantity of beams, planks, and other materials which we possessed, rendered our work less difficult than we had at first imagined.

The floor of our chamber was covered by a thick bed of clay, over which was placed a quantity of small pebbles, laid closely and evenly together. The plaster with which we had covered our walls, I calculated, would be properly dried by the end of the summer. The idea occurred to us to utilise the hair of our goats and the wool of our sheep in the fabrication of carpets for the floors of our dining- and sitting-rooms. In order to do this, we placed on a piece of sail-cloth a layer of hair, which we had previously carded and which I wetted with fish-glue melted in boiling water. I then rolled up the cloth, and we set to belabouring it with all our might with large sticks. The operation with the glue was again gone through, as was also the beating, which was this time long and vigorous. We then unrolled the sail-cloth, and removed from it a long strip of felt, which when dried in the sun, answered perfectly the object we had in view. Our carpets were not Turkish ones, but they had their merit for us.

CHAPTER XXIV

The anniversary of our deliverance

One morning I awoke earlier than usual, and getting up without disturbing the rest of the family, I tried to make a reckoning of the time that had passed since we first set foot upon the island on which we now found ourselves.

My calculations, to my great astonishment, led me to the conclusion that we were on the very eve of the anniversary of that day which was at once so unfortunate and so fortunate for us.

That evening at supper, as I had not decided upon my course for the morrow—'Children,' I said to my boys, 'tomorrow is a memorable day—a day to be remembered as long as life lasts. Let us never forget it. It is the anniversary of our miraculous deliverance from the wrecked vessel, and our debarkation upon this charming island. I intend that we shall keep it as a solemn feast-day, so be up early to celebrate it.'

This news astonished the children. They could not realise the fact that we had already lived a year in our delightful solitude.

'Are you not wrong in your calculations?' asked my wife, much moved. 'Is it possible that we have been here a year already?'

'I am not mistaken, my love,' I replied. 'We were stranded on the 30th of January, twelve months ago. A calendar, which I was fortunate enough to save, carried us through eleven months. Since then, four weeks and three days have passed by, and tomorrow is the 1st of February, the day we landed on this island. Tomorrow, therefore, we will celebrate the anniversary of our deliverance. And as our library fails to supply us with a new almanac, we must henceforth take care of our chronology for ourselves.'

'That is easy enough to do,' said Ernest. 'We have only to follow Robinson Crusoe's example—to cut a notch in a stick every day, and then divide the product into weeks and months and years.'

The boy's plan appeared to me to be an excellent one. I asked him several questions upon the calendar and the methods of regulating it; and as his answers astonished me by their invariable correctness, I good-humouredly named him astronomer of the whole colony, and gave him charge of the chronology of our domains.

We talked late into the evening, and then prepared for bed.

'I shall cook you a grand dinner for the fête tomorrow,' said my wife, as she kissed the children and bade them good-night.

Preoccupied with the thought of what was in store for them, the boys lay awake for a long time; and I heard them asking each other in whispers what they thought I had in preparation, and of what the fête would consist?

I feigned to hear nothing, and left them to their conjectures and to sleep.

Immediately after breakfast, which we took in the open air in front of our grotto, I opened the solemnities of the day by reading my journal, in order that we might have fresh in our memories all the circumstances of our deliverance.

Then came the usual Sabbath exercises, with a special thanksgiving added for the day; and after that we took a walk to the spot where we had first landed, at the mouth of Jackal River in Deliverance Bay.

On our return my wife served us up a delicious repast, consisting of two roasted fowls and a dish of prepared cream, which was appetising in the last degree.

'Now, boys,' I said, 'prepare to give brilliant proofs of your skill in gymnastics. Splendid prizes will be rewarded to the victors!'

Then followed a shooting match, a race to Falcon-nest, a tree-climbing competition, and, finally, a swimming competition.

As the sun was sinking slowly behind the horizon we returned to our dwelling, whither my wife had gone before in order to receive us with all the dignity belonging to a distributor of prizes—to which office I had, with the consent of all my children, appointed her.

We found her seated upon a chair of state decorated with leaves. The prizetakers defiled before her and stood in a half-circle round her improvised throne, awaiting, like knights of old, the rewards of their valour.

With charming gracefulness she handed to each his prize, giving with it a few words of praise and encouragement and a tender maternal kiss.

Fritz received, as his prizes for skill in shooting and swimming, an English double-barrelled gun and a beautiful hunting-knife which he had long desired to possess.

Ernest, who was the winner in the running-match, received a gold watch similar to that possessed by Fritz.

Jack received a pair of spurs and an English whip, which pleased him better than anything else that could have been given him. To smack his whip loudly seemed to be the one business of his life.

As to little Francis, we gave him a pair of small spurs and an ivory-handled riding-whip.

I then advanced to the foot of the throne, and, amid the plaudits of all my children, presented the queen of the jousts with a handsome work-box containing a number of useful articles for a housewife—such as scissors, thimbles, needle-cases, bobbins, threads, and so on.

My dear wife was as much surprised as she was charmed with her present, and begged me to tell her where I had obtained the little treasure.

I told her that I had found it one day upon the wreck, and had hidden it in order to give her an agreeable surprise some day and an acknowledgement of all her care of us.

Night crept on apace. After supper and prayer, we laid ourselves to rest on our soft beds of cotton, and a night of peaceful repose followed a day which left behind it the pleasantest memories.

CHAPTER XXV

Birdlime—preparations for the winter—divers labours—the rains again

About a month later, we were spending a day at Falcon-nest, when we noticed that the trees were filled with thrushes, ortolans, and wild pigeons, as they had been at the same period last year; and we resolved to lay in another stock of these delicate game, to be preserved in butter or fat. We were all to take part in the sport; and, as I desired to economise our powder as much as possible, I hit upon the notion of having recourse to a birdlime which I fancied I could make with resin, caoutchouc, and a little grease.

Our supply of caoutchouc being nearly exhausted, I sent Fritz and Jack to the wood where the trees whence it exuded grew. They had no trouble to renew our store, for when we were last there we had made numberless incisions in the trunks, and placed large gourd-vessels below to receive the gum as it trickled out.

They returned in the evening, bringing not only a plentiful supply of caoutchouc, but also of turpentine. They brought, too, a crane which Fritz's eagle had killed flying, a plant of anise, and a number of roots which they had taken upon themselves to christen the Monkey-roots, because they owed the discovery of them to a troop of monkeys that they surprised digging them out of the earth with extraordinary labour, and devouring them gluttonously.

I recognised in these roots the ginseng, a plant to which the Chinese attribute the most extraordinary nutritive and medicinal properties, and which, in their country, no one but the emperor has a right to cultivate.

The excursion would have given us unmingled satisfaction if the boys had not told us that they had pushed on to Forest Grange, where they found our farmery completely devastated. So far as they could judge, the destruction had been the work of monkeys.

The cabin had been partly demolished, the fowls had been strangled, and the goats and sheep had strayed away into the neighbouring woods.

I secretly determined to take signal vengeance upon the detestable tribe of animals that had thus laid our little colony in ruins. I said nothing, however, of the intention to my family.

I made the birdlime, with which we smeared some sticks that Fritz and Jack placed among the higher branches of the trees. In less than a week we had taken enough birds of different kinds to fill a cask, even after we had prepared them for preserving in the same manner as we did twelve months before.

Two of our old tame pigeons which we had brought off the wreck with us were taken in our snares one day, and we recognised them at once.

Jack begged their lives, saying, 'Look, father! how with their eyes they seem to greet us as old friends!'

It is needless to say that Jack obtained the boon he asked.

To keep the two travellers at home for the future, we constructed in the side of our rock at Undertent a pigeon-cote, half of which was excavated and the other half made of trellis-work. This dwelling-place proved so acceptable to them that they not only took up their abode there themselves, but in the course of time induced a number of wild pigeons, which soon became domesticated, to do the same.

I made use of some reeds to prepare parts of the loom which my wife had asked me to construct. I took two of the largest, which, split longwise, furnished the frame that carries the warp. I then employed the boys in cutting some small pieces of wood between which the warp was to pass.

As I finished each part of the loom I hid it, determining to put the pieces together in secret, and some day surprise my wife with an unexpected present of the machine she so much desired.

At about this time the onager presented us with a beautiful foal, which was unanimously devoted to my use; for up till now I had had no mount of my own at all. I called him Racer, a title which he soon justified by his swiftness of foot and elegance of form.

As the rainy season was again approaching, it now became necessary to lay in an abundant stock of provisions and forage, and to take measures for preserving our animals.

I also took means to lay in a supply of fresh water to our winter quarters, of which we had just finished the interior arrangements.

To this end we made a long conduit with hollow bamboo-canes, which we spliced together, and made watertight at the joints with resin. The conduit was much longer than it would otherwise have been, for by the fortifications and hedges with which we had surrounded our dwelling we have completely cut off all access to the nearest point of Jackal River, and had therefore to obtain our supply of water higher up the stream.

One pipe, which was laid upon a long row of forked sticks, emptied itself into a large cask; and when this cask was full, we corked the conduit till we required a fresh supply.

My wife thanked us warmly for our system of waterworks, assuring us that she was better pleased with it than she would have been with a marble fountain adorned with dolphins and statues.

Day by day we devoted ourselves to getting in potatoes, rice, maize, acorns, and every variety of useful plant that we could think of. The savoury ananas, you may be sure, was not forgotten.

As we had not vessels enough to hold all our spoils, my wife made us some sacks out of the remains of the sail-cloth, and we even broke up our raft for the sake of the tubs of which it was made.

In the midst of all our labours, I had not forgotten that our farmery had to be made safe from the monkeys.

'How would it be if we were to put some little windmill sails at each corner of the hut? Would not that keep the monkeys away?' asked Jack.

We all set to work at once, and a few hours afterwards as many as thirty miniature windmills were spinning away all over the estate.

I was not myself at all sure about the efficiency of this method of keeping off the monkeys; but as the end which the boys had in view was good, and as the work which they were engaged in pleased them, I neither interfered nor imparted to them my doubts.

It took four whole days to repair the damage done by the monkeys, but, both by reason of our improved carpentry and our knowledge of the kind of attacks to which our work might be subjected, we left the farm in better condition than it had ever been in.

Before long the storms set in, and the fine weather was at an end.

Thunder, lightning, and driving rain compelled us to take refuge in our grotto. The sea took part in the general convulsion of nature, and the noise of the waves as they roared inshore and burst booming upon the rocks filled us at first with an involuntary and indescribable terror.

I had not expected these storms till the month of June, but they came upon us long before that; and we were obliged to remain confined for twelve weeks to our winter quarters.

We only kept four of our animals in the stable at the grotto—the cow to provide us with milk, the onager to feed its little one, and the buffalo and the donkey to carry us to Falcon-nest from time to time to look after our poultry, feed our animals, and bring back supplies of forage to the cavern.

It is hardly necessary to say that we also kept near us the dogs, the eagle, the jackal, and the monkey, whose antics diverted us amazingly.

With our spare timber, and some pieces of rock taken from the cavern, we laid a terrace along the front of our new abode, and thereupon erected a bamboo veranda surmounted by a balcony, from which we could survey the surrounding country.

We soon found that the fitting-up of the cavern, although it had been the object of all our cares, was in no sense complete. The three openings in the rock which served for windows, for instance, admitted but a feeble light into the interior. It is true we determined to remedy this defect thoroughly when the rains were over, but it was necessary to do something immediately, for it was by no means pleasant to remain buried in the dark for weeks together.

I thought the matter over for a long time, and hit at last upon a plan which the skill and agility of Jack rendered easy of execution.

I took a long and thick bamboo, one end of which I solidly fixed in the floor of the cavern, while the other touched the vaulted roof.

Jack climbed up this pole, and with a hammer drove securely into a natural crevice in the rock a stout wooden stake, upon which was fixed a pulley whose ropes reached to the ground.

While he was thus engaged, his mother cleaned and trimmed with oil a lantern which he had found on the wreck. We then lighted its three wicks, fastened it to the ropes of the pulley, and drew it up to a convenient height. The crystal facets of the vaulted roof flung back its light in a thousand sparkling forms.

The arrangement of the different apartments occupied us several days. Ernest and Francis put up shelves for the books. My wife and Jack fitted up the sitting-room and the kitchen. Fritz and

I reserved to ourselves the arrangement of the workshop, as that involved the heaviest labour.

In this apartment we placed the captain's lathe, the carpenter's bench and tool-chest, and all the cooper's and gunsmith's tools that we had brought away from the wreck.

In one corner we fitted up a forge. We had a pair of bellows, an anvil, and some hammers; but we required a great many more tools than we had to enable us to set up the trade of blacksmith.

No day passed, indeed, in which we did not feel the want of one or other of a crowd of European contrivances which are never valued till they are missed. Among them were chairs, tables, chests of drawers, and many other things equally homely and equally useful.

In order to keep the children from idleness, we set vigorously to work to supply many of these wants; and, if complete success did not crown all our efforts, we nevertheless managed to keep ourselves employed, and to show many useful results of our labours.

Thanks to the industry of our young scholar and Jack, the library soon began to look quite like a museum. Upon the shelves were ranged the books which had belonged to the captain and officers of the ship. They consisted of works of natural history illustrated with coloured engravings, treatises on botany and zoology, and other works not less useful. To these were added an excellent supply of mathematical and astronomical instruments, and a large terrestrial globe. Besides these, again, were ranged the natural history specimens which we had collected since our sojourn on the island.

Among the educational books we found several grammars and dictionaries of different languages. We determined to make use of these to perfect our knowledge in the tongues of which we knew so little, and to learn others of which we knew nothing: so that we might be able to converse with the sailors of any ship that might chance to call, if God so willed it, at our island. We knew French well. Our mother tongue was German. Fritz and Ernest proposed to learn English. Jack decided in favour of Italian and Spanish, which seemed to him to sound more pompously on the ear.

Ernest made up his mind to learn Latin also, a very useful language in the study of natural history and medicine, of which we had several treatises in our library.

Furthermore, he took upon himself the duty of instructing his brother Francis, who progressed so well that, far from being frightened at books, as was formerly the case, he waited with impatience the hour at which he was in the habit of receiving his lessons.

For myself, I resolved to learn the Malay language, thinking it not impossible that we might some day be favoured with a visit from some Indians of an adjacent island or mainland.

CHAPTER XXVI

New treasures—the dead whale

When the more pressing of our needs had been supplied by our various labours, we broke open the chests which we had brought from the wreck or which had been washed up by the sea.

We at once found ourselves in possession of several looking-glasses, two console tables with marble tops, a chest of drawers, two handsome writing-tables, and other articles.

My wife had the first choice among these unexpected treasures, and, assisted by her boys, who were never so delighted as when helping her, fitted up a little chamber, of which she was very proud.

In the chests were also discovered several clocks, and a sea-watch, which I confess I did not know how to use. In short, we found ourselves rich beyond our most sanguine expectations, not only in the absolute necessaries, but even in some few of the luxuries of life.

The twelve weeks which we spent in the grotto passed away so quickly that I was not able to carry out one-half the projects I had formed for occupying our time.

The children during this period obtained my permission to find a name for our subterranean dwelling.

They selected Rock-house, and I approved of their choice.

At the end of August we were visited by fierce hurricanes. The sea roared in upon the shore in large breakers that seemed to threaten even the rocks with destruction. The thunder, lightning, and rain menaced the whole land with devastation. We devoutly thanked God that He had given us our grotto for shelter from the terrible fury of the elements. We dwelt as in an Arabian Night's dream.

At length the weather changed. The sky became blue, and we were able to leave our retreat to breath the fresh air again.

While we were engaged in contemplating the phenomena of the new vegetation that surrounded us, the lynx-eyed Fritz saw something lying near a small island in an inlet of the bay, which looked like a capsized boat. I took the telescope, but could not make out at all clearly what it was.

We thereupon determined to make an excursion across the intervening island in order to get a nearer view of it. Besides, we had need of air and exercise after our three months' seclusion.

Having emptied our pirogue of the rain-water with which it was filled and furnished it with its rigging, we set out—Fritz, Ernest, Jack and I.

As we came nearer to the object of our journey, our first conjecture vanished, and we soon saw that what we had fancied to be an overturned canoe was neither more nor less than a huge whale, which the violence of the sea had flung upon a jutting point of the island. The waves, which beat furiously upon the coast where the whale lay, forced us to make a detour to get to land.

I quickened my steps, and soon overtook the boys, who had walked round the beach. They showed me their caps, filled with coral and sea-shells, which they had picked up on the way, and concerning which they overwhelmed me with questions.

The boys, who found working at the oars a somewhat laborious occupation, asked me if I did not think I could invent some contrivance whereby the pirogue might be made to glide over the waves without so much effort on our parts.

I smiled as I thought of the unlimited confidence they placed in my ingenuity.

'I am not a sorcerer,' I said, 'nor have I a fairy always at my elbow. Nevertheless, if you will undertake to find me a large iron wheel, I will at least promise to do the best I can to meet your wishes.'

'An iron wheel!' cried Fritz. 'Why, there is a capital one on one of our roasting spits!'

On the following day we furnished our pirogue with tools and provisions, and also put on board a few tubs. We then embarked and weighed anchor. The sea was calm, and we had no difficulty in landing close to the whale, whose size and hideous aspect frightened Francis and his mother not a little. It was, indeed, an enormous beast, measuring not less than seventy feet in length, and weighing several tons. It was as ugly as it was large. My children were overcome with fear as they reflected upon the fate that would have befallen us had we met such a creature as this during any of our voyages to the vessel.

We set to work at once to cut the monster up.

We did not carry on our offensive but useful labours alone. A multitude of birds of prey, undaunted by our presence, settled upon the carcass, and carried their effrontery to the point of flying away with the slices which we cut off with our knives. The boys killed several of them, and as our good housewife said she would be glad to have their feathers, we put them in our boat.

We filled our tubs with pieces of blubber cut off the flanks of the whale, and with our precious cargo—of which, however, the odour was not very agreeable—we returned to Rock-house.

The next morning I announced a new plan of procedure, but my wife and little Francis declined to be of the party, the work we proposed to do being to repugnant to them. I had determined to open the body of the animal.

Before beginning work we took off our ordinary garments, and dressed ourselves in some rough ones which my wife had prepared for the purpose.

Fritz and I then opened the body of the monster with our hatchets, and drew hence the liver, the sinews of the tail, and lastly the entrails, of which I intended to make bags to hold the oil which we extracted from the blubber. This task achieved, we hastened to set out for land again.

My wife regarded our odorous spoils with no great pleasure. I softened her a little by promising that, however unpleasant our cargo might be at present, I should extract from it unheard-of treasures.

The next morning at daybreak we proceeded to convert our blubber into oil.

After having, by heavy pressure, obtained a first running of fine, pure oil, with which we filled two of our tubs, we fed our cauldron several times with pieces of flesh, and, with the assistance of a brisk fire, obtained ten large skinfuls of ordinary train-oil.

Although we took care to perform this operation at some distance from Rock-house, the insupportable smell which exhaled from the cauldron failed not to penetrate even to the inner chambers.

'Why on earth,' asked my wife, when we assembled at dinner, 'did you not carry on this abominable manufacture on the island? You would have found enough wood there to melt down a hundred times as much oil, and we should not have been poisoned by the stench. While on the point, too, I may as well tell you of an idea that has occurred to me. Why cannot we establish a colony of poultry on this same island? There, at least, there would be nothing to fear either from jackals or monkeys.'

'A capital notion!' cried I. 'We will endeavour to carry it out as soon as possible.'

CHAPTER XXVII

The loom finished—the palanquin—the boa

It was at this time that, with the assistance of Ernest, I finished the loom which I had so long intended to present to our good housewife, who was growing more and more anxious as she saw our stock of linen decreasing daily without any apparent means of replacing it.

I had reason now to congratulate myself for having, in my youth, taken every pains to examine and understand the mechanism of such looms as it has been my good fortune to see in the workshops of my own country. Almost up to the point of elegance and finish, my own machine was perfect.

My wife knew not how to sufficiently thank me when I brought it from its hiding-place, and showed it to her ready for work.

My success encouraged me. I resolved to try my hand at the manufacture of saddles and harness for the beasts which my boys rode.

The saddles were already cut out, and I re-covered them with kangaroo's skin and stuffed them with moss. I also made straps, bridles, traces, and other articles, but as the trade was quite new to me. I found it necessary to do as the tailors do, measure my customers by fitting their new garments on from time to time during the process of manufacture.

I had scarcely finished these labours when we were visited, as in the preceding year, by a shoal of herrings, of which we laid in a plentiful supply.

To the herrings succeeded the dog-fish, of which we killed a score or so, and pickled their skins with salt for future use. The fat and the bladders were carefully put on one side. As to the flesh, we cut it up and threw it into Jackal River for the crabs, of which, thanks to this bait, we took a large quantity, to replenish our exhausted store in the dam we had made for their reception twelve months before.

These fisheries at an end, I determined to see what I could do at making baskets, of which my wife had great need for carrying her seeds and vegetables to and from the garden, and for other purposes.

Our first attempts were made with the common osier, and we took to the work fairly; for although our first productions were rough and unshapely, they did well enough to carry dirt in, and with practice we soon acquired greater skill. Two large baskets that we made were of such excellent form and finish, that Jack and Ernest, proud of their share in the work, put Francis into one of them, and, thrusting a couple of poles through the handles, carried him upon their shoulders in triumph.

'Oh, father!' cried Fritz, all at once, looking and laughing at them for some time, 'could we not make a similar litter for mamma? She would find it so much easier than riding on the truck when she accompanies us on our excursions!'

'No doubt, my good Fritz,' I replied, 'but where are the porters with shoulders strong enough to carry this new palanquin?'

'Have Storm and Grumbler!' cried Jack, putting down Francis, and joining in the conversation. 'We can easily harness them, one on the left and the other on the right, to the two poles which support the basket. May we try, father?'

I consented willingly, and the two animals were at once led out.

We put on their saddles, to which we securely fastened the poles that were to support the basket.

Then Jack mounted upon Storm, and Francis upon Grumbler. The beasts knelt at the command of their masters while Ernest got into the basket, and at a second command they got up and walked leisurely away with their load between them.

The palanquin swung as easily and as pleasantly as a carriage upon light springs. Little by little, however, the two burly porters quickened their pace, and though this delighted Ernest at first, he soon became so alarmed that he shut his eyes and laid hold of the sides of the basket. Thereupon Jack and Francis, who had remarked the growing fear of their brother and were much amused at it, began whipping their beasts furiously, and they started off at full gallop.

Poor Ernest, tossed hither and thither and jolted up and down, bounded from one side of the basket to the other like an india-rubber ball, and cried out with all his might to be put down. The two animals, however, seemed to enjoy the fun as much as their giddy-witted riders, and, after making a wide detour upon the beach at Undertent, brought themselves upon their knees in front of us, as if begging for our applause.

Ernest, red with anger, was no sooner out of the basket than he began to load his brothers with indignant reproaches, to which they were not slow to reply sharply.

I was obliged to intervene, and tell the madcap Jack that though, as it turned out, their fun had done no harm, yet that in some circumstances it might have led to broken limbs.

Both he and Francis saw at once that they had been in the wrong, and begged Ernest's pardon.

Ernest, who was of a very easy disposition, not only forgave them there and then, but helped to unharness the animals who had played him the trick, and even begged his mother to give them a little extra barley and salt as a reward for their readiness to obey the word of command. We heard him afterwards arranging with his brothers for another palanquin journey when opportunity occurred.

As my wife and I sat quietly conversing in front of the grotto, I noticed that Fritz, who was some paces off, was looking intently towards the avenue which led from the bridge crossing the river to Falcon-nest.

In a moment or two he came up and said, 'There is a strange animal of some kind below there, father. I don't know what it is, but it seems to be coming this way, if one may judge from the movements of the clouds of dust it raises.'

'It is no doubt one of our own animals rolling in the sand,' said his mother.

'No, it can't be that,' returned Fritz; 'all our animals are shut up for the night. Besides, this one, as far as I can make out, is altogether different in form. It looks like a huge cable, now unrolling itself on the ground, now rising erect and swaying from side to side.'

At these words my wife, in great alarm, re-entered the grotto, and I sent my boys in after her to get the arms ready.

I then took the telescope and directed it towards the bridge. An exclamation of horror escaped me.

'What is it, father?' asked Fritz anxiously.

'It is an enormous serpent,' I replied in a low voice.

'Then I won't be the last at the fight,' cried the courageous boy. 'I will go and fetch the guns and the axes.'

'Prudence before all,' I exclaimed. 'This animal is too terrible for us to venture to fight face to face with him.'

In saying these words I drew Fritz after me into the grotto, when we set to work preparing to receive the monster.

Our terror was too well grounded. We could distinctly see the fearful reptile trailing his enormous folds along the bank of the river. As soon as he had crossed the bridge, he stopped from time to time, raising his hideous head and surveying his surroundings, as if he were upon new ground and uncertain of his way.

We barricaded the door and stopped up all the openings but one, where we could see without being seen. There, gun in hand, and ears and eyes on the alert, we watched every movement of the approaching enemy.

It was a boa of the very largest size.

The monster made straight towards the grotto. But all at once he seemed to hesitate, as if troubled by the evident traces of human beings.

At this moment Ernest, overcome by excitement, dropped the trigger of his gun, and the piece went off. Jack and Francis, thinking the time had come for action, did the same.

At this triple discharge the serpent raised his head rather in surprise than fright. It may have been that neither shot reached its mark; it may have been that the scales of the creature were impervious to bullets; at any rate, he seemed to have received no wound.

Just as Fritz and I, after taking careful aim, were about to fire in our turn, the monster glided swiftly away towards Goose Marsh, where he disappeared.

A unanimous exclamation of satisfaction rose to our lips. We felt that we had been preserved, at least for the time being, from imminent peril.

At the same time, the presence of the boa in the neighbourhood disquieted me not a little. At any moment the terrible animal might reappear, and I knew no means of getting rid of it without risking a great deal of danger.

I expressly forbade every one to leave the house, under any pretext whatever, without first obtaining my permission.

During three whole days fear held us prisoners in the grotto. The least noise outside put us in mortal terror. We dared scarcely venture over the threshold.

However, the monster gave no sign of his presence, and we should probably have come to the conslusion that he had left the neighbourhood, had it not been for the way in which our poultry and pigeons cackled and flew from rock to rock, as if they feared the attack of some terrible enemy.

Our anxiety increased hourly while the obstinate refusal of the serpent to show himself only left us the more time to reflect upon the horrors of our situation. On the other hand, our stock of provisions was diminishing rapidly without our being able to renew them, and all our projected employments were suffering from our enforced inaction.

The forage was coming to an end; and we foresaw that the time would shortly arrive when our own food would fail, if we continued to divide with our animals the slender supply of provisions that remained to us.

I determined, therefore, to set the beasts at liberty, in order that they might find fodder for themselves.

We decided to drive them up towards the source of the river in the opposite direction to the marsh, where we concluded the boa still lay concealed.

Fritz took this hazardous duty upon himself.

He drove the beasts out, and was making ready to escort them, while the rest of us stood at the window with our loaded guns, in readiness to fire should he be interrupted in his work. The buffalo and the cow were already yoked together, when the ass, to whom three days' rest and an abundance of good food had imparted an extraordinary amount of vigour and playfulness, dashed off into the open ground, he-hawing so loudly and indulging in so many grotesque gambols, that, in spite of the grave cause we had for seriousness, we could not help bursting into a hearty laugh.

Fritz leapt upon the onager and was preparing to set out in pursuit, when I stopped him, pointing out the danger he would incur in approaching the marsh, towards which the ass was now making as fast as he could.

We attempted to call the fugitive back, but he only looked round at us from time to time, shaking his mane with an air of bravado. We showed him fodder and salt; all was useless. He was evidently determined to enjoy his liberty, and galloping farther and farther away, made straight for the supposed lair of the serpent.

All at once we saw a terrible head raise itself from among the reeds.

At first sight of it the poor donkey appeared petrified with fear, uttered a strange, hopeless kind of groan, and looked towards us mournfully. One would have thought him transfixed to the earth, for as the serpent approached him, he neither moved nor gave any indication that he even contemplated flight.

In an instant the unhappy beast was wrapped in the monster's fatal folds, and suffocated in the horrible embrace.

We looked upon the scene in sad silence: it rent our hearts.

The children asked me if they might not fire upon the reptile, to release their favourite.

I forbade them, observing that they would only irritate the monster, which might perhaps turn its fury upon us without profit to the ass, who already gave no sign of life.

'Let us wait,' I said, 'till the boa has swallowed his victim, for when he is glutted with food there will no longer be any danger in attacking him, and we shall be sure of our prey.'

'But,' said Jack, 'the frightful beast will not swallow our donkey at a mouthful ,will he?'

'As serpents have no teeth to enable them to rend their prey,'

I replied, 'they crush and swallow it at one and the same time. But look! See how the hideous creature is crushing the unfortunate animal's body with its rings, in order to bring it down to the size of its throat!'

As I spoke the boa was making ready his repast with horrible avidity.

My wife, fearing that the barbarous spectacle would leave a too vivid impression upon the mind of our youngest child, and not caring personally to be witness of it, retired with Francis into the dining-room.

I was myself well-nigh overcome with horror.

Not only was the ass dead, but its body was crushed into a shapeless mass, of which one could distinguish nothing but the head hanging bleeding and hideous.

The boa, to get more strength, had twined his tail round a small jutting piece of rock, and was gradually pressing the broken flesh into a soft paste.

He then covered the whole carcass with a slimy saliva, and, opening his enormous jaws, made ready to commence his repast.

He first laid himself out at full length in front of the mass he had so carefully kneaded. Then seizing the ass by the hind-legs, he began swallowing it; and, little by little, the thighs, the body, and the fore-legs were engulfed in the monster's body, which gave as many signs of pain as of pleasure as it swallowed the still bleeding mass.

When he came to the head, which he had neglected to crush, his hunger was appeased, and he rolled over completely motionless.

This was the moment I was waiting for.

Seizing my gun, I cried to my boys, 'Courage, children! courage! The monster has fallen into our hands!'

I hastened towards the serpent, followed by Fritz and Jack, but not by Ernest, who, always more timid than his brothers, remained at the post of observation.

The boa keenly watched our approach, his eyes glistening with impotent malignity.

He was literally unable to move a muscle of his body. Fritz and I, therefore, had no difficulty in sending the contents of a couple of barrels, well loaded with bullets, crashing into his skull. An intensely evil light played in his eyes for a moment—his tail beat the ground feebly once or twice as he writhed in anguish—he was dead!

At this moment Jack, who desired to have his part in the victory, fired his pistol into the reptile's belly. The wound produced a kind of galvanic effect on the tail of the serpent, which flew up suddenly and struck our young giddy-head so smart a blow upon the chest that it knocked him down.

It is hardly necessary to say that, finding himself thus laid upon his back, he fully believed for the moment that the boa had come to life again, and trembled in every limb at the thought of following the donkey to his last resting-place.

Happily this was the last evil deed for which our formidable enemy was responsible.

We sent up a shout of victory, which speedily brought my wife, with Ernest and Francis, upon the scene of action.

We embraced each other warmly in an ecstasy of joy. It seemed as if we had received a new lease of life.

'So far as I am concerned,' said Ernest, always ready to display his erudition, 'I honour our poor donkey for having devoted his life to our salvation, as those noble Roman heroes, the Curtii, did theirs for the citizens.'

'What are we going to do with the body of the serpent?' asked Jack, recovering from his panic.

'Skin and stuff it,' said Ernest, 'and put it in the museum as a trophy of our victory and a valuable curiosity.'

'But,' said Francis, 'could not we eat this huge eel? We should have stews and broiled meats which would last us for weeks.'

'Eat the flesh of a serpent!' exclaimed his mother; 'of a serpent which is perhaps venomous.'

'The boa, my dear wife,' I said, 'is not venomous; and even if it were, there would be no danger in eating its flesh, provided we threw away the head. It is in that part of a serpent that the fangs and the glands are found which contain the poison.'

CHAPTER XXVIII

Epitaph on the ass—stuffing the boa

Our long conversation beguiled us into taking a long rest, during which we forgot, for the time being, both our past troubles and our anxieties for the future.

We were seated under the shadow of a huge rock, with our guns and pistols beside us.

In order to tease Ernest, and as a sort of punishment for his unwillingness to take part in the attack on the enormous reptile we had just killed, I told him that we should require him to write a suitable epitaph for our donkey, observing that since he had many times shown poetic longings, now was the time, or never, to make proof his talent. The subject, I added, was worthy his genius.

The young poet saw not the least joke in what I had said. On the contrary, he accepted my invitation with the utmost gravity, and resting his head, overcharged with sublime thought, upon his hands, proceeded to obey me.

Ten minutes afterwards he lifted his eyes, his countenance glowing the while with an amount of self-content which would have done credit for Archimedes or Pythagoras in the moment of their highest achievement.

'Father,' he said, 'I have hit upon an epitaph! But,' he added, seeing a smile playing across my face, 'you must not make fun of me, you know.'

I encouraged him to speak out and give us the results of his meditations.

He did so, blushing with all the modesty of youthful genius. Here are the lines which the dear child had composed:

> 'An honest ass lies buried here,
>   By disobedience killed;
> A hero though he was 'tis clear,
>   For from a death which all with terror filled,
> He saved father and mother and children four,
> Shipwrecked on this uninhabited shore.'

'Capital! capital!' I cried, laughing. 'By far the best poetry that was ever composed in this island! Here are six splendid lines, the fourth of which—if not the following two—ought to count for several more, for it has nearly as many feet as a centipede! Nevertheless, the rhyme comes in at the end exquisitely. As a reward, I decree that the stanza shall be written on that part of the rock which is nearest to the spot where our regretted donkey met his disastrous fate, until we find time and talent to correct it and shorten its lines a little.'

Saying this, I drew from my pocket a large red pencil, which I always carried with me for marking wood, and wrote upon the smooth face of the rock the six halting lines which Ernest had dictated.

The young poet, the while, was a victim to contending emotions. Proud of his authorship, he yet had a lurking suspicion that he had not achieved a very brilliant success.

I had just finished my writing when Fritz returned from the grotto, whither he had been to fetch the animals to remove the carcass of our vanquished enemy.

First of all we dragged the mangled body of our poor friend from the boa's jaws, and buried it in a deep grave, upon which we piled several boulders to protect the sad remains from the ravages of wild beasts.

Then we yoked the cow and buffalo to the serpent, and dragged it up to the entrance to Rock-house.

Arrived there: 'Father,' said one of the young people, 'how are we going to skin this terrible beast? We should like to preserve him as a curiosity, but I do not see how it is to be done.'

'I am going to tell you,' I said, 'of a very simple method of overcoming your difficulty. You must first of all make a circular incision round the neck, and turn back the skin a little. Then you must fasten the under part of the skin so turned back to the ground by small stakes, and the upper and side parts to a tree by cords. All you have to do now will be to re-harness the oxen to the head and let them pull gently. They will thus draw the body of the animal out of the skin, and everything will be ready for stuffing. To proceed with this operation, you will have to take the skin, which will be inside out, and salt it well, and sprinkle it with ashes. This done, turn it right side out again, fill it with moss, prepare and sew the head to it, and, after giving the creature the position you want, dry it in the sun.'

These instructions were immediately followed by the four boys, directed by Fritz. I also lent a hand, the better to encourage them in their labours.

The stuffing was not achieved without several amusing incidents.

Jack, who stripped himself to his trousers, was ordered inside the skin, which we had hung to the branches of a high tree. Then we all handed him up moss, which he trod in. On reaching the chest, he suddenly popped his head out, red and perspiring from his labours, and asked whether we did not think he looked pretty well for one who had so long been inside a boa.

With such pleasantries did the light-hearted boys beguile their labour.

The skin stuffed, the next thing to be done was to give the creature a characteristic attitude. This was a task of no small difficulty. One proposed this, another that, but none of them arrived at a satisfactory conclusion.

I came to their help, I rolled the stuffed boa round a stake some three feet in height, fixed into a small hillock, and rested the chest upon the top of it in such a manner that the head and neck were thrown forward horizontally, as if the creature were about to strike a victim. The jaws were placed wide open, and the tongue drawn out, and both were painted a blood-red with the juice of the Indian fig.

For want of the necessary glass, I replaced the eyes with prepared pieces of gypsum varnished with fish-glue.

Although dead, the horrible beast looked so much like life, that during the whole of the time it was exposed to the sun our animals never passed it without trembling.

When dry, we removed it to the entrance of our museum and library, and the children pinned a paper to its jaws, on which was written this sentence, whose double meaning is apparent:

'NO ADMITTANCE TO DONKEYS'.

For a moment I thought of blaming the boys for treating a sad subject so lightly. But I had laughed myself when I read the inscription, and therefore could not rebuke them: I was disarmed.

CHAPTER XXIX

An excursion—another grotto—fuller's earth—rock crystal

Although relieved from our present danger, I did not feel at all easy in my mind. I feared, and not without reason, that since the reptile we had killed was a female, we might have before long to encounter other members of her family—the male, or the young ones, for instance.

I therefore determined to beat the whole neighbourhood around both Rock-house and Falcon-nest. The latter excursion I resolved should extend as far as our house of call on Prospect Hill, for on the road thither lay a rocky defile through which I doubted not our terrible visitor had made its way.

When time came for setting out, I noticed a sort of hesitation in the movements of Ernest and Jack. They still retained so vivid a recollection of the impression made upon them by the destruction of our donkey that they did not care to risk encountering another boa. The feeling was natural at their age, and I could not well rebuke them.

'I declare,' said Jack, 'it sends a thrill through me even now when I think of the way in which the tail of the dreadful beast knocked me down. I thought every bone in my body was broken.'

I reassured them as well as I could, and appealed both to their feelings and their reason.

'Reflect,' I said, 'that the serpent we have killed may probably have left young ones, which may grow up and some day fall traitorously upon your mother and little Francis! It is a matter of life and death to us that we should put ourselves out of this peril before our enemy gains strength enough to overcome us.'

This decided them.

We set out with our best guns and hunting-knives, carrying with us some bamboos, a plank or two, and a few inflated skins to assist us in crossing Goose Marsh, where we intended commencing operations.

Arrived at the edge of the morass, I proceeded with the utmost caution to get my little caravan over. The swamp was both wide and in some parts deep, and it was very uncertain all over; but we alternately threw our planks and bamboos in front of us to walk upon, and in this way got across without meeting with any accident.

Here and there on the way we found unequivocal traces of the boa; but to our great joy nothing indicated that she had left either eggs or young behind her.

A little farther on, upon the sharp acclivity of a small hill, we discovered a good-sized grotto, from the bottom of which there issued a clear stream, while the vaulted roof above was hung with glittering stalactite. The floor was covered with a fine earth, as white as snow. To my great satisfaction, I recognised in it the mineral called fuller's earth.

128

'See!' I said, filling my handkerchief with several handfuls of it, 'here is a present for your mother which I will undertake to say will prove most acceptable. It will do to clean our clothes with when we return travel-stained from our excursions, and it will also serve the purpose of soap, and save me the trouble of baking lime.'

'Is lime used in the making of soap?' asked Ernest.

'Yes,' replied I. 'Soap is made by mixing fatty substances with soda or potash, and without lime it would seriously injure the hands of those who used it. It is also made of ashes soaked in lime-water and mixed with fat. But all these preparations are somewhat costly, and they are replaced in most cases by this earth which we have just found, and which is called fuller's earth, because it is used in the fulling of cloth.'

Examining the stream a little more closely, I saw that it ran out of a fissure in the rock at the back of the grotto. Our curiosity was excited. The stone round about the opening was so soft that we had no difficulty in removing it, and Fritz and I went in, leaving Jack and Ernest outside to await our return.

In a few moments we found ourselves standing side by side in profound darkness.

In order to get some idea of the extent of this second grotto, I fired a pistol straight before me. The cave was quite as large as the one we had just left. As I wished to assure myself concerning the state of the atmosphere, I struck a light in the tinder-box and applied it to a candle-end which I carried in my pocket. It burnt steadily.

We advanced cautiously, peering round on every hand as far as the rays of our dim torch extended, when Fritz cried out excitedly, 'Father! father! it is another salt grotto! See these marvellous crystals! Look at these glittering blocks!'

'They are not salt crystals, my boy,' I said, 'for I have just tasted the water which runs down the centre here, and find it destitute of savour. My own opinion is that we are in a cavern of rock crystal.'

'You are right, dear father; I am sure you are right!' cried Fritz, growing more excited every minute. 'What a splendid treasure we have found!'

'Splendid enough,' I replied, 'but of no more use to us than was the ingot of gold to Robinson Crusoe. We can neither eat it, nor wear it, nor sell it.'

'At any rate,' said Fritz, 'it is beautiful to the eye, and I will carry some away to put in our museum.'

With that he chipped off a piece with a hammer that he had with him.

'How is this?' he asked suddenly. 'When it is broken off it is no longer transparent.'

'That,' I replied, 'is because you have not broken it off properly. This pyramid of crystals, each hexahedral in form, clings to a very hard crystalline stone, called the mother crystal, which may easily be mistaken for the argillaceous earth in which it is found. A careful examination, however—it may be made with the naked eye—will show that there runs through it a delicate tissue of needle-like spars. These are in some sort the germ of the crystal; for the crystals grow to them, and each set of needles and crystals forms a perfect and independent group. Now if, in getting such a piece as you have got just now, you separate a group, rending only one needle from its place in the mother crystal, there follows a general breaking up of the whole stone—a series of almost imperceptible cracks—changing what was before as clear as water to an opaque milky hue.'

'How should one proceed to avoid this difficulty?' asked Fritz.

'You must raise the mother crystal whole,' I replied, 'taking care to strike that only with your hammer: if you strike the other crystals, you will destroy them.'

Conversing in this wise, we made our way across the grotto, Fritz pressing me with questions which showed a laudable desire for instruction, and I answering him to the best of my knowledge. Then, with the utmost care, we got out a perfect group of crystals, worthy to be placed in our museum.

Our candle being nearly burnt out, I told Fritz it was time to return to the daylight. Before going, however, he begged and obtained leave to fire off his pistol, in order to enjoy the imposing effect of the detonation as its echoes reverberated through the vault.

When I reappeared with Fritz at the opening through which we had entered the grotto, I saw Jack standing in a state of utter desolation, sobbing heavily.

At the first sound of our voices he ran towards us, clapping his hands and shouting for joy.

'What is the matter, dear child?' I said. 'Why so sad and so gay at the same time?'

'My joy, father,' he said, 'arises from seeing you again. My grief arose out of the fears which your prolonged absence caused me. Twice I heard a terrible report, followed by a rattling noise which sounded as if everything were falling into ruins in the cave in which you and Fritz had disappeared; and I did not know what to think.'

'Dear little heart,' I said, 'let us embrace. Thanks to the gracious protection of Heaven, we have not even run into danger, much less suffered harm. But where is Ernest?'

'He is down below in the reed-bed,' replied Jack.

Leaving Fritz with Jack, I went in the direction taken by Ernest, and was not long before I came upon the young gentleman, squatting tranquilly upon a bed of reeds. He had heard nothing and was quite undisturbed. He was occupied in weaving a new kind of landing-net of a very ingenious pattern, and I complimented him upon his work.

'And that is not all I have done, father,' he said with a self-satisfied air. 'I have killed a young serpent about four feet in length. There it lies under those reeds by the side of my gun.'

'A serpent!' I exclaimed laughingly, as I moved the reeds to look at the young scholar's prize. 'It is better than a serpent, Ernest. It is a fine fat eel, which will furnish us with an excellent supper this evening.'

The other two boys now came up, and learning the mistake Ernest had made, they teased him.

I interposed.

'My dear Ernest,' I said, 'I am proud of what you have done; not because the creature you have killed will make us a good meal, but because you have given me a proof of that courage which I have always wished you to possess. You have only fought an eel, it is true, but you believed you were fighting a serpent, and in my eyes the two things are the same.'

That said, we took up Ernest's fish and net, and Fritz's crystal, and set out for Rock-house. When we got there my wife was engaged in washing clothes. I leave you to imagine her surprise and pleasure when we handed her the fuller's earth.

The crystal was added to our collection, to the great joy of Francis, who could never sufficiently admire what he called 'the great diamond.'

CHAPTER XXX

Excursion to the farmery—the cabiai—the cinnamon-apple

Satisfied that there were no snakes on the Goose Marsh side of the country, I determined that our second expedition should be to the farmery.

I had for a long time entertained the idea of fortifying this part of our domains.

We set out full of confidence and good spirits.

As it was our habit when we started on an expedition to give the goats, the sheep, and the poultry their liberty, my wife laid out plenty of food for them in the neighbourhood of Rock-house, to keep them together till we returned.

At last we were fairly on the road to Forest Grange, where we intended to pass the night. We determined to fill our bags with corn by the way, and to make a more detailed survey of Swan Lake and the neighbouring rice plantation.

There were no signs of our old enemies the monkeys.

Our farmery was in excellent condition. We dined with a good appetite, and after a substantial repast, set out to reconnoitre in the neighbourhood.

I took little Francis with me this time, arming him with a gun proportionate to his size, and teaching him how to carry, load, and fire it.

Ernest was left with his mother at the upper end of Swan Lake, which we were about to explore. Francis and I took the left bank, and Fritz and Jack the right.

As we could not think of setting out without the more nimble of our four-footed allies, each party was accompanied by a small detachment of them. Ernest and his mother had Fan and Nip; Turk and the jackal were with Fritz and Jack; Francis and I had Brown and Fawn for our companions.

Francis and I followed the left bank of the lake. We were much impeded in our progress by the underwood and reed-beds, but our dogs, on the contrary, ploughed through these obstacles with as much enjoyment as if they were in their native element.

All at once we heard a strange lowing sound in the reeds. It was so much like the muffled braying of an ass that Francis took it to be the young onager escaped from Rock-house.

'That cannot be,' I said. 'In the first place, the animal is too young to bray so loudly. Secondly, it is impossible that he should have passed us without our seeing him. I am rather disposed to think it is a bittern, or a kind of heron called the marsh ox, because of its cry, which resembles the lowing of cattle in the distance.'

Heron or bittern, Francis was impatient to fire his first shot at the extraordinary bird. In order to assist him in his very natural desire, I called the two dogs, and indicated to them the direction in which the heron lay.

In a few moments there was a rustling among the reeds, and almost immediately thereafter a report of a gun, followed by a cry of triumph on the part of my little sportsman. I doubted not that he had made a successful debut.

I ran up to where the little fellow was standing proudly over his prize, which had just been retrieved by one of our young dogs. It was a cabiai, cavia, or cavy, about two feet six inches in length. This animal has short, stiff hair, very sleek, and of a blackish-brown colour, which becomes lighter as it reaches the belly. It lives upon aquatic plants, and can remain a long time under water.

When we were preparing to set out again, Francis, like a true sportsman, insisted upon carrying the cabiai slung over his shoulder. Unhappily, however, he was not strong enough to carry so heavy a burden.

'Ah! ah! I have it!' he cried at last. 'I shall throw my game across the back of Brown, who seems, so far as I can judge, quite strong enough to carry it.'

Francis, disembarrassed of his burden, which the honest Brown received upon his back with the utmost docility, set out again with the same vivacity and the same satisfaction that he had shown all along.

We soon reached Pine Wood, where we made a short halt, and

then returned to Forest Grange, without having lighted on any traces of the boa.

In returning to our good housewife we met Fritz and Jack, who did not appear to us to be very well satisfied with the results of their expedition. Nevertheless, Fritz brought in a pair of heath-birds, and Jack a dozen eggs wrapped up in a kind of fur.

The children, united again, talked over the results of their sport, speaking with enthusiasm of those of their exploits which had been successful, and passing lightly over their failures.

As to Francis's cabiai, it was cut up there and then. Part of it was placed upon the spit and eaten at once. The remainder was put by for the next day. We did not enjoy the flesh much: there was a marshy smell and taste about it.

Towards the end of the dinner, Ernest, always a young Sybarite, complained that we had nothing to take the abominable taste of the cabiai out of our mouths.

Fritz and Jack at once pounced upon their game-bags, and presented him with some pine-cone kernels, two little coco-nuts, and some light green apples which had a very agreeable smell.

'Stay! stay, boys, stay!' I cried. 'What is this new fruit that Jack has brought us? Has he tasted it himself before offering it to his brother?'

'No, dear father,' returned the young giddy-head. 'I should have done so if Fritz had not stopped me, saying that it might possibly be the poisonous fruit of the mancinul. But it looks so delicious a fruit that I hope he is wrong.'

While praising Fritz for his prudence and blaming Jack for his thoughtlessness, I cut open one of the unknown apples, remarking that, at all events, it did not resemble the mancinul inside, inasmuch as it contained no stone. Master Nip, approaching cunningly at this moment, snatched the half of the fruit which I had just cut off, and ate it up, at a convenient distance, with evident satisfaction.

This was taken as a general signal. All the boys pounced upon the fruit with so much avidity that I had some difficulty in saving even one for my wife.

Ashamed of their greediness, the boys at once hastened to offer their mother what was left in their hands, which, truth to tell, was not much.

'Many thanks,' said she, 'for your kindness, but I have a whole apple here.'

They blushed under the good-natured rebuke.

I questioned Jack anew as to the kind of tree from which he had gathered this delicious fruit. As I had supposed, it was the cinnamon of the Antilles.

I saw that sleep, the result of the fatigues of the day, was invading all four of the boys. I invited them to take their rest upon the cotton bags, and set them an example myself.

CHAPTER XXXI

Halt at Sugar-cane Grove—the peccaries—an Otahitian roast—the giant bamboos—continuation of our journey

We awoke at daybreak, after a peaceful and refreshing sleep, and renewed our journey in the direction of the plantation of sugar-canes, to which we had given the name of Sugar-cane Grove. We had previously constructed a hut there with the interlaced branches of trees, and this did away with the necessity of putting up the tent during the short time we expected to halt on our way.

Whilst my wife busied herself with preparing our breakfast, I and my children scoured the neighbourhood, to see if there were any traces of the boa. We returned without having discovered any indication whatever of its passage through this part of our domains.

We were hardly seated at table, regaling ourselves with fresh sugar-canes, of which we had been deprived for some time, when we were interrupted by the persistent barking of our dogs. We took our guns, and ran towards a thicket of reeds, whence proceeded all the tumult. After some minutes there appeared a number of little pigs, which were running with all their strength, in a row one after the other, like soldiers disciplined though routed. We had a fine time to fire before they were out of reach. Three or four discharges from our guns killed about a dozen of them, but did not interfere at all with the methodical and rapid retreat of the troop. This uniformity of movement, and the grey colour of the animals, convinced me that we had before us a kind of wild pig, very different from the European species. It was possible that they were musk-pigs or peccaries.

As we were some distance from the hut where we had left my wife, and as it was impossible to carry our spoils without the help of our cart, I sent Jack to fetch it, and he was not long in bringing it to us.

Whilst we were waiting I was not idle. Remembering to have read somewhere that the flesh of the peccary is not good unless care is taken, as soon as it is dead, to remove its little scent-bag, I hastened to perform this necessary operation. When all was finished we packed our booty upon the cart, which we covered with flowers and green boughs, and returned to the hut singing joyously.

Notwithstanding the keenness of our appetites, the produce of this last hunt was too plentiful for us to finish it whilst the flesh was still sweet. It was therefore necessary to take some measures for its preservation.

While a special smoking-room was being constructed by Jack and Fritz, whom I entrusted with this duty, desiring them to make all speed, I cut off the hams and other choice parts of the animal, for future use. The carcasses, as well as the heads, were left to the dogs and the eagle. The good flesh was carefully washed, salted, and placed in sacks open at the top, which we hung to the branches of the trees. A large gourd-vessel caught the drippings of salt water, which were poured over it again through the openings at the top.

The morning of the next day was employed in preparing an Otahitian roast, with which Fritz wished to surprise his mother. Under his direction his brothers dug out a cylindrical hole of a certain depth, in which they made a fire of branches and brushwood, so as to heat some stones. Whilst superintending the heating of his improvised oven, Fritz busied himself in the preparation of one of the pigs. He singed it, washed it, stuffed it with potatoes and sweet herbs, and finally salted it, not in the Otahitian, but in the European manner. I had told Fritz that, in default of banana-leaves, which are the best for this purpose, he had better envelop his animal in bark, so that it might be a little better protected against the dust and ashes; and, well for him, Fritz had scrupulously followed my recommendation.

The flesh, after having been prepared as I have described, was buried in a bed of red-hot stones, mixed with charcoal, wood-ashes, and earth; and whilst it was roasting quietly in this primitive oven, we returned to hasten the construction of the smoking-room, which we did not finish until evening. As soon as the hams were hung on the roof of the hut, which had been built by Fritz, we lighted upon a rude hearth, erected on the floor, a fire made up of damp turf and dry leaves, and it was not long before a thick smoke filled the hut, which we closed carefully in every part. I need not add that the smoke was kept up for several days, until the hams of the peccary were thoroughly penetrated by it.

Three hours sufficed to cook the Otahitian roast perfectly. When lifted out of the bed of earth, sand, and stones which covered it, there rose from the bottom of the hole in which it lay an agreeable savoury odour, which prepossessed us favourably, and which reconciled our good housewife to that which she had ironically called, some hours before, a barbarian piece of cookery. Fritz was triumphant. After the repast, as there was no reason why the stomach should not be grateful, I thought over the exquisite flavour which had been communicated to the dish by the bark I had advised my eldest son to use instead of the banana-leaves. I examined the bark and the tree which had produced it attentively, and came to the conclusion that it could be no other than the ravensara of Madagascar. In Madagascan language this word signifies 'good leaf', and from this the botanists have given it the Greek name of *Agathophyllum*, which has the same signification. It unites to the perfume of the nutmeg that of cloves and cinnamon, and an oil is extracted from it with which Indian cooks flavour all their dishes.

The preparation of our hams kept us for two days near our smoking-room, and my wife, under the protection of one of our sons, kept the fire moderately replenished, whilst the rest of us made some excursions into the neighbourhood. Every time we returned, which was at meal-times, we brought with us some booty. Amongst other treasures we discovered in the bamboo thicket a number of reeds about sixty feet in height, and proportionately thick, which we could easily use for casks, being careful to saw them near the knots. The thorns with which these knots were covered were as hard as nails, and were hailed by us with as much satisfaction as the reeds themselves. Also the young bamboo shoots, which we had gathered with the gigantic reeds, were specially appreciated by our good housewife, who preserved them in vinegar, covering them over with ravensara-leaves.

On a journey to Prospect Hill, I saw with great disappointment that the monkeys had, as before, committed serious depredations at Forest Grange. The goats and sheep, too, had dispersed themselves in the neighbourhood, our fowls were become almost wild, and the cabin was in such a deplorable condition that I felt obliged to postpone to a future period the labour of repairing it.

Some days were employed in laying out our route, as well as in preserving the peccary flesh. When it seemed to us sufficiently smoked, we made ready to set out and continue our journey. We took some hams to increase our stock of provisions; the rest we put into the smoke-house, which we carefully barricaded with sand, earth, and thorns, to protect it from the attacks of birds of prey, wild beasts, and apes. Then, early one morning, our little caravan gaily set out, with undoubting confidence in the protection of Providence.

CHAPTER XXXII

*Excursion in the savannah—the herd of ostriches and their eggs—
the Green Valley—fright of Ernest—the bears*

After a walk of some hours we arrived, without adventure, upon the outskirts of a small wood. The situation was charming, and well sheltered. The wood was bounded on the right by a steep rock, and on the left by the mouth of a river which emptied itself into the large bay. Within the distance of a gunshot lay the narrow defile, between the river and the rocks, which gave access to our domains. It was an agreeable and advantageous position from every point of view. We pitched our tent, and made the necessary arrangement for a more lengthened stay there. During the preparations for dinner I proposed an excursion into the wood, to assure ourselves that we had no unpleasant neighbours, and we met with nothing worse than some wild cats, which were occupied in hunting badgers, and which fled at our approach.

After dinner the heat became so suffocating that we could not dream of undertaking anything. The evening was spent in preparations and projects for the following days, principally for the morrow, when we intended taking a longer excursion than any we had hitherto made. At sunrise we were ready, my three eldest sons and I, and, having taken breakfast, we set off, escorted by our four-legged skirmishers, Fan excepted. In passing through the defile we saw our barricade of bamboos broken and overturned, doubtless by the late hurricanes and inundations, and we concluded that it must have been by this opening that the boa had entered our domains. We determined to repair these ravages on our return. Before entering the savannah, we paused to survey the vast and magnificent landscape that was spread before us. To the left, on the far side of the river, which we had named provisionally the Eastern River, there stretched away to the far-distant horizon an undulating chain of mountains, crowned with green woods and palm-trees, which stood out sharp and clear against the calm sky beyond. On the right, proceeding step by step to the skies, rose innumerable groups of steep rocks, which, barren and frowning, seemed to be ascending from the plain to take a habitation in the clouds, among which their farthermost ridges were already lost. These immense rocks formed a natural boundary to the magnificent country upon which we were looking. We forded the stream, whose shores appeared to us still pleasanter when, seated on the eastern bank, we saw the side of the mountains covered with clusters of shrubs smiling with verdure. But in proportion as we advanced the country grew more barren and arid. There was not a single trace of water. The grass became scarcer and scarcer. The only plants which we saw were dry, thorny, and without beauty; indeed, such as one would expect to find upon a soil so scorched. Fortunately, we had taken the precaution to fill our gourds at the stream before leaving it behind us.

After a painful walk of two hours, during which my three young companions had only opened their parched mouths to rail against the heat and the fatigue, we arrived at the foot of a hill which we had fixed upon as the farthest point of our journey. Here, with no desire to go farther, we sat down under the shade of a rock for rest and refreshment.

We contemplated in silence the magnificent view spread out before us, as it swept down from the blue mountains, which cut the horizon at a distance of fifteen or twenty leagues, and lost itself beyond Eastern River, which ran winding across the plain like a silver riband in the yellow sand.

We lay there for some minutes, when Master Nip, smelling here and there in an excited manner, rushed hissing and crying towards the rocks, followed by our dogs, to whom he had given the signal of attack. We were little disposed to disturb ourselves, in the first place, because we thougt there was nothing particular the matter, and in the second, because we had just fallen-to upon our provisions, to which we were doing every justice.

All at once, however, Fritz, who, whilst eating, was looking attentively before him, rose suddenly.

'What do I see below?' cried he. 'It looks like two men on horseback. A third is approaching them at a gallop. They are coming in our direction. Father, can it be the Arabs of the desert?'

'It is impossible, my dear boy,' replied I. 'However, as we cannot be too prudent, take my telescope and look attentively. What do you see now?'

'I see a large herd of cattle grazing here and there; then some haycocks walking, and loaded waggons which go and come from the wood to the river. What can all this be, father?'

I smilingly took the telescope, and told my three boys, who were much excited by the adventure, that what they took for mounted cavaliers on large horses were only giant ostriches, to which, if they liked, we would give chase, since we had so fine an opportunity. They agreed with pleasure.

The ostriches came nearer and nearer to us. I resolved to wait and surprise them, if that were possible. I therefore ordered Fritz to call in the dogs and the ape, whilst Ernest and I hid ourselves in a crevice of the rock, where Fritz and Jack, leading our animals, soon joined us.

We could see the ostriches very distinctly, and they gradually drew near to us. There were five, four of which were females, the male being easily distinguished by his white feathers.

'My dear boys,' said I, 'if we intend to capture one of these creatures we must be careful not to startle them, for we could not dream of hunting an animal which could beat a horse at full gallop. Our eagle alone can match them in flight.'

The ostriches had now approached to within a hundred paces of us. On seeing us they stopped, looking disquieted and irresolute; but as we kept in the dogs, and ourselves remained all but immovable, they took courage and innocently came to meet us, swaying their necks first on this side and then on that, examining us with an air of mingled curiosity and astonishment which was very amusing. They might have familiarised themselves with our appearance, and come close enough for us to capture them by means of the lasso, if our dogs, who were very impatient, had not at this moment escaped and thrown themselves upon the ostriches with a great noise of yelping and barking. Like feathers carried away by the wind, the ostriches dispersed over the plain, using their wings as sails. They had the appearance of ships sailing over an immense sea of sand. In a few minutes they had vanished out of sight.

Fritz meanwhile, following my recommendation, had quickly unbound the eyes of his eagle, and let him loose at the moment the ostriches took flight.

The male, which we admired more than all on account of his beauty, was a little in the rear of the rest—for the purpose, no doubt, of protecting his companions. This circumstance proved fatal to him. Fritz's eagle precipitated himself upon him, struck him in the neck, and knocked him down in less time than I can tell. The jackal continued the work. We came up just in time to secure a few feathers for our hats.

We then continued our journey. Before long, Ernest and Jack, who were walking in front, stopped and called to us with all their might.

'Come quickly!' cried they. 'An ostrich's nest! an ostrich's nest!'

We ran, and there we saw in a hole in the sand about twenty eggs, as white as ivory and as large as the head of a child.

'It is a splendid find,' said I; 'but do not disturb the order in which these eggs are placed, for fear the hen should abandon them when she returns.'

'Do you not think they are already abandoned?' said Fritz.

'No,' said I. 'In this scorching climate the ostrich generally leaves her eggs to the heat of the sun in the daytime, and returns to cover them during the night.'

The children could not, however, resist the temptation of taking one or two eggs of these to show to their mother. I therefore lifted two, which were on the top of the others, as gently as possible, and after having raised a little pile of stones, to enable us to find the nest again, we went on our way.

We did not stay to explore a verdant valley which formed a very agreeable contrast to the *calcined* plains we had just traversed, and to which we gave, with one accord, the name that it deserved so well—Green Valley. Here and there, in the distance, herds of buffaloes and antelopes were peacefully depasturing, and we should doubtless have been able to approach them easily had it not been for the barking of our dogs, who always ran before, seeking prey on their own account.

By degrees we approached the cavern where Jack had caught his young jackal.

We were only a short distance from it, whem we saw the valiant Ernest come running towards us, pale and agitated, accompanied by his friend Fawn. He had set out on his own account to take possession of the cavern, in which we had determined to rest awhile.

'A bear, father! a bear!' cried he in a voice tremulous with fear, and he threw himself into my arms, clasping me closely, as if begging my protection. Ernest's fright had a serious cause, for with the barks of our dogs were mixed growls of a by no means doubtful nature. I pressed forward, gun in hand, recommending courage and prudence to my children.

In a few moments a huge bear dashed out of the cavern, with a dog hanging to each ear; behind him came another, stil larger.

Fritz, who followed me closely, chose this last for his adversary, whilst I prepared to do battle with the first. Jack, a little agitated but ready to do his part, stood a short distance off. Ernest alone, I am sorry to say, failed to form one of our group. He had not yet recovered from his emotion.

Fritz and I fired together. Unfortunately, neither of our shots was mortal, for, being afraid of wounding one of our dogs, who pulled their dangerous enemies hither and thither, and had at times seemed to form part of them, we could not choose a spot to aim at. Still, I had shattered the jaw of one of the bears, and Fritz had broken one of the fore-feet of the other, so that if they were not precisely unable to fight at all, they were both rendered rather less formidable. However, the two bears continued to defend themselves energetically—sometimes seated, sometimes upright—menacing us, and filled with rage, which expressed itself in growls that resounded in echoes through the cavern.

It was necessary to finish the combat, for if prolonged it might have proved fatal to our courageous companions. I loaded one of my pistols, and, advancing a few steps, I chose the moment when the head of one of the bears was exposed, and quick as lightning fired a ball at it; while Fritz, not less fortunate than myself, hit the other one in the heart.

'God be praised!' cried I earnestly, seeing our two enemies fall down in the last agonies of death.

Jack, who had witnessed our victory, ran joyously to announce it to Ernest, and persuaded him to approach the scene of conflict.

'Why,' said I, without thinking of reproaching his inaction in the face of danger, 'were you so eager to go first into the cavern?'

'Father,' he replied in a guilty tone of voice, 'God has punished me, for I only went in there with the intention of concealing myself, to frighten Jack by imitating the growlings of a bear. I never thought that two real bears would come to enact naturally a part which I was only intending to play as a joke.'

These animals were in truth terrible. One, the largest, measured about eight feet in length, and the other rather more than six. Their powerful paws, their strong shoulders, their enormous necks, their glistening hides, which shone with a metallic lustre, excited the admiration of my boys, who, seated on the two still warm carcasses, occupied themselves by examining them in detail. We certainly had before us two examples of the silver bear met with by Captain Clarke, on the north-west coast of America. However that might be, the skins of these beasts would furnish us with magnificent furs, But, as it was impossible for us to skin them at once, I contented myself with dragging the two bodies into the cavern, whose entrance we closed up with a thick trellis-work of branches.

Fritz and Jack left the ostrich's eggs there also, as the weight inconvenienced them; for it was late, and we should have to make all haste to return to our hut before nightfall.

CHAPTER XXXIII

Occupations of my wife during our absence—the condor—skinning and curing the bears—an expedition by the four boys—the Angora rabbits—the antelopes—Fritz's narrative—the cuckoo—Jack and the bees

By sunset we were again with our good housewife, who gave us one of the warmest of those pleasant greetings to which we had become so well accustomed after the day's toils were over. Our nightly labours, to which we had looked forward with no great pleasure, were all accomplished. The repast was prepared. Even the fires which we burnt during the night to keep off beasts of prey were lighted.

During supper we were called upon, naturally enough, to give an account of our expedition, which we did as briefly as possible, in order not to encroach upon the time necessary for our repose.

My wife, on her part, told us how she, in company with Francis, had opened up a passage through the little wood to the foot of a hill, where she had found an extensive bed of fine argillaceous earth, known as pipe-clay. This, she thought, might be made the means of supplying her with a set of china, and she had brought home two or three bagfuls. Afterwards she had cut some bamboos, and with the tubes of these had constructed a spout to carry a stream of water from a small rivulet among the rocks to the place where our cattle were housed. Also, with her clay and some pieces of stone, she had contrived to build an oven in one of the crevices of the rock. She had had some difficulty with the door, but overcame it at last in such a way as to render her contrivance all but perfect. Finally, she had harnessed the oxen, and brought in a large supply of bamboo-canes, to assist me in building the wall of defence of which I have previously spoken.

I was gratified but not surprised. We—that is, my wife and I—had by this time reached a point at which we believed nothing to be impossible, if we set about it with patience and a determined will. We were no longer astonished at the results we achieved, whether as a family or as individuals: we were pleased, and sometimes proud of each other, but that was all.

Of the numberless discoveries and inventions which the necessity of our situation had forced upon us day by day, during our sojourn in this island, time fails me to speak now.

I hope some day to take up the narrative, when I am more at leisure in my own dear fatherland.

To return: I thanked my brave wife cordially for the industry and thought she had displayed during our absence; and in order to test at once the nature of the clay she had found, I made up a few balls of it, which I placed among the glowing logs of one of our night-fires.

141

After this, we sought upon our pillows the rest we so much needed.

A little before daybreak on the following morning, I got up—not without a sharp struggle with a certain degree of lassitude, very excusable after the labours of the preceding day—and called the family.

As I expected, the pipe-clay balls had become hard. I noticed, however, that the heat had been too intense, and that our pottery was, in consequence, vitrified to an extent which would have rendered it useless had it been made up in the form of cups and saucers.

I determined that, when we came to make the famous china tea-set, I would remedy this evil by constructing a furnace which should moderate the action of the fire.

We offered our morning prayer.

Then, breakfast finished and the oxen harnessed, we set out for Bear Cavern, which we reached without accident.

Fritz—who, as usual, led the van of our little caravan—cried out, the moment he got in sight of the entrance of the cavern, 'Make haste! pray make haste, if you wish to see a regiment of turkeys! I do not know whether they have assembled to do honour to the funeral of our huge enemies; but there is a fine proud fellow up in front there, who seems to be a sort of royal guard, keeping away the crowd of humbler people from the place where the two sovereigns of the forest are lying in state.'

That which Fritz had termed the royal guard was a bird of high stature, with a bright red comb, long wattles clinging like a strip of flesh to its neck, a collar of white feathers falling about its breast, and a bare pink neck, much wrinkled. His plumage was black, flecked here and there with white.

He paced gravely up and down in front of the cavern, which he entered from time to time, as if to superintend the arrangements for some ceremony there.

We were contemplating this strange spectacle with the utmost astonishment, when we heard a great noise in the air over our heads. We looked up, and saw a huge bird with an immense spread of wings.

In an instant it fell among the turkeys, pierced by a ball which Fritz had sent after it.

The feathered band, which we had seen assembled together at the entrance to the grotto, at once took wing and dispersed in all directions. The large bird, the supposed guardian of the dead, alone remained, contemplating with his great round eyes the body of his newly-arrived friend, upon which our dogs were on the point of precipitating themselves.

He was not slow, however, to follow the example just set him by his companions. He started off at full speed, and there was left us only the bird Fritz had shot and a turkey which it had crushed in its fall.

I entered the cavern cautiously, and soon found that the tongue and eyes of one of our bears had disappeared. A few hours later, and their magnificent furs and succulent hams would have been lost to us to the manifest advantage of the aerial marauders which we had just dispersed.

I returned to the two dead birds, and after an attentive examination, I came to the conclusion that that which we had taken for a turkey was a vulture found in Brazil, where it is called the uruhu, and that which Fritz had killed was a condor, as indeed was shown by the extraordinary size of its wings.

We spent the remainder of the day in skinning the bears, a labour which we found to be very unpleasant and very difficult. To complete, it took us two days, during which time we bivouacked in the tent that we had erected a few steps from the mouth of the cavern.

Our occupation during these two days was not quite to the taste of the boys, who, with the exception of Ernest, were burning with a desire to resume our expedition in search of serpent-tracks.

I saw my children growing up around me, and becoming more manly and hardy every day, with a pride which I cannot well express. I could look forward to death without anxiety now. My birds were able henceforth to fly with their own wings, the eldest protecting the younger ones as I had protected him, and supplying my place should I, in the providence of God, be removed from my headship over them.

Feeling this confidence in them, I yielded to their earnest solicitations, and permitted Fritz, Jack, and even little Francis, who loved adventure as ardently as his brothers, to undertake with their dogs an expedition to the savannah, while I, contrary to my habit, remained at the tent with my wife and Ernest.

They set out after I had addressed a few words to them on the value of union and prudence.

While my active wife, assisted by Ernest, proceeded with the curing of the bears' flesh, I found plenty of occupation in the cavern.

I had remarked, during a careful examination, that the interior rock was formed of a species of mica, traversed by long threads of amianth. I proceeded to dig, and was not long in finding sheets of the former mineral, as much as two feet square, and transparent as crystal. It was a most valuable discovery, for henceforth we had a kind of glass with which to glaze our windows in lieu of the fish-glue, or isinglass, which was useless in the wind and rain.

Towards the evening, while we were grilling a few appetising slices of bear's flesh, and growing somewhat uneasy at the prolonged absence of our young huntsmen, a sound of distant hoofs and a faint echo of hurrahs borne upon the wind announced the return of the excursionists.

I went to meet them. They leapt from their beasts at once, unsaddled them, set them free to depasture themselves, and walked home with me to the tent.

Jack and Francis each carried a kid slung over his shoulder. Fritz's game-bag was of a size that looked significant.

'Splendid sport, father! splendid sport!' cried the lively Jack. 'Do you see these kids?'

'Yes, to say nothing of the Angora rabbits which Fritz has in his game-bag!' added Francis precipitately.

'Yes, and to say nothing either of—' Jack was saying, with even more precipitation, when:

'Stay!' I cried. 'Stay! proceed in order, pray. Let Fritz begin; he will be able, I doubt not, to give us a correct account of your adventures.'

Fritz went on to tell his story.

'An hour after we left you,' he said, 'we crossed Green Valley at a brisk trot, passed through a ravine to the great plain, and found ourselves upon an eminence which commanded the surrounding country. From the spot on which we stood we could see the rocky defile, where a number of animals, which I believed to be either gazelles, goats, or antelopes, were quietly feeding. We determined to give chase to them. I led the way cautiously, and in order to avoid frightening the game, we held our dogs in leash.

'Arrived within a short distance, Francis took a course to the left, Jack rode straight on, while I, mounted on the onager, set off to the right to cut off the retreat of any animal which should try to escape us. We advanced cautiously and quickly, you may be sure; but, in spite of that, the herd took alarm. Several of them bounded from rock to rock, staying every now and then to toss their heads and prick up their ears. At this point we let the dogs loose, and galloped after them at full speed.

'Distracted by the unusual sight and sounds, the poor creatures sought safety in flight; but we had so ordered our plans that, start from where they would, they were compelled eventually to pass through the place we had chosen for them—that is to say, the defile. The first difficulty was over, but it now became necessary to devise some plan of turning our conquest to account. We determined to make the herd prisoners in the defile, and drive them home to Farm Grange. And this is how we did it. We stretched a piece of string across the road about three or four feet from the ground, and tied upon it the ostrich feathers which we had in our caps, and some pieces of rag that were lying in the bottom of our game-bags. The wind blew these about, and the animals as soon as they saw them came to a dead stand, not knowing which way to turn. I had read of something similar being done in an account of a voyage made by Captain Levaillant, the naturalist; and I thought I might as well try my hand at the experiment. It was perfectly successful.'

'Well done, brave boy!' I said, interrupting him. 'I am happy to see that you have profited by your reading. Now tell me how you took the Angora rabbits, and tell me also what you propose to do with them. I warn you that I am not very much disposed to admit them to our domains, for they multiply almost to infinity, and will prove very injurious to our fields and gardens.'

'The capture of these rabbits,' said Fritz, 'is due to my eagle, which pounced down upon a flock of them that were frisking at the foot of a little hill. He brought me two alive and one dead, which latter I gave him to eat for his trouble. As to the introduction of them into what you call our domains, have we not two little islands at our disposal which we could people with these pretty little animals without any danger or loss to ourselves whatever? We should thus be assured of a delicacy for our table, and fur for our caps and other garments.'

'You speak wisely, my son,' I replied, 'and as you seem to be both able and willing to carry out your plan, I will leave its execution wholly in your hands.'

'Is it not our turn to speak now?' asked Jack, who was growing very impatient.

'Undoubtedly,' I replied, smiling. 'Let us hear how you brought down these beautiful kids.'

'By hunting—sheer hunting!' he cried excitedly. 'Fritz was some distance off, engaged with his eagle and the rabbits. Our dogs were sniffing about in the underwood, when they put up two animals resembling large hares. They took to flight instantly, bounding and capering in the most extraordinary manner. We and our dogs followed them at the top of our speed. In about a quarter of an hour they were out of breath, and fell down as if they were dead. We got down from our cattle, drove away the dogs, and found that what we had supposed to be large hares were young kids. We tied them by the legs and slung them over our shoulders. There! that is the history of the day's sport so far as Francis and I are concerned.'

'Good, my children!' I said, 'you have done well. The only remark I would make is that the kids, as you term them, are very fine specimens of the dwarf antelope. And now, Jack, I want you to explain how it is that your face is so swollen? Have you been fighting a legion of mosquitoes?'

'Oh, no,' said Jack gaily, 'my wounds are more honourable than that. I will tell you how I came by them. We were all three returning home, when I noticed a bird that kept flying from tree to tree in front of us, and seemed to invite us by his song to follow him. I thought the bird was playing us some impudent trick, and put my gun to my shoulder to take aim at it, when Fritz stopped me, observing that it was of no use to fire, as my gun was loaded with a bullet: small shot, he said, was the only thing for such a bird as that at such a distance. 'Besides,' he added, 'the bird resembles the Indicator cuckoo spoken of by Buffon and Latham, and it may be giving us counsel that it would be well to take.'

'Upon that we determined to follow the bird, at all events for a short distance. After a few minutes it settled on a tree and ceased its song. We stopped also, and were not long in discovering that the trunk of the tree upon which it had posted itself was the retreat of a swarm of bees. The bird, which lives upon honey, no doubt coveted that store which it knew was concealed within, and, as its habit is, led us to the place where it was in the hope that we should leave it part of our booty in repayment for its services.

'We were trying to hit upon some means of taking the bees, when Fritz proposed to suffocate them with a sulphur match as you had done. I lighted one at once, and without stopping to plug up the hole, threw it in among the buzzing colony. In a moment the whole swarm poured out and set upon me. I was assailed in so many places at once and saw such clouds of fresh enemies pouring down upon me, that it seemed as if all the bees in the world were at my heels. They stung and tormented me until there was nothing left but to leap upon my buffalo and make off at the top of my speed. That is the story. You see the state I am in. It is not my fault, for I rubbed myself with damp earth as soon as I could get clear of my enemies, remembering that was the remedy which you applied when I was attacked by bees before.'

'It was not the remedy alone that you should have remembered, my poor boy,' I said; 'you should have recollected how to avoid the danger which made the remedy necessary. You cannot expect me to sympathise with you very deeply, for, having been stung in the same manner once before, I can only put down your second misfortune to want of common prudence.'

My wife dressed the poor boy's face and neck with salt-water bandages, which relieved his pain and left him free to make a hearty supper.

Afterwards, assisted by the other boys, I made a sort of cage in which to transport the Angora rabbits, first to Rock-house and then to Shark Island.

Then we retired to rest.

CHAPTER XXXIV

Spurge-oil—Arab Hill—capture of an ostrich—the return to Rock-house—another large eel—training the ostrich—hydromel—hat-making

There were many things still remaining to be done before our return to Rock-house—a return which it was necessary to hasten for more than one reason, the most important being the approaching recurrence of the rainy season.

Our bears' flesh had been salted and smoked; but I did not wish to leave behind either the ostrich-eggs, which we had found, or some spurge-oil which I had lighted upon in a little wood during one of our expeditions.

I determined, therefore, to make a final excursion into the savannah.

We set out, leaving at home with our good housewife, not little Francis, who desired to distinguish himself in our company, but the indolent Ernest, who now made no secret of his distaste for fatiguing journeys.

Fritz on this occasion handed over to me his onager, and himself mounted young Swift, her foal, which was destined to become an excellent hack. Francis mounted his calf, and Jack his buffalo.

Brown and Fawn very much wished to accompany us, but I thought it better to leave them behind for the protection of my wife, and I told Ernest to look after them.

We took the Green Valley road, but in an opposite direction to Bear Cave, and eventually came to Arab Hill—the name we gave to the eminence from the top of which we had at first mistaken the ostriches for mounted Arabs.

Arrived there, I permitted Jack and Francis to push on ahead, but without losing sight of them for an instant.

As to Fritz, he stopped with me to assist in securing a supply of spurge-oil from the trunks of the euphorbia shrub, in which I had been careful to make incisions when I was there before. The sun had dried the exudations, of which we collected a large quantity, and placed it in some bamboo vessels that we had brought for the purpose.

This valuable harvest achieved, we set out to overtake our advance-guard, who had got far beyond the ostrich-nest without knowing it. The two boys were strongly desirous of knocking over some of these couriers of the savannah, as well as of taking one or two alive for their brother Fritz, who had often expressed a wish to possess one. He now determined to join in the chase, and obtained my leave to remount the onager for the purpose.

We had not long to wait for the result of the sport. Before we had advanced far, four ostriches—three females and a male—came out of the thicket in which our nest lay.

As they made straight towards us, they fell in with our young companions, who were accompanied by their dogs. There was but little chance of their escaping us.

When they were fairly within range, I threw my lasso at one of them; but the cord, instead of getting entangled in the legs of the creature, at which point I aimed at, entwined itself round the upper part of the body. The motion of the wings was at once paralysed, but the vigorous animal began struggling fiercely to disembarrass itself of the ill-adjusted cord; and I felt certain it would have escaped me if Fritz had not immediately dispatched his eagle, whose beak he had bound with cotton in order that it might not seriously wound our victim.

The eagle pounced upon the ostrich, laid hold of it by the top of the head, and arrested it in its impetuous course.

Jack, arriving at a gallop, threw his lasso, and, more adroit than

I was, succeeded in entangling the legs of the animal, which fell heavily upon its side.

To rush up and bind it more securely was the work of an instant. After having tied a handkerchief over its head—a precaution without which we should never have been able to master it—I strapped its wings down with a strip of dog-fish skin, through which I passed a strong cord. One end of this cord I attached to the collar of Storm, the other to that of Grumbler. I had determined that the bird should be thus led home between the two oxen; and, as I did not wish that its kicking and struggling should in any way incommode these two faithful servants, I fettered its legs in such wise that it could walk with tolerable ease without having the power to do any harm. These precautions taken, I removed the handkerchief with which I had blindfolded it, and the lasso-ropes which pained it unnecessarily, and awaited the result.

At first, irritated and humiliated at finding itself vanquished, the bird remained absolutely immovable upon the ground. Then, fancying itself free again, it all at once leaped up and tried to take wing. But the straps and cords held it back, and it fell upon its knees.

It was soon up again, struggling furiously; but, thanks to the strong necks and shoulders of Storm and Grumbler, it strove in vain. At length, being powerless to do otherwise, it gave up the unequal contest, and submitted to follow the gentler forward movement of its two brave conductors.

While Jack and Francis, mounted upon their oxen, led our captive to Arab Hill, Fritz and I made our way to the ostrich-nest which we had discovered during a former visit to the spot. We were not many paces from it, when a female ostrich rose from the eggs so unexpectedly that we had time neither to fire at nor follow it before it was far beyond our reach.

The bird's presence there proved clearly that the nest had not been abandoned, and we had some hope that we might find among the eggs at least one or two that were far enough advanced to be hatched artificially. We carried away ten of them, leaving the others buried in the sand, in order that the mother upon her return might continue her maternal office.

We carefully slung our spoils to our saddles, and rejoined our young companions, with whom we set out for Bear Cavern, passing through Green Valley on the way.

On our return we were at first saluted with cries of admiration. But soon our good housewife grew alarmed at the bare thought of the prodigious quantity of food which our majestic prisoner would devour.

'My good husband!' she exclaimed, 'to what possible use can you put this huge glutton that will repay the drain it will cause upon our scanty stock of provisions during the rainy season?'

'It will supply me with a swift steed,' said Jack, with enthusiasm; 'and if our little country is joined anywhere to the continent of

Asia or Africa, I will, thanks to our ostrich, make a journey thither in a few days, to seek help and news of our fatherland of the first European colony that I meet with. In anticipation of its future exploits, therefore, I name it "Tornado"; for it shall travel as swiftly, or I have no skill in ostrich-breaking. So soon as he shall be taught to obey the bit, I will be his rider, and Ernest shall have my dear buffalo, Storm.'

After a little pouting and recrimination on the part of Francis, the ostrich was unanimously awarded to Jack, who from that moment took possession of it and began its education.

It was too late today to think of returning to Forest Grange; but early the next morning we were all on the way thither, human beings and cattle.

The ostrich marched with bandaged eyes between the two oxen. The car was harnessed to the cow, on whose back Ernest rode. Jack and Francis naturally mounted Storm and Grumbler. I was upon Lightfoot, and Fritz upon Swift. My wife rode on the car. Altogether we formed a highly picturesque caravan.

We made a short halt in the defile. The children desired to carry away the ostrich feathers which they had put up to catch the antelopes; and I was not sorry of the opportunity to take in a supply of pipe-clay and of aromatic beans with the scent of the vanilla-tree about them, which my wife had discovered during one of her useful rambles.

Before setting out I took care to repair our barricades, so that they might be impregnable as well to rodent animals as to beasts of prey. I also effaced from the soil all traces of our journey, in order that when we came again we might have no difficulty in detecting the footsteps of strange animals.

This done, we set out, intending to reach Forest Grange before nightfall. The only halt we made was at Sugar-cane Grove, where we collected our peccary hams, by this time properly smoked.

Directly we reached the farmery we unharnessed our beasts, partook of a hasty supper of cold meat, and flung ourselves upon our beds of cotton: for we were worn out utterly by fatigue.

At daybreak I went out to the poultry, and saw with pleasure that among the chickens hatched by our hens were several fine fat pullets. My wife desired to carry these to Rock-house, our favourite dwelling-place, towards which we seemed to be drawn after our long absence by a kind of nostalgia, or homesickness.

We arrived there towards noon.

The first care of our good housewife was to throw open the door and all the windows, and begin dusting, sweeping, scrubbing, and washing so vigorously that, absorbed in this highly commendable labour, she altogether forgot to prepare dinner, and we were obliged to content ourselves with a cold meal.

While the two younger boys were helping their mother, I proceeded with two others to the unpacking and provisional stowing away of our booty.

The ostrich, relieved of the bonds which attached it to the oxen, was tied up in front of our dwelling, under the arbour of branches, where I decided it was to remain until properly tamed.

The ostrich-eggs were placed in tepid water for some time; and those in which we believed there were young were afterwards placed on a cushion of cotton, and deposited in the oven, which with the aid of a thermometer, I raised to the necessary temperature for their incubation.

The Angora rabbits were the same day transported and left on Shark Island, where their mission was to acclimatise themselves and propagate their species. We resolved to pay them a visit soon, and prepare them a proper dwelling-place for the rainy season.

In our new division of territory, Whale Island fell to the dwarf antelopes, which, though nearly dead when taken, revived, and with care became as strong and active as ever. We were particularly desirous of keeping these graceful creatures in our immediate neighbourhood; but we feared that the dogs, unable to withstand so tempting a prey, might worry them when we were out of sight.

As to some land-turtles which we had found in the vicinity of Sugar-cane Grove, and of which we had left a couple at Forest Grange, I at first thought of turning them loose in the kitchen garden to rid it of snails that infested it. But as my wife had less fear of the ravages of the latter than of the damage which the turtles might do among the young plants, I told Jack to go and place them among the reeds in Goose Marsh.

The boy carried the creatures off at once. Scarcely had he reached his destination, when I heard him calling for Fritz at the top of his voice, saying, 'Make haste, Fritz! Pray make haste! And bring a stick with you!'

I thought at first that it was some frog-hunting freak, for there were a great many of these creatures in the marsh, and Jack liked nothing better than to pursue them till they leapt souse into the water. Great was my surprise, therefore, to see the boys returning with a magnificent eel, which had been taken upon a line secretly laid by Ernest before we set out on our excursion. A portion of the delicious fish was immediately prepared for our dinner. The remainder was preserved in butter and salt for a future occasion.

Previously to this we had run out a veranda in front of the grotto, supported by slender bamboo columns, around which trailing plants of all kinds crept up and depended in graceful luxuriance. We now planted at the base of these columns some pepper-vines and the aromatic beans which we thought resembled in odour the fruit of the vanilla-tree.

My wife claimed for her pantry the bear and peccary hams, as well as a little keg of fat which we had extracted from these animals. The skins of the bears were laid to soak in the sea, huge stones being placed upon them to prevent their being carried away by the tide.

The fat pullets which we had brought from Forest Grange were kept in a cage out of the reach of Master Nip and the jackal.

The condor and the vulture were laid provisionally upon a shelf in our museum. We postponed our stuffing of them till the rainy season, when we should have more leisure.

The amianth, the mica, and the pipe-clay were carried, also provisionally, into our workshop, where I intended to put each to its proper use as soon as time should serve for the purpose.

Having handed over to my wife everything that was of an eatable character, I reserved to myself the gum of the euphorbia, which I tied up securely in a triple packet, writing thereupon in large letters, as a precaution against the too curious appetites of my children, the forbidding and fatal word 'Poison.'

The skins of the musk-rats were strung together in a bundle and hung in the roof of the veranda, in order that they might not become offensive to us.

These arrangements lasted two days. When they were completed, I began to think of digging up and sowing a field of grain, training the ostrich, and preparing the skins of the bears—all which projects had suffered nothing by a little delay.

Our agricultural labours—so little were we used to work of this kind—were very irksome. Notwithstanding that the whole family assisted me, I was not able to dig and sow more than a single acre of land. The spot chosen was the neighbourhood of my wife's small plantation of sugar-canes. My boys and I were able now to comprehend the truth of the Word of God, 'Thou shalt eat thy bread in the sweat of thy brow.' A third of the acre was sown with wheat, a third with maize, and a third with barley, while here and there, as heretofore, we scattered over the uncultivated land a few handfuls of other species of grain, relying upon Providence and the fertility of the soil to cause them to bring forth fruit in their season. Also, on the other side of Jackal River, I set apart a piece of land for the culture of those valuable roots, the potato and tapioca.

As, owing to the heat of the noontide sun, we only devoted four hours a day to these labours—two in the morning, and two in the evening—there remained in the intervals a good deal of time which we employed otherwise.

We undertook, for instance, the training of Tornado (this, the reader will remember, was the name Jack gave to the ostrich); but I am bound to confess that we did not at first succeed very well therein.

I was obliged to stupefy the poor creature with the fumes of tobacco, as Ernest had done with Fritz's eagle. When she was in this state the children mounted her in turn, to accustom her to the weight of their bodies and the novelty of being ridden after the manner of a horse. This she permitted us to do, not having any will of her own during the existence of the state of torpor into which the tobacco threw her. But in spite of our patience and perseverance, in spite of our caresses, in spite of the excellent litter we had provided for her, in spite of the care we had taken day by day to lengthen the cord with which she was attached, in order to give her more liberty as an earnest of still greater freedom in the future, she remained quite intractable. The poor creature indeed, refusing all nourishment, seemed at last to have resolved to perish of hunger, to punish us for having separated her from her companions in the savannah.

She became so feeble and wretched that I began to fear we should not rear her, and to regret that we had ever deprived her of her native freedom. Happily my wife one morning hit upon a plan of relieving us of our difficulties. She prepared some balls of bruised maize and butter, such as they fatten capons with; and these we gave to the ostrich who swallowed them eagerly. From this day the creature ate everything we placed before it. So robust did its appetite become, indeed, that our fears underwent an entire change. From doubting whether it would live, we came to doubt whether we should be able to find food enough for its support. Fortunately, however, about this time Madame Tornado took to alternating pebbles with her other food—a fact which led the boys to think that she might probably come to eating pebbles altogether, till I told them that she swallowed stones only for digestive purposes.

Her strength thus revived, her education was proceeded with vigorously. In less than a month, she knew how to sit down, get up, turn, walk, trot, and gallop at the command of her young driver, Jack.

As we desired to use her as riding-horse, it was necessary to make her a bit and bridle; and I was much embarrassed to know what to do in the matter. A bit was indispensable to guide her with; but who ever saw a bit adapted to a beak?

I was on the point of giving the thing up, when I recollected to have noticed that the alternation of light and shade had a great influence over her; and I conceived the idea of making for her a leathern hood, something like one which Fritz had made after the manner of falconers to manoeuvre his eagle. Bringing the cap far enough down the neck to fasten it securely, I cut in it two square flaps like the blinkers of a horse's bridle, and these I attached to reins which could easily be managed by the rider. By shutting one of the blinkers, the ostrich would at once be turned in the direction of the other whence the light came. By shutting both, she would be stopped altogether. By opening both, she would be directed straight ahead.

The saddle also required a good deal of ingenuity: but in spite of the difficulties of the enterprise, I came out of it with so much honour that, could the sovereign of England have heard of me, I doubt not I should have received a royal patent affirming that I was the best saddler for ostriches in the neighbourhood of Cape Disappointment.

The equipment of the ostrich finished, we tried her capabilities, which were beyond our expectations. If she declined to do much as a draught beast, she justified her name of Tornado by her performances as a saddle-horse. She accomplished, for instance, the journey between Falcon-nest and back again before Fritz upon his onager was able to traverse more than half the distance.

So superior, indeed, was she in speed to any of our other animals, that Fritz, Ernest, and Francis grew jealous of Jack, her master, and begged me to withdraw the gift we had made him. But I held steadfastly to our first decision, and Jack continued to retain possession of his ostrich which, however, was none the less the property of his three brothers, for they rode it almost as often as they pleased, and were allowed equal rights in its services when they required them.

Also they were able to console themselves with the thought that the eggs in the oven might possibly furnish each of them, some day, with as good a mount as their fortunate brother's. Their hopes were of short duration. The eggs were hatched well, and the chickens at first looked healthy; but after a few days, notwithstanding our solicitude and almost maternal care, they died for want of that nourishment which Nature alone can provide in her own benignant way.

The preparation of the bears' skins had proceeded simultaneously with the training of the ostrich and other small labours. In place of bark, I tanned them with a vinegar made of honey; and for a fleshing-knife, I used the blade of an old sabre. To soften them and render them fit for use as leather, I rubbed them well with a compound of grease and ashes, which produced the precise effect intended.

Speaking of this vinegar, I may mention here in passing that while making it for the use I have mentioned, I obtained, without any intention of doing so, an excellent hydromel, or honey-water. The attempt to achieve the useful had brought forth the agreeable, and henceforth my boys and I were assured of a refreshing drink during our thirst-producing daily labours.

My double success as tanner and distiller emboldened me. I took a turn at the trade of the hatter, and essayed to make a beaver hat of the skins of the musk-rats for little Francis. As, however, this was a kind of industry for which none of my previous occupations had fitted me, I at first failed to achieve my ends. But I was not thereby discouraged. After several attempts, I obtained a sort of felt, to which, for want of a more sober dye, I imparted a brilliant red colour obtained from the cochineal insect. To render the fabric impervious to wet, I impregnated it with caoutchouc. When it was thus prepared, I moulded it upon a block, and placed it in the oven for a night to dry. The next morning we had the satisfaction off drawing out a magnificent red Swiss biretta, light in weight, and sufficiently strong for all reasonable wear.

My wife, delighted to witness the pleasure with which Francis contemplated his new cap, added thereto a lining of silk, a band of gold lace, and a plume of ostrich feathers.

At first the child was not at all at ease in his new hat; its brilliancy contrasted so ludicrously with the old caps worn by myself and his brothers. I was, therefore, obliged to promise that I would make similar birettas for the whole family, provided the brothers would supply me with the skins.

They brought enough to make fifty hats.

CHAPTER XXXV

Return of the rainy season—manufacture of pottery—building a cajack—voyage to Shark Island

These several occupations had so engaged our attention that we failed to note the approach of the rainy season. As it set in, my success as a tanner, distiller, and hatter induced me to seek new laurels as a potter.

The dining-room served me for a workshop. My lathe was constructed of a cannon-wheel, adapted to a wooden axle, to which I fixed a piece of board cut in a circular shape. By way of a beginning I made some bowls, intended to replace our calabash vessels, which did not keep the milk sufficiently fresh. With the view of beautifying my work a little, I mixed with the clay some particles of mica. Also I sought amongst the spoil from the wreck for a case containing glass trinkets, which had been shipped for the purpose of barter with the savages. I pounded on the anvil a certain quantity of the blue and yellow contents of the case, reducing them to an extremely fine powder, which I sprinkled over my porcelain when it was about half-baked. It melted and formed an excellent enamel. I then obtained, after one or two unsuccessful attempts, and not a few misfortunes, several coffee-cups, a sugar-basin, and six small plates.

What I have so briefly set down here occupied, as you may well imagine, a good deal of time. I had first to make models in wood—a work which, owing to my unskilfulness as a turner, was at least but imperfectly done; and then upon these I had to mould others, which were eventually to become the utensils we desired to manufacture.

My stock of clay being exhausted, and the rain not permitting me to renew the supply, I occupied myself, to the general satisfaction, in stuffing the condor and the vulture. I laid the skins to soak in tepid water, into which I threw a little of the gum of the spurge-tree, to prevent the future ravages of insects. Thus softened and rendered impervious to corruption, I stretched them over pieces of wood, carved out in the form of the birds to be represented. Small rods, covered with cotton wire, were placed in the neck, while the wings were supported in their proper positions with the aid of wire. For eyes I made four small balls of porcelain, of the requisite size, which I painted and baked, and which restored to the two birds their natural appearance.

These occupations were succeeded by others, for the rainy season kept us prisoners, and we determined to make good use of our leisure. It was repugnant to my feelings to see my boys unoccupied. We set up daily readings. Ernest gave lessons to little Francis, which Jack voluntarily turned to his own profit. I gave a course of lectures on natural history, which was fully as instructive to the master as to his pupils; for our island yielded thousands of specimens which in Europe were unknown.

For all this, however, we were not able to wile away the monotony of the long days.

Fritz came to the rescue.

'Now,' said he, 'that we have in the ostrich a rapid traveller by land, we ought, I think, to have another for a sphere a little more extended. I mean the sea, What if we were to make a Greenland canoe, or cajack?'

I fell in with the proposition at once; it was hailed by the youngsters with enthusiasm; but my dear wife received it with a sigh of apprehension. Completely ignorant of what a cajack was, she dreaded that we were about engaging in an imprudent enterprise. I tried to reassure her by explaining that a cajack was a wonderfully safe kind of canoe, covered with the skin of the dog-fish and very strong and buoyant. Hearing this, she was constrained to give her assent to our project, in spite of the aversion with which any vessel designed to traverse the sea inspired her.

We set to work at once, in order to have, at least, the body of the canoe finished before the return of the fine season. First of all, with the aid of our largest whalebones, which were of a curved shape naturally, and which I joined together end to end, I made two keels fitting into each other, and of about twelve feet in length.

I gave them a coat of resin, and underneath cut three holes, into which I fitted some small castors to facilitate the transport of the skiff on land. I then fastened the two keels securely together with bamboos, and ran up at each end a new whalebone, which was intended to form the prow and stern of the cajack. I also bound the keels together with a band of copper, to which I fixed an iron ring for mooring purposes. Split bamboos served to build up the sides of the vessel, excepting the higher parts of it, which I formed of reeds similar to those which grew in Goose Marsh. I also worked some of these reeds in amongst the split bamboos, and so shaped the vessel to my liking. The deck extended over the whole surface of the cajack. I cut a circular opening in it for the oarsman, and round the opening placed a rim over which he could fasten his waterproof cape, and so keep the sea from entering the hole. In an ordinary cajack the Greenlander who rows it is obliged to kneel during the process—a fatiguing position if long continued. Among other innovations upon the ordinary form of the boat, I placed in the opening a movable seat, which the occupant could either use or not as he pleased.

The body of our canoe was finished. Owing, perhaps, to the seat, it was a little higher than it should have been; but happily that modification did not appear to affect its lightness or its elasticity.

Much as we had accomplished, our task was but half completed. After having carefully caulked all the joints with a mixture of tar and moss, we covered the skeleton of the boat inside and out with two of our largest dog-fish skins, so as to cover over the bamboos and reedwork.

Dog-fish skins were also strained over the deck, and fastened down by bamboos, which formed two bulwarks to the boat. I forgot to say that the hole cut in the deck for the rower was placed a little farther back than is usual, because I wished to put up a mast forward. For the present the skiff had to be rowed with a paddle, to one of whose blades I fastened a bladder coated with wax, the better to assist its occupant in swimming to shore should he be capsized.

At length, to the general satisfaction, the cajack was finished. But before I could permit its owner, who could be none other than he who had at first conceived the idea of making it, to venture to sea, I begged my wife to try all her ingenuity to the utmost to make him a suitable swimming dress. This dress, by my advice, was to be so constructed as to form a covering adapted to the size and shape of the hole in the deck, and to envelop the rower completely—of course, leaving his movements unfettered. Besides this, as it was necessary to provide against every contingency, the dress was made double throughout, so that air could be injected into it by means of a small tube provided with a stopper. The rower would thus be able to inflate himself like a balloon, and to float on the surface of the water by his own specific gravity.

The wet season passed away in these interesting occupations, and in other employments more or less important; but in spite of the rapidity with which time flew by, we did not the less joyously salute the return of the fine weather; for it was also the return of our journeys in the open air, and in our fruitful woods and savannahs. Fritz, especially, longed ardently to make a trial of the Greenland-Swiss cajack, and I was not less curious than he to know how it would succeed.

At last, on a fine afternoon, our strange craft was launched into the sea. Fritz, in order to honour the life-coat which I had devised and my wife had made, put it on, inflated it, and walked boldly into the water, where he floated as securely as if he had been walking on land. His brothers were as much amused as astonished at the strange figure he made, and because of the protuberances which the coat made both before and behind, laughingly gave him the nickname of Punch.

Fritz, however, without paying attention to them or their jokes, pushed forward and at length reached Shark Island, to the great delight of his mother and myself, who had arrived there in our pirogue, in which we had set out to follow him. We paid a visit to our dwarf antelopes, and left them a supply of bruised maize, salt, and sweet acorns. We could see by the condition of the place that they often took refuge beneath the shed we had built, and we had therefore no fear but they would find the food we left them.

Before setting out again, we made a tour round the island in order to collect some corals and shells for our museum. We found an unusual quantity of sea-wrack and other marine plants, of which, at the request of our good housewife, the boys carried away several armfuls.

On our return to Deliverance Bay, she selected from amongst these plants several serrated leaves of about six or seven inches long, which she carefully washed and spread in the sun to dry, afterwards placing them in our oven with a sort of mysterious solemnity; on which I bantered her, but without, for the moment, obtaining any satisfactory explanation. Some days afterwards, when we had returned wearied, hungry, and thirsty from a tour to Falcon-nest, the dear woman set before us, in a large gourd-dish, the finest transparent jelly we had ever seen. It was neither more nor less than the product of the famous leaves which my wife had prepared unknown to us in order to give us a surprise. I leave you to judge whether her ruse succeeded, and also to imagine the avidity with we fell-to upon the new dish. My wife told us afterwards that during our excursion to Shark Island she had recognised amongst the marine plants some leaves similar to those which she had seen prepared with sugar and the juice of citron, or of orange, by the housewives of the cape where we put in for a time during the ill-fated voyage which brought us to these parts. She had simply substituted for the citron, which alone was lacking, vinegar, honey, and a little cinnamon.

Our plantations of mangroves, cotton-plants, pines, and coco-trees in Shark Island were in excellent condition. We therefore hoped to find those in Whale Island, towards which we soon directed our steps, equally prosperous. On our arrival I perceived that the number of our rabbits had increased, and the little gourmands had gnawed the bark of our young trees, and entirely devoured the coco-nut shoots. The pines alone were spared, no doubt owing to the unpleasant taste of their sap. In order to preserve our nursery from similar devastations in future, we surrounded it with a thick, prickly hedge.

We saw again on the coast the carcass of the whale, so cleanly picked by the birds, and blanched by the action of the wind and sun, that I had no difficulty in carrying away those parts which seemed to me likely to be of use—as, for example, the vertebrae of the dorsal fin. I took at the same time some specimens of two marine plants which I had seen the rabbits eating—one of a disagreeable marshy smell, which might possibly be the *Fucus saccharinus;* the other of a most decided violet perfume, which might be the *Fucus palmatus.*

We returned to our favourite habitation, revolving new projects for the future.

CHAPTER XXXVI

A rat-hunting expedition—ravages by pigs—return of the hunters—skinning the animals—the harvest—the herring-shoals and dog-fish again

One morning, while three of the boys were absent with their mouse-traps, seeking the first elements of their future hats, I set out alone, leaving Ernest reading in the library, to find a tree of the right shape and size to be used in the making of a pounding-mill to braise our corn. I also desired to renew our supply of loam, which by this time was getting very low.

I harnessed Storm to the old truck, and, accompanied by Fan and Brown, directed my course towards the nearest wood to Jackal River.

Arrived on the other side of the bridge, I went to look at our potato and tapioca fields, and, to my annoyance, found them well-nigh laid waste by the ravages of some kind of marauders which, judging from their foot-marks I took to be pigs. Their tracks, which I followed, led me along by the rocks, and through a coppice to the old potato-field not far from Falcon-nest.

Evidently the invaders were very numerous, or they could not have committed so much devastation. However, none of them put in an appearance, and I had already despaired of meeting even one to chastise him as a warning to the rest, when the furious barking of the dogs, mingled with a dull grunting sound, satisfied my legitimate impatience. I ran to the spot whence the sound proceeded, and saw, facing the dogs, our old sow—now become almost a wild animal—surrounded by eight little pigs of about two months old, and a larger pig—one of her first litter—which we had left for the purpose of increasing the race. This latter animal was now almost as large and savage as its mother.

Overcome by the anger which the devastations of these marauders had caused me, I fired off both my barrels among the herd that stood before me grunting and showing their teeth. Three of the little pigs fell, and the remainder made off at once for an adjacent thicket, pursued by the dogs, which I immediately recalled. I carried the carcasses to the truck and again set out in quest of my tree.

I found one at some distance from the loam-pit. The trunk measured about two feet through and was straight and smooth.

Having marked it, after the manner of other woodmen, I returned to the grotto.

Our young rat-hunters had not yet returned. My wife was still alone with Ernest, who had not long finished his reading for the day.

Towards evening, just as we were beginning to grow anxious about them, the three boys returned, heralded by Jack, who was mounted upon his ostrich.

Fritz and Francis escorted two large sacks, carried by Grumbler, and containing four duck-bills, twenty ondatras, a kangaroo, a monkey, two animals of the hare species, and a half-dozen beaver-rats of a different kind from those we had found before.

Fritz also brought with him an armful of large thistles, to which no one paid any attention for the moment, because of the enthusiasm excited by the contents of the sacks.

'Oh, father!' cried Jack, 'what a splendid steed my ostrich makes! She runs with the swiftness of the wind. A score times I lost breath and was near upon falling off, being overcome by giddiness. She goes with what I may call a blinding rapidity. You must at once make me a mask with glass eyes for our next expedition.'

'Impetuous boy!' I replied. 'That is not the way to talk. There is no "must" in the matter.'

'Why, dear father?' he asked.

'In the first place,' I said, 'because it does not become a child to impose his desires upon his parents in this manner; in the second place, because I have to do many things, in the general interest, far more important than the making of a mask with glass eyes for a young gentleman who is very well able to try to make one himself, if it were only to surpass his brothers in ingenuity.'

Jack became silent, and left his eldest brother to take up the narrative.

'We have diverted ourselves,' said Fritz, 'to admiration today. We have had splendid sport, and have brought home an enormous booty. Nevertheless, we will willingly exchange all our treasures for a small glass of wine, if the price of it is not too high for us.'

'Well proposed, Fritz,' cried I. 'I shall willingly give each of you a glass of wine because you have so well deserved it. But another time do not set out upon such an excursion as you did this morning, without first obtaining the consent of your mother and me. And now, boys, go and unsaddle your animals and take them to stable. A good horseman never attends to himself till he has properly cared for his beast.'

When the family were assembled at supper, our good housewife served out to each in turn his share of a delicious joint, saying, with comic gravity, 'This, gentlemen, is a European sucking-pig, under the guise of an American marcassin. Here also,' she continued, 'is a young and savoury European salad, grown and gathered in my garden, which is, as you know, at the antipodes of Europe. It has, in consequence, its roots where European gardens have their leaves. And here, to finish with,' she cried, uncovering a large gourd-basin, 'is an excellent Hottentot jelly, drawn from the garden of the sea.'

The good-humour of our housekeeper secured her the praise she so well merited. She was applauded a second time when she brought in a dish of cassava fritters and a bottle of hydromel for dessert.

Never was there a better supper, or a merrier company to enjoy it.

Fritz told us the story of the day's expedition: how he and his brothers had remained all day in the neighbourhood of Forest Grange, laying their traps; how they had taken the ondatras with yellow carrots, and the beaver-rats with small fish; how with the same kind of bait they had taken the duck-bills; and how his brothers and he had dined off fresh fish roasted with ginseng and anise roots.

'And my jackal!' cried Jack. 'You have not spoken of him—how he turned up the two hares under my very nose, and helped Francis to catch the kangaroo, who for the first and last time in his life made acquaintance with gunpowder.'

'While wandering about in search of adventure,' said Fritz, 'I found these large thistles, at the end of which there are strong thorny hooks, that I fancied might be useful for carding the felt. I also found among the thickets small cinnamon-trees. And with my gun I gave a sharp lesson, which he has no doubt forgotten now, to a huge ape that took a good deal of trouble to throw coco-nuts upon my head.'

The spoils of Fritz were not to be disdained, and his mother thanked him warmly for them.

As to the skinning of the game, I pretended that I would take charge of this labour myself. To that end I fetched a large syringe out of the surgeon's instrument case, and in the piston of it made an opening in which I fixed a couple of plugs. I thus obtained an air-pump, which, although not perfect, would serve my purpose. When I drew out the piston, the air passed between the two plugs in the cylinder; and when I pushed the piston in again, the lower plug opened into the nozzle of the syringe, and allowed the compressed air to pass out with tremendous force.

When the boys—who had awaited patiently, but not in the best of humours, the completion of my preparations for skinning the animals—saw me marching off with my surgical weapon under my arm, like a field-marshal with his baton, they burst into loud laughter, and asked me what I intended to do with an instrument which seemed to be altogether out of place at such a time.

The only reply I gave them was to lay hold of the kangaroo, hang up by the hind-legs, and make an incision in its skin, into which I passed the nose of the syringe, and proceeded to pump air with all my might.

Gradually the animal was blown out of all proportions, and

became twice its natural size. Still I continued to pump until I saw that, excepting in two or three places of no importance, the skin was everywhere separated from the flesh.

I then handed the kangaroo over to the astonished boys, to finish the work so near completion.

'Wonderful!' cried Jack.

'Father must be a conjurer!' added Francis.

'Rather an odd-looking magic staff for a conjurer,' muttered Ernest under his breath.

'But how does the air remove the skin?' asked Jack.

'Very simply,' said I, 'and there is not a savage tribe which is not well acquainted with this method of inflation, though I suppose they know nothing about the cellular tissue. Between the skin and the flesh there are thousands of little vecisles which contain a fatty substance. If these are filled with air they dilate and burst, and the skin, deprived of its adherent qualities, detaches itself naturally. Thus the grand secret is explained.'

I again set to work with my syringe, and my task progressed rapidly; but as we had a large number of animals to skin, I determined to set apart a whole day for the purpose.

The next day, early in the morning, we started off to cut down the tree which I had marked out for destruction near Falcon-nest. We took with us our truck, a good supply of ropes, and the necessary tools.

On the way thither, I showed the boys the devastation committed by the pigs, and the place where they had recieved their punishment.

Arrived at the tree, I told Jack to climb up and cut off the branches, which in their fall rested upon neighbouring boughs. He also, by my instruction, fastened some ropes to the upper part of the trunk, which ropes were carried out to a distance that left us nothing to fear if the tree should happen to fall in a direction contrary to that which we intended.

These preparations made, we took a strong saw and cut two large notches in the lower end of the trunk, one on each side, and one a little higher up than the other. Then we all pulled vigorously at the rope. The tree cracked, tottered, and fell, without misadventure of any sort. Once upon the ground, the trunk and the principal branches were sawn into lengths of about four feet. The remainder, destined to become firewood, was left where it was to dry.

When one is not a woodman by trade, one advances very slowly with this kind of labour. What I have just recounted took us nearly two days to accomplish. But I achieved what I desired. I found myself in possession of exactly the kind of timber which I required to construct my pounding-mill according to the best models.

The mill finished, we tested its powers with some rice, which at the end of a day was completely braised, and, to the general satisfaction, fit for use without further preparation. The operation was a little more lengthy than would have been the case with a grinding-mill; but it had succeeded, and that was the essential thing to be considered.

While surveying the working of the mill, I remarked that our domestic poultry, on their return from a neighbouring field to which they had made their way with unusual haste, had very full crops, and appeared to be altogether in a state of high satisfaction. At first I wondered who could have been thoughtless enough to give the fowls so much of the grain, which it was our duty to economise till we were able to grow more. But soon the secret was revealed. On going in the direction whence the fowls had come, I found that the acre of land we had sown only four or five months since was covered with an abundant growth of ripe corn. I concluded therefrom that for the future we should be able to reckon upon two harvests a year.

This was certainly a satisfactory discovery. Nevertheless ,it caused us some embarrassment, because the unexpected labour it involved coincided with the annual visit of the herrings and the dog-fish. Our good housewife was even more troubled than I was. She saw not how it was possible that we could attend to our fisheries and our harvest, or salt down the herrings and gather in corn, at one and the same time. Notwithstanding, she never for an instant failed in gratitude to the Divine Giver of all our wealth.

'Truly,' she said, 'Good is good above all that we can ask or think! We have never been so rich in all our lives before.'

'I am not so sure about that,' I said laughingly. 'We have not a penny in hard cash to bless ourselves with.'

'Well,' said Jack, 'what do we want with money here? I never think of it now. Do you not remember, father, how, when you used to give us half-pence for pocket money once a week, we jumped for joy every time we received them? Why, we should not care now for a bushel of sovereigns.'

So abundant were our riches that my wife lost her head in the mere contemplation of them; speaking of fishing for rice and harvesting dog-fish, of salting down potatoes and reaping herrings.

I begged her not to harass herself, but to rest assured that the good God who had given us all this profusion would not neglect to provide us with the means of appropriating it to our needs.

I determined—rather in opposition to her wishes, I think—to begin upon the grain, and cut it in the Italian method, which, although not nearly so economical as other methods, is far more expeditious; and expedition in our case was true economy. I proposed, after that, to leave the potatoes and tapioca, which I judged would not hurt for a few days in the ground, while we proceeded with our herring fisheries.

Without delay, therefore—in order that we might commence our harvest on the following morning—I cleared a piece of ground in a sheltered spot near the field, where we could place the grain to be trodden out by our oxen. We adopted this old-fashioned plan of threshing, as being the one involving least labour; but we were prepared, after the oxen had done their best, to complete the work ourselves with such extemporised flails as we could command.

The next morning, armed with our sickles, we set out for the field which we were about to reap, and at once began work. Our plan—the Italian one—was to lay hold of as many ears as we could with the left hand, and cut them off with the right, taking away as little straw as possible, and throwing away the decapitated ears into a basket. The method was a new one, and, like everything that was new to them, pleased the youngsters immensely— so much so that when evening came the whole field was reaped, and the basket, filled, emptied, and refilled all day long, was pronounced to have done its work well.

'Fine economy, in truth!' exclaimed my wife with some asperity as she saw us begin our work. 'All the short ears and all the straw remain in the stubble!'

'My dear wife,' I replied, 'you are mistaken in your ideas of economy. The Italian is not so foolish as you suppose him to be. That which you fancy he wastes is not lost: in place of eating, he drinks it.'

'I never heard a better than that!' returned my wife. 'How can one "drink" ears of grain and straw? Heavy work for the throat, I should think!'

'The Italian,' I replied, 'drinks it after a manner. His soil being better fitted for husbandry than for the support of cattle, there is a dearth of pasturage there. This leads him to cut his corn as we have done. At the end of a few days—a week or two, perhaps—the herbage begins to grow up among the stubble until together they form a thick mass. Then the Italian mows it close to the earth, and uses it for forage in the winter-time. What the straw wants in succulence is furnished by the herbage and the short ears of corn, which thus contribute largely to the abundant yield of milk for which the cows of Italy are famous. This is the whole mystery.'

My wife allowed herself to be persuaded of the excellence of this method of reaping, although in her heart she protested, in honour of just principles, against the anti-economic expedient.

It was now necessary to proceed to the threshing of our corn. This was a rare occupation for the boys, who, astride of their favourite animals, trod out the corn wonderfully.

My wife remarked that this celebrated Italian method not only wasted a third of the standing corn, but allowed the animals to appropriate to themselves a tithe of it while engaged in the process of treading it out; and she desired me to muzzle them.

I reminded her of the Divine command: 'Thou shalt not muzzle the ox when he treadeth out the corn.'

This quotation removed her scruples at once. I may add that when we had done threshing we had a hundred measures of wheat and maize, and nearly the same quantity of barley, to stow away in our granary in the grotto.

In order to obtain a second harvest, it was necessary to begin sowing again at once. In this operation we adopted the Swiss method—that, namely, of changing the crop periodically. We had just reaped English wheat, maize, and barley, we now sowed spelt or German wheat, rye, and oats.

Before we had finished our task the shoal of herring arrived and we were in a great strait as to what course to pursue.

My wife suggested that we should not take more than a couple of barrels of them, and we followed her advice. As to the dog-fish, we were able to take as many as usual, because we only wanted their skins, and my pneumatic instrument helped us to these much more quickly than we had been able to get them before.

CHAPTER XXXVII

Trial of the cajack—disappearance of Fritz—the walrus—a storm—anxieties concerning Fritz—saved!—the drawbridge—the salt-lick—a longer expedition

The cajack had been ready to put to sea a long time, and Fritz, who had been appointed captain of it, was consumed by the desire to approve his title.

The most important of our labours being now at an end, we resolved to give him the opportunity he sought of distinguishing himself.

On the appointed day we all assembled upon the shore. Fritz desired to be solemnly invested with his command before embarking. Each of us, therefore, hastened to perform the office of valet, helping to dress and arm him for his expedition. Thus clad, our young Greenlander seized his paddle and harpoons, and cast a look of sublime defiance towards any invisible monsters of the deep that might be disposed to question his sovereignty of the seas. Then, like another Neptune, he installed himself in his vessel.

Assuming the requisite kneeling posture in the central opening of the cajack, he fastened his sea-dog-skin dress around the edge of it, so as to exclude the outer air, and, with his harpoons placed in their supports to the right and left of him, proceeded to inflate himself until he resembled in form a gigantic frog.

Ernest and Jack, with a strong rope, drew the vessel down the beach, while Francis pushed it behind; and Fritz set up a song of triumph on thus seeing himself abandoned to the mercy of the waves.

I was proud to see the ease and grace with which he managed his canoe, and partook of the gaiety of the three boys who remained with me. Our laughter formed an admirable chorus to Fritz's improvised song.

My wife, on the contrary, stood looking on seriously, if not sadly. She thought only of the perils which the eldest child of her bosom was about to encounter.

To reassure her, I was obliged, in spite of my own confidence in the skill of my son, to get the pirogue ready for sea, and promise to follow him to render assistance should he need it.

After riding at its ease upon the tranquil waters of our little bay for a few moments, the cajack began its trial evolutions. With the assistance of its paddle, Fritz first sent it swiftly ahead, cleaving the waters as it went. Then he inclined it to the right, then to the left. At last, to show that he could not be submerged, he completely capsized it, to the great fright of his mother and the great delight of his three brothers.

Fritz, excited beyond his wont by our plaudits, and not hearing the exclamations and appeals of his mother, who every moment expected some catastrophe, directed his vessel into the current at the mouth of Jackal River, which, before he had time to reconnoitre, carried him swiftly out into the open sea.

This imprudent act alarmed me. I embarked in all haste in the pirogue, and, accompanied by Jack and Ernest, set out in pursuit of the fugitive, praying my wife to have no fear, for that I should soon overtake Fritz, and would scold him roundly for his thoughtlessness.

By this time he had completely disappeared, and it was only by passing out of Deliverance Bay into open sea that we could hope to discover his whereabouts.

Our canoe glided swiftly away, under the impulsion of our six oars, skimming over the waves like a sea-mew.

We were not long in reaching the shallows where the vessel which brought us to these parts had been wrecked, and where I supposed the current had carried my eldest son. There were sunken rocks there, and others which lifted their heads out of the sea, and upon these the waves broke heavily in foam and spray—portending, as I thought, rough weather.

In searching among the shallows for a place where we could rest in security upon our oars for a time, we found ourselves in a labyrinth of rocks, which completely shut out the horizon on all hands.

We wandered backwards and forwards in this species of archipelago for some time, unable to find a way out, but impatient to do so, in order to get sight of the dear, but imprudent, fugitive.

Suddenly, at a considerable distance, I saw a thin wreath of smoke curling upwards, followed, at the end of a second or two, by a feeble noise which I recognised as the far-off report of a gun.

'There is Fritz!' I cried, with a joyousness which it is impossible to set down in word.

'Where? Where?' asked Ernest and Jack, looking impatiently in every direction.

At the same moment I heard another report like the first.

I fired one of my pistols, and it was replied to by a third report.

I assured my boys that Fritz was not more than a quarter of a league from us, and bade them lay on to their oars with a will.

A few minutes later we came up with the fugitive.

After Fritz had shown us a sea-cow, or sea-horse—as it is indifferently the custom to term the walrus—which he had just killed, and which lay dead upon a neighbouring fragment of rock, I gravely reproached him for the anxiety into which he had plunged all of us, and especially his mother, by his imprudence.

He excused himself by throwing all the blame upon the current, which he said had carried him away against his will. He passed by in silence any desire he might have had to try his cajack and his harpoons in the open sea.

I forgave him frankly, being only too happy to bring him safe and sound home to his mother; and, after removing from the walrus its head and tusks, as hunting ornaments for the cajack, we set out to return to port, Fritz leading the way.

On the voyage, Ernest asked me upon what I had based my calculation when, after the third report of Fritz's pistol, I had affirmed that he could not be more than a quarter of a league away.

'We are taught by the science of physics,' I said, 'that light travels at the rate of seventy thousand miles a second. Sound, on the contrary, does not travel more than three hundred and fifty yards a second. Having counted three seconds between the time that I saw the smoke of Fritz's pistol and the time that I heard the report of it, I concluded that he must be something over a thousand yards away, and a thousand yards is about a quarter of a league.'

'Has the same kind of calculation been applied to the light of the stars?' asked Ernest.

'Without doubt,' I replied. 'It takes eight minutes, seven seconds and a half for the light of the sun to reach the earth, and there exist fixed stars so far distant from us that it takes thousands of years for the light from them to reach us. If, for instance, one of them were suddenly to cease shining today, we should see its light for thousands of years to come.'

'What an abyss is science!' said Ernest musingly; 'and what a glorious thing it would be to know everything!'

'It is a glorious thing to know what we do,' I replied, 'and it is still more glorious to strive by study to know more. But the secret of all knowledge rests with God alone.'

In conversing in this wise, we had not travelled a third of the distance towards land when the storm which I expected, but did not think was so near, suddenly burst upon us with indescribable fury.

Unhappily Fritz was so far in advance of us that, what with the roaring of the winds and the waves, and the terrible torrents of rain which poured down from the overhanging clouds, we could give him no signal to come on board our safer craft. My heart was torn with an anguish which I will not attempt to describe. But I had to watch over the fate of others no less dear to me; and

I ordered the boys to at once put on their swimming jackets and attach themselves to the canoe with straps, in order that, in case of our being capsized, they might not be carried away by the waves.

I afterwards took the same precautions myself, and we abandoned ourselves to the mercy of Heaven.

The storm increased every minute. The waves rolled up mountains high, obscuring even the heavens with their foaming tops, and then fell like menacing avalanches, mingling their glistening facets with sinister glare of the lightning.

Moment by moment we feared that we should be swallowed up in the large abysses that opened beneath our frail craft. Moment by moment we found ourselves mounting with terror the glassy slopes of the enormous valleys that yawned before us.

Happily our canoe sustained bravely the clash of the waves, riding now upon their crests, now in their huge crevasses, so lightly and easily that I was even tempted to try to direct its course with the rudder. But in this I very naturally failed.

The agonies of our own situation were as nothing compared to those I experienced concerning my unhappy son, who was the prime cause of our being brought into danger.

The tempest was not likely to deal with him less roughly than with us, and, in spite of the superior swiftness of his cajack, I dared not hope that he had reached the shore before it came on.

What had become of my first-born? Now I imagined him dashed with his frail bark upon some rock, and lying there broken and bleeding. Now I fancied him buried for ever in the depths of the sea, and become prey to the very monsters against which he had launched his playful defiance.

My heart suffered an age of anguish; but my lips were silent. I dared not alarm the two dear children of whom I still had charge, and who, perhaps, had fewer fears than I had, owing to the holy and ingenuous confidence with which my presence inspired them.

They placed their trust in me: I placed mine in the Divine Ruler of the seas.

I was altogether lost in this painful train of thought, when, through the dread obscurity that surrounded us, and in spite of the mountainous waves that reared themselves on every hand, I perceived that we were near the entrance of Deliverance Bay.

I now took an oar myself, and we all worked with so much energy that in a few minutes we found ourselves in the well-known avenue of rocks which, after our disastrous wreck upon the shallows we had just visited, led us to our deliverance long ago.

We were saved! And I was once more able to pour out my heartfelt thanks to God for an almost unhoped-for escape from the perils of the merciless sea.

How can I express the ecstasy of joy with which I at length beheld upon the shore my wife and little Francis, and, above all, my dear boy Fritz, kneeling together and fervently praying that we might be restored to them out of the jaws of the great deep which seemed ready to swallow us up!

I shall not attempt to depict the overflowing joy with which we were received, nor that with which we ourselves once more embraced the dear ones whom we had hardly hoped to see again. My wife and I were so happy to see the children reunited, that we thought not for a moment of reproving Fritz for his disastrous imprudence.

After offering together our warmest thanks to our Heavenly Father for this new proof of His tender care over us, we partook of a comforting repast, prepared for us by our excellent housewife, and then went out to draw the pirogue and the cajack, which had served us so well, up the beach.

This heavy and unexpected rain had so swollen the streams which poured down from among the rocks, that in several places, and especially at Falcon-nest, the floods were out and did damage which required immediate attention. Jackal River rose to so great a height that it almost carried away our bridge, and committed other ravages no less serious.

The reparation of these injuries, and divers other employments, such as salmon and sturgeon fishing (for which the season had again come round), occupied us for several days, and time flowed by so peasantly that we well-nigh forgot the terror we had undergone during our adventure upon the open sea.

One night, when the moon was shining clearly, I was awakened by the barking of the dogs, responded to by strange growling sounds at a distance. Fancying that the jackals had taken in into their heads to make another raid upon us, I got up in great haste, armed myself with my gun, and thrust my head through the upper part of the door, which we always left open during the summer to allow the fresh air to circulate through the house, I looked on this side, on that, and straight before me, to find out what was the matter, when I heard the voice of Fritz.

'Father,' he asked, 'are you up?'

'Yes,' I replied. 'Get up too, and come with me.'

Fritz was soon by my side, and we set out in the direction whence the sound of the tumult proceeded, to discover what occasioned it.

We found that our dogs were engaged in repulsing an invasion of pigs.

As nearly as I could make out, they were some of our own brood which had become wild; and I doubted not that they had made their way across Jackal Bridge, the planks of which the boys had probably neglected to take up, as it had been our invariable custom to do nightly since the visit of the boa.

We had some difficulty in untying the dogs, and our enemies got the start of us. In pursuing them to the other side of the stream, I saw that it was not by the negligence of the boys that the marauders had been enabled to cross over, but by their own cunning. They had crept along the three beams which formed the main support of the bridge, and which therefore could not be removed.

Seeing this, I determined on the spot to turn our bridge of planks into a drawbridge; and next morning I and my boys commenced operations with that view.

We obtained two strong posts, which we fixed in the ground on the grotto side of the river, strengthening them above and below with stout cross-beams. A number of steps were placed across, by which we could easily reach the top. Here we fixed a pulley, over which we threw a rope, whose far end was fastened to an iron ring, fixed securely in the timbers at the other extremity of the bridge. A balancing weight or plyer was next extemporised, and, with very little exertion, we were able to lift up the whole bridge, and retain it on one side of the water till we required to use it again.

We were thus, henceforth, completely sheltered from attacks like those which had put us in a commotion on the night of which I have spoken.

During the first few days which followed the completion of the bridge, the boys did little else but lower and raise it, or climb to the top of its posts, whence they could see on the other side of the river herds of antelopes and gazelles, which vanished as soon as they perceived that they were watched.

'What a pity, father,' said Fritz one day, 'that these graceful creatures cannot be tamed! It would be delightful to see them going and coming amongst us like our other domestic animals, without being frightened by the noise and bustle of our daily labours.'

'Yes,' said Ernest, 'we ought to establish here a buffalo-lick like there is in Georgia, the gazelles would then tame themselves.'

'What is this buffalo-lick of which Ernest speaks?' asked Fritz.

'It is a spot determined by nature,' I said, 'for the capture of certain animals. There is one in New Georgia, between the Savannah River and the Alleghenies. It is not more than three acres in extent, and its peculiarity is that the soil is mixed with a kind of marl, or saltish earth, which wild and even tame ruminant animals, and particularly the buffalo, take great pleasure in licking—so much so that large cavities are the result of their visits. Hence places of this kind are called buffalo-licks. In certain countries of Europe, also, as upon our own native mountains, artificial licks have been established, and are called "salt-licks".'

'Oh, let us make a salt-lick!' exclaimed the boys, dancing with joy at the thought of being able to catch without trouble every variety of deer, antelope, goat, gazelle, and buffalo.

'Willingly,' I replied, 'if it will please you. With our pipe-clay we ought to be able to lay an excellent bait. Let us go, then, and get a fresh supply of this earth, and at the same time we will bring in some large bamboos, which are necessary to execute a project which I have in my head.'

My children consulted each other apart for a few moments.

'Father,' said Fritz at length, 'my brothers and I have long had it in our minds to make another expedition, if we can get your consent. We wish to visit Forest Grange and Prospect Hill, and to push our explorations both to the right and left of this route. What do you say?'

All eyes were fixed on me, and sparkling with desire.

'If you wish it, my dear boys,' I said. 'I ask nothing better. The eye of the master has been lacking at our farmery for a long time.'

'Let us go! Let us go!' they cried.

'In that case,' said Fritz, 'I will at once prepare some pemmican for the journey, if mamma will have the goodness to give me some pieces of bear's flesh.'

'Pemmican!' said my wife. 'What barbarous dish is that?'

'It is,' said Fritz,' a preparation of bear's and deer's flesh, cut into small pieces and pounded into a lump, which the fur-dealers of Canada carry with them during their long excursions into the interior of their country. There is nothing like it for portability and nourishment combined. It is a very substantial food, and occupies a very small space. So, dear mother, as we are about to undertake a lengthy expedition, please give us some bear's flesh, and I will see to the making of the pemmican.'

Although my wife was less favourable than ever to excursions which removed her husband and the children from her, she, as usual, allowed herself to be persuaded of the necessity of the expedition, and even went so far as to assist Fritz in the preparation of the 'barbarous dish'.

While this was going on, the other children busied themselves in preparing their arms and outfit, and, from their more than ordinary care and activity in the matter, I concluded that they placed a very high value upon the importance of the expedition they were about to undertake.

The old truck, turned into a wagon by the addition of a couple of cannon-wheels, was loaded with bags and baskets of all kinds, with the tent, and with the cajack.

Master Jack, thinking he was not seen by me, added a few pigeons to our supply of pemmican, with the object, I suppose, of varying his food a little when he grew tired of pounded bear's flesh.

I affected not to be conscious of the innocent trick, and hastened the preparations for our departure.

CHAPTER XXXVIII

Expedition to Forest Grange—the hyena—the carrier-pigeon—Fritz's letter—the black swan—the royal heron—the tapir—the cranes—the bird of paradise—more ravages by monkeys—how they were punished—serious devastation by huge beasts

On the morning of the day fixed for the setting out of the expedition, my wife declined, much to my surprise, to take part in it, saying that she preferred repose for a time. Ernest also, after many warm discussions with his brothers, declared that he was equally in need of rest, and should stay at home with his mother.

Seeing our project thus modified, I determined to let the three boys undertake the expedition alone while I remained at Rockhouse, and, with the assistance of Ernest, tried my hand at the construction of a sugar-press.

Our three young hunters made their adieux, and set out gaily, with a notable provision of good wishes, exhortations, councils, and advice.

I will not weary the reader with the details of my attempt at making a sugar-press. It differed so little from an ordinary sugar-mill that it is not worth describing. I prefer to replace a dry recital of my own with a summary of a far more picturesque one, made to me by my three adventurous sons when the expedition was over.

After leaving us they pushed swiftly on to Forest Grange, where they had determined to remain during the first and following days.

On approaching the farmery they were not a little surprised to hear a succession of short and sharp bursts of what seemed to be human laughter. Their oxen and their dogs showed considerable alarm; while Jack's ostrich, a creature singularly impressionable—I might almost say very nervous by nature—took fright and bolted with its young rider on its back, in the direction of Forest Grange River.

The lugubrious bursts of laughter which had thrown the whole caravan into confusion were repeated, and the oxen, more and more alarmed, made wild attempts to turn back again. The dogs were not less terrified.

Fritz and his brother dismounted to discover the cause of this panic; and while the former tried to calm the terror of the animals, the latter advanced cautiously through the copse to take further observations. He was simply to do this, his brother instructing him to return at once in case of encountering any peril.

Little Francis, although much daunted by the terrible laughter which still broke forth from time to time, pushed on with stealthy steps. His gun was held in readiness to fire, and in a low voice he encouraged the dogs, who seemed but little disposed to follow him.

In the course of a few minutes, on softly pulling aside a bush, he saw, some eighty paces ahead of him, a huge hyena in the act of devouring a ram which it had just killed.

On catching sight of the young hunter, the hyena repeated for the fourth or fifth time—without, however, for one instant relinquishing its hold upon its victim—the weird bursts of laughter which the boys had previously heard.

Francis, although he fully comprehended the risk of the act, did not hesitate to at once fire at the beast. His ball smashed one of its fore-feet and passed thence into its chest, leaving a large gaping wound.

Fritz, after having succeeded—but not without considerable trouble—in restraining the backward course of the oxen, fastened them securely to a couple of trees, and hastened to the help of his brother, who, however, had now no need of his assistance.

The two dogs, who from a state of the most incomprehensible timidity had passed to a condition of extreme fury, had flung themselves upon the prostrate enemy.

Fritz, therefore, dared not fire for fear of shooting Fawn or Brown, who, happily, in a short time made themselves masters of the field of battle. Though the hyena was dead, and they had torn from him his prey, they still stood over him menacingly, ears erect, teeth displayed, and eyes sparkling with malice.

A short time afterwards, Jack rejoined his brothers with his ostrich, which had become more docile since the cessation of the horrible laughter that had excited it so much.

The three boys then set out for Forest Grange, carrying their booty with them upon the truck. They resolved to skin the beast during their sojourn at the farmery.

We who remained at Rock-house, while sitting under the sheltering foliage of the veranda when the labours of the day were ended, found little else to talk about beyond the probable course taken by the three adventurous young travellers.

My wife from time to time gave indications of her motherly apprehension of dangers.

I questioned Ernest about certain mysterious whisperings which I had heard among the boys when the caravan set out.

At first he replied only in words that were somewhat enigmatic, but towards the end of our supper he condescended to observe: 'Pray calm yourself, dear mother; and you also, dear father. I hope to be able tomorrow to give you satisfactory tidings of our three travellers.'

'How so?' I asked. 'You do not intend to join them, surely? It will be very inconvenient to me if you do, for I want your assistance particulalry.'

'I shall not leave you, dear father,' he said with a smile; 'but, nevertheless, I promise that tomorrow you shall have news of the wanderers. Who knows? I shall dream perhaps of what they have been doing today, and be able to tell you where they are.'

'What is that?' I exclaimed, interrupting the young dreamer as something flew past me. 'It is a belated pigeon, I suppose, entering the dove-cot. I wonder where it has been. It is too dark to see whether it is one of our own brood or a stranger which has mistaken its roosting-place.'

'Shut down the trap! Shut down the trap!' cried Ernest excitedly. 'Who knows but it may be a carrier with news from Sydney? Were you not speaking today, father, of the likelihood of our being in the neighbourhood of the colony of which that is the capital? If the pigeon which has just entered should really turn out to be a courier thence, we might use it to open up a correspondence with New South Wales.'

'I could heartily desire that it might be so, my dear child.' I replied sadly; 'but it would be without the remotest hope that the desire would be realised. But it grows late: let us to bed. The first thing tomorrow morning, you can, if you so wish it, go and consult your good courier from Sydney, and read to us the news which you hope to find under its wing. In the meantime do not dream too wildly while you are asleep tonight.'

The next morning, rising much earlier than was usual with him, Ernest went out to the dove-cot, and afterwards spent some time in the library.

As his mother and I were sitting down to breakfast, we saw him coming gravely towards us, bowing as he approached. Then, with an air of mock dignity, he presented us with a paper, folded and sealed in the form of a government dispatch.

'To you, most noble owners of this domain,' he said, 'the humble Postmaster of Rock-house presents his respectful compliments, and begs that you will not too severely condemn him for delaying until now to present you with the dispatches from Forest Grange and Sydney. The post arrived last night, but, owing to circumstances beyond his own control, your devoted servant was not permitted to open the bag until this morning.'

My wife and I greeted this solemn exordium with a hearty burst of laughter; and, scenting beneath it some pleasantry imagined by Ernest to soften down his mother's fears concerning the absence of her three dear boys, I entered willingly into the humour of the thing.

In a precisely similar tone of voice and solemnity of accent, I said: 'Accept, Mr. Postmaster, we pray you, our pardon and the assurance of our high esteem both for yourself and your office; and let us know, without further delay, what dispatches you have for us from Sydney, our capital. Nay, inasmuch as we are fatigued with the burden of our royal duties, read, we command you, that which our trusty and well-beloved Secretary of State has to communicate touching the welfare of our subjects in that part of our dominions.'

Deliberately unfolding his paper. Ernest again saluted us, and in a clear, measured voice proceeded to read as follows:

'THE GOVERNOR-GENERAL OF NEW SOUTH WALES, TO HIS EX-
CELLENCY THE GOVERNOR OF ROCK-HOUSE, FALCON-NEST,
UNDERTENT, FOREST GRANGE, SUGAR-CANE GROVE, &C, &C.,
GREETING,

'Most noble, well-beloved, and trusty Ally,

'We learn, with high displeasure, that within the week last past,
to wit, this morning, three disreputable adventurers have set out
from your Colony with the object and intention of living by
brigandage, to the no small hurt and detriment of the game, large
and small, of this Province.

'We learn also that a ferocious troop of hyenas, as destructive to
property as they are dangerous to human life, have recently made
an irruption into a certain portion of the territory under your
Government, to wit, that portion of it known by the name and
style of Forest Grange, and have already caused considerable
damage to the flocks and herds depasturing thereabouts.

'In consequence, we pray you to advise yourself speedily of
some means whereby these disorders may be promptly suppressed,
and to take measures both for the arrest and return of the fugitive
brigands, and for maintaining the legal rights of man and the
domestic animals, as against the ravages of wild beasts.

'Accept, most noble, well-beloved, and trusty Ally, the assurance
of my highest consideration and esteem.

'Given at Sydney, New South Wales, this 12th of the present
month, in the years 34 of the Colony.

'(Signed) PHILLIP PHILLIPSON.

'GOVERNOR'

His reading achieved, Ernest burst into loud laughter, and
began dancing so wildly that a small note escaped from his pocket
and fell to the ground. I ran to pick it up, but Ernest was before
me.

'This,' said he, 'is a private letter from Forest Grange. Nevertheless, if you desire it, I will give your highnesses the contents of it.
It may not be so pompously nor so elegantly worded, perhaps,
but I fancy it contains more truth than the official dispatch of the
good Sir Phillip Phillipson, who, so far as I can judge, seems to
have lent too ready an ear to mere exaggerated rumours concerning
the condition of this colony.'

'You are giving us a strange enigma to solve,' I said. 'Did Fritz,
before he set out, hand you a letter for me with instructions not
to deliver it till he was far upon his journey? Because if—'

'No, dear father,' replied Ernest, who saw that his mother was
growing anxious. 'The truth is, that this note which I hold in my
hand was brought last night by the belated pigeon that you saw
enter the dove-cot, and I should have read it to you last night had
I been able to get at it in the dark. These are the contents of it,
word for word:

' "Well-beloved Parents and dear Ernest,

' "An enormous hyena killed two of our lambs and a ram. Francis behaved gloriously. He knocked it over with a shot which struck it full in the breast. The dogs finished it. We have passed the remainder of the day skinning it. It is a magnificent skin. Our pemmican is wretched stuff. Mother was quite right in showing her contempt of my new-fangled cookery.

' "Yours affectionately,
' "Fritz

' "Forest Grange, the 12th instant." '

'A true hunter's letter!' I said, laughing. 'And Heaven be praised that my little Francis was able to achieve so easy a victory over his terrible enemy! But how, I wonder, could the creature have found an entrance into our farmery?'

'I pray they may be prudent!' murmured my wife, as she thought of the three boys exposed to dangers so serious at a time when they were so far away from us.

She desired that we should at once set out to join them, and, if necessary, bring them home again by main force. But while, on the one hand, we had only very scanty news, which might be supplemented by a letter dispatch sent by the same means, there was, on the other hand, every probability that we should miss them on the road if we set out to join them. We therefore determined to stay where we were, for that day at least.

Towards sunset a second carrier-pigeon entered the dove-cot. Ernest at once caught it, and brought us the following note:

'All well during the night. Splendid morning. A cruise on Forest Grange Lake in the cajack. Capture of black swan, royal heron, cranes, and black diver-ducks. Unknown animal, escaped. To Prospect Hill tomorrow. Adieu to all.

'Fritz, Jack, Francis'

This note reassured us. It showed, at all events, that no other hyena had put in an appearance. As to its enigmatical details, they were explained by the young adventurers after the expedition.

They had made up their minds to explore Forest Grange Lake, and especially those parts of it which could not be approached from the land because of the depth of the mud. To that end Fritz had embarked in his cajack and cruised round, while his brothers followed him along the shore behind the reed-beds. Wherever Fritz had indicated a spot to which he wished to return, Jack and Francis had set up a tall bamboo-cane to serve as a landmark.

In setting out upon his explorations, Fritz had determined, if possible, to take some black swans alive. Arming himself, therefore, with a long bamboo, furnished at its ends with a wire noose, he contrived to approach three young ones of the species, which, being less wild than the older ones, suffered themselves to be taken without much trouble. Brought living to Rock-house, the feathered prisoners, with their shining black plumage and brilliant red beaks, became handsome ornaments to the glassy waters of Deliverance Bay.

Scarcely had the black swans been secured, when a royal heron made its way out of the reeds. Fritz at once cast a lasso, which caught his prey by the neck. The noble bird made a desperate struggle to escape, flapping its wings, kicking with its long legs, and endeavouring to break asunder the rope with its beak. So great was its strength that Fritz had to run his cajack aground before he could take it. Once unable to draw the boat after it, the bird fell half strangled and became an easy prey to the determined young hunter. Tying its wings and legs, and bandaging its eyes, he brought it home alive.

While the three brothers were standing on the bank of the lake, admiring their captures, a large quadruped came out of the marsh, hissing loudly, and so disconcerting them that they did not think to fire at it till it was out of range. By the description they gave of it afterwards, I recognised it as the tapir or ant-eater, a sort of incomplete elephant, perfectly harmless, which inhabits the banks of the large rivers of South America. Fritz went in pursuit of it while his brothers remained behind to take charge of the black swans and the heron.

As Jack and Francis were passing by the rice-field they saw a large flock of cranes flying overhead, and sent a few arrows among them. Four or five fell, and among them were two of the species *Numidian demoiselle*.

It was a splendid take of game; and Fritz, who at that moment returned to his brothers without having captured his intended prey, manifested some little pique. So much was he put out, that on reaching the farmery he put his eagle on his shoulder and strayed away into the guava-wood, to take his revenge on the first animal that crossed his path.

He had walked on about a quarter of an hour, when the dogs put up a covey of birds resembling the English pheasant. They were soon scattered far and wide among the trees. The eagle, however, on being let loose, took one of them, while Fritz brought down another with his gun. They were magnificent creatures, with a brilliant tuft on the top of the head, and long-flowing tails. Fritz's capture was worthy to compare with his brothers': he had taken two birds of paradise.

The dinner hour found all three of the brothers reassembled, and talking of their several exploits. They dined with the best possible appetite off a peccary ham, potatoes roasted among the embers of a wood fire, the fruit of the guava, and some cinnamon apples. As to the pemmican, they found it so little to their taste that they gave it to the dogs, who enjoyed it immensely.

The evening was employed in procuring a supply of cotton and rice, which they proposed to take with them to Prospect Hill, on their journey thither next day. Also, for the execution of a project they had conceived, they collected an abundant stock of coco-nuts and palm-tree wine, cutting down the trees to get at the fruit, after the manner of the Caribbeans. I reproved them for this act of gross wastefulness when they told me of it, but they excused themselves by saying that for every tree cut down they had taken care to plant eight or ten coco-nuts.

I shall here transcribe, as nearly as possible in his own words, the account Fritz gave us of the journey he made with his brothers to the hut at Prospect Hill, which they reached at noon on the day after their exploration of the lake.

'Scarcely had we entered the little pine-wood,' said he, 'when we were furiously attacked by a horde of monkeys, who sat among the branches of the trees, chattering, grinding their teeth, and literally raining down pine-cones upon us. Although the fruit was for the most part ripe, the quantity of it became very embarrassing, and in order to put and end to the attack, we fired a few shots at random. To our great regret, four or five of our aggressors fell dead at our feet. Their numerous comrades, justly alarmed at our method of rewarding their ill-timed pleasantries, became immediately silent and invisible.

'In passing through Sugar-cane Grove, I was astonished to find that the new growth, which had reached a height of eight or ten feet, was beaten down and broken as if a fierce storm of hail had fallen upon it.

'At length we got to Prospect Hill, where, after attending to our beasts and unloading our spoils, we made an inspection of the place. You will be sorry to hear it, dear father, but not more sorry than I am to have it to tell—the abominable monkeys have committed even worse ravages here than they did at Forest Grange: everything is laid waste; we even had to rebuild the little hut before we could inhabit it for the night.

'Before we set out we had feared something of the kind, and were prepared to visit the monkeys with condign punishment. To that end we, in the evening, filled a number of gourd-vessels and coco-nut shells with fresh goat's milk, palm-tree wine, and pounded millet. Into each of them we poured a few drops of a poisonous drug which Ernest had prepared for us, at my request, and which we carried in a gourd-bottle. This done, we hung our deadly chalices to the branches of the neighbouring trees, and went to bed upon our bags of cotton.

'In spite of our fatigue, we found it almost impossible to sleep. At first we were disturbed by the cries of strange animals and the barking of our dogs, and then by the invasion of monkeys, who, however, soon found out and lapped up with avidity the choice repast we had prepared for them.

'At daybreak the next morning, curious to know what had passed during the night, we got up and went abroad. We were astonished to witness the effects of our essay in toxicology. You may rest quite satisfied: I will undertake to say that there is not a living monkey remaining for two leagues round Prospect Hill. Nor do I think it likely that a fresh colony will establish itself to partake of the feast with which we are prepared to provide them. Seeing the terrible destruction the monkeys had wrought, we did not think you would reprove us for our wholesale slaughter, which I assure you left no traces whatever upon our own consciences.

'It was now that we sent you our third carrier-pigeon, with a dispatch penned by Jack in a style pompous and altogether Oriental, giving you an account of our grotesque expedition, and at the same time news of our intended return.'

I here take up the narrative myself.

The letter of which Fritz spoke just above quite reassured us as to the safety of our three young hunters. But shortly after dinner on the fourth day, a fourth carrier-pigeon arrived, bringing the following letter:

'The defile is forced. As far as Sugar-cane Grove everything is laid waste. The new growth of sugar is pulled up, broken down, trampled upon, destroyed. Numberless and enormous footprints of huge beasts are seen in the soil. Hasten, dear father, to our help. We dare not go forward nor retire; and although quite safe at present, we know not how to prepare for a danger of which we know not the gravity nor the quarter from which it may menace us.'

This news was of a totally different character from any that had preceded it, and you may be sure I did not waste time in idle comments upon it.

Without the least delay, I saddled the onager, and, telling my wife and Ernest to follow me next day to the defile, I set out at a gallop.

CHAPTER XXXIX

Construction of a summer residence—the fruits of the cacao- and banana-trees—the mysterious sack—the sultan fowl—the elephants —the panthers—the amphibious monster—the biter bit—restoration of Falcon-nest—fortification of Shark Island

I accomplished in three hours a journey which ordinarily occupied six. My prompt arrival, upon which my boys had hardly ventured to count—not knowing whether the carrier-pigeon had reached us—was hailed with shouts of joy and warm embraces. Without losing a minute, I set out to survey with my own eyes the extent of the disaster of which the letter apprised me. It did not take long to convince me, much to my chagrin, that my sons had in no wise exaggerated the injury which had been done.

Devastation met my gaze on every hand. The posts which had

served to close the narrow defile between the ricks, and which we had been at so much trouble to place there, lay trampled into the soil, snapped off at the base like so many dry reeds. A neighbouring grove of trees, which we had begun to train in such a manner that they would, in the course of a few months, form a sort of Kamskatka cabin for our summer residence during the heat of the season, were torn down by the branches, and completely ruined. In the bamboo plantation all the young plants were either trampled down or devoured. But the worst part of the devastation was apparent in Sugar-cane Grove. Those of our plants which were not hopelessly trodden underfoot were either broken to pieces or half-eaten. There was nothing, even down to the hut we had used for curing flesh, which did not bear marks of the prevailing ruin.

What was the origin of this terrible devastation? Who were the prime movers in it? I had remarked on approaching the mouth of the large river in that neighbourhood, to which we had given the name of Oriental River, a number of heavy footprints, which I fancied were those of the hippopotamus. I had also remarked other footprints, smaller in size, which might be taken for those of wolves or hyenas. These tracks, however, all tended towards the water, and were not seen near the defile.

We hastily erected the tent, and got together a large quantity of wood, with which we lighted fires to protect ourselves against the attacks of wild beasts during the darkness. As you may conceive, we did not pass a very tranquil night. Fritz and I, gun in hand and ears and eyes on the alert, sat up till daylight, awaiting whatever danger might present itself.

The next day, towards noon, Ernest and his mother arrived upon the cow and the ass, which were laden with baggage, and we prepared for a lengthy sojourn in the neighbourhood. I intended, indeed, to repair all the damage that had been done, so as once more to leave everything in security.

When the re-fortification of the defile had been completed—an undertaking which occupied us for a week—I set about constructing a summer residence, after the Kamskatka fashion. I chose four fine trees whose branches interlaced each other at height of about twenty feet from the ground, and across these branches I laid a floor. The foliage formed the side walls and the roof. I devised a ladder which, while strong and convenient both for ascent and descent, could be lifted up upon the floor whenever we pleased. The aerial cabin finished, it presented a highly picturesque appearance, and served at once for a sleeping chamber, an observatory, and a fowl-house. We were henceforth in no fear about our Prospect Hill colony of poultry.

This new dwelling was unanimously called the Hermitage.

The labours I have mentioned were not our sole occupation during this period. While I was at work upon the Hermitage, and my wife was employed in her domestic duties, which were neither light nor unimportant, the boys made several excursions, each time bringing home some novel kind of booty.

For instance, Fritz returned from one of his later journeys, bringing with him two kinds of fruit which he had taken for gherkins or young cucumbers, but which in reality were the fruits of the cacao- and banana-trees. We tasted both, and I am bound to say that neither of them came up to its reputation in point of delicacy. The pips of the cacao, buried like those of the apple in a sort insipidly-sweet pap, were exquisitely bitter. The banana fruit was hardly agreeable: it had a neutral kind of flavour on the palate, something like half-rotten pears.

'It is very strange,' I said, 'that these fruits, so highly prized elsewhere, should seem to us to have a flavour so disagreeable. In the West Indies, the pulp of the cacao, well sprinkled with sugar, is held in the highest esteem, while its pips, which we find so bitter, are dried to form chocolate, pounded with sugar, and pronounced delicious. In both the Indies the fruit of the banana, whether roasted or boiled, is found to be extraordinarily agreeable to the taste. Perhaps it is because it is gathered at some particular period —before it is ripe, maybe.'

'If that is the case,' said my wife, 'I will take possession of some of these fruits and plant them in my garden. I hope that, by this means, we shall be able to find them as delicious as other people.'

'Be careful, then, my dear,' I said, 'to set the pips of the cacao in well-watered soil, and do it the moment you take them out of the pulp in which they are embedded, otherwise they will not grow. As to the bananas, they are usually reproduced by slips. If you wish it, Fritz shall get you some, and also some more cacao fruit.'

Accordingly, on the day before that appointed for our return to Rock-house, Fritz received a commission from his mother to supply her both with banana slips and cacao fruit, and from me to seek, during this last excursion of the present expedition, as many new specimens as he could find both of the animal and the vegetable kingdoms.

He set out on the river in his cajack, towing behind him a kind of Californian raft, very light but very strong. He returned in the evening laden almost to sinking point.

Jack, Ernest, and Francis ran to assist him in unloading the cargo of the little flotilla, and dividing the spoils among them, carried them up the bank to the cabin. Ernest and Francis had already set out with their loads, when Fritz, saying, 'Here is something for you,' handed over to Jack a large wet sack, in which singular movements and noises manifested themselves.

Jack hid himself behind a bush and opened the bag. At sight of its contents he uttered an exclamation of surprise, and executed a joy-dance. Then, thanking his brother for his present, he carried the sack along the bank of the river, and placed it half in the water and half out, in a retired spot where he could find it next morning.

Fritz leapt to land with a great bird, whose legs and wings were tied and its eyes bandaged, and presented it to us with an air of supreme satisfaction. It was a fine sultan fowl.

He then gave us an account of his excursion. The country all along the opposite bank of the river, he said, was extremely fertile. He had seen dense luxuriant forests, which extended from the water's edge to the foot of the mountains in the distance. He had been half stunned by the ceaseless clamour of multitudes of magnificently plumaged birds, such as guinea-fowls, turkeys, peacocks, and so on; and among them, with the assistance of his lasso, had taken the sultan fowl.

Still cruising up towards the source of the river, he passed Buffalo Plain, and a little farther on came upon a large wood of mimosa-trees on his right, where a number of elephants, in herds of ten or twenty, were tranquilly feeding upon the branches, which they broke off with their trunks and crunched up in the mass as a horse does hay. Neither the cajack nor its occupant disturbed their serenity in the least.

Higher up the same bank of the river opened into a little creek or bay, to whose margin a number of panthers had come to quench their thirst. Their lithe forms and beautiful furs imparted a picturesqueness to the scene which was as pleasing as it was novel to our young adventurer.

'I felt for an instant,' he said, 'the strongest desire to try my skill upon one of these magnificent animals; but I knew it would be imprudent to do so, and very soon my bellicose ardour melted away like snow before the sun. I was suddenly seized with a desire not less powerful than before to put about and make a speedy return. While occupied with these contending thoughts, I saw the water, about a couple of gunshots ahead of me, boil up all at once as if some large spring were welling forth, and immediately thereafter an enormous reddish-brown head hoisted itself our of the water and began to bellow a loudly in a manner which somewhat resembled the neighing of a horse. I had only time to remark during its bellowing that its huge mouth was filled with a double row of terrible teeth, which seemed to be driven into its gums like pointed stakes. Three or four strokes with my paddle removed me to a safe distance from the animal, and in three or four more I lost sight of him altogether, hoping with all my heart that he would not attempt to rejoin me lower down the stream.

'This done, I took possession of my Californian raft which I had moored in a creek while I made this brief inspection of the upper part of the river, and returned hither in all haste by the shortest way.'

Such, in brief, was the narrative of our eldest son. It gave us much to reflect upon, for it proved that we had in our neighbourhood a number of huge beasts, such as elephants, hippopotami, and panthers, which it would be very difficult to keep out of our domains if they made up their minds to pay us a visit. Apart from awakening these very natural fears, Fritz's expedition had been a highly satisfactory one, for he had brought us a large number of new specimens, both animal and vegetable.

We had none of us been idle during his absence. We had prepared everything for our departure on the following day.

In the morning, therefore, we set out. My wife and I, and the three younger boys, with our equipage, took the ordinary route. Fritz, who had previously asked my permission, went by water. Embarked in his cajack, his intention was to descend the river, double Cape Disappointment, and explore all those parts of the coast hitherto unknown to us.

We made the journey to Rock-house without misadventure. Jack, mounted upon his ostrich, went on before to lower the draw-bridge, and took advantage of the opportunity thus afforded him to deposit in the soft mud of Goose Marsh the mysterious sack which his brother had given him on the preceding evening.

As soon as we arrived at the grotto, Ernest and I, while waiting for Fritz, proceeded to unpack and dispose of our spoils. At first, the number of our feathered captives alarmed me not a little, for I foresaw that, with the poultry we already possessed, they were likely to do infinite damage among our crops whilst we were absent on hunting excursions. To obviate this inconvenience as much as possible, I determined to distribute the larger members of our feathered tribe among our marine territories.

The turkey and guinea-fowls, the cranes—whose wings were clipped a little to prevent their escape—and a few other birds were carried to Shark and Whale Islands. The black swan, the royal heron, and the Numidian demoiselles, whose pretty coquetry was very diverting, were placed in Goose Marsh. The old bustards were accorded the privilege of remaining near us. They were very grave, and were generally to be seen standing soberly by, waiting for crumbs, whenever we dined, as we often did, in the open air.

Soon after the arrival of Fritz, who paddled in about two hours before sundown, we sat down to a comfortable repast.

Dinner over, we were seated under the veranda of the grotto, chattering peacefully as our custom was, when we were startled by the roaring of some strange animal. The noise at first sounded like distant thunder. It came from the neighbourhood of Goose Marsh.

Our dogs, no less alarmed than we, bounded off barking loudly.

I leapt up at once, ordering Jack to get the guns and ammunition, while my wife and Ernest and little Francis were making their way to seek refuge from the unknown animal in the grotto.

Fritz, who in such cases was usually the first to fly to arms, did not move from his seat, but sat smiling in a manner that almost reassured me.

'Do not alarm yourselves, my dears,' I said. I dare say that which we have so readily taken for a wild beast is nothing more than a bittern or marshpig.

'At all events,' said Fritz, 'it may only be a small serenade given in our honour by Jack's giant frog.'

'Ho, ho!' replied I, laughing, 'so it is a trick that young giddy-head is playing us, is it? I can understand now all about the mysterious sack: it was used, I presume, to carry this huge frog home. Well, well! since Jack has seen fit to frighten us, let us see if we cannot frighten him. When he returns, pretend, all of you, to be in the greatest possible state of excitement.'

The three boys played their parts in this improvised comedy to perfection. Ernest and Francis, stopped upon the threshold by my remark, ran hither and thither in the utmost confusion, with wild staring eyes; while Fritz, with his hand shading his eyes, seemed to be anxiously peering all round the neighbourhood.

'What's the matter?' asked Jack, returning with the guns, and looking as pleased as possible at the state of fright into which he supposed his frog had thrown us. 'Whatever is the matter?' he repeated, on seeing Fritz look as frightened as the of us.

'Do you not see it?' said Fritz, with a faint and trembling voice. 'Do you not see it?'

'What?' asked Jack, growing very pale.

'That huge cougar there, glaring among the trees.'

'A cougar!—no. What is a cougar, papa?' asked Jack, becoming more alarmed still.

'It is,' I said, 'an American tiger, otherwise known as the puma. Its skin is of one colour throughout, whence it is called by the naturalists *Felis concolor* It is a terribly ferocious animal. Its skin is much valued, and——'

'I do not care to know any more about it!' said young giddy-head, and he made off at the top of his speed for the grotto.

As soon as he had taken refuge, we followed him with loud bursts of laughter, which were redoubled when we saw him, gun in hand and pale with fear, looking out of one of the windows as if he expected to be instantly devoured. He could not understand our laughter, till he came down from his watch-tower and all was explained to him.

He promised that we should never catch him in a similar trap again.

A few days afterwards, when we had recovered a little from the fatigue attendant on our last expedition, my wife urged me to repair our old dwelling at Falcon-nest.

I consented willingly; and, after we had laid out a salt-lick near the bridge, in the manner described some pages back, we all set out for the old aerial dwelling.

Thenceforward the restoration of what we were now pleased to call Fig-tree Castle proceeded with rapidity. The arched roots at the base were planed up and polished, and the terrace on the top of them was relaid with loam, and made impervious to the wet with a coating of tar and resin. The house in the branches was roofed with bark, carefully closed at the joints, while the flooring around it was garnished with a balcony of trellis-work, which gave it a very picturesque appearance. In short, our old nest, unsightly and ill-contrived as it was at first, now became, thanks to our improved skill in carpentry, a very charming-looking and very comfortable dwelling.

This, so to speak, was but a labour of pleasure. Fritz was for doing something more useful. To that end he determined to fortify Shark Island.

The enterprise was a difficult one, but we achieved it without any great expenditure of time or any overwhelming fatigue. I began by constructing a winch upon the upper rocks, with the view of placing our four cannon there. This done, we set to work to raise the guns. As the height was between fifty and sixty feet, and the ordnance was heavy, you may be sure this was no light labour. However, we accomplished it without accident.

Behind the cannon, which were mounted upon their carriages and pointed towards the sea, we built a sort of watch-tower with planks and bamboo-canes; and, hard by, raised a mast, with running cordage attached, for the hoisting of signal-flags. These were to be white in times of tranquillity, and red when we appre-hended danger.

The restoration of Falcon-nest and the fortification of Shark Island took us about two months, and when we had finished we determined to celebrate the event.

We fired off six rounds of ordnance as a grand salute, and for the first time hoisted the Swiss flag over our dominions.

CHAPTER XL

Condition of the colony at the end of ten years—excursion by Fritz in the cajack—the sea-birds' nests—Pearl Bay—the dog-fish—the albatross

Chapter has added itself to chapter as year has added itself to year —insensibly and uniformly—since I began to narrate the history of my life, or rather that of my family, during the decade that we have lived upon this lonely island, far from our fellow-men, far from our native country, without any other resource than our industry, and without encouragement or consolation other than those derivable from our sincere faith in God and our affection for each other, which time has only broadened and deepened.

During these ten years what undertakings, small and great, have we not achieved? What events, trivial and serious, have not occurred in our midst? Each day has brought with it its labours and its anxieties; each day has also brought with it its rewards and its pleasures.

And during these ten years—passing so slowly with the idle and the infirm, passing so swiftly, on the contrary, with those who like myself, had a family to provide for, to love, and to protect—our little colony went on prospering beyond even our most hopeful expectations. Thanks to our unremitting attention and incessant toil, our plantations and establishments were all in a thriving condition, and our means of living increased indefinitely.

Putting aside a few inevitable failures and vexations, putting aside also a few passing attacks of sickness, equally inevitable, everything had grown around us—our trees, our gardens, our cattle and poultry, our children, and our love. The eaglets had become eagles. All four of our boys, as it appeared to me, had grown as handsome as they were good, each following the peculiarities of his own humour and temperament. They loved each other tenderly, with an affection at once manly and child-like. They worked like strong men and played like boys. Fritz had attained his twenty-fourth year, Ernest his twenty-second, Jack his twentieth, and Francis his seventeenth.

Time had laid the lightest touch upon the features of my beloved wife, who still remained, as she always had been, the angel of our solitude. Her pure soul shone youthful as ever through the sweet expression of her countenance. The children adored her, and loaded her with tenderness. Each strove to outdo the other in anticipating her lightest wish, in sparing her an unnecessary anxiety, in giving her an unexpected pleasure, in doing her will upon the slightest hint.

'I never before felt so happy,' she often said to me; 'indeed, it is more than happiness, and if we could only live always for our dear children's sake—if inevitable death never threatened to come in and separate us from them—if, in this dreadful solitude we were not doomed to disappear one after the other, leaving our survivors overwhelmed with grief and loneliness—I should bless Heaven for bringing us to this paradise upon earth. But, alas, alas! a day must come, my love, when our eyes will be closed for ever!'

As to myself, my hair was silvering fast, but I was still strong and hearty. Age had weakened none of my faculties, and my faith in God grew stronger daily. I felt myself to be near Him and in His holy keeping.

Our animals, who were our companions and friends, had prospered as we had. Grumbler had achieved his full growth. The cow had presented us with a calf yearly, and of her numerous progeny we had spared two, one of which had become a fine milch cow, and the other a powerful bull. We called the first Swan, because of the whiteness of her coat; and the second Roarer, because of his terrible voice. We had also added to our stock two young asses—a male and a female—one of which we christened Arrow, and the other Sprightly. Lastly, we had saved out of the far too numerous offspring of the agile Jackal a specimen which promised to become an excellent hunter, and to which Jack had given the grotesque name of Cocoa.

I have not spoken here, be it understood, of our flocks and herds, which, of course, had multiplied exceedingly; nor of our poultry, which had abundantly supplied our table. There never was a richer farmer than I was, and nothing would have been wanting to complete our felicity if, as my wife said when more depressed than usual, we could have seen our boys growing up the midst of a populated country, instead of living so far removed from their kind.

One day, when Fritz, unknown to us, had set out early in the morning in his cajack, we went in the afternoon to the fortifications on Shark Island, to endeavour to get a sight, if possible, of the adventurer. The white flag floated from the top of the mast; the cannon lay loaded and ready to speak, at the word of command, with their formidable throats.

We waited some time without being able to see anything of our runaway. At last, by the aid of the telescope, I perceived a black speck on the water. It speedily assumed larger dimensions, and at last a definite shape. It was Fritz. His paddle dipped regularly in the tranquil mirror of the sea, but, as far as I could judge, much more slowly than usual. He was making his course towards Deliverance Bay.

'Fire!' cried Ernest, in his character of captain of artillery.

Jack brought his match to the touch-hole, and at the same time as he heard the noise of the cannon our sailor was greeted with loud hurrahs.

We then descended in all haste to receive Fritz as he landed near Rock-house.

I was now able to account for the unaccustomed slowness of his progress.

At the prow of the canoe—that is to say, at the point where we had fixed the head of the walrus, was suspended a large bundle of what appeared to be stout thorny feathers. It was, in point of fact, a new supply of the gelatinous sea-weed of which my wife made jelly. At the poop hung a large sack well filled, half in the water and half out. At one side of the cajack floated an important capture, the nature of which we could not quite make out.

'You seem to be well attended, Fritz,' said I. 'Whence do you come thus laden? Have you been in any danger?'

'None, thank Heaven,' replied Fritz. 'On the contrary, the voyage has been the luckiest I ever made, as you shall presently hear.'

The cajack having been drawn up on the beach and unloaded, we surrounded Fritz to hear the story of the voyage, which, on his part, he was only too ready to recount.

'First of all, dear father,' he said, 'I have to beg your forgiveness for setting out this morning without obtaining your leave to do so. Having a craft so light and so altogether suitable, I could not resist a desire that sometimes comes over me to make a voyage in it. I have for a long time wished to become better acquainted with the coast west of Deliverance Bay, and also to explore the part where I killed the walrus. If you had forbidden me I should not have disobeyed you, and it was because I feared you might have forbidden me, on account of the supposed danger of the cruise, that I set out without your knowledge. To provide against unforeseen exigencies, which might have prolonged my journey, I took with me, besides provisions, a boat-hook, a harpoon, some fishing-lines, my axe, my gun, my pistol, a compass, and my eagle.

'The weather was everything I could have desired. The sea was calm and the sky cloudless. I took advantage of a few minutes, when you were engaged in the grotto, to jump into my cajack and pull into the river current, which in a very short time carried me out of your sight. On reaching the spot where ten years ago our vessel was wrecked, I found the water so clear that I could see on the smooth sandy bottom several cannons, a quantity of shot, a number of bars of iron, and other objects, which we shall do well to get up when you have made the diving-bell you were talking about the other day.

'Thence I directed my course to the west, towards the coast, doubling a promontory formed partly of rocks, piled one on the other, and partly of sunken rocks scattered about in the sea below them. Here I found innumerable flocks of sea-birds, and a little farther on a number of marine animals, such as bears, walruses, seals, etc.

'As I did not feel quite at my ease in the neighbourhood of these monsters, I made the best of my way among the various channels that ran between the rocks, and in the course of an hour found myself in front of a kind of triumphal arch, built by nature of huge rocks flung at hazard one upon the other. Beneath this massive arcade, which looked strong enough to bid eternal defiance alike to wind and seas, a vast population of sea-birds had made their nests. They flew screaming around me by hundreds, perhaps to stun or perhaps to frighten me, without thinking for a moment that my curiosity was stronger than their rage, and that, for all their uproar, I could examine them at my leisure. They were about the size of wrens, with under-plumage of a dazzling whiteness, and feathers of a deep black on their backs. Their wings were grey as ashes. As to their nests, there were thousands of them, skilfully built, and adhering to the juttings of the rocks. Each of them rested upon a little suport resembling a spoon without a handle. I carefully removed several, and have brought them with me, in order that you may taste them, if your stomach will allow you to do so. I read that they make excellent food, in virtue of the gelatinous substance of which they are formed. I suppose they are the famous salangave nests of which the Chinese are so fond.

'I continued my voyage, and, when I passed the rocky vault, found myself in a magnificent bay from the shore of which a splendid savannah stretched away till it was lost to view on the horizon. Here and there clumps of verdant foliage sprang from the clefts of the rocks, while into the centre of the bay poured a large river whose banks were lined with magnificent cedar-trees.

'In cruising round the coast of this bay I perceived in the depths of the water, which was transparent as crystal, millions of shell-fish that seemed to be tied together and fastened to their shells by numberless filaments, which looked like tufts of hair. Thinking that these fish would probably be more agreeable to the taste than the oysters which we take in Deliverance Bay, I detached some with my boat-hook and fished them up with my lines. I threw upon the beach those which I intended to eat, and put the rest into a sack, which I tied to the stern of my canoe, in order to bring a few home to you. Then I landed to take a rest. On opening my oysters, which appeared to be very tough, I found in them several little round bodies of the size of peas, very brilliant, and resembling pearls. I leave you to judge whether I am right in my conjecture. There they are—examine them.'

At these words, Ernest, Jack, and Francis hastened to look at the shells which Fritz handed to me. Our brave adventurer was right: the small round bodies of which he had spoken were indeed pearls of a dazzling whiteness, and of rare purity and fineness. Many of them were unusually large.

'You have found a real treasure, my dear Fritz,' I replied. 'Whole nations would envy you your discovery, for it is a mine worth millions, is a pearl-bank such as you describe. Unhappily, it is impossible for us to profit by it, or even to make a market out of sea-swallows' nests, for sea-swallows they are. We have no relations with the rest of the world, and for our own use these inestimable treasures are not worth nearly so much as a bag of nails or a measure of wheat. Nevertheless, as it would be ungrateful to neglect the gifts which Providence throws in our way, and as we may be permitted some day to join our friends in Europe, we will make an early expedition to this opulent bay. For who knows but the seemingly useless labours of the present time may in the future contribute to the well-being of all of us? Now, my dear son, continue your narrative.'

Fritz proceeded:

'After a short repast,' he said, 'to recruit my failing strength, I continued my journey round this smiling coast. I found it indented along its whole course with verdant bays, which seemed to invite me every moment to pause and make another landing. At length I arrived at the mouth of the river of which I told you. Its shallows were covered with aquatic plants whose leaves were so broad that, as they floated out upon the water, huge long-legged birds ran over them with as much safety as if they had been upon dry land. I thought for an instant that I had been transported in a dream to the great river St. John, in Florida, of which I lately read a description in one of the books in our library.

'After replenishing my stock of fresh water, I set out again, and soon reached the promontory which shuts in Pearl Bay. It faces

Sea-gull Arch, and is distant from it about a league. There is a long ridge of sunken rocks, which completely separates the bay from the open sea, except in one part, where there is a deep clear channel, somewhat narrow but very convenient. It would be impossible to find a situation more advantageous for a seaport.

'As I was making my way through this sea-pass, an unexpected current brought me to a sudden standstill, and I was obliged to coast along the promontory to find an opening similar to that by which I had entered on the other side. But I did not succeed. On my way I saw an immense number of marine animals of the size and shape of dog-fish, playing upon the rocks and in the water, and leaping from the one to the other in turns. I was too far off to draw upon them, but I nevertheless had a strong desire to make their acquaintance. I therefore rowed a little nearer, and put up my eagle, which swiftly pounced down in the midst of the thoughtless shoal. Quitting my canoe, I leapt from rock to rock, and arrived just in time to seize the prey, which the eagle was already rending. The entire shoal had disappeared as if by enchantment.'

'But,' I asked, 'how did you manage to bring your booty home? It must be very heavy.'

'That consideration gave me some trouble,' replied Fritz. 'I did not like to leave my dog-fish behind at any cost; and yet I knew that, unless I could hit upon some means of lightening its weight a good deal, it would be impossible to bring it with me. While casting about for a plan, I was struck by the enormous quantity of sea-birds that were circling and screaming around me. There were sea-swallows, mews, gulls, petrels, albatrosses, and several other kinds unknown to me. Their noise became so insupportable that, to rid myself of them, I hit out wildly with my boat-hook. One fell at my feet stunned, and lay there with wide-extended wings. It was a kind of albatross, which I believe is called by sailors the frigate bird.

'Remembering then a device in use among the Greenlanders, I pulled out one of the bird's largest feathers, and used it as a pipe to inflate my dog-fish. In this state I tied the creature to the side of my cajack, and it rode buoyantly upon the sea. But it was time now to think of returning, and I stopped no more.

'I found my way out of the labyrinth of rocks in safety, and laying on upon my paddle soon found myself in known waters.

'There I saw our white flag floating in the breeze afar off, and heard the welcome report of our artillery.'

CHAPTER XLI

*A confidential conversation with Fritz—the English girl on the
Burning Rock—a pearl-fishing expedition—Cape Flat-nose—
pearl-fishing—the return*

So far Fritz had ended his narrative. But while his mother and
brothers were examining with much curiosity the spoils he had
brought home, he took me mysteriously on one side and led me to
a distant bank, upon which we sat down. He there completed his
account as follows:

'I have not told you all, dear father,' he said. 'The strangest
part of the story remains at present for your ear alone. As I was
searching over the albatross which I knocked down, to select a
feather suitable for my purpose, I found a piece of linen rag tied
to one of its legs. I at once detached it, and saw written upon it in
English, in a kind of red ink, these strange words:

' "*Whoever you may be to whom God bears this message from an
unfortunate girl, seek out a volcanic island, which you will recognise
by the flame that rises from one of its craters. Save the unhappy lost
one of the Burning Rock!*"

'Amazed, I read and re-read the message a half-score times, to
assure myself that I was not dreaming. "What!" I cried, "is it
possible—a human being living in these uninhabited parts? How
came she here? Without doubt like we did, by shipwreck. Oh, that
I may be able to find her in time to save her life!"

'Thereupon I endeavoured to revive the poor bird, which happily
was only stunned. I poured a drop of hydromel into its beak, and
it seemed to be recovering. Then with a feather dipped in the bleeding wound of the dog-fish, I wrote in English upon a piece of my
handkerchief:

'*Have faith in God. In all probability succour is near.*'

'I tied the two pieces of rag to the leg of the albatross, now
completely recovered from its swoon, and allowed it to try its
wings. It at once flew off to the westward with a swiftness that
vexed me not a little, for I had hoped that it would go at a slower
pace, and thus enable me to follow it, and discover the Burning
Rock.

'This is what I wanted to tell you alone, father. And now, think
you that my message of comfort has reached the poor unfortunate
who yearns for it? Where is she? How can I find her?'

'My dear son,' I replied, 'I rejoice extremely in the prudence
with which you have conducted this matter, and I congratulate
you upon it. You did well to reserve your account of it for my ear
alone, because in divulging it to your mother and brothers you

would have caused them an amount of anxiety which it was your duty, as a son and a brother, to spare them. It may unhappily be the case that the message you found tied to the leg of albatross is an old one written many months since. It may also be that the unfortunate whom you desire to save is separated from us by a wide tract of ocean; for the albatross is a powerful bird upon the wing, and traverses inconceivable distances in a few days. The country whence it came, and to which it has probably returned, may therefore be leagues away from our colony. However, we will speak of that later on. For the present, let us return to the family, who will wonder what business we have on hand to hold us in this mysterious converse.'

Saying this, I got up. Fritz followed my example, and we walked arm-in-arm to meet the other members of our family, who, as I expected, had begun to grow curious as to the nature of our conversation.

'My dear wife,' I said, with much gravity, 'and dear children,' I added, addressing Ernest, Jack, and Francis, 'your son and your brother, Fritz, whom you now see linked arm-in-arm with me, has so long proved, by his courage, his ability, and his intelligence, that he is worthy of the fullest freedom of action, that I have determined to declare him henceforth responsible to no one but himself. He will remain, without doubt, our son and your brother, but he is now his own master, and for the future he will receive from me not the orders of a superior, but the counsels of a father and a friend. The boy has become a man.'

Each of my auditors, I could see, was deeply impressed by the solemn decree of emancipation which I had just pronounced. My wife took Fritz to her bosom, weeping over him tears of joy, and bestowing upon him a hearty benediction, which came not only from her lips but from her heart. Then she hastily left us, under pretext of preparing our supper, but in reality to indulge her tenderness in solitude. The three younger boys also embraced Fritz affectionately, and attempted a few lugubrious pleasantries, the better to hide their emotion.

'I wish you joy and happiness with all my heart,' said Ernest. 'You have just quitted the *toga praetexta* for the *toga pura et libera*.'

'Hide me beneath your manly vesture, Fritz, whenever I am about to commit a foolish action,' added Jack.

'Take me with you wherever you go, in order that I may enjoy part of your independence,' said he, who, during the whole ten years, had been still known as our 'little' Francis. Fritz smiled, but made no reply, and we sat down to supper.

Our conversation during the meal turned naturally upon the pearl-oyster, and I was compelled to describe the manner in which the gem forms itself in the shell, the method of fishing, the devices of the divers, the dangers to which they are subject, and so on.

These points settled, we decided that, having so inexhaustible a mine of wealth in the immediate neighbourhood, it was our duty to possess ourselves of some of its riches as soon as possible. We had, however, no implements suitable to oyster-fishing, and it became necessary that each of us should set to work to make some. I myself forged four iron hooks, two large and two small which were intended to be hung to the bottom of the canoe in such wise that they would drag the bottom, and bring our prey to the surface. Francis assisted his mother in making some landing-nets, to get them ashore when brought there. Ernest employed himself in making, after a design I had given him, a long instrument that would serve to detach the nests of the sea-swallows; while Jack, having the same end in view, knotted a rope and fastened a hook to it, with the intention of climbing where Ernest would only venture to reach with a pole.

As to Fritz, he thought of but one thing. It was how to make a second opening in the skins which covered the deck of his cajack. His brothers naturally supposed that he was desirous of providing a seat for one of them during his coming excursions. I alone divined, without, however, revealing anything, the purpose he had in view. He was providing for a new member of our little colony—one who had doubtless been shipwrecked on the rocks, and was probably dwelling in a solitude worse than our own.

These preparations made, we got ready to set out on our voyage. Our provisions were varied and plentiful—fresh pemmican, made on an improved plan since Fritz's failure six or seven years ago, cassava cakes, maize, almonds, and a small cask of hydromel. These, with our arms and baggage, were placed on board the pirogue, and on an early day, when the weather was favourable, we set sail, leaving my wife at home under the care of Francis.

The companions of our voyage were Nip the Second (Nip the First had been dead a long time); Jack's jackal, rather old for such a journey, but still an excellent hunter; our good dog Fan, also growing old; and our two vigorous dogs Brown and Fawn, who, what with good nourishment and a healthy climate, had grown so powerful and courageous that I could only compare them to the animals which, presented by King Porus to Alexander, did battle valiantly with lions and elephants.

Jack had insisted on taking the second seat in the cajack, in order to serve as our pilot—assisted by Fritz, be it understood.

Ernest and I followed them round by the rocks where Fritz had seen the walruses and other marine animals, and where the waves now beat in furiously. Here and there we saw the skeletons of dead monsters blanched by time, and, by the desire of our younger companions, took some specimens away with us, to be deposited in our museum.

Arrived at length in the tranquil waters of a large bay, we saw, playing upon its smooth surface, as upon a mirror, a large quantity of the elegant shell-fish known as argonauta, or nautili. Our pilots possessed themselves of some fine specimens, which were carefully laid away in the pirogue.

Soon afterwards we reached a promontory which looked as if it had been crushed in by a blow, from which circumstance we at once named it Cape Flat-nose. When we had doubled it we saw in the distance, through Rock Arch, the famous object of our search —Pearl Bay.

The gigantic vault, under which we passed, merited all the praises which Fritz had bestowed on it. Like him, we were assailed on reaching it by myriads of sea-swallows, which circled round, and rose and fell on every side of us, like gnats on a summer evening.

As you may imagine, we wasted no time in admiration, but set to work at once upon the nests nearest at hand. Jack's knotted rope was of the first utility to reach the juttings of the rocks; but as the adventurous spirits of my sons carried them beyond the bounds of prudence, I was obliged to order them to desist from their harvest. Our booty was placed in the pirogue, and, after partaking of some refreshment, we again set out upon our voyage.

The rising tide helped us, without misadventure, through the dangerous defile of sunken rocks of which Fritz had told us, and before long we found ourselves in one of the most magnificent bays I had ever seen. It was about six or eight leagues in circuit. Several small islands, scattered about its surface, rendered it the more picturesque in appearance. It was shut in from the sea by a belt of broken rocks, in the centre of which was a defile of some fathoms in width, offering a commodious entrance to the largest vessels. The only objection a sailor could have had to it was that here and there it was dotted with sandbanks and shallows; but these latter, being partly composed of oyster-beds rising to the level of the water, were easily seen and consequently not very dangerous.

It was with a sensation of vivid delight that we found ourselves floating over this beautiful sheet of water; and, as we coasted round its shore, the verdant prairies beyond it, the shadowy woods, the undulating hills, and the picturesque river, gave pleasure to our eyes, and seemed to put hope into our hearts. A creek a few paces from the bank of pearl-oysters was chosen for a landing-place. Our dogs, to whom we had doled out water sparingly during the passage, waited not for our invitation to leap over the side of the pirogue and make for a small clear stream, running into the bay, to slake their thirst.

The monkey also scented the stream, and, being as desirous as his four-footed comrades to taste fresh water, made the oddest grimaces as he went and came from the poop to the prow, looking imploringly at the sea, at the sky, and at us; desiring much to try his hand at swimming to shore, but not daring to make the requisite leap into the sea. I at first laughed heartily at his pitiful contortions; but, taking compassion on him, I at length threw a rope to land, with a billet of wood tied to the end of it, and thus afforded poor Nip the Second a means of gratifying his legitimate desires. He set out upon the swinging cord, and followed it cautiously to the end, being aided therein by a stick which I gave him, and which he carried as a tight-rope dancer carries his balance-pole. He reached dry ground at last, but not without several slips that caused him to scratch his ear in an agony of anxiety.

We were not long in following the example of our animals. The day was declining, and the first thing to be done on landing was to prepare our supper and provide a lodging for the night. We were not long in improvising a repast. It consisted of pemmican soup, boiled potatoes, and maize cakes.

A great fire was lighted with waifs and strays, washed up during the course of ages by the sea, and dried in the sun. Our dogs were left on the beach. We ourselves slept on board the pirogue, which was anchored in the creek, and upon the deck of which we had set up our tent.

CHAPTER XLII

*Jack's fright—the wild boar—truffles—nankin cotton—the lions—
death of Fan—Fritz's expedition—the spermaceti whale*

During the earlier part of the night we were disturbed a good deal by the distant howling of jackals, to which, according to its detestable custom, our own insisted on replying.

At daybreak we were all afoot, and, after a good repast, proceeded to the pearl-bank, where the supply was so abundant that I determined to stay three days. Our plan was to take our oysters and spread them out upon the sand, where the sun speedily opened them for us, and leave them to putrefy; after which, as I had read, we could take our pearls easily. While thus employed, we lighted upon two kinds of soda among the rocks. With one of them I hoped to make a better kind of soap than we had hitherto been using, while with the other I thought I should be able to purify our sugar.

Each evening. about an hour before preparing our supper, it was our custom to make a pedestrian excursion into the savannah, whence we brought in specimens of rare vegetables or birds.

On the evening of the third and last day of our fishing expedition, we had the curiosity to penetrate a little farther into a wood, where we fancied we had heard the cries of turkeys and peacocks.

Enest and the brave Fawn went first. Behind them went Jack and the jackal, strolling idly among the long grass. Fritz and I, who were repairing some of our implements upon the beach, had not yet set out.

Suddenly we heard the report of a gun, followed by a cry of alarm. Then came another report.

Fawn and Brown at once dashed off the direction of the noise, followed by Fritz with his eagle. I also hastened forward, to see what was the matter.

The cry of distress that we heard at first was soon succeeded by another altogether different, and, peering through the trees, I saw

Jack limping and moaning, and only able to walk when supported by his brothers.

'What is the matter? What has happened, my dear son?' I asked in a trembling voice. 'Are you injured? Where is the wound?'

'Here,' sighed Jack feebly, 'and here. Here also, and there. I am injured all over!'

I at once proceeded to examine him carefully. But I found no fracture, no wound; nothing but a few slight contusions here and there that would soon pass away. Jack was astonished, but still continued to sigh and moan as if he were terribly injured.

'You seem, my dear Jack,' I said, quite reassured, 'to be very effeminate for a hunter.'

'Effeminate!' he cried, with a sort of comic indignation. 'Effeminate! when I have been knocked down, half-killed, trampled under-foot, crushed to death almost! When I was within a hair's-breadth of being ripped open! Ah. father! if it had not been for our brave dogs and Fritz's eagle, I should not have been here. I should certainly have fallen a prey to the monster.'

'But,' I said impatiently, 'what is this monster that has so excited your fears? You have neglected to tell me that.'

'A wild boar, dear father.' said Ernest, 'an enormous wild boar. He has tusks at least six inches in length, and a snout as long as your hand. We surprised him as he was grubbing in the soil, and ploughing up great furrows in it. But for the two balls which we managed to lodge in his body, Jack, whom he had knocked down, would have been torn to pieces by him.'

'Let us thank God,' I replied. 'The peril is now past, and Jack shall have some medicine to cure him of his fear, which, after all, is like any other complaint, I suppose, and must be treated accordingly.'

Saying this, I gave the imprudent hunter a glass of Canary wine, and bathed his bruises with a solution of the same liquor. Afterwards, I carried him on board the pirogue, where he soon fell fast asleep.

To this accident, which happily was unattended by any serious consequences, we owed the discovery of a bed of truffles. The wild boar, which had caused poor Jack so great a fright, was engaged in grubbing for these delicious tubers when he was disturbed. No wonder he took it ill when deprived of so agreeable a repast.

The truffle, although of a very secondary value to people who live so plainly as we did, is reckoned a great delicacy in Europe, and we thought our good housewife would like to have a few. We therefore procured a supply, and placed them on board our vessel.

My boys asked for some account of this singular product of the earth, and I told them that by naturalists it was classed among the fungi family, and that it grew without leaves, without stalks, and without roots.

'In order to discover them,' I said, 'it is necessary to take with you either dogs or pigs. These animals, guided by their keen sense

of smell, soon find the places where they grow, and will indicate
their whereabouts to you by digging into the earth, the former
with their paws, the latter with their snouts. Large quantities of
them are found in France, in Italy, and in many other countries.
They are very choice and very highly esteemed, on account of their
rarity, perhaps, more than their flavour, which, so far as I can see,
has nothing extraordinary about it.'

It was now time to think of repose. We arranged to sleep in our
pirogue, as we had hitherto done, and we passed a night as tranquil as if we were at Rock-house.

The next morning, at daybreak, I proposed to go after the
wounded boar, which I judged could not long have survived the
two bullets that had been lodged in his body.

My two elder sons accompanied me. Jack, still suffering from
his fright of the previous evening, preferred his bed, and we left
him fast asleep.

On reaching the edge of the wood, our dogs and jackal approached
us with the liveliest demonstrations of satisfaction, and led us
direct to the carcass of the boar, over which they had kept faithful
watch all night. The prodigious size of the animal surprised us.

'What a splendid opportunity to replace our Westphalian hams!'
said Fritz, after examining the enormous thighs of the animal.

'So far as I am concerned,' said Ernest, 'all I ask is that I may
have the head to place in our museum. But first of all it will be
necessary to devise some plan of getting the carcass down upon
the beach, where we can cut it up much more easily.'

'That will be an easy thing to do,' said Fritz, 'if my father will
give us his permission.'

'I have no opposition to offer,' I replied; 'but I give you fair
notice that, excepting the head and the hams; the flesh of the
animal is very tough. You will, therefore, do better to take these
parts, and leave the remainder of the enormous carcass here.'

My advice was taken. My boys cut off the hams and head of the
boar, and we placed them on some branches, which the dogs, being
harnessed thereto, dragged down to the beach.

Fritz remarked that upon the branches we had used for this
purpose there still hung a kind of food which, having burst, was
found to contain a ball of yellowish cotton. I recognised in it the
cotton of the nankin-tree, which is by nature of the bright colour
we all know so well.

Thereupon we returned to the wood, and gathered an abundant
supply of the new material which we put carefully on one side,
to serve as an unexpected present for my wife.

On reaching the beach again we found Jack awaiting us, perfectly recovered from the effects of his tussle with the boar. He
at once offered to assist his brothers in salting and smoking the
hams, and was the first to indulge in a few pleasantries concerning
his fears of the previous evening, which nevertheless were, to
some extent, justifiable.

On the evening of this day we lighted our fires upon the beach as usual, and, as everything seemed tranquil, were about to retire to rest, when we were startled by a succession of loud roarings which, proceeding from the depth of the forest, were re-echoed by the distant mountains.

Our dogs and the jackal set up a fearful howling, as if they were overcome by terror.

A great fear fell upon us, for, for the first time since our sojourn upon the island, we felt assured that we heard the voice of some one or other of the largest beasts of prey.

'What a satanic concert!' cried Fritz, leaping up and taking his gun, with determination visible upon every lineament of his countenance. 'You stay in the pirogue; I alone will go and find out what the enemy is like.'

In an instant the courageous young man leapt into his cajack, and disappeared in the darkness.

I had no time to advise him before he was out of sight. So I got all the arms ready, and awaited the result.

The roarings continued, approaching every minute nearer and nearer. The boys became a prey to their fears, and nothing that I could say or do tended to reassure them. For myself, persuaded of imminent danger, I stood, gun in hand, awaiting the gleam through the darkness of the flaming eyes of a leopard or panther.

In a few moments, by the lurid glare of our fires, we saw a beast of enormous size approaching with a lithe and stately tread.

It was a lion.

On arriving in front of the pile of glowing timber, he came to a dead stand. The flame lighted up his face, in which we read power, fierceness, and hunger. He lashed his tawny flanks furiously with his tail, and looked as if he were about to spring upon us. This fearful pantomime lasted for some time. We dared not move, and I was reflecting whether it would even be wise to fire, when we heard the report of a gun.

'It is Fritz!' said Ernest in a voice trembling with fear.

The lion leapt up, uttering a roar of pain, and fell fainting in a stream of blood that poured from its huge breast.

'We are saved!' I cried. 'We are saved! The lion has been pierced to the heart! Fritz is a dead shot indeed!'

I drew up the anchor, and with a few strokes of the oar brought myself near enough to the beach to leap ashore.

I advised Ernest and Jack to remain where they were.

The dogs came bounding up to lick my hand, but in a moment began to howl again, and directed my attention towards the wood. It was a notification not to be disregarded.

I at once paused, and it was well I did, for at the same instant there emerged from the darkness of the forest a huge lioness—the female, no doubt, of the superb animal Fritz had just killed.

The lioness, by her hoarse purrings, seemed to be calling her companion. Becoming suspicious that all was not well with him, she began sniffing on all sides, and lashing her flanks with her tail as if in the deepest anguish. Presently she caught sight of the corpse. She hastened towards it, and tenderly licked the still bleeding wound. Then, comprehending that her companion was in truth dead, she uttered a terrible roar, ground her teeth fiercely, and, her eyes flaming with vengeance, peered into the surrounding darkness as if seeking a victim to offer up as a sacrifice to her combined rage and despair.

At this moment the report of a gun resounded through the air. The lioness uttered a cry of pain and drew up one of her enormous paws, which had been pierced by the ball. But she was only wounded, and was dangerous still. Seeing this, I in my turn drew upon her. The ball crashed into her jaw, which fell useless. Thereupon the dogs flung themselves upon her flanks, and a terrible combat ensued.

A mute spectator to the fight, I dared not move. Another shot might have put an end to the sanguinary encounter, but the fear of wounding one of our dogs withheld my hand.

At length, seeing our faithful old dog Fan fall, rent from breast to flank by a blow from the lioness's paw, I no longer hesitated. Rushing forward, without thought of danger. I presented myself before the enraged beast. She raised herself upon her hind-legs to spring upon me, when I leaped forward and plunged my hunting-knife into her heart.

The noble beast, with a roar, rolled over upon the sand, never to rise again.

Fritz arrived upon the scene of action at once, forestalled only by a few minutes in the execution of an intention similar to my own.

For safety, I discharged a pistol into the head of the lion, and, feeling now quite secure, called Ernest and Jack.

They were already on the way to render us what assistance they could, for the moment they saw us in danger their fears vanished. They rushed into our arms, well-nigh overcome by excess of joy at finding us unhurt, after the great peril we had encountered.

The two lions lay extended upon the sand, and although we had nothing more to fear from them, we could not look upon their huge carcasses without experiencing a sensation of terror.

The inanimate body of poor Fan lay stretched in death beside that of her huge enemy.

'Brave animal!' said Fritz, wiping away a tear that did him honour. 'Thou art a cruel sacrifice to thy unselfish devotion! Once more, my dear Ernest, a sad opportunity presents itself of putting to the proof your literary ability. You must write an epitaph for our faithful companion.'

'I will do so,' said Ernest, 'but my heart is too full to write it in rhyme. I will give you an epitaph in simple prose.'

This said, our scholar walked apart, to think over a suitable inscription.

Fritz and Jack, meanwhile, dug a grave for the reception of the body. For myself, I set to work bathing the wounds of Fawn and Brown, and also those of the jackal, who had fought valiantly on the side of the dogs against his natural companions, and had received, like his comrades, several wounds from the lioness's talons and teeth.

When the grave was ready, we tenderly lowered our old friend into it, and filled in the earth. A large slab of rock, with a smooth face on one side of it, was placed over the mound, and Ernest, in a voice broken with emotion, pronounced the following epitaph, which served as a funeral oration for our brave and faithful friend:

> SACRED TO THE MEMORY
> OF THE
> GOOD FAN
> A PATTERN OF WHAT A DOG SHOULD BE
> A MODEL OF FIDELITY.
> SHE DIED THE DEATH OF THE BRAVE,
> FALLING, A MARTYR TO HER DEVOTION, BENEATH THE PAW OF A
> GIGANTIC LION.
> THIS STONE WAS ERECTED
> BY HER BEREAVED HUMAN FRIENDS,
> WHOM SHE UNSELFISHLY SAVED FROM A FATE SIMILAR
> TO HER OWN

'Excellent!' said Fritz, pressing Ernest's hand. 'We will engrave this epitaph as soon as possible upon the tomb of poor dear Fan.'

Jack, inconsolable, said nothing. He wept. 'Poor Fan! dear Fan!' he exclaimed presently. 'Best of friends! I can offer you nothing but tears!'

Our eyes were all moist.

The night air, however, had sharpened our appetites, and we turned away from the grave to prepare a repast, of which we stood much in need after our unwonted exertions.

'Bless me!' cried Jack, drying his eyes, 'I had almost forgotten. We put the boar's head in the fire yonder, and I should think that by this time it must be well baked.'

My younger sons went to withdraw the joint, which to their great disappointment, they found burnt black as a cinder.

They were about to throw it away.

'Stop! stop!' I cried, and plunging my knife into the head, I came upon the meatiest part of it, done to a turn, and exhaling a most appetising odour of truffles. I had dressed the head myself.

During the meal, eulogiums upon Fan formed the staple of our conversation.

We then retired to rest.

The first thing in the morning we set to work skinning the lions. Thanks to my system of inflation, our task was neither long nor difficult. At the end of it we found ourselves the possessors of two superb hides.

We had now been absent from Rock-house several days, and I knew that my wife would be getting anxious about us. Besides, our pearl-oysters, lying scattered upon the beach, were beginning to putrefy, and gave forth gases that were likely to prove injurious to our health. We determined, therefore, to return to the grotto, and to make the best of our way back again in a week or two, to take possession of the pearls which by that time, we felt sure, would be detached by decomposition from their fleshy beds.

We set out. Fritz, the sole occupant of his cajack, preceded us. When we were fairly outside the belt of rocks he approached the pirogue, and with the end of his paddle presented me with a letter, which he said, with a smile, 'the postman had forgotten to deliver'.

In order that I might give his brothers no cause for anxiety, I fell in with a pleasantry that had become familiar enough with us since the adventure of the carrier-pigeon, and withdrew to the stern of the boat to open the missive.

I was more troubled than surprised to learn that Fritz was about to quit us, in order to go in search of the unfortunate English girl who had written the message from the Burning Rock.

This project seemed to me to be both too adventurous and too romantic; but I felt that it would be in vain to oppose it. My heart fell within me as I saw my boy skimming lightly away from us, like a swallow, upon the great waste of waters.

'Farewell, Fritz!' I cried. 'Be prudent, and return as soon as you can, my dear son. Think of us and of your mother.'

He kissed his hand from afar.

It was his only answer.

He disappeared behind the promontory, and, praying for his safe return, I set sail for Rock-house, feeling very lonely.

My wife—from whom, to save her unnecessary inquietude, I concealed the real object of Fritz's adventure—received our spoils with the liveliest satisfaction. The discovery of the nankin especially delighted her; and she saw us all, in imagination, habited from head to foot in brilliant yellow. She thanked us warmly, and gave us the strongest proofs of the pleasure she experienced in seeing us safe home again.

But the absence of her eldest son caused her much anxiety, and all that I could say concerning the prudence of Fritz, and his perfect knowledge of navigation, failed to calm her fears.

During three whole days we were engaged in cleaning, classifying, and storing away the treasures we had brought home. On the evening of the fourth day, finding Fritz still absent, I began to partake in the fears and anxieties of his brothers and my wife; and I proposed to set out with the pinnace in search of our dear fugitive.

My wife, from whom I was wholly unable to conceal my inquietude, approved of this project, and proposed to accompany us.

After laying in abundant stock of provisions, and assuring ourselves that the pinnace, which we had not used for a long time, was in good condition, we set sail.

A fresh land breeze was blowing at the time, and our craft sped out to sea so swiftly that I was unable, for the time being, to manage it. On reaching the opening of the bay, it came into collision with a huge mass of something floating upon the water with so much force that it threw us all upon the deck. My wife and children uttered a cry of alarm. At the same moment we saw the floating mass sent up into the air, with a tremendous hubbub, two great streams of water, and then plunge into the boiling and foaming sea.

We had come into collision with a spermaceti whale. The proximity of such a monster was by no means pleasant, and I laid our cannon ready to fire upon it.

The huge creature reappeared at some distance.

Ernest at once did his best to take accurate aim, and Jack fired off one of the pieces.

Our gunner had sighted his mark well. We saw the ball strike the monster full in the flank; and he at once buried himself in the depths, leaving a long trail of blood behind him, and making the sea boil again.

Some few moments afterwards he reappeared upon the surface. A second shot struck him in the head. He struggled violently for a time, and then, his strength failing him, he made for one of the rocks at the entrance to Deliverance Bay, and became stranded.

I was congratulating my son upon his skill and presence of mind, which had delivered us from so formidable an enemy, when all at once Jack cried out:

'A savage, father! A savage!'

We all looked in the direction indicated, and saw in the distance a strange canoe gliding over the waves with incredible swiftness.

The savage we fancied we had sighted seemed to have seen us, and to have at once disappeared behind a jutting rock.

Thoroughly alarmed, I ordered Jack and Ernest to re-load our guns, and hold themselves in readiness for an attack; for I doubted not that the man in the canoe was the precursor of a band of barbarians.

My sons made a good show of bravery, and my wife sought to inspire them with a tranquillity which she was far from feeling herself.

The savage soon showed himself again, and seemed to examine us more attentively. Then he disappeared behind the promontory again, but only to reappear a few minutes afterwards.

Seeing that he continued to observe us, I took the speaking-trumpet, and, with all the strength of lung I could command, hailed him in the Malay language. He did not appear to understand me, for he still maintained his position.

'I fancy,' said Jack, 'that if we treat him to a few English sea-sayings, such as "Shiver my timbers!" "Lay-to, you lubbers!" "Avast there!" and so on, he will the better comprehend our meaning.'

Thereupon he laid hold of the speaking-trumpet, and carried out his intention.

Almost at the same moment the savage raised the branch of a tree above his head, in sign of peace, and began rowing swiftly in our direction.

The other boys laughed heartily at the success of Jack's device. But they soon changed their tone when they recognised in the savage, black as he was, and wearing a plume of feathers on his head, our dear Fritz.

In a short time he was upon the deck of the pinnace embracing us.

His mother, intoxicated with joy, overwhelmed him with kisses and caresses, without troubling herself about his strange costume or the colour of his skin.

It was not until we all burst into a laugh, on seeing her face disfigured with Fritz's war-paint, that she came to herself.

CHAPTER XLIII

Return of Fritz—Miss Jenny

I judged it wise now to tell my wife the secret of Fritz's expedition. Her surprise and, I am bound to add, her anxiety were extreme.

The three younger boys, scenting a mystery, plied Fritz with so many questions that he would have had some difficulty in answering them, even if his examiners had not spoken all at once.

At length, when this flow of words had ceased, I asked him to satisfy me upon two points. Had his expedition been successful? And to what end had he metamorphosed himself into a savage?

'My expedition has ended most satisfactorily,' he replied, giving me a significant look, 'and I cannot tell you how glad I am that I undertook it. As to my disguise, that was a measure of precaution. I saw you a long way off, and took you for Malay pirates. The reports of your cannon led me to think that you were in great force, and I therefore judged it prudent to change my garments and blacken my face, lest my European appearance should unduly attract your attention and curiosity.'

My wife here interrupted us to wash Fritz's face. She could not bear to see him looking like a negro, she said. When he had been restored to his natural, colour he continued:

'Father,' he said, 'God has heard my prayers, and vouchsafed an answer to them. I have discovered the volcanic island, with the Burning Rock upon it; and, as the rising tide will soon compel us to seek an anchorage, I will, with your permission, conduct you to a neighbouring bay, where we shall find——'

I interposed at this point, and, leading Fritz apart, asked him in a low voice to tell me what kind of a person it was that he had discovered; 'because,' I added, 'in some contingencies it would be better, perhaps, that you and I should go alone.'

He reassured me in an instant.

'Father,' he said, 'I thought when I saw her that I was looking upon my mother at the age of fifteen, or rather, perhaps, upon one who should have been your daughter, if we had been granted the happiness of having a sister worthy of both her and you.'

'Forward, then!' I cried, delighted. 'Conduct us to the rock at once!'

Fritz immediately set out with amazing ardour and swiftness. Seated in his canoe, he shot ahead to guide us through the channels among the sunken rocks, and at length brought us to the far side of an island situated at the western end of Pearl Bay. A long tongue of land ran out into the sea, and formed a natural port, at which we landed.

Fritz leapt upon the beach without saying a word, and ran towards a clump of gigantic palms, among the umbrageous branches of which we descried a kind of hut, something like that at Falcon-nest, but constructed wholly of boughs. We naturally followed in the footsteps of our guide, and soon found ourselves standing before a fire composed of large stones, upon which was placed, in lieu of a pot, a large shell.

Fritz fired one of his pistols in the air, and at this signal we saw descending from a neighbouring tree, not a girl of fifteen as I had expected, but a trim young sailor, slender in form, and of a modest and charming mien.

I know not how to describe the sensations we felt at this moment. For ten years the human race had been dead to us, and now all at once recollections of it were suddenly raised to life in the person of the fair creature standing before us. She looked almost a child, so beautiful and so ingenuous was her countenance.

We stood for an instant dazed and silent. My children, especially, could hardly believe their eyes. The stranger, upon her part, seemed to be equally undecided as to the line of conduct which she ought to pursue.

Fritz put an end to our embarrassment.

'My dear mother, dear father, and dear brothers,' he said, 'I present to you a friend—the young Lord Edward Montrose.' At this point he looked at me significantly. 'May he be welcomed as a son and a brother of our family circle!'

'He is welcome!' we all replied enthusiastically.

The young sailor looked so inexpressibly happy, that our sympathies were won over at once.

As head of the family I stepped forward, and, taking the stranger's hands in both my own, saluted her in the English manner, with as much warmth and kindness as if she had been one of my own sons, restored to us after a long separation.

She thanked me in a low, timid voice, and then, addressing my wife, recommended herself particularly to her care and kindness.

I had understood from the look given me by Fritz, when he introduced the stranger as a man, that for the present he did not wish his brothers to know she was a girl. Both I and my wife kept the secret, and I desired the children to show their young comrade every hospitality.

My recommendation was needless. The young lord had already become the object of the most delicate attentions. Even the dogs greeted him with joybarks and caresses.

The younger boys, in their ardour, ran pell-mell to the pinnace, and brought thence the table, the seats, and all sorts of provisions for our evening repast. Our good housewife displayed to the best advantage her brilliant talents as cook, while the innocent young Edward almost betrayed himself by the ease and knowledge with which he assisted my wife in her household duties.

Our supper was a joyous one. My boys, enlivened a little by some Canary wine which I had brought out in honour of the occasion, gave free vent to their youthful sprightliness; and we gossiped mirthfully, but not foolishly, till a far later hour than was usual with us. At length I put an end to the conversation, and ordered a retreat.

We all rose from table. The stranger was about to bid us good night with the intention of retiring to her hut in the tree, when my wife prevented her, saying that she had prepared a bed for her on board the pinnace.

Meanwhile my sons, who had taken the precaution to light safety fires upon the beach, sat chatting round the braziers. The three younger ones plied Fritz with questions to find out how it was that he had at first hit upon the idea of making an excursion to Burning Rock.

Straightway he proceeded to tell them the story of the albatross, and of his subsequent expedition, with so much precipitation that he completely forgot to substitute the name of Lord Edward for that of Miss Jenny, which was the real name of the young lady.

'Ha! ha!' cried the three listeners. 'Master Fritz has betrayed himself, and our new brother is changed into a charming sister! Hurrah! hurrah!'

Fritz was for a moment disconcerted; but he put the best face upon the matter, and joined heartily in the laugh against himself.

Francis was dumbfounded. 'This is a most extraordinary thing!' he said. 'I did not know there was any other woman in the world besides mamma.'

The next morning the three younger boys met the stranger with an air half of embarrassment and half of mischief, and saluted her by the name of Miss Jenny, which they strongly accentuated. The poor child blushed and lowered her eyes at first, but, recovering herself almost instantly, she frankly held out her hand to the young monkeys, and with charming grace commended herself to their brotherly friendship.

After breakfast—which, thanks to some chocolate prepared by Fritz, was a very substantial one—we determined to set sail, in order to recover what remained of the whale we had killed on the previous day. Its carcass was too valuable to be abandoned wholly to the birds.

We cut the monster up as best we could, and by the advice of Jenny—who saw clearly enough that, circumstanced as we were, a half-loaf was better than no bread—we determined to take away at once as much blubber as we could put in our sacks and stow away in the pinnace, and leave the rest to the vultures.

When this labour came to an end we returned to Burning Rock, to bring away the baggage of the young Englishwoman, who, moved by a praise-worthy sentiment, wished to preserve every object that recalled the circumstances of her isolation, and the special protection which Providence had vouchsafed to her. The whole of her movables—they were not many, poor thing!—were placed on board the pinnace; and then, after bidding adieu to Burning Rock, and christening the creek where Fritz had landed by the name of Happy Bay, on account of our fortunate discovery of Miss Jenny, we set out for Pearl Bay, where it was necessary to make a short sojourn before returning to Rock-house.

On arriving there we found that the lions had become a prey to vultures and other birds, and that nothing was left to them but a few bones bleaching in the sand. We put up our tent, intending to stay only as long as was necessary to harvest our pearls from the shells of the decomposed fish. But a discovery which I made delayed our departure.

Among the rocks, I remarked one which appeared to be calcareous or chalky, and I thereupon determined to build a kiln, and endeavour to prepare some lime.

We set vigorously to work. The kiln was built and filled with chalk, and a fire was lighted above and below, which it was necessary to leave burning for several days.

During this operation we had plenty of leisure on our hands, and, being pressed by his brothers, Fritz set apart a portion of each evening, after Miss Jenny had retired to rest, to recount his adventures in search of Burning Rock. He began his narrative as follows:

'You remember the circumstances under which I left you, after handing our father a letter, in which I explained to him the object of my excursion. Well, on setting out the sea was calm and the weather fine, but I had no sooner passed Pearl Bay than a terrible tempest arose. My cajack, not being strong enough to do battle with the waves, I allowed it to float at will, and, without giving all up for lost, commended myself to the protection of God. My confidence was not misplaced. After three hours of tumult the sea grew calm again, the heavens became serene and my little craft glided gaily over the waves.

'But I was far from any point that I could recognise. The country around me was different to anything I had yet seen. The coasts of the islands among which I found myself were fringed with enormous rocks whose points pierced the clouds, while inland I could see

gigantic forests, in which birds of varied and brilliant plumage
flew from bough to bough, and majestic rivers that roared down
to the sea.

'Several times I was sorely tempted to ascend one or other of
these great watercourses, but the fear of making my excursion too
long withheld me. I had but one desire, and that was to find
Burning Rock. To arrive there, I would have encountered any
obstacle. Nevertheless, the heat of the day became so overpowering that, in spite of my resolution not to loiter by the way,
I felt compelled at last to seek the welcome shade of the hanging
bowers of foliage that adorned the coast. I had no sooner alighted
upon the sands of this fertile and enchanting shore, however,
before I saw at no great distance in front of me a numerous herd
of hippopotami, disporting themselves in one of the rivers. And,
what was worse, a number of serpents, with glistening scales,
were writhing in and out among the underwood at the foot of the
trees, like the roots of some huge mangrove endowed with motion.

'Nothing more was needed, you may be sure, to cause me to
prefer the hottest sun at sea to a shade so treacherous; and I paddled away again for miles without finding a spot at which I could
debark. Every ten minutes revealed to me some huge denizen of
the forest, such as a lion, a panther, or an elephant.

'After a journey of some hours, the face of the coast changed,
and I found myself opposite scenery of a far more pastoral character. The songs of inoffensive birds alone broke the silence of the
peaceful-looking solitude. I landed in perfect security, and, having
fastened my boat to a large boulder, made a hearty meal of
oysters and other shell-fish, which I found lying in large quantities
along the beach.

'By this time day was on the wane, and, as I did not think it
prudent to pass the night in a region so altogether unknown to me,
I determined to sleep in my cajack. I anchored the craft a few
fathoms out, by tying a large stone to a rope fastened to the prow,
and throwing it into the water. Although feeling tolerably safe
from attack, I fired off my gun as a warning to evil-disposed beasts,
and then, wrapping myself in one of our skins, fell soundly asleep.

'The next morning I awoke early, and, having returned thanks
to Almighty God for the tranquillity in which I had spent the
night, I again set out on my voyage.

'I felt full of strength and spirits. My cajack cut through the
waves like an arrow. I abandoned myself to the enjoyment of the
magnificent scenery that lay spread out before me.

'Towards noon, fatigued by several hours of continual rowing,
I decided to land near a little wood, the aspect of which was most
inviting. The luxuriant foliage of the trees was peopled with
humming-birds, paroquets, and a thousand other feathered
songsters, who kept up a continuous and harmonious concert. At
once surprised and delighted, I pushed on beneath overhanging
bowers, formed of branches and trailing plants, which stretched

from tree to tree, and dropped in graceful festoons almost to my head.

'I unhooded my eagle, who, feeling himself free, took wing, and soon returned with a little paroquet, which I took away and was examining, when all at once I heard behind me a crackling among the branches, as if some large animal were making its way through them.

'I turned round, and what think you I saw? A huge striped tiger, not more than ten or twelve paces away from me! I saw at once that it was too late to think of flight. I was so terrified that I could hardly hold my gun, which, besides, would be but a feeble protection against so redoubtable an enemy.

'A cold perspiration broke from every pore in my body, and I verily believed that my last hour was come; when suddenly my eagle, who no doubt well understood the danger in which I was placed, precipitated himself upon the head of the tiger, and with beak and claws began to tear out its eyes.

'I was saved! The tiger, fully occupied in defending itself against the furious attack of the bird, took no further notice of me. Seeing this, I approached, drew my pistols, and fired them. One shot crashed into the creature's skull: he uttered a terrific roar and fell over dead.

'The joy which I felt on achieving this victory was tempered, however, by a most poignant grief. One of my shots, aimed hastily, had struck the eagle, which fell dead at the same moment as the tiger. I took the faithful bird up, and, weeping tears of regret, carried it down to the cajack, to be brought home and preserved in our museum.

'Quitting this place sad at heart, without even staying to skin the tiger, I rowed away listlessly, overcome by disappointment. Indeed I was just upon the point of tacking about, in order to return to Rock-house, when, among the peaks of a small rocky island to my right, I saw a thin wreath of fiery smoke curling slowly up towards the sky.

' "The Burning Rock!" I cried, lifting my hands to heaven in an attitude of devout thankfulness.

'My ardour at once returned, I laid on to my oars with all my might, and in a short time effected a landing, not without some risk, upon the rocky coast of the island.

'I managed to climb with difficulty, using both my hands and my feet, to the top of a rock, whence I hoped to be able to survey the whole island. After looking about me for an instant, I followed a narrow pathway, which led me down to a sort of platform, some few yards square, sheltered on all sides by the neighbouring rocks.

'Arrived there I cautiously approached the entrance to a large cavern, which I thought perhaps might be the lair of some beast of prey. I was walking on tiptoe, with my pistols in my hand and my eyes and ears on the alert, when, through a break in the rocks, I perceived, with an emotion I cannot describe to you, a human creature, dressed like a man, but bearing every appearance of being a young girl, lying asleep, with her head resting on her arm, upon a bed of moss and dried leaves. I stood immovable and speechless. My surprise was as great as if the discovery, which had been the sole object of my expedition, were wholly unexpected. For the first time during ten years I was looking upon a human creature who was not one of our own family! For the first time during ten years I should, in a few minutes, hear a strange voice, and be looked upon by one who had never seen me before!

'I hardly dared breathe. I stood gazing steadfastly upon the sleeping castaway. My joy was extreme to find that, instead of some poor creature worn out with age and fatigue, I was to rescue a young and charming girl. The features of the sleeper wore an expression so altogether infantine, that I did not think she could be more than twelve or fourteen years old. Her costume was that of a young midshipman. Long light hair fell about her face and upon her neck, and her little hand peeped out from among a mass of ringlets.

'I thanked God that He had chosen me to be the means of rescuing this lovely creature, and of presenting to my father and mother so beautiful a daughter, and to my brothers so amiable a sister. Her costume, after I had once examined her features, did not deceive me for an instant. Francis himself, who was so beautiful in his infancy, had not a softer or more delicate skin. I could only compare her to what I supposed our mother to have been at her age.

'My heart beat so loudly against my breast that I was afraid it would awake her. How long I stood there, contemplating her beauty, I know not. All I can say, that nothing in the world could have induced me to disturb a sleep so tranquil.

'A thousand confused thoughts agitated my mind. I would have given anything could my mother have stood in my place, so that the fair stranger on awaking might have looked upon first her sweet face. I might have stood there dreaming I know not how long, but that a little bird, untroubled by scruples like my own, skimmed noisily into the cavern and posted himself upon the fair young sleeper's forehead.

'Waking with a start, she raised herself into a sitting posture, and peered round with her large lustrous eyes to see what it was that had disturbed her repose. The real offender had flown, and her eyes rested upon me.

'She uttered a cry of mingled surprise and terror.

'I could not, however, have looked very terrible, for I never in my life felt so much embarrassed.

'With a gesture almost of supplication, I strove to calm her. "Fear nothing," I said. "I am far more alarmed than you are, and do not intend you any harm."

' "Who are you?" she asked. "Whence come you? How did you get here?"

'Then leaping lightly to her feet:

' "Whoever you are," she said, "so that you be an honest man, I bid you welcome to this solitude."

'The sound of her voice, the anxiety depicted on her countenance, the emotion which agitated her whole frame, brought me to myself.

' "I am," I replied, "the unknown knight to whom you appealed by the message which you confided to the care of the albatross. I have quitted all to come to your rescue. I am not an Englishman, as you may tell by my accent, but I am a citizen of a free country, where we know the respect which is due to misfortune. A tempest, no doubt, cast you upon this rock. A tempest cast me and my father and mother and three brothers upon a neighbouring island. Ten years have we been separated from the rest of mankind, dwelling upon a corner of the earth which has now become our world. If you can put confidence in me, I will conduct you to my family."

'After hesitating an instant, during which I could read in her face the thousand contending doubts that were passing in her mind, she advanced a step and tendered me her hand.

' "Heaven reward you!" she said in a voice broken by emotion—'you and yours! You have rescued me from a life that was worse than death, from a solitude that was fast becoming unbearable. If your father and mother will not turn me from their door, if your brothers are willing to receive me, I shall strive to become to the former the most grateful and submissive of daughters, and to the latter the most devoted and affectionate of sisters."

'The similarity of our misfortunes soon established a perfect confidence between us. Miss Jenny—this, she said, was her name—told me that she had been cast half dead upon the rock where I found her; and, once there, she had achieved miracles of courage, of patience, and of industry to find the where-withal to satisfy the first cravings of nature. Burning Rock is not nearly so productive as our island. Nevertheless, being alone there, dependent wholly upon her own woman's strength, surrounded by a soil far less fertile than ours, and having nothing whatever cast up from the wreck, she had contrived to drive away hunger, thirst, and cold, and to live on from day to day, though suffering the most terrible privations. In such circumstances, the little she was able to do was the more worthy of admiration.

'I listened to her story with amazement, being neither able to question her nor to interject observations upon it; and I went with her to visit the barren wilderness where she had neither despaired of herself nor lost her faith in God.

'Miss Jenny was the first to recover her equanimity. She gave me a proof of it by asking me to assist her in preparing a repast. This recalled to my mind my good mother.

'Thanks to the excellent stock of provisions with which she had furnished the cajack, I was enabled to lay before my new-found friend a supper which she pronounced exquisite.

' "I always had a famous appetite," she said laughingly. "I think I was spoiled at home. Ah! poor papa! If he had only known the fate reserved for his child!"

'And her laughter was succeeded by a passionate burst of weeping.

' "Restrain your tears, dear Miss Jenny," I said. "God will return to you all that you have lost a hundredfold." ·

'We then retired for the night—I to my cajack, she to her hut in the tree, to which she climbed with the agility of a squirrel.

'In the morning I used every effort to induce the young lady to take one of the seats in the cajack, and return with me to Rock-house; but she resolutely refused to leave behind her the thousand little objects which she had either made or found, and applied to useful purposes in her solitude.

'I therefore set out alone, with the double purpose of procuring a larger vessel and of bringing my mother to give the poor stranger a maternal welcome.

'It was while on my way to Rock-house, with these objects in view, that I sighted the pinnace, and, taking you for pirates, disguised myself as you saw. It was not with any malicious intention that I made myself the subject of your fears, for, if you will believe me, I was far more alarmed than you were. I had now not only my own life in my keeping, but that of another, the place of whose forlorn habitation was altogether unknown to you.'

CHAPTER XLIV

The history of Miss Jenny—a family feast—musical recreations

Fritz told us all that I have recorded in the foregoing chapter on the three first nights of our sojourn in Pearl Bay. The narrative was a long one, but it was not too long. As, however, we had to be on foot early in the morning of the fourth day, I gave the signal for retreat at the point where Fritz was telling us why he had assumed his strange disguise. The younger boys, who were burning to hear the remainder of the story, protested loudly; but it was of no use. I was firm, and we all retired to rest.

On the following morning, after breakfast, Ernest, Jack and Francis took possession of their eldest brother, and begged him to continue the history of our young friend.

Fritz suggested that Miss Jenny should recount the circumstances under which she became wrecked upon Rock Island; but she was too timid to do so.

Thereupon Fritz himself took the word, and this, in brief, was his story:

Sir William Montrose, a major in the British army, had obtained the command of an important post in India, and went out there.

While fulfilling his command he lost his wife, and was left with an only daughter, scarcely seven years of age—Miss Jenny. He lavished all his affection upon the little one thus committed to his charge, undertaking her education himself, and wisely determining so to train her that in the event of any reverse of fortune, she might be able to confront peril bravely, and do battle with adversity. Miss Jenny's natural aptitude rendered his task easy of accomplishment. At fifteen years of age she was as clever in the management of a gun or a horse as she was fitted to move with ease and good breeding in the best society.

A circumstance now occurred which for the first time separated the father and daughter. Sir William was promoted, and named commander of an expedition destined for a distant part of the country. Not being able to take his daughter with him, he confided her to the care of a friend, the captain of a British war vessel, who undertook to convey her to England, and place her in charge of one of Sir William's sisters, who was childless. At the end of a year the father hoped to bring his expedition to an end, when he proposed to obtain leave of absence and rejoin his daughter in London.

The young lady embarked in the costume of a midshipman, because women were not allowed to travel on board a man-of-war.

The voyage was a prosperous one during the first few days; but after that a terrible tempest arose, which drove the ship leagues out of her course, and eventually carried her to the same coast where we ourselves had been wrecked ten years before. Having struck upon the rocks, the vessel broke her back and foundered. One boat alone could be put to sea. In it was placed Miss Jenny and as many of the officers and men as it would hold, lots being cast to select those who were to take this last chance of deliverance. Hardly had the frail craft received its living freight, when a huge wave struck and capsized it. By a miracle almost, the young girl, who had become insensible, was carried on the crests of the breakers to the top of a rock on the volcanic island, where we found her. She saw no more of the men, some thirty in number, who had embarked with her in the boat.

The first days of solitude were full of horror for the unfortunate young castaway. Thrown upon an unknown coast, she had little in prospect beyond a slow death by starvation, or a quicker one by the attack of some terrible beast of prey. How happy to her now was the reflection that she had received and education which had developed in her courage, fortitude, and ingenuity—qualities so necessary in the new mode of life she was about to commence!

She commended herself to the care of God, an at once set about constructing a hut, or rather a nest, in the trees as we had done ourselves at Falcon-nest. Hunting an fishing supplied her with food. Among the few pieces of wreck washed up by the tide, she found some nails, which she bent and used as fishhooks, plaiting threads drawn from her garments to serve as lines. With the larger iron-work thrown up she made a number of rude tools for daily use, and weapons for her defence against unknown enemies. She was thus enabled to cut out arrows, which she used with great adroitness in her hunting excursions. Her food, however, consisted chiefly of fruits, shell-fish, roots, and, dried fish—especially during the rainy season, which had reduced her to the most terrible state of privation.

One of her favourite pastimes had been to catch young birds, which she tamed and trained. It was thus that she had obtained the albatross, which, after involuntarily delivering her message to Fritz, had faithfully carried my son's reply back again.

Such, in few words, was the story Fritz had to tell us.

When he had concluded his narrative, we gave Miss Jenny the warmest proofs of our affection; and the young girl, pleased to be the subject of so effusive a display of goodwill, responded with deep emotion—the grace with which she tendered her thanks adding to the charms of her lovely face and figure.

Meanwhile, our lime-burning experiment had succeeded to perfection. Several pieces were submitted to the action of water, and crumbled away, hissing and sputtering.

During the day Miss Jenny bustled about bravely to assist us in our several labours, so that I was able to see with my own eyes how dexterous and useful she was, not only in those employments which appertained to her own sex, but in those rougher kinds of labour which fall to the lot of men; and I thanked God that He had sent me an adopted daughter at once so beautiful and so able.

By sunset the pinnace was loaded with everything that we intended to carry with us.

We desired much to return to Rock-house, my sons especially, for they were impatient to do the honours of the establishment to their young companion.

They had painted for her a picture of our island home so enchanting, that when we raised anchor in the morning she could not restrain a cry of joy. We needed no other proof that our society had become more pleasant to her than the dear, though forlorn, home of her solitude on Burning Rock.

On nearing Deliverance Bay, and seeing Cape Disappointment in the distance, I proposed to sail on to Prospect Hill, to ascertain whether the farmery was still in good condition. Fritz and Francis, who preceded us in the cajack, went straight to Rock-house to prepare for our reception.

On walking over our grounds at Prospect Hill, Miss Jenny manifested the liveliest surprise and admiration. It was two years since she had seen a trace of a human habitation, and our farmery, peopled with sheep and goats and poultry, recalled to her mind the dear home she had been obliged to abandon in India.

We stayed at Prospect Hill all night, and on the next morning set sail again, touching at Whale Island, where the colony of rabbits proved a fresh source of delight to our newly adopted daughter.

The two young men, who had gone on before, had ,as I expected, used every effort to receive us with distinction. Our approach to the entrance of Deliverance Bay was signalised by two rounds of ordnance, to which I replied with the guns of the pinnace.

As we doubled the cape of Shark Island, we saw Fritz and Francis in the cajack, coming to meet us. Once in sight, they tacked about, and piloted us to land. When we had cast anchor Fritz leapt ashore, and with imperturbable gravity announced himself as the Governor of the Castle of Rock-house, to which mansion he invited us, to partake of the refreshments there awaiting our arrival. Then with knightly courtesy he offered his hand to Miss Jenny, and conducted her to the umbrageous veranda in front of our grotto.

In the open air, in front of the door, we saw with surprise a table laid out with all the choicest productions of the island. The calabash dishes were filled with magnificent ananas, intermingled with fresh green leaves; while pyramids of oranges stood side by side with baskets of figs and guavas. Canary wine, hydromel, and fresh milk from our cows invited us temptingly to slake our thirst. In the centre of the table lay a couple of roasted fowls and a dish of fried fish. Over the table was suspended a double garland of leaves, on which were picked out in flower-blooms these words:

'*A thousand welcomes to our dear sister Jenny! May the day be long remembered on which she first set foot in the dwelling of the Swiss Robinson!*'

It was a magnificent feast—a reception such as I scarcely thought could have been provided out of the means we had at hand in our island solitude.

Miss Jenny took her place between my wife and me: it was only right that she should occupy the seat of honour. Ernest and Jack faced us. Fritz and Francis would not sit down at all. Napkin on arm, like waiters at an hotel, they ran hither and thither, cut the joints, changed the plates, and poured out wine, with a gravity and agility which was as admirable as it was droll.

The afternoon was made a complete holiday. Each of the boys did his best to entertain our young guest. She was taken all over the grotto and all over the adjacent ground.

'Dear Jenny, do look here!' cried one. 'Pray examine this first!' said another. 'That will do presently,' rejoined a third, 'come here and see something that you have never seen before!' In spite of her tact and native graciousness of demeanour, the amiable child found it utterly impossible to satisfy everybody. At length my wife rescued her from her tormentors, and led her into the kitchen, which, in the eyes of a good housewife, is by no means the least important element in the organisation of a home.

The next morning early, the whole household was afoot, for we had determined to make an excursion to Falcon-nest, with the exception of Miss Jenny, who was still weak in health, and to whom therefore Jack lent his buffalo: we all went on foot. ·

The house in the tree had again suffered from the weather, and we all set to work to restore it. Three days sufficed to put it into habitable condition.

While we were engaged in this labour, a few showers of rain fell, and warned us to gather in our harvests and stores of provisions for the winter.

In these latter occupations Miss Jenny displayed an amount of ingenuity and willingness which rendered her aid invaluable to us. She did my wife a thousand nameless services, and crept deeper into her love every day. We all worked so vigorously that we had nothing to fear when the rainy season set in.

Although habituated to the periodical occurrence of the heavy rains, we never contemplated their approach without a feeling of commingled sadness and terror. Our long seclusion, the roaring of the sea upon the shore, the howling of the wind, the boom of the thunder, the terrible glare of the lightning, and the ceaseless hissing of the rain, all concurred to render us melancholy. But this year, thanks to the agreeable society, the incessant industry and the never-failing sprightliness of our fair young friend, the rainy season was one of the most pleasant we had ever spent upon the island. Since we had an amiable companion with whom to share our joys and sorrows, that which was new to her became new to us, and we seemed to live over the past again.

I shall not attempt to describe in detail the events of this pleasant, this joyous season. The even flow of a happy life is incapable of narration.

Suffice it to say that Miss Jenny perfected us in the pronunciation of the English language. Fritz and Ernest, if I may trust her report. acquired as pure an accent as a born Englishman. On her part, she learnt in a very short time to speak German with a charming accuracy, and even with grace; and this, to my wife, was an accomplishment which she could never find words to praise sufficiently.

The union between the two women was perfect—so much so that when, one day, Jenny asked in a voice trembling with apprehension whether she might be permitted to call my dear wife by the sacred name of 'mother', her only answer was a passionate burst of tears and a warm maternal embrace. It was a touching scene, awaking emotions known only to the hearts of those who love each other tenderly.

'Once more, then,' cried Jenny, weeping for joy, 'I have a mother —a beautiful and loving mother.'

'And I,' said my wife, not less moved, 'have found a charming daughter, as good as she is brave and courageous,' and she took Jenny to her heart.

And when the boys laughingly disputed with Jenny her right to their mother's kisses, 'Fy! fy!' she said, 'I am ashamed of you!

So jealous as that! Are you such misers that you cannot spare a few of the good things which you have in plenty, and which I have not enjoyed for many long years? And you pretend to be brothers who love me!'

Jenny had a remarkable voice, and a rare talent for music. Her memory, also, was such that she knew by heart the choicest *morceaux* from all the great masters. She not only charmed our solitude by her singing, but she taught Francis, who had great aptitude in that direction.

It was quite a revolution in our lives to hear her sweet voice, and the improvised concerts which she arranged at unexpected times with Francis.

Jenny's own voice was so clear and musical that it filled the whole grotto: we listened to it, and were compelled to silence. Her peaceful melodies raised our souls nearer to the Divine Giver of music.

You can understand now how it was that our winter passed so pleasantly.

For the first time the sun reappeared without finding us bemoaning his absence.

CHAPTER XLV

A grave incident—on the look-out—visitors—new friends

Notwithstanding all the charms of our enforced solitude, my sons felt, as the fine season again approached, an insatiable desire for liberty and independence. They left the grotto as birds escape from their cages, flying on swiftest wing to fields bathed in light.

Fritz, the intrepid sailor, proposed to make an excursion to Shark Island, for the purpose of ascertaining whether the sea, during its tumult, had thrown anything valuable upon the rocks. As I could not accompany him, he set out with Jack.

I desired them, in accordance with our invariable custom at the end of the rainy season, to fire off two rounds of ordnance on their arrival at their destination. We had a double purpose in pursuing this course. The guns would serve as a signal to any poor creature who might have been wrecked upon our coasts, and also it would enable us to establish communications with any vessel that might find itself in our neighbourhood.

The boys were not likely to forget my instructions, for nothing pleased them better than to make play with our cannon.

But what was their astonishment when they distinctly heard, far out at sea, the report of a gun in response to their double detonation!

At first they were in doubt, thinking it an echo; but in a short time the first report was succeeded by another. Some minutes after, while they were listening in silent anxiety, a third report resounded over the waves.

In the first ecstasies of their emotion they embraced each other for joy.

At length Fritz cried: 'A rescue! A rescue!'

'God grant that it may be!' ejaculated Jack.

'What shall we do?' he added.

'Go at once and tell father,' replied Fritz.

And without more ado they leapt into the cajack, which, impelled by two pairs of vigorous arms, literally flew across to the beach.

'What has happened?' I asked, seeing their scared look.

'Oh, father! father! Have you heard nothing?' they exclaimed, throwing themselves into my arms.

'Nothing,' I replied, 'absolutely nothing.'

Then they imparted their astonishing news.

At first I thought they had been deceived; but they affirmed so energetically and so seriously that they had distinctly heard three cannon-shots, that it was impossible for me any longer to doubt the fact. But were we to rejoice or to be alarmed? Had we in our neighbourhood Europeans or Malay pirates? Such were the grave questions I asked myself.

I hastened to assemble the family and take counsel with them, for I found the subject too grave to decide upon myself.

Darkness surprised us before we had come to a conclusion. I gave the signal to retire to rest, advising my boys to keep watch by turns during the night in front of the grotto, lest we should be surprised.

The weather was lovely at first, but later on a terrible storm arose. The rain fell in torrents, and the howling of the wind and the dash of the waves prevented us hearing any other sound seaward.

During two days and two nights, it seemed as if the rainy season had recommenced. It was quite impossible for us to go out, as we intended, to take observations.

On the third day the wind fell, the sea became calm, and we were able to make a voyage to Shark Island. I went thither with Fritz, taking with me a couple of flags, with which to make signals either of joy or alarm to our dear ones who remained at home at Rock-house.

If I lowered the flag three times and finally cast it into the sea, they were to take instant flight to Falcon-nest. If, on the contrary, I waved it over my head, they were to remain where they were and fear nothing.

You may imagine with what beating hearts we landed and climbed to our observatory. We swept the horizon carefully on all sides with our telescopes, and, discovering nothing, I told Fritz to charge and fire the cannon.

He obeyed me, and a few minutes afterwards we heard, in the direction of the south-west, which we had never explored, first one report, then a second, then a third, and so on, to the seventh report.

We had no doubt whatever now that there was a vessel in our neighbourhood.

It only remained to ascertain its character.

We returned to the family without having given them a signal.

They overwhelmed us with questions, to which, as you can well understand, we were unable to reply.

I told them that I had determined to set out on a voyage of discovery, in company with Fritz, and this project had their unanimous assent. Jenny, indeed, ordinarily so calm and business-like, gave expression to the wildest hopes, She was certain, she said, that the strange ship could belong to no one but her father, who, having returned to London and heard of the wreck, had set out instantly in search of his lost daughter. I could not find it in my heart to discourage the dear child, but I confess I did not share her pious confidence in the romantic chivalrousness of her father.

I had all the provisions put in safety, and as Fritz and I set out in the cajack, my wife, Miss Jenny, and my three younger sons departed for Falcon-nest, taking with them the cattle.

Utilising the idea which Fritz had hit upon some months before, we disguised ourselves as savages, thinking that, in any case, this device would lay us less open to suspicion as to our intentions. This, however, did not prevent us from concealing our best arms in the bottom of the canoe.

I was near upon midday when we set sail, and more than an hour elapsed before we rounded the western cape of Deliverance Bay.

After rowing straight on for something like three hours in waters quite unknown to us, we found ourselves under a cape, which we determined to double by coasting, so that while we saw everything before us, we might be seen as little as possible.

Judgel of our astonishment when, on rounding the promontory, we saw ying at anchor in the bay behind it a large three-master, flying the English flag!

I had the greatest difficulty in preventing Fritz from throwing himself into the water to swim to the vessel. Nothing but my suggestion that the unknown captain might be flying English colours as a cover to piracy could restrain him.

Then we put in behind a cliff, which, while hiding us from view, enabled us to see clearly everything that was passing on board and on shore.

A little distance up the beach a large tent was erected, and a fire was burning, before which some joints of meat were in process of roasting. The crew of the ship appeared to be very numerous. Two sentinels were pacing backwards and forwards on the deck. We ventured out of our concealment, whereupon one of them disappeared, and quickly returned with an officer, who held a telescope under his arm.

'That is the captain,' said Fritz. 'I recognise him by his uniform. We have nothing to fear, father, for his features are undoubtedly those of a European.'

Fritz's remark was a shrewd one; nevertheless, I did not think it wise to venture nearer at present.

Taking up the speaking-trumpet, I shouted with all my might in English: 'Englishmen! Good men!' without adding anything else.

The captain, who evidently took us for the savages we appeared to be, made signs to us to advance, at the same time displaying before us some pieces of red cloth, together with axes, nails, beads, and other articles which it is usual to exchange with the indigenous inhabitants of the New World.

His mistake caused us a good deal of amusement; but we were not yet satisfied that we should be safe in putting ourselves in his power.

We consequently determined to go away, and to present ourselves on the morrow in our proper persons, and with more pomp before our European visitors.

We made signs of farewell, and disappeared briskly behind the promontory.

Joy had doubled our strength, and in a very short time we were again with our family, who awaited us with impatience.

The prudence and reserve with which we had conducted the interview with the captain were approved on all hands.

After we had taken counsel together, it was decided that we should all embark next moring in the pinnace, and visit the European ship in state.

We employed the remainder of the day in putting the armament of our craft in order, in bedecking her gaily with flags, and in the preparation of the old uniforms which we had brought off the wreck ten years before. We also laid in a stock of our choicest fruits and the principle productions of our islands, which we intended to present to the captain; for we judged it wise to inspire him and his crew with an exaggerated idea of our wealth and power.

Next morning after breakfast we lifted anchor. Near the guns, which were loaded, stood Jack and Ernest. Fritz, in the uniform of a naval officer, preceded us in the cajack.

As soon as we got within a mile of the English vessel—the sight of which awoke in us, and in Jenny particularly, the deepest emotions—I ordered the British flag to be hoisted, and in a few moments it was floating gaily out to the winds from the foremast of the pinnace.

The astonishment of the English crew on seeing a vessel with flags flying and all sails set, advancing proudly into the bay, was so great, that if we had been pirates I verily believe we should have been able to make an easy prize of the ship in the first moments of confusion which our appearance had brought about among her crew.

Having taken in sail at some distance from the vessel, I and

Fritz embarked in the pinnace's boat, which we towed behind us, and rowed on to salute the captain, who from the quarter-deck replied to us most amicably, and invited us on board without delay.

The worthy officer received us with all a sailor's frankness and cordiality, and leading us into his cabin, inviting us to drink a flagon of old port with him, asked us under what circumstances it was that we found ourselves upon an island which, as he had understood, was only inhabited by savages.

I briefly narrated to him the history of our shipwreck, and of our life upon the island. I also spoke to him of Miss Jehny, and asked if he had ever chanced to hear of her father, Sir William Montrose.

He said he knew the name of the gentleman well, and had heard that after distinguishing himself in his expedition in India, he had returned to England, and retired from the service. As for himself, his name was Littlestone, and he was commander of the frigate *Unicorn*. Overtaken by a storm, he had been driven out of his course, but had been fortunate enough to find an excellent port at a moment when he had almost given his vessel up for lost. As the parts in which he found himself were wholly unknown to hin, he thought perhaps I could give him some information which would be of value; and for that reason and many others, he was proud to make my acquaintance.

When the captain had finished speaking, I begged him to do me the honour of paying a visit to the pinnace, in order that I might present him to my family.

He at once accepted my invitation, and embarking in one of his own boats, which was rowed by two of his sailors, was soon on board our vessel. It is unnecessary to say that he was received with every manifestation of joy. Miss Jenny, especially, displayed the liveliest satisfaction at being able to speak of her father to a compatriot.

The captain had among his passengers an English family, whose acquaintance we were happy enough to make. It consisted of Mr. Woolton, a distinguished engineer and shipbuilder, whose health had suffered much during the voyage; his wife, Mrs. Woolton; and their two charming daughters, one aged fourteen and the other twelve. Notwithstanding the tenderest attentions of his wife and children, Mr. Woolton had been growing feebler and feebler daily. The sea air was too bracing for him, and to save his life it was necessary that he should land as soon as possible. We offered him and his family an asylum at Rock-house, placing at their service everything in our possession.

Our proposition was accepted with gratitude, and the same day the amiable family was transferred to our island home.

The surprise with which the newcomers surveyed our possessions would be difficult to express. Their exclamations of astonishment, repeated enthusiastically over every object that met their view, amused my sons hugely. They could hardly bring themselves to believe that six persons had been able to achieve so much by their own unaided exertions. In the evening we took supper under the veranda, and until bedtime conversed together with gaiety and animation.

During the night my wife and I were occupied by the gravest thoughts. The opportunity we had so long prayed for, of returning to our friends in Europe, had at last offered itself. Should we profit by it? Why, we asked ourselves after reflection—why should we abandon a home where we had been so happy, with the object of renewing relations which time and absence had probably destroyed for ever? Had we not reached an age when tranquillity and repose were far more pleasing to us than the risk of a voyage to the Eastern Hemisphere? Nevertheless, we had no desire that our own decision should influence that of our sons, if they wished to return to their fatherland—though the idea of parting from them rent our hearts.

Miss Jenny, since she had learned that her father was in England, ardently desired to go thither and rejoin him.

I doubted not that her departure would be the cause of deep grief to my eldest son, who had never concealed the profound affection which the young girl had inspired in him.

No time was to be lost in coming to a decision upon these points, delicate as they were for all of us.

The next morning, at breakfast, Mr. Woolton, who already felt the better for his brief sojourn on land, gave me his hand and said: 'The life which you lead in this solitude pleases me immensely. I feel that I should grow young again in this magnificent country, and I should esteem myself fortunate if I could obtain your consent to take up my habitation in some corner of it.'

The proposition was received with joy. We all of us expressed the happiness we should have in admitting him to our colony with his wife and daughters. I also took advantage of the occasion to announce that I and my wife had come to the resolution to end our days in that beautiful island—to which I desired to give the name of 'New Switzerland.'

'To the prosperity of New Switzerland!' cried the whole party, raising their calabash vessels filled with palm-wine.

'And long life and prosperity to all who dwell in it!' added Ernest, Jack, and Francis.

I remarked that Fritz kept silence, from which circumstance I understood that he secretly wished to accompany Miss Jenny. The poor boy hoped, no doubt, that her father would consent to her union with one who had been the means of rescuing her from her cruel solitude.

Although my heart bled as I looked forward to this double separation, I concealed my emotion, in order that I might not augment the grief of my wife, who had great difficulty in restraining her tears.

She, poor woman, however, had herself noticed Fritz's ominous silence as I had done. A deadly pallor overspread her face. The heart of the mother, far tenderer than that of the father, was broken. She fell into a swoon.

Fritz threw himself upon his knees. 'My mother! My mother!' he cried, 'I will not leave you—no, never. I will die at your feet rather.'

Jenny wept piteously. 'Pardon—pardon!' she sobbed. 'Oh, pray forgive me!'

She also had comprehended the meaning of Fritz's silence.

When my wife returned to consciousness, Jenny gently led her into her chamber.

What passed there between the mother and her adopted daughter I know not.

In a short time my wife returned to us calmed—sad still, but resigned. Her arm encircled the waist of the young girl, whose head reposed upon her shoulder.

Mr. Woolton and his family, feeling that their presence was a restraint upon us at this sacred time, went out and left us alone.

Jenny approached me. 'My father,' she said, in a voice broken by emotion—and it was the first time she had called me by this name—' My father, bestow upon me your blessing, as my mother has done; let me—let *us* go. We shall come again to see you. Do not think that we are about to part from you for ever. Sir William Montrose is a man of honour and of the tenderest heart. He will certainly discharge his daughter's obligations when he knows that his daughter's happiness depends upon his doing so. He returned to Europe on my account, and on mine alone: he will quit Europe for my sake and for yours.' Then, looking tenderly at Fritz: 'Have confidence in us both,' she said. 'Fritz will answer for me, and I, knowing him as I do, will answer for him.'

'I have.' she continued, 'had a long conversation with the captain of the ship which is going to take us away. The purpose of his voyage, he told me, was to find some port in these seas which would be suitable as a refuge for British ships driven out of their course by stress of weather. And he added that the accident of his being cast upon our island had provided him with that which he came to seek. Now my father, Sir William Montrose, is on the best terms with the Lords of the Admiralty. Your island will cease to be your island, but it will become a portion of the powerful realm of Great Britain—a centre of life and activity, whence your children, no doubt, may set out and leave you for a time, but to which they will be able easily to return and dwell among you to the end of their days. Do not think that I am embracing a chimera. If all this of which I have spoken is not accomplished, there is one thing at least which shall come to pass, and that is our reunion on this spot before six months is over. Dear father, put confidence in her who will always remain your child. Under the spur of misfortune children become men. Fritz and I have been trained up in this school—put faith in us!'

I embraced the noble child.

My wife gave her consent.

I gave mine.

Fritz, distracted by joy and grief, embraced first one and then the other, laughing and weeping by turns.

At length we grew calmer. I took Fritz aside and gave him counsel, which I hoped would be of value to him in the event of his meeting with disappointment on his arrival in England.

'Rest assured, dear father,' he said on leaving us, 'your son will always do his duty. I shall not be worthy of success if I am not prepared for reverses.'

I have little to add. A year had not passed away before all that our charming young prophetess had predicted had come to pass, with one exception. Her father was dead before she reached London, and she had not the consolation of seeing him again.

Five years have passed since then, and what changes have taken place! The sailors of the *Unicorn*, on their arrival in Europe, spread the account of our history in every land, and their relation, as may readily be supposed, became more wonderful every time it was repeated. I have often heard them say since that, even before the end of the voyage, the strange facts of which they had been witnesses had ceased to gratify their appetite for the marvellous, and that they had found it necessary to their enjoyment to amplify our plain story with added circumstances of their own invention. And on their arrival in England, finding eager listeners to whatever they had to say, vanity, and above all greed, became new incentives to deception, and from cheating themselves for pleasure they took to deceiving others for pecuniary advantage. Our history, it might be thought, narrated in its simplest form, contained enough of marvels, and yet they soon came to look upon it as a story that would hardly repay the pains of telling without receiving some embellishments of their own. We became, as represented by them, beings more resembling the creatures of fable than those of everyday life; but what probably gave their auditors a greater interest in the story was that the wealth at our disposal in the natural resources of the island was said to be almost unlimited. In a little while these stories produced their natural results, the tide of emigration began to flow in the direction of this remote place; and the first settlers, unwilling to own themselves duped, and perhaps not altogether averse to duping others, did not take particular pains to correct the false impressions which prevailed at home. But fortunately this culpable exaggeration on the one side, and equally culpable cowardice and deceit on the other, had no very serious results. The settlers, as I hope my reader is by this time aware, had not been attracted to a barren spot. The island contained abundant resources for the support of a large colony, and as those who came out were for the most part not wanting in energy, they soon found themselves provided with the necessaries of life, which are comforts to those who have known privation. In a little time all the mists which had been raised by ignorance and interest were dispersed; the true state of the island and the real nature of our connection with it became known; the population rapidly increased; and at the present hour we number more than two thousand souls.

Ernest and Jack are wedded to the two amiable daughters of Mr. Woolton.

Jack followed the trade of a shipbuilder, and is at the head of a considerable establishment, organised under the superintendence of his father-in-law. His gains are rapidly increasing, for in an island community like ours shipbuilding is of the first importance, and my son practically enjoys a monopoly of the trade.

A more splendid destiny seems to be reserved for Ernest. He was always of an adventurous character, and, young as he is, he has already returned from his second voyage to Europe. He did not land on its shores as a simple sailor; his mind was enriched with a knowledge of natural history, which he had acquired mainly from his observations on the island during his boyish rambles; though I am bound to admit, in justice to myself, that he had been assisted not a little by the instruction I had been able to give him, and by the books I had put in his way. These acquisitions have made his society extremely valuable to the naturalists of Europe, and he has been enrolled a member of several learned bodies. It has ever been his custom to impart the knowledge he possesses as freely as though he were unconscious of its value, though this is by no means the case, and he has shown his accustomed generosity in presenting the museums of London, France, and of Holland with numerous objects hitherto known only by the reports of travellers. These spontaneous acts of generosity led to a very warm recognition of his merits on the part of those who had benefited by the opportunities for study thus supplied to them. My son has been complimented, not to say fêted, by many men of learning and of position in England; and I please myself by picturing a future for him worthy of his merits and fulfilling my desires.

Francis, 'little' no longer, and handsome as well as tall and stout-built, is captain of a merchantman. He is (to use an expressive phrase which I picked up during my residence in England) 'every inch a sailor', and, sailor-like, he regards his ship not only as his home and his refuge, but as his bride. In other words, he does not think of falling in love and marrying like his brothers, and he laughingly announces that his vocation is to be merely 'son' and 'uncle'. And it would be difficult to say in which part he shines most, so admirable does he appear in both. His tenderness and respect for us, his father and mother, constitute one of the main blessings for our declining years; and his kindness to the children of his brothers would almost seem to exceed that of their own parents. He brings them presents from all parts of the world, and these are often of such value that they are judicially laid aside by the parents, for the use and enjoyment of the little recipients when they shall have arrived at a more mature age. Uncle Francis is, therefore, as it may easily be supposed, the harbinger of joy in the house for both young and old, and his arrival is invariably made the occasion for the liveliest manifestations of delight in the family.

My dear wife and I are old, no doubt—at least we are bound to believe it when we consult our mirror, though, thank Heaven, we find no special intimation of the fact in our hearts. The freshness of feeling of our youth has been permitted to remain with us, and in caressing our children's children we seem to forget the time that has passed away since we fondled our own. Our sons, too, are still our 'boys', in spite of the fact that the gravity engendered in them by the cares and responsibilities of an active life sometimes makes them seem older than ourselves—according to the good-humoured banter of our friends. It is an unspeakable pride to us to see them all doing well in the world; industrious, handsome to look upon, content with their lot, esteemed and worthy to be esteemed by their acquaintance, beloved and revered by their children and by all whom Providence has made dependent on their bounty or their care.

And when the time shall come for us to render up our souls to the Sovereign Lord of all, we shall be found ready. The grand voyage—that which leads us to God—has no anxieties for those who during their whole lives have loved and served and honoured Him—those who never knew without a keen sense of ingratitude what it was to doubt His mercy and His loving-kindness.